RACHANEE LUMAYNO

A Retold Story

SEEING RED

Seeing Red: A Fairy Tale Retelling of Little Red Riding Hood

ReTold, Book One

Editing by Tom Loveman

Cover art by Fiona Jayde Media

Thank you for reading, I hope you enjoy Seeing Red! I'd love it if you'd leave an honest review on Goodreads or wherever you purchased this book. Thanks!

ALSO BY RACHANEE LUMAYNO

Kingdom Legacy

Heir of Amber and Fire

Heir of Memory and Shadow

Heir of Magic and Mischance

Heir of Crowns and Curses

Heir of Secrets and Spectres

Heir of Illusions and Others

Heir of Immortals and Empires

ReTold

Seeing Red: A Fairy Tale Retelling of Little Red Riding Hood

Midnight Rose: A Fairy Tale Retelling of Beauty and the Beast

CONTENTS

JOIN THE
NEWSLETTER

Hello Dear Reader!

I have always loved fairy tales and fairy tale retellings, but surprisingly, as a writer, that's not where I started.

My writing journey actually began with a character in a Dungeons and Dragons campaign that I never got to play. (Thanks, pandemic!) That character became the basis for the first book in my Kingdom Legacy series, ***Heir of Amber and Fire***.

Since the first book had such strong ties to tabletop gaming, a friend suggested I create a campaign set in the world of the Kingdom Legacy series. And so *The Mysterious Magical Emporium* was born, and I'd love to send you a FREE copy! Just sign up for my newsletter at www.rachanee.net/newsletter, and your new campaign will be sent to you right away.

So grab your friends, grab some dice, and grab a copy of *The Mysterious Magical Emporium*, and get ready to spend some time in the kingdom of Calia with your new friends, Jennica, Beyan, and Taryn!

A Notice

To the citizens of Woodside:

There has been a recent rise in violence in the neighboring Littlewood Forest that gives our fair town its name. Several animals, both small and large, predator and prey, have been found dead, the cause unknown but a result of obvious unnatural attacks. We have also had an increase in reports of attacks on people traveling through the forest. The attacker or attackers move with such stealth and speed that the victims have been unable to identify who or what is attempting to harm them.

The majority of the attacks have occurred between sunset and dawn.

Caution is advised if you choose to traverse the woods.

Signed,

Joven Marley, Mayor of Woodside

PRELUDE

MUSINGS FROM THE PAST

W HEN I WAS A child, my mother used to call me O.A. O.A., as in *overactive*. An overactive imagination, one that couldn't be tamed no matter how much she scolded me to calm down or tried to curb my fancies.

I'd often play on the kitchen floor in our family bakehouse, pretending the spilled flour was fairy dust that would change my appearance or grant me wishes. Mama wasn't pleased with my whimsy, but she dismissed it as harmless play.

Until *that day.*

It was Daypito, the end of the week and our kingdom's traditional day of rest. The shops in our sleepy town of Woodside would be closed, and Rowena's Bakeshop, my mother's namesake bakery, was no exception. I loved Daypito, because it meant that I would get to spend uninterrupted time with my Mama. And my beloved grandmother, my Lola Cerise.

Lola Cerise, my mother's mother, had lived in the neighboring town of Cedarbrook for as long as I could remember. Well, perhaps *neighboring* was a bit of a stretch. Cedarbrook was close by, but it was on the other side of the large forest that lay in between our two towns. Nearly every Daypito, Mama and I would make the hours-long trek through the woods to visit Lola Cerise. My lola resided in a quaint little cottage that I could spot as soon as we reached the forest's edge.

Seeing the cottage's chimney smoke curling cheerfully up into the sky, I had released Mama's hand and ran ahead, calling out, "Lola! Lola Cerise!"

The front door had opened, revealing my grandmother standing in the doorway. With a happy smile and arms open wide, she had scooped up my little five-year-old self into a big, enthusiastic hug. I had laughed and squealed as she carried me inside and set me down, then waved my mother in.

The visit had gone as usual, with my mother and grandmother chatting over tea and me playing at the table and, later, on the floor. And as usual, I had not paid attention to what the grown-ups were discussing.

But what had grabbed my attention were the funny little faces I saw staring at me, peeking out from behind potted plants or between knickknacks on my grandmother's bookshelf.

One face had slightly resembled Mister Arran, who lived down the street from Mama and me. The portly gentleman always had a smile on his face for Mama and a wrapped sweet in his pocket for me. Except this face was rounder and ruddier than Mister Arran's, and much smaller—about the size of my outstretched hand.

Other faces hadn't looked human-ish at all. And yet, despite their strange features, my innocent self hadn't been scared of them.

One little creature with pointed ears and overly large eyes, whose entire body was just slightly taller than my chubby pointer finger, had flitted about me and landed on my head, then my shoulder. Its tiny feet had tickled, making me giggle and clap my hands in delight.

My mother and my grandmother had turned to look at me, curious as to what was causing me such glee. Looking around in wonder, I had said, "Lola. Mama. Who are all these funny little people?"

Both women had stilled, with two very different reactions. At first startled by my question, Lola Cerise's face grew proud, her eyes misty. But Mama's face looked thunderous. She started to rise from her chair, like she wanted to grab me and run out of the cottage right then and there.

Later, when we had returned home, Mama had knelt down so she could look me in the eyes. "Claret, whatever you thought you saw at your lola's today ... you didn't."

"But, Mama ..."

"It was just a figment of your overactive imagination," she had said firmly. "You didn't see anything. So don't say anything about it, to anyone."

A few weeks after that visit, Lola Cerise came to Woodside, in one of her rare visits to our side of the forest. Much to Mama's annoyance, she had presented me with a special gift.

A cape that swirled around my ankles, it was made of a lovely rich red velvet and had an oversized hood. When I pulled the hood over my head, Lola Cerise had laughed at the sight. I could barely peek my head out from under all that fabric.

"It's a bit big still, but you'll grow into it," she had said, showing me how several inches of fabric had been sewn into the cloak, creating an extra wide hem, but allowing for the cloak to be lengthened later, when I grew taller.

"It's too much," Mama had protested. "The fabric alone probably cost two months' wages."

"Oh, hush," Lola Cerise had told her daughter. "Don't you worry about the cost. Claret will have this for years, so the price doesn't matter."

"Mother—"

"Besides," Lola Cerise had continued. "You know as well as I, she might need this someday. Best for her to have it sooner rather than later."

Mama had fallen silent at that, her lips pursed in obvious disapproval. But she had only huffed, then turned on her heel and walked back into the kitchen. Baking was her answer to everything. If she was happy, she baked. If she was mad, she baked. When my father had died after his horse had thrown him, Mama had baked. Perhaps that was why she had decided to open the bakehouse in the first place. What else was she going to do with all the things she created?

As the sound of clanging pots and pans punctuated the air, Lola Cerise had knelt down to look me in the eyes.

What is it with grown-ups and them wanting to be on my level? I had wondered.

Out loud, I had said, "Thank you, Lola Cerise. I love my new cape."

My grandmother had put her hands on my cloaked shoulders as she regarded me solemnly. "Claret, my darling. I'm so glad you love it. A lot of care went into making this cloak. I sewed it with my own hands, and wove my own charms into it."

I had nodded. I didn't understand what she meant, but I also didn't know the right questions to ask. So I had just nodded.

"Every time you come to visit me, wear it," Lola Cerise said. "If you keep it safe, it will keep you safe. Do you understand?"

I hadn't, of course, but I couldn't say that. Instead, I said, "Yes, Lola Cerise." She had smiled. "Good."

She had kissed me on the forehead and then stood. "My darling, darling girl. I know you'll do me proud someday."

Since then, I had kept my promise. Whenever I traversed the forest to see my grandmother, I wore the red cloak she had given me. Whether or not it actually kept me safe, I didn't know, but the joy in her eyes whenever she saw me in it was enough reason for me to keep wearing it.

As the years passed, I forgot about the strange tiny beings I had seen in Lola Cerise's cottage. Mama never talked about it, and since the topic instantly upset her, I stopped bringing them up. And despite my grandmother's urgings, I never saw those little creatures again. So, it was easy to dismiss them as just what Mama had said they were—figments of my overactive imagination.

Although the two most important women in my life were often at odds with each other, there was one warning they both agreed on. Once I was old enough to visit Lola Cerise on my own, they drilled this caution into me: always stay on the forest path.

Lola Cerise would tell me that if I strayed off the path, I might very well find myself stepping into Faerie, as Littlewood Forest served as a gateway to that mythical land.

For Mama's part, she just said that it would be too easy for me to get lost if I left the road. The forest, ancient and wild, had a way of claiming unwary, unsuspecting travelers. It was the closest admission to magic that Mama had ever gotten.

And as I grew taller, Lola Cerise had lengthened the cloak as she had said she would, and it still was as soft and vibrant as it had been on the day she had presented it to me.

Perhaps that was the cloak's true magic.

CHAPTER 1

"Claret? Claret, dear, can you come here and mind the shop for a bit?"

I stopped mid-sneak and sighed. Turning on my heel, I called out, "Sure thing, Mama. I'll be right there."

The interior door that separated our home from the bakeshop clicked shut. I cast a longing look at the gorgeous day framed in the window, then trudged away.

Really, it was my own fault. I had just been about to slip out the back door that served as the primary entrance for our private home, but as I reached up to take my red cloak from its peg by the door, I had gotten lost thinking about the time my beloved grandmother had gifted it to me.

I don't know why. I had worn this cloak countless times, and usually didn't reminisce on its history. But today, for some reason, thoughts of the past had snuck into my mind and distracted me from leaving.

Sighing, I hurried down the hallway, towards the front of the building and our bakeshop. Grabbing a plain linen apron from where it hung, I pushed through it and entered the family bakery.

It may have been Daypito, the traditional day of rest, but the inside of the shop looked anything but restful. The counter was swarmed with impatient customers, with many more crowded behind them.

My poor mother rushed around, her stress palpable. "Claret, I'm so glad you're here. If you could fill some orders while I check on the ovens ..."

"Go, go." I shooed her away.

The next few hours passed by in a blur of taking orders, fetching items, getting payment. And then, repeat and repeat and repeat. Mama ran in and out of the bakeshop, refilling various food trays before going away to bake more.

Through the two large windows up front, I could see the store's wooden sign, "Rowena's Bakeshop," hanging outside. As time wore on, I eyed the light outside. The day was going by fast, but hopefully there would be a break in customers soon and I would be able to leave.

Finally, the crowd thinned. Mama came through the door, holding yet another tray of bread.

"This should be the last of it," she told me, placing the tray down on the counter. "Whatever we have out is it for the day."

"Oh, good," I said. "Do you still need my help? Otherwise, I'm going to head out."

Mama frowned. "Head out? Where?"

I sighed as I started to undo the strings of my apron. "It's Daypito. My day to visit Lola Cerise."

Mama's frown deepened. "It's been so busy, I forgot." She paused. "I guess we'll be closing soon, though."

"You don't really need me anymore, then, right?" I prodded.

"Honestly, Claret, I would prefer it if you didn't go over there every week. I know she's your grandmother, but the stories she tells ... I'm just glad you're old enough to have discernment."

"Oh, Mama. You know they're harmless—"

The bell over the bakeshop door rang out, signaling the arrival of a new customer. I stepped back from the counter, hoping I could slip away. But I was trapped, with Mama on my right and the bakery wall to my left.

I gave an annoyed sigh. "We're closed!"

Mama hissed, "Claret!"

But I was beyond caring. I wanted to get to Lola Cerise's. "I mean, we are still technically open, but what's left is it. No more special orders to—"

My voice trailed away as I looked up into the most hypnotizing pair of green eyes I had ever seen.

The owner of said green eyes startled. "Uh, hello. I hope I have the right place." He glanced around, then turned to look out the window and peer at the sign. "This is Rowena's Bakeshop, correct?"

"Yes it is, young man," my mother said, nudging me slightly so she could address the newcomer squarely. "Forgive the confusion. How can I help you?"

"Oh." He cleared his throat and eyed me sidelong. Belatedly, I smoothed my face into ... well, if not a welcoming expression, at least something more neutral. "Mayor Marley wanted me to give you this."

He plunked a piece of paper down on the counter. Mama picked it up and carefully looked it over. Her eyes widened. "Oh my goodness! He wants *how many* pastries in two weeks?"

The young man shrugged, brushing back a strand of dark hair that fell in his face. "I didn't read the message, madam. I'm just the messenger."

I narrowed my eyes at him. "I've never seen you before. Are you really the mayor's messenger? Or his secretary, perhaps?"

"Neither. I'm the new sheriff, just arrived in Woodside this morning." He extended a hand. "Hunter Tavish."

I gaped. "But you're so young!" Our last two sheriffs had been much older, the prior one around my Mama's age, and the one before him closer to Lola Cerise's age.

The man laughed, rich and melodious. "Please accept my sincerest apologies for that, Miss ...?"

When I still didn't make a move, Mama swooped in. Taking Sheriff Tavish's hand, she gave it a firm shake. "Well met, sheriff. I'm Rowena Pangati, and this is my daughter, Claret."

"A pleasure, Madam Pangati." He looked at me, eyes twinkling. "And Miss Claret."

I nodded stiffly, just barely polite. Goodness, how much deeper could my embarrassment get?

"I'm glad I was able to get the mayor's order to you before you closed for the day," Sheriff Tavish said.

"Yes," Mama said, looking over the note again. "My goodness. Between this weekend's festival and now this order, I'll be working overtime. If I'm going to get everything done on time, I should probably start right away." She began muttering to herself. "I'll need to check my stock. Do I have enough flour? And other supplies ..."

"I'll stay and help you, Mama," I said, resigning myself to forgoing the visit to Lola Cerise.

Mama waved away my half-hearted offer. "No, no. You go on and see your lola. Don't forget to bring the basket with you."

"Where does your grandmother live?" Sheriff Tavish inquired politely.

"Past the forest, in the next town over. Cedarbrook."

Was it my imagination, or did the sheriff suddenly stiffen? "Oh. I'd be happy to escort you, if you like."

"Thank you, but I really don't need—"

"What a lovely idea!" Mama interrupted. "If it's not too much trouble, Sheriff Tavish—"

"It's not."

"—Then I would feel much better if you accompanied Claret. Really, that's just wonderful."

Glad Mama thought so. I had been looking forward to a quiet walk—by *myself*—to my grandmother's. After the flurry of customers, I just needed some silence to decompress. It didn't look like I'd get my wish.

Although the new sheriff was terribly handsome, and he seemed nice enough. As walking companions went, he wasn't a bad choice.

Not wanting to waste any more of the day, I sighed and pasted what I hoped was a grateful smile on my face. "Again, I thank you, sheriff. Let me hang up my apron and get my things, and I'll meet you out front."

Sheriff Tavish nodded. "I'll be waiting. Good day, Madam Pangati."

He left the shop, the overhead bell ringing decisively in his wake.

"Go on," Mama said. "Don't keep the new sheriff waiting."

"First you didn't want me to go, now you do?" I grumbled as I removed my apron. "Make up your mind."

Mama clarified, "I didn't want you to go *by yourself*. Not that I can stop you anyway."

She added under her breath, "So stubborn, like some other women in this family." Then, in a louder voice, "Now that you have that handsome young man to accompany you, I'm not so worried."

I'd be just fine on my own, I thought, but I knew better than to say that aloud. Ever since the mayor's notice about the attacks in Littlewood Forest had been posted around town two months ago, Mama had, understandably, fretted about my weekly visit to Lola Cerise's. I had even stopped visiting my grandmother for a little bit, just to appease my mother.

But I missed my grandmother, so eventually I pushed to start visiting her again. And when I had made several trips into the forest and returned home unscathed each time, Mama had relaxed. Somewhat.

Mama locked the shop door. "Go out the back, honey. Send my love to your lola. And don't forget the basket!"

"I will! And I won't!" I promised. I pushed through the door that separated the bakeshop from our private residence, grabbing the basket from the counter and hanging up my linen apron. I continued through the house. Before I exited out the back door, I made sure to grab my red cape, hurriedly throwing it around my body and tying the strings at my neck.

Rounding the house, I walked towards the front, where Sheriff Tavish waited at the bakery entrance. Seeing me approach, he stood straighter.

"Oh, Miss Claret! I didn't expect you to come from that direction." There was a slight question in his voice.

"Shall we?" At his nod, I began walking. Sheriff Tavish fell into step beside me. "Mama would prefer we use the front entrance only for the bakeshop. Anything personal, we use the back door. It's just a way to keep business stuff separate."

"That makes sense." He eyed my cloak appreciatively. "That's a beautiful cape. It's certainly eye-catching."

"Thank you." I beamed. "My Lola Cerise—my grandmother—made it for me, some time ago. I always wear it when I visit her."

"It's very fine craftsmanship. And what a lovely red color." His eyes twinkled. "For some, it's a lucky color, too."

"I don't know if it's brought me any luck," I shrugged. "But it makes me feel closer to my lola to wear it. And it makes her so happy to see me in it."

We turned down Main Street, passing the small complex of buildings that housed the mayor's office, the courthouse, and the sheriff's office. "There's your new office."

"Yes." Sheriff Tavish smiled. "It will be a while before I can settle in, though. There's quite a few repairs that need to be made, first. The building's a bit ... unusable, right now."

I chuckled. "That's a generous way of putting it."

He chuckled along with me. "I will admit, I was a bit dismayed when I saw how bad the building had been allowed to get. Holes in the ceiling, cracks in the walls. Not to mention the hay and manure on the floor?"

"Oh, yes. I think it was used as a temporary barn after the main one burned down."

"That explains it, then." He shook his head. "I'll do my best to get it repaired quickly, but that depends on how long the investigation takes."

"Investigation?"

We continued down the road, out of Woodside. The cobblestone of Main Street gave way to the dirt path that would lead through the forest to the next town, where my grandmother lived.

"Yes," Sheriff Tavish affirmed. "I was hired to investigate the recent attacks."

CHAPTER 2

I SHIVERED, DESPITE THE early spring sun's warmth overhead. I pulled my cloak tighter around me, finding comfort in the familiar, worn cloth as Sheriff Tavish and I entered the wood.

"That makes sense, given all the tacked up notices around Woodside," I said. "And you should always be careful in Littlewood Forest. Any forest, really. But still, I don't think it's that bad."

"It's not?" Sheriff Tavish raised an eyebrow. "And why do you say that?"

I shrugged. "I've traveled through these woods by myself most every week, since I was a child. And I'm still alive."

He smiled, his eyes twinkling. "Then you must know some special secret. Care to share?"

I blushed in spite of myself. "There's no secret. I'm just watchful, I guess."

A surprisingly easy silence fell between us.

"My goodness, where are my manners?" Sheriff Tavish said out of the blue. "Here, let me carry your basket."

"It's all right, you don't need—" But my protests went unheeded as he gently removed the basket from my arm.

"Wow, what's in this thing?" He sagged slightly under the weight, but I couldn't tell if he was exaggerating or not from his teasing tone.

"Go ahead and look, if you're so curious. Just don't spill anything."

The sheriff tweaked aside the bright red cloth and peeked inside. "Well, now I know your secret. If you get lost in the woods, you have enough food here to last you for at least a week."

I chuckled. "It's for my lola—my grandmother. Mama puts any bakery items that she deems unfit for selling in this basket, and then we give it away. Usually to the neighbors, or for charity. Or to Lola Cerise. And since Mama can be a perfectionist, the basket gets full rather fast."

"Ah. That's very kind of you both."

"It's more Mama than me."

"But you're taking the time and braving the forest to deliver it." He tucked the cloth back around the top of the basket. "Don't worry, your secret is safe with me."

I smirked. "Thanks." Eyeing my companion sidelong, I asked, "So how did you end up in Woodside?"

"I have roots here," Sheriff Tavish said. "My family goes back several generations in and around Woodside, although they left a while ago. When I heard that the sheriff's position was open, it seemed like a great way to return to a place with so much history for my family."

"Oh, that's lovely. Although it's a shame that you were hired under such troubling circumstances. We haven't needed a sheriff in Woodside for a few years. When the last one moved away, Mayor Marley didn't bother to hire a new one. It's kind of a sleepy town. Hardly anything bad happens here. Except the recent attacks, of course."

"When did they start?"

I frowned, thinking. "Just after the winter thaw. Before that, the townsfolk had found a few dead animals in the forest, but we all thought some poor beast had woken up during the winter and was cold and hungry and trying to find whatever it could. But when people started getting hurt, the mayor thought something else might be happening."

"Well, I hope to figure it out soon, so Woodside can get back to being quiet and safe."

The rest of our walk passed pleasantly, with Sheriff Tavish asking me general questions about life in Woodside. I didn't think there was much to tell—as I had told him, Woodside was a sleepy town—but, as my mother ran a beloved bakeshop, we knew most of the townspeople. After all, everyone needed bread, right?

I'll admit the conversation distracted me a bit, but Littlewood Forest didn't seem any different than usual. Aside from the occasional bird flying through, or the brief glimpse of a deer, it felt pretty safe to me. We passed through the deepest part of the forest without incident, and soon the trees began thinning.

"We're almost to Cedarbrook," I said. "My lola lives on the outskirts, just outside the forest."

"Not far, then."

"Not far at all." I paused. "Will you be heading back to Woodside right away? Or ...?"

"I don't have any business in Cedarbrook to keep me there. Unless you would like an escort back?"

"Not really." At his amused look, I added, "Not that this hasn't been pleasant. But I don't want to detain you, if you have other things to attend to. I'll be able to get back to Woodside on my own just fine."

"If you're sure?"

"I am." I nodded for emphasis. "Lola makes sure I leave well before sunset. If our visits run late, then I just stay overnight with her and return in the morning. But I don't usually stay that long anymore. As she's gotten older, she wears out easily, and I hate imposing on her like that."

"All right, then," Sheriff Tavish said as we broke through the tree line. "I did want to hunt some game before the light fades."

The dirt path continued on, leading to a small house just a few feet away. Beyond that, we could see chimney smoke rising from the town of Cedarbrook.

"I guess this is where I take my leave," I said, holding my hand out expectantly, palm up, for my basket.

But instead of giving it to me, Sheriff Tavish turned my hand over and kissed the back of it. Then he held out my basket, closing my fingers over the handle.

"It was a pleasure, Miss Claret," he said. "I hope to have the pleasure of accompanying you again soon."

With a nod and slight wave, he turned and headed back the way we had come. I watched him disappear into the forest, trying to ignore the tingly feeling that his kiss on my hand had created.

I shook my head, then shook my hand out for good measure. Nope, the tingles were still there.

Silly Claret, I told myself as I approached the house by the road.

I stepped up to the door and knocked. From within, an elderly woman's voice called out. "Who is it?"

"It's Claret, Lola Cerise."

"Oh, my darling Claret! Come in, come in!"

I tested the door. Unlocked. Smiling to myself, I went in.

CHAPTER 3

I STOOD IN THE doorway, letting my eyes adjust to the dim interior. The curtains were closed, but I knew this house by heart.

From down the hall, my grandmother's voice called out. "Claret! Claret, my dear, sit down. I'll make us some tea."

I heard rustling, and hurried into her bedroom. Lola Cerise was struggling to get out of bed. I rushed to her bedside to help her sit up.

"Oh, there you are, my dear. Thank you. What a good girl you are."

I reached down and hugged her, noting her frail frame. "I'll take care of it, lola. You stay in bed."

"Nonsense. I'm perfectly capable." But she didn't try to stand.

"Take your time. I'll get things ready."

I went back into the main room, opening the curtains to let in some light. And promptly sneezed at the dust that kicked up. When was the last time she had cleaned in here?

I left the basket of baked goods on the small wooden dining table by the window. I took my red cloak off and hung it up near the door.

In the kitchen, I put the kettle in the fire to boil, then rummaged around the cupboard. Finding two mugs and two plates, I brought them over to the table.

My grandmother lived in a modest one level house, with the kitchen and main room in the front and two small bedrooms in the back. Lola Cerise usually kept a clean home, so if it was dusty in here, it meant her hip must be bothering her again.

And the other thing about my grandmother—she loved the color red.

It wasn't just the cloak that she had so lovingly made me years ago. Everywhere I looked around the cottage, items in all shades of red met my eyes. Crimson curtains. Burgundy furnishings. Rose and ruby colored knickknacks on display. Pictures with red as the dominant color. Even one scarlet painted accent wall, despite the high price for such colored paint.

It wasn't all red—there were several lovely green plants on display, as Lola Cerise also loved the outdoors. And of course, not everything she purchased could be red. But if it was, then she most likely owned it.

I paused, narrowing my eyes as I stared at the wall. Perhaps my eyes were still blurry from my earlier sneezing fit, but it looked like part of the wall had moved? Just a little shadow, no bigger than my hand. But that couldn't be right. Lola Cerise's inanimate knickknacks couldn't move.

I sniffled and wiped at my eyes, then took up a rag and began cleaning.

A high-pitched giggle floated on the air. I looked around sharply, but didn't see anything. The laughter came again, followed by a hasty shushing.

I shook my head in disbelief. I must have been hearing things. Imagining sounds into existence, as my overactive mind sometimes did.

And there—now I heard real sounds. Uneven footsteps, coming down the hallway. I looked up to see Lola Cerise making her slow way towards me.

Throwing down the rag, I hurried to her side. "Lola! I told you not to get up!"

She chuckled, a slight wheeze coloring her laugh. "And I'd be a pretty poor hostess if I just let you do all the work."

"Come, grandma." I helped her over to the little dining table, making sure she was settled before I began cleaning again.

"You don't have to do that." She waved a weak hand at me.

"I don't have to, I want to." The kettle whistled. I went back into the kitchen and took it off the stove. "Sugar?"

"No, thank you, dear." Lola Cerise sighed and leaned back. "How did I get such a wonderful granddaughter?"

I laughed. "I don't know. Just lucky, I suppose."

I finished arranging the tea tray and brought it over to the table. After I poured cups for both of us, I sat down. "Mama sent you some sweets."

"Mmm, I can see that," Lola Cerise said approvingly. She pulled off the cloth covering the basket and began looking over the contents.

"Lola," I chided her, "you really shouldn't leave the door unlocked. There have been some animal attacks in the woods lately. What if some wild animal broke in here?"

My grandmother leaned over and patted my hand. "There's nothing to worry about, my dear. That door—and this house—is fully warded. No human can break in here, and no Fae creature can come in, unless invited. I'm perfectly safe."

"Oh, lola. While I love your confidence, I don't know where you get your superstitions from."

Lola Cerise tsked. "It's not superstition, silly girl. It's bona fide fact. The Fair Folk can only enter a building if expressly invited by one who is deeply connected to it."

"If you say so," I chuckled, used to Lola Cerise's fanciful tales. She often talked about the Fair Folk, one of the many names for the magical otherworldly beings known as the Fae.

Not that the Fae, or their realm of Faerie, existed. No one in Woodside or Cedarbrook had seen a Fae in several generations. The old traditions—such as leaving little offerings in the woods or in one's home to appease them—had long since died out.

She knew I didn't believe in her silly stories. But that didn't stop her from telling them, or insisting that they were true.

She stilled, her eyes honing in on mine with surprising focus. "Oh, my Claret. You used to listen and believe when you were little. As much as I love your mother, I know Rowena has closed your mind to believing. But you must remember the things I've said. For as sure as your red cape will keep you safe from the evils outside, so will all the stories I've told you."

Her seriousness unnerved me. "Of course, lola. If you say so," I repeated, this time with more gravity.

I changed the subject to lighten the mood. "Speaking of Mama, she tried to play matchmaker today."

"Oh, really?" My grandmother's eyes twinkled. "Do tell, my dear."

"He's new to Woodside. A little older than me, about mid-twenties, I think. He's the new sheriff."

"Ooh. I must hear more."

The afternoon passed in a blur of conversation and good company. In between cups of tea, I made sure to clean up as much of the house as I could, despite my grandmother's protests.

Finally, Lola Cerise looked out the window and frowned. "It's later than I thought, my dear. You should get going, before it gets dark."

"Right after I'm done with this." I held up the broom I was using to attack the dirt on the wooden floor. "I'm about halfway done."

"No, no," my lola said. "I can finish up. You shouldn't waste any more time."

"Spending time with you is never a waste," I said. But I put the broom down against a wall.

I hugged Lola Cerise and kissed her cheek. "It was so good to see you, lola. I'll be back next week."

"It was so lovely to see you, my dear." She gave me an extra squeeze. "Now, get home safely."

"I will." I put my cloak on and grabbed the basket. As I opened the door, I turned and gave a little wave. "I love you, lola."

"I love you, Claret."

"Don't forget to lock this behind me!" I closed the door on my grandmother's laughter.

CHAPTER 4

I WASN'T TOO WORRIED when I passed the tree line, but as I walked
deeper into Littlewood Forest, I realized lola had been right about my
needing to leave. It was much later than when I normally went home, as
evidenced by the deep shadows already forming around me.

It was no matter. I would be fine. I had walked this path countless times,
and nothing had ever happened to me. I knew these woods, and I knew how
to take care of myself. I would be fine.

Still, I started to walk faster.

My skin started to prickle, but I didn't know why. The light was fading,
but I knew it was still too early for true night.

I stopped, realizing why I felt so uneasy. Usually, the woods were full of
sounds. Birds and bugs, chirping and buzzing. Small animals darting about
in the undergrowth, or larger animals making their way through.

But the entire forest was quiet.

I suddenly became acutely aware of the noise I was making. Each footfall
against the dirt path. My increasingly panicked breathing.

Should I stop and hide? Or keep moving?

If I hid, it would be too easy to get disoriented in the dark forest. I didn't know how long the danger would be present. Or what the danger even was. And sunset was fast approaching.

I was about halfway through the forest. It wouldn't matter if I turned around to go back to Lola Cerise's or continued towards home. Either way, it would take me the same amount of time.

I didn't want to wait in the forest for whatever was out there to go away. I would much rather be inside—either my home, or my grandmother's—tucked away in a nice, cozy bed.

I shivered. It was getting colder, quickly. I pulled the hood of my cloak up, wishing I was already in that nice, cozy bed.

That decided me. I was going home. I crept forward, trying to minimize the sound of my passage. I gripped the basket handle tighter in my sweaty palm, brandishing the makeshift weapon.

A few steps. And a few steps more.

Nothing happened.

I relaxed a little. Perhaps whatever was out there had gone.

I hoped.

I continued on for a few more moments, but something still seemed wrong. I stopped, straining to listen.

Silence.

I started walking again. Stopped. And started again.

There—that was it.

I could hear the sound of my steps, but with a strange echo. They seemed a little too loud to my ears.

Some creature was tracking me, matching me footstep for footstep.

I picked up my pace. So did whatever was following me.

I kept going, willing my mind not to dwell on the notices Mayor Marley had posted all over Woodside. Or my earlier conversation with Sheriff Tavish.

I've traveled through these woods by myself most every week, since I was ten. And I'm still alive.

Was that a snarl I heard coming from the trees?

Oh, dear. Please, let this not be the day that I'm proven wrong.

Another guttural growl sounded, louder and more menacing.

Without breaking stride, I turned my head ever so slightly to my right. A small glint flashed in the growing darkness.

Forget caution. Breaking one of the cardinal rules of woodland survival—*never run from a predator*—I broke into a run. The mysterious creature stalking me followed suit.

I ran as fast as I could. At any moment, I expected my follower to jump out from the trees and attack me. But, surprisingly, it just kept pace with me.

The trees began to thin out up ahead. I was nearly to the forest's edge.

The last of the light faded. Twilight settled around me.

With a low moan that crescendoed into a loud roar, my pursuer sprang at me.

I screamed. The creature swiped at me, catching the edge of my cloak. It hissed and yelped, dropping the cloth as if it had been burned.

It was a close call, but I wasn't going to stick around to give it another try at me. With the last of my energy, I sprinted down the path, through the tree line—

—And ran right into something solid and unmoving.

I screamed again. Wielding my basket like a club, I swatted at the obstacle over and over.

Strong arms encircled me. Perhaps to calm me down, but I suspect also to still my attacks. "Woah, woah. Hold on, there."

I twisted in the person's grasp, to no avail. With my arms pinned, I moved on to the next best thing.

My booted foot made satisfying contact with a leg.

"Ow!"

The arms around me loosened, and I stepped back, breathing hard, basket weapon at the ready.

"Miss Claret! Please, stop! It's just me, Sheriff Tavish."

His words clicked in my head just as the town lamplighter finished his task on Woodside's Main Street. The soft yellow glow bathed the sheriff's face and form, proving the truth in his words.

"Oh my goodness!" I clapped a hand over my mouth, embarrassed. "Sheriff Tavish! I am so sorry. I didn't mean to hit you. I was just so scared. I thought you were ..." I broke off, realizing I was babbling.

"It's all right," he said. "I know you weren't trying to hurt me. At least, I don't think you were?" Amusement laced his voice.

"No," I affirmed. "I was coming back from my grandmother's, and something was following me. I tried to make it back to Woodside as fast as I could. I was able to escape it. Barely."

The sheriff's face was grave as he regarded me, then the woods behind me. "Did it harm you at all?"

"N-no. I don't think so. But—" I paused, thinking of my unknown attacker's hiss of pain when it had touched my cloak.

"But what?"

I hesitated. Should I tell the sheriff about it? But it seemed so bizarre. And I had been so panicked. Maybe I had imagined it. I decided against saying anything.

"Nothing. I'm just surprised I managed to get away. It tracked me halfway through the forest, and hardly seemed winded."

"Hmm. Interesting." He looked between me and the forest again. But we were—thankfully—alone. "You look shaken, Miss Claret. Let me escort you home."

"Oh, no. I'm fine." I took two steps and my knees buckled underneath me.

Sheriff Tavish's arm shot out, grabbing my elbow to keep me upright. When he was satisfied I was steady on my feet again, he said, "I insist. Allow me."

He took the basket from my unresisting hands and offered me his arm. Gratefully, I took it and allowed him to escort me home under the comforting, safe yellow lamps of Woodside.

CHAPTER 5

THE NEXT DAY WAS so normal that I began to doubt that the event in the woods had ever happened. I woke up, got dressed, and, after a quick breakfast, I went to help Mama with the bakeshop. The morning passed by in a blur of baking (mostly Mama) and fetching things for patrons (mostly me).

I had just finished wrapping up the purchases for a group of three women when Mama asked me, "Claret? I was putting some rolls in the basket and couldn't find the red cloth that covers it. Do you know where it is?"

I waved at the exiting trio, then turned to Mama, my eyebrows furrowed in confusion. "Isn't it with the basket?"

Mama shook her head. "No. And I searched all around, but it wasn't on the floor or in the house anywhere."

Oh, dear. Apparently I hadn't imagined my twilight trip through the woods. I must have dropped the cloth when I was fleeing the mysterious creature.

But I hadn't told my mother about what had happened. If she found out, she would understandably worry—and then probably forbid me from visiting Lola Cerise unless she could accompany me. But since the bakeshop always kept her so busy, it would be weeks before she would be able to get away and go with me.

I loved my lola dearly. And frankly, I was much closer to her than I was to my mother. I didn't want to go that long without seeing her.

But now, since I had lost the covering, I would have to confess. I braced myself for the inevitable, and opened my mouth to speak.

The bell above the shop door jingled.

I promptly closed my mouth as Sheriff Tavish strode into the shop.

"Hello, sheriff," Mama said. "How can we help you today?"

"I believe this is yours." He held up a red cloth.

Oh dear, oh dear. I was in for it now.

Mama reached out and took it from him. "Wherever did you find this?" She ran loving fingers down the length of the cloth. "My mother gave this to me as a gift, years ago, when the bakeshop first opened. She said it would bring the business luck. It's silly, I know, but I like having it nearby."

I gave Mama a sharp look. She didn't often talk about Lola Cerise—at least, not in such a wistful manner.

"I'm glad I could return such a valuable keepsake, then, Madam Pangati."

Mama shook out the cloth, dislodging some dirt and leaves. She frowned. "Oh, my. Why is it torn?"

She was looking at the sheriff, who was looking at me. He paused. I stared into his eyes, imploring him not to give me away.

"It was just outside the bakeshop door," he said smoothly. "Please forgive me. I stepped on it, that's how I noticed it, and when I tried to pry it from my shoe, it stuck to the bottom and I ripped it by accident."

I finally found my voice. "I must not have noticed it fall when I came home last night. It was a bit later than when I usually return. Thank you for returning it."

With a giddiness I didn't expect, I added, "And it was probably leftover honey glaze, that caused it to stick to your shoe. Take care that you don't have a line of ants following you home."

"It was my pleasure. And I'll be sure to do so." His emerald eyes danced with amusement. And a question.

"I think such a chivalrous act deserves a thank you," Mama said. She swept a hand around the room. "Pick whatever you like. On the house."

"Thank you. Hmm. How about that?" He pointed at a berry tart.

Mama wrapped one in paper, but when she was about to wrap a second, he stopped her. "Madam Pangati, I'll only take one."

"Nonsense," she said. "Please. I insist."

He paused, then smiled. "All right, then. I'll eat it right away. Thank you, again."

"Of course." She turned to me after she handed Sheriff Tavish the tarts. "Claret, while it's quiet, can you run to the mayor's office? Tell them I'll have the order ready on time, but we'll need to borrow a cart and horse from them, if possible. Also, if they have any special requests, they should let me know right away."

"All right, Mama."

"And when you get home, please take care of this." She waved the basket cloth at me. "Since you're the one who lost it, you can be the one to clean it and patch it up."

I groaned. I hated sewing. "All right, Mama."

"I'd be happy to escort you to Mayor Marley's, Miss Claret," Sheriff Tavish said.

I was about to decline—after all, the mayor's office was located in town, not in the woods—but then changed my mind. With a smirk, I said, "That sounds lovely, sheriff."

Mama beamed, as if she had suggested he accompany me herself. "Take your time, Claret. I can handle things back here."

"I'll see you out front."

Sheriff Tavish nodded and left. And for the second time in as many days, I found myself walking around Woodside with the handsome new sheriff.

As we walked away from Rowena's Bakeshop, I asked him, "Where *did* you find that cloth?"

"It was inside the woods," he said. "From the way you were swinging that basket around last night, I'm not surprised it dropped from it."

"Inside the woods?" I frowned, thinking. "But I didn't hit whatever was following me with my basket. Just you."

The sheriff smirked. "How fortunate I am, then, that I'm the only one you deigned to attack."

I nudged him lightly with my shoulder. "Yes, consider it a privilege."

"I was surprised it blew so far in, though," he continued. "I don't recall having a heavy breeze last night."

We hadn't, that I remembered. At least, I didn't think we did? I had been really tired when I got home, and had fallen asleep almost immediately.

"How is your office looking?"

Sheriff Tavish chuckled. "It's slow going. I need to repair the roof and the walls before the weather turns, otherwise it will be another season before I can move in. But the inside is just so filthy...."

"I'd be happy to help you clean up the place." I'm not sure who was more surprised—Sheriff Tavish at my offer, or me for actually offering.

"If it's not too much trouble—"

"It's not. Mama works better without me getting in the way."

"Are you sure? You've got that order from the mayor coming up. And didn't she say something about another event? I'm sure she'd welcome the help."

I smirked. "Not from me. The last time I was in the kitchen, I burned the rolls and spoiled the next two batches of dough. I'm allowed to help the patrons, but that's it."

An answering smile played around his lips. "I see. Then I accept your offer, gratefully. When do you think you could start?"

"Honestly? Later today, if that's all right with you. I just need to deliver Mama's message to the mayor's office, then run home to tell her whatever they say. We usually close the bakeshop in the early afternoon anyway, so I'll be able to get away then."

"Perfect. And thank you."

"I should be thanking you," I said.

"For what?" But the arch of Sheriff Tavish's brow told me he had a good idea of *for what*.

"For not telling my mother where you did find that cloth. If she knew what had happened ... I'll tell her, eventually. Just—not yet."

He shrugged. "With the way your eyes were boring holes into my head, I knew something was going on. But you must be more careful."

"I will be."

Our conversation died down naturally as we approached Woodside's municipal center. "I'll be at my office for the rest of the day," Sheriff Tavish said. "And here."

He handed me the wrapped berry tart.

"Oh, I couldn't. This is for you."

"One's plenty for me." He winked at me. "Just don't tell your mother. Come find me when you get back."

"I will. See you then."

CHAPTER 6

I APPROACHED MAYOR MARLEY'S office just as his secretary was locking the door. She turned when she heard me behind her, her eyebrow arched in disapproval. "The office is closed. Whatever business you have will have to wait until after we take our midday meal. Come back after first bell."

After first bell? I didn't want to wait that long. "I'm here on behalf of my mother, Rowena Pangati. Of Rowena's Bakeshop. Please, I just have a simple question...."

"As I said, we're closed. Come back later."

I began to clench my fists in frustration, but stopped when I realized I was holding a delicate baked good in my hand. Inspired, I held out the wrapped item. "Well, at least take this, and enjoy it with your luncheon. It's a sample of what my mother will be providing for the mayor's event in a few days."

The mayor's secretary took it, noticeably thawing. "Why, thank you. That's very kind of you, and your mother. You said you just had a simple request? I suppose I could wait a few more moments before leaving...."

"Oh, thank you. Yes. My mother just wanted me to tell the mayor that his order will be fulfilled on time, and if there are any specific items he would like, to please let us know immediately. And finally, we would like to borrow a horse and cart to help transport the food."

"That's easy enough. Just come back when you're ready to borrow it, and it should be available for you. As for any special orders, I don't believe Mayor Marley has any." The secretary peeled back a bit of the paper covering and bit into the berry tart. Her eyes grew wide. "Strike that. We—he—would definitely like some of these included on the menu."

I grinned. "Consider it done."

With my errand completed, I headed back home. As I had suspected, Mama was fine with me helping Sheriff Tavish clean his office. In fact, once I told her, she practically shoved me out the door.

Cleaning tools in hand, I headed back to the civic complex and Sheriff Tavish's office. I pushed open the wooden door—not hard, considering it was hanging off one hinge. "Knock, knock."

Sheriff Tavish's head popped up from behind an old wooden desk near the back of the room. "Ah, Miss Claret! Hello aga—aga—*achoo!*" He sniffled, swiping a dusty hand across a forehead smudged with dirt.

I giggled. "I don't think that helped."

"No, I don't think it—*achoo!*" He grimaced. "Sorry about that."

"No need to apologize." I surveyed the room. "Wow. This is ... pretty bad."

Sheriff Tavish eyed the broom I had brought. "I don't know if that will cut through all the dirt around here."

"That's why I also brought this." I grinned and held up a shovel.

Between the two of us, we made good headway on making his office more presentable. By the time it was nearly sunset, I had shoveled and swept the floors from half the building and removed all the cobwebs from the ceiling. Sheriff Tavish had fixed the door so it hung properly, closed, and locked. He had also patched several holes in the walls and hauled away all the dirt and manure I had piled up while cleaning.

"There's still much to do, but we've made good progress," Sheriff Tavish said he looked around. "The rest of the floors, plus a thorough scrub down. And I need to patch up the roof. I'll start with the cells first, I think."

"We don't get that much trouble in Woodside," I said. "But I guess it wouldn't do to lock someone in a cell, only to have them escape out the roof."

"I'd be a pretty poor sheriff if I let that happen," he agreed, grinning. "Still, it's looking much, much better than it did before. I thank you again, Miss Claret."

Acutely aware of my dirty hands and dusty hair, I curtseyed, an impish smile on my face. "You're very welcome, Sheriff Tavish."

He glanced over my shoulder to look out the window. "It will be dark soon. Shall I see you home?"

"You don't have to. I'm sure you'd like to get home yourself to clean up. Besides, it's not like I've left Woodside. I'll be perfectly safe."

The sparkle in his eyes faded. "I believe that's what you told me on our first meeting, and then had a near encounter in the woods."

I fell silent. He was right. There wasn't anything I could say to counter that. Finally, I nodded. "All right. Let's go."

Leaving the shovel and the broom behind, we closed up the office and headed back to the bakehouse. The orange and pink sky overhead bathed Main Street in a lovely warm light as we walked.

"Will you be visiting your grandmother again soon?" Sheriff Tavish asked.

"I hope so," I said. "I try to visit her at least once a week. But she's been a bit forgetful lately, and I worry about her, so I'd like to go more."

"I'm sorry to hear that, but I suppose as we get older, some things are inevitable."

"Yes. Despite all that, she's a lovely lady."

He smiled at me. "I'm sure she is. Perhaps I'll get to meet her someday."

I smiled back. "Perhaps."

We had reached the bakehouse, and my home. "Will I see you tomorrow?" Sheriff Tavish asked.

"In the afternoon, if that suits you?"

He nodded. "It definitely does. With your help, I should be able to move some things in this week. The sooner I can set up, the sooner I can investigate the attacks in earnest."

"Have you discovered anything of interest yet?" Then I laughed—at myself. "Silly me. It's only been two days since you arrived in Woodside."

He smirked. "I've discovered many interesting things. One, travelers should not be alone in the woods as darkness approaches. Two, baskets can be used as deadly weapons."

The smirk faded and his emerald eyes softened as they looked into mine. "Three, I think I will enjoy living in Woodside."

I blushed. Clearing my throat, I said, "Well, with investigative skills like that, *I* could be sheriff."

"I would welcome any insights you have, Miss Claret."

With that, we said our farewells. For a few moments, I watched Sheriff Tavish walk away, then headed to the back of the building to let myself in.

As I entered, I heard Mama call down the staircase, "Claret? Is that you?"

"Yes, Mama."

She poked her head over the railing. "Goodness, Claret! I think you brought half of Woodside's dirt home with you!"

She wrinkled her nose. "And I can smell you all the way from up here," she said teasingly.

I chuckled. "I need to draw a bath."

"Let me. You just stay right there. That way you won't be tracking any more dirt in than is necessary."

I waited by the front door while Mama readied a bath for me. A few hours later, I was clean—and so was our back hall from all the dust and grime on my person—and settling into bed.

The candle by my bedside burned brightly, enough light for me to read by. Or sew by. Which was the unfortunate task ahead of me. I threaded my needle, nearly going cross-eyed in the process, then examined the red basket cloth that I was to mend.

And stopped short, staring.

Mama had mentioned that the cloth was ripped, but she must not have looked at it too closely. Sheriff Tavish had told me that he had found the cloth in the forest, not just outside it, which would have been a more likely place, given that that was the only place I had used my basket as a weapon.

I would have expected a small tear or two, or maybe a little hole or snag where it would have caught on a bush or a branch.

But no.

There were several large rips down the middle, in perfectly parallel lines. Like long, sharp fingernails had done this. I placed my hand over the torn cloth. Whoever owned these nails had a bigger hand spread than mine. And much sharper fingernails.

There were some other odd markings, too. Two puncture marks, close together. I held the cloth up to my eyes, then slowly pulled it back, examining it. I couldn't say for certain what they were, but what they reminded me of were bite marks. Such as I had seen when happy patrons bit into their pastries or bread rolls in our bakeshop, too excited or hungry to wait until they had left the shop to eat.

Except these were much bigger and deeper looking than any teeth marks I had ever seen before.

Uneasily, I looked out the window to where full night had fallen. But there was nothing unusual outside, just the cold white stars and the peaceful, silvery moon holding court in the nighttime sky.

I tried to shake off the unsettled feeling. *It's nothing, Claret. Your imagination is just working overtime, that's all.*

I picked up my needle and thread, ready to get to work. And promptly swore at the pinprick of pain. I had jabbed my needle into my thumb, and was rewarded with a bright bead of blood welling from the tip.

Rummaging around in my bedside table's drawer, I found an old strip of cloth and bandaged my thumb. But even as I slowly, clumsily worked on darning the cloth, my injured thumb throbbed, as if it, too, was disturbed by the task at hand.

CHAPTER 7

MY NEXT FEW DAYS settled into a busy, but not unpleasant, routine. Mornings, I would help Mama run the bakeshop. Then in the afternoons, I would stop by Sheriff Tavish's office. While he wouldn't let me up on the roof to help with repairs, there were other things I could assist with. I swept up the rest of the dirt, washed down the walls, and tackled the overgrown garden outside.

Slowly, day by day, the building transformed from a messy former makeshift barn to a respectable-looking office. As he had hoped, Sheriff Tavish began moving his things in. Including his personal effects, like clothes and bedding.

"I've been working out of Mayor Marley's office, and he and his wife have been kind enough to let me stay with them until I could get this office in working order," the sheriff said. "It's not ideal, but I'll stay in the office until I save up enough for my own place."

"Are you sure?" I surveyed the office. It was serviceable, with enough room for a desk, a few chairs—and a small cot in the corner. Still, it could hardly be comfortable.

Sheriff Tavish shrugged. "I'd rather that than rent a room. It may be cramped, but at least I can call the space my own."

The worn furniture that had been passed down from the previous sheriff would have to suffice until funds were allotted for him to buy replacements, but he didn't seem to mind. "Compared to how this place was when I first got here, a threadbare cushion is hardly worth complaining about."

By Daylima, which was the end of a usual work week in Woodside, the sheriff's office was pretty much done. All the major repairs had been completed, and the tasks that were left—namely, Sheriff Tavish settling in—were things I wasn't needed for.

"Again, I couldn't have done this without you," he told me.

I chuckled. "You could have—and you would have. It just would have taken much longer."

He smiled. "Just saying thank you doesn't seem like enough. Will you be at the festival tomorrow?"

"Of course. All of Woodside will be there. And most of Cedarbrook too, if I'm not mistaken."

"Good. I'll see you then."

The promise in his voice caused a happy shiver to run down my spine.

The next day I was up early, waking up with the sunrise. The annual Woodside Spring Festival marked the start of the season, welcoming the warmer weather and longer days. As was tradition, Rowena's Bakeshop would have a booth at the festival. It was usually one of our best-selling days.

Mama had been baking like mad all week, preparing for the event. Fortunately, our booth was just in front of the shop. But there was still much to do. While Mama put the finishing touches on her creations, I got our stall ready, hauling baskets and trays of baked goods outside.

After all that, I must have looked a sweaty mess. And I wouldn't have much time before the festival officially started. I looked towards the bakeshop door anxiously. Where was Mama? I couldn't leave the stall unless she was here, and I wanted to freshen up before—

"Good morning, Miss Claret," a familiar voice said.

Too late.

I gazed up into mesmerizing green eyes, well aware that wisps of my dark hair clung to my forehead and cheeks. I swiped a hand across my face, which only made things worse. I blew at a particularly clingy strand in the corner of my mouth. No luck. It still stuck stubbornly to my cheek. "Good morning, Sheriff Tavish. You're up early."

"I'm a morning person, for sure. Although I tend to stay up late too." He shrugged. "I'm able to get by on little sleep."

"Lucky you." I was a morning person out of necessity. Rowena's Bakeshop did its best business in the morning. But on the occasional holiday when the shop was closed? I'd happily sleep in until midday.

The door behind us opened. I could hear the jingle of the shop's bell. Mama appeared by my side, holding a tray of freshly baked bread. I could feel the heat wafting from it, and the delicious smell was sure to attract potential buyers.

But I couldn't help feeling a little sour. Why couldn't she have come outside just a few moments earlier?

"Sheriff Tavish," Mama said, delighted.

Even though other merchants were setting up their booths around us, it was clear he had singled us out. We were situated in the middle of the street and the rows of stalls, so our booth was an unlikely one to start with for festival goers. Not that there were many walking around at this early hour.

"Good morning, Madam Pangati," the sheriff said politely. "Would you object if I borrowed your daughter for a few hours? I'd like to take her around the festival."

"I need to help Mama here," I said. "Perhaps in—"

"Of course you can," Mama interrupted smoothly. "I can take care of things here for awhile."

I looked at Mama incredulously. This was the Spring Festival. One of the busiest days of the year for Rowena's Bakeshop. She would surely need my help.

She met my gaze and gave me a slow, deliberate wink.

Okay, Mama. I could take the hint.

I kissed her cheek. "Thank you, Mama. We'll walk by every so often to see if you need any help."

"Sure, sure." She winked again. "I'll see you around."

Before we left, Sheriff Tavish bought two pastries from Mama. "Keep the change," he said over her protests.

I had a sneaking suspicion that he had just paid for the other day's complimentary berry tarts, as well as today's treats. Which would only serve to endear him to my mother more.

As we walked away, Sheriff Tavish handed me one of the pastries. "Here you go. I thought you might be hungry." He suddenly looked embarrassed as a thought struck him. "Although I'm sure you eat these all the time."

I took the pastry from him gratefully. "Actually, I don't. Whatever Mama bakes is for the customers. If there are any imperfect items, they go to charity or my Lola Cerise. But I've always loved her baking."

I bit into the treat, enjoying the sweet-and-savory combination of honeyed lamb.

We wandered around the Spring Festival, lingering to look at wares from various stalls. We came across a puppet show in mid-performance, a group of children sitting on the ground in front of the makeshift theater, paying rapt attention. When the performance ended, the sheriff and I clapped as enthusiastically as the rest of the young audience.

The day was growing warmer and the crowds larger. "It seems all of Woodside is out today," Sheriff Tavish commented.

"They are," I said. "And not just them. Just wait until more people from Cedarbrook arrive."

"Does Cedarbrook have—"

A shout caught our attention. We exchanged a brief look, then both took off running in the direction the sound had come from.

A crowd was forming, whispers floating on the air.

"What's going on?"

"Someone's been hurt!"

"Anyone we know?"

"I'm not sure. I don't think so? I can't tell for sure."

Sheriff Tavish gently but purposefully pushed his way through the crowd. I followed on his heels, curious to see what was causing the commotion.

A merchant was leading his skittish, spooked horse, tethered to a cart full of goods, into the town square. One of the wheels bumped against a rock in the road, causing the cart to jolt.

A limp hand flopped over the side.

CHAPTER 8

I GASPED. THE SHOUTS started up again.

"Who is that?"

"What's happened?"

"Is he dead?"

The merchant, winded and equally as spooked as his horse, just shook his head.

Sheriff Tavish took charge of the situation. Turning to the crowd, he blocked the cart with his body and waved them away. "Please, everyone, go about your day. Enjoy the Spring Festival. I'll take care of this."

He pulled one man aside. "Can you fetch Doctor Zonta here, please?" The man nodded and ran off.

One by one, the crowd began to disperse. One person called out, "Thank you, Sheriff Tavish!" and instantly whispered questions spread through the group.

"That's the new sheriff?"

"Glad someone finally filled Arnon's spot."

"He's a handsome one, isn't he?"

Sheriff Tavish ignored the comments and turned back to the cart, leaning over to examine whoever was lying inside. Even though I was probably part of the "everyone" that the sheriff had addressed, I didn't leave.

Besides, I recognized the poor merchant who had brought the unconscious—*hopefully not dead*, I thought—person in his cart.

"Mister Thoms?"

He looked over at me, bewildered. His brow furrowed. "Miss Claret?"

"Yes, that's right. Rowena's daughter."

"Goodness, girl! Here's no place for you." He glanced at the cart.

I followed his gaze, then pointedly turned my back on the cart and focused completely on him. "How are you doing, Mister Thoms? And what happened?"

A torrent of words poured out. "I got a late start from Cedarbrook. I should have been here a few hours ago. If I had, maybe I wouldn't have seen ... as it was, I was the only one on the road ..."

I steered the merchant towards a low stone wall that bordered the road. Gently, I pushed his shoulder until he sat, then sank down next to him.

Mister Thoms kept talking. "I was riding on the wagon seat. We were close to Woodside, maybe just another hour and we'd arrive. Then my horse Bitsy just stopped moving. Something had her spooked, but I couldn't see anything in the road. I'd heard the stories about the attacks in the woods, so I figured Bitsy was smelling some dead animal or something."

He took a deep, shaky breath. "And then I saw the leg sticking out of the bushes. A human leg."

I patted his hand, hoping it would calm him. What should one do or say in a situation like this?

Sheriff Tavish approached us. "Sir? If I might have a word?"

Mister Thoms nodded and stood. The two men walked a short distance away, talking in low voices.

I stood as well and wandered over to Bitsy. Poor beast. She stood stiff and straight, just barely obedient to her master. I could tell she wanted nothing more than to bolt and run, except she was tethered to the cart. But she knew something unnatural or wrong was near her, and she didn't like it at all.

I stroked the horse's nose, talking to it in soft tones. I hadn't finished my savory pastry from earlier, so I now fished in my pocket and offered some of it to Bitsy. She snuffled and eagerly took the treat.

While she ate, I peered into the cart curiously. The hand I had seen earlier belonged to a man, his salt and pepper hair falling in his unconscious face. His shirt was torn in three places, long gashes that revealed equally long, bloodied cuts. I stared at the rips, wondering why they seemed both familiar and unsettling.

In one hand—the one not hanging over the side—the man clutched a red knitted cap.

The man's chest rose and fell, nearly imperceptible. I breathed a sigh of relief. Although he was in bad shape, he was alive. He stirred slightly, and I stared. Something was sticking out from his head. Maybe twigs or leaves from when he had had fallen in the forest?

I reached out to brush the twigs—if that was what they were—away.

The hand hanging over the side of the cart suddenly grabbed my arm.

The man's eyes flew open and fixed on me. I gasped.

I could have sworn they were blue when he first opened them, but as I stared, his eyes turned gold. Instead of normal round pupils, his were odd vertical slits. They grew bigger and rounder as he looked at me.

"Where is it? Where is it?" he demanded.

Eyes wide, I could only stammer, "W-what? Where is what?"

"My cap. Where is it?"

"I-it's in your h-hand, sir."

He clenched his fist, relaxing once he registered the feel of his cap in his hand. He chuckled weakly. "Good. Wouldn't do to lose it. She'd have my hide, if that other one didn't try to take it."

"What do you mean, sir?" I didn't understand his ramblings.

"Red for safety. Red for life." With that, he fell back unconscious. His hand dropped from my arm. Shaken, I moved away from the cart.

"Miss Claret? Are you all right?"

I turned as Sheriff Tavish joined me. I nodded numbly.

He looked from me to the cart. "What happened?"

"The man woke up briefly. He was worried about his hat, until I told him he was holding it. He's out again."

The sheriff frowned. "Where's that doctor?"

As if summoned, Doctor Zonta hurried towards us. "I came as soon as I heard. Where's the patient?"

Sheriff Tavish and I both pointed at the cart. Doctor Zonta nodded. "Bring him along."

We made our way to the physician's office. I eyed the unconscious man while we walked, but he didn't wake up again.

With the help of Doctor Zonta and Mister Thoms, Sheriff Tavish got the man out of the cart and into the office. After a few moments, the sheriff popped his head out. "I might be here for a while. I apologize, Miss Claret. I was hoping we could go around the festival some more ..."

"I completely understand," I said. "I should probably go help Mama with our booth, anyway. Thank you for a lovely day."

He smiled, but his eyes were grim. "If I can, I'll come by your booth again."

"I'd like that." And I was surprised to realize I meant it.

The sheriff went back inside. I slowly headed back towards Rowena's Bakeshop. I could have walked around the Spring Festival by myself, but after what had happened, I wasn't in much of a festival mood anymore.

I spent the rest of the day working the bakeshop stall. Mama didn't say it outright, but I could tell she was glad I had returned early. She had barely been keeping up with the large crowds and huge demand for her food, and my presence was able to relieve her burden a bit.

Sheriff Tavish didn't come by our booth again.

It wasn't until I was safely tucked away in my bed that I was able to ponder some things that had been bothering me. For one, I knew Mister Thoms wasn't the only person from Cedarbrook who had attended the Spring Festival. In fact, he had said he had been running late. So why did no one else from Cedarbrook, who had gone before him, find the man on the side of the road?

Who—or what—had attacked the man? For what purpose?

What had the man meant about "red for safety, red for life"? Who was the "she" that would be upset with him if he lost his cap? Or had they just been the murmurings of a hurt, delirious man?

I put all the questions to the back of my mind. Perhaps Sheriff Tavish would be able to enlighten me when I next saw him.

The handsome sheriff, who had wanted to give me a pleasant day at the festival. Who had kindly returned my basket cloth when I dropped it....

I sat upright, realizing what the tears on the man's shirt had reminded me of. Slash marks, like that of a large animal's claw.

Marks similar to the ones I had mended on my basket cloth.

CHAPTER 9

THE MAN MISTER THOMS had brought on the day of the Spring Festival was the talk of Woodside. By sunrise the next day, the entire town knew about the mysterious man's arrival, his injury, and that it was connected to the string of attacks in the forest.

Mister Thoms had identified him as Brantley Feldan, of Cedarbrook. As Mister Feldan was still injured and unconscious, the Woodside physician would be taking care of him until he was better.

Once Mama heard about Mister Feldan, she was wary, but didn't curtail my visits to Lola Cerise.

But when the body was discovered in Littlewood Forest a few days later, she forbade me to go into the forest.

It was Mister Tabend who reported it. Mister Tabend was one of our neighbors, and his wife was a frequent patron of Rowena's Bakeshop.

He had been in the woods, checking his snares. He had been surprised at how few animals had been caught for it being springtime. Although, with the recent unrest in the forest, perhaps he shouldn't have been. Animals, after all, have a more acute sense of danger than most humans do.

Which may have explained why he didn't notice the figure lying facedown until he was nearly upon them.

Mister Tabend recoiled in fright, then, once his breathing steadied, called out to the figure. "Hello? Hello, sir? Or madam? Are you well?"

When there was no response, Mister Tabend cautiously approached the unmoving form. Although he was sweating from his exertions and the midday sun, Mister Tabend felt a chill creeping down his spine.

He reached out, turning the person onto their back.

And instantly turned and heaved up the contents of his breakfast onto the base of the nearest tree.

The man Mister Tabend had found sported deep gashes, punctuated by dark, dried blood, down the sides of his face and arms. Mister Tabend also saw a small trickle of dried blood falling from one corner of the man's mouth. Eyes wide, jaw slack, the man's pale face was forever frozen in a terrified tableau. Mister Tabend wondered what the poor man had seen before his obviously untimely and gruesome end.

Mister Tabend didn't recognize the man, nor the marks on the deceased's arms. The claw marks were much larger than that of a bear or wolf, the two largest predators in Littlewood Forest. Nor did the animals usually attack humans, unless they were starving or provoked.

A bear's or wolf's claw marks would have come in a set of four, mirroring the swipe of the animal's paw. But the marks on each cheek and arm were a single, long stripe—almost like they had been created by a lone finger with one wickedly sharp nail at its tip.

And, strangest of all, the poor soul had been left mostly intact. Mister Tabend would have expected a wild, starved animal to have ravaged the man until there was hardly anything left. Aside from the cuts that had made him bleed out, the body was in recognizable condition.

Upon his discovery, Mister Tabend went to Sheriff Tavish for help in identifying the dead man. The unfortunate man was from Cedarbrook, and was returned to his town and loved ones. But not before rumors about the man's mysterious murder began flying around Woodside.

"But today is Daypito. Lola Cerise will be expecting me." I couldn't help the small whine that crept into my voice.

"She'll understand," Mama said. "And she wouldn't want you to be in any danger. No, you'll stay here in Woodside until these attacks stop."

"But I'm not—" I stopped. I couldn't argue that I wouldn't run into trouble, because I had. I had just been lucky. But I also couldn't tell Mama about my own near attack experience. Not if I wanted to have the slightest chance of ever going to Cedarbrook again.

"What? You're not what?"

I sighed. "I'm not going to argue with you. You're right."

The surprised look on Mama's face was almost worth my little white lie. Almost.

More days passed in a flurry of activity. Mama was busy preparing for Mayor Marley's event, which left me to cover as many of her duties as I could in the bakeshop. I welcomed the busyness. It took my mind off not being able to visit Lola Cerise, as well as Sheriff Tavish's absence.

I hadn't seen the sheriff since our failed day out at the Spring Festival. With Mister Feldan's unexpected arrival, and then the discovery of the Cedarbrook man, I was sure Sheriff Tavish had much to do. But even knowing that, I still looked up in anticipation every time I heard the shop bell ring.

As usual, we closed in the afternoon and Mama continued working on the mayor's order. I was wiping down a counter when I heard Mama sigh from the back. "Oh, dear."

"What's wrong?" I called to her.

Mama pushed through the door separating our private residence from the shop. She leaned against the closed door, her arms crossed as she looked at me.

"Uh-oh. Am I in trouble?" I asked uncertainly.

She gave another loud sigh. "No, you're not. I'm just not happy."

With me? I refrained from asking. Frantic, I thought back over the last few days. I had been a model daughter, aiding her in the shop without complaint. So, I couldn't be the reason she was upset.

Right?

"You're not in trouble," Mama reassured me again. She must have seen my thoughts on my face. "It's just—I'm low on several things. I've already gone through our garden multiple times, but there's no help for it. I need you to go into the forest tomorrow to gather some items for me."

"Really?" I tried not to sound too happy. "Are you sure?"

"No, I'm not. But what am I supposed to tell Mayor Marley? 'I couldn't fill your order because the woods are scary'?" She ran a frustrated hand through her dark hair, leaving a white streak of flour down several strands. "I'd go with you, but someone's got to run the shop. The Spring Festival was lucrative, but it also made me run through supplies faster than I thought."

"May I ... may I visit Lola Cerise while I'm out there?" I held my breath, afraid she would say no.

Mama paused. "Yes, you may," she began.

I couldn't stop the cheer that escaped my lips.

"*But*," she emphasized, "if you do so, I want you to stay overnight with her. I don't think you'll have enough time to search the woods for what I need, visit your grandmother, and get back here before nightfall. So take your time tomorrow, and then stay safely in Cedarbrook. Come back the next day, by sundown. If you're not here in two days' time, I'll worry. Do you understand?"

"Yes, Mama. And thank you. I promise I'll stay alert and be safe. Now, what would you like me to gather?"

Mama gave me a list of the items she needed. Berries, herbs, nuts. Even little flowers or leaves that could be used as decoration. She also gave me a sizable purse, to purchase extra supplies in Cedarbrook and secure a ride back to Woodside, if I could find anyone traveling this way.

I was so excited to see my lola that I could barely sleep that night. I was up before the sun was, getting ready for the day.

Mama was also up and moving about, although with much less energy. She yawned as she handed me the basket, with the newly mended red cloth lining the bottom.

"No pastries for lola?" I asked, surprised the basket was empty.

Mama shrugged. "Supplies have been so low, I've even been selling the less-than-perfect items. No one seems to notice, as long as they taste good."

I smiled. "And they always do. See? You worried over nothing."

She gave a sheepish smile. "Maybe. But I still don't like selling anything less than my best. And once the mayor's event is over and our supplies are back to normal, I want to get back to having charity items on hand."

I kissed her on the cheek and gave her a quick hug. "Soon, Mama. Soon. And speaking of soon, I'll need to get going shortly." Already the sky was growing lighter outside the shop windows. By the time I reached the edge of town, the sun would be peeking over the horizon.

And I would be safe traversing through the forest.

"Of course. Go on, and say hi to your lola for me."

I headed out, feeling much lighter than I had in days. My red cape billowed around my shoulders, warding off the morning chill. That giddy feeling lasted me well into my walk, and I spent a pleasant hour or two strolling through the forest, stopping occasionally to gather something from Mama's list.

As I wandered deeper into the forest, my happiness faded. My basket was about halfway full. A presentable amount, but nowhere near what Mama needed to fulfill Mayor Marley's order.

Daylight filtered through the trees. I couldn't tell exactly what time it was, but I judged it to be about mid-morning. Perhaps even midday, from the rumbling of my stomach. I still had plenty of time to stay in the woods.

Also, it was getting hot under my thick cloak. I removed it, folding it over my arm.

I spied a small shrub growing near the forest path, and eagerly headed towards it. I hung my cloak on a nearby tree branch and put the basket on the ground. Kneeling by the shrub, I rooted around in it, retrieving a small handful of wild blueberries.

Perhaps I could get more? But additional searching turned up nothing. I sighed.

"Why so glum, miss?"

CHAPTER 10

I STARTLED, MY ARM scraping against one of the shrub's twigs. Carefully, I extracted my arm before turning around to face the speaker.

"Oh! Sheriff Tavish! I didn't expect to see you out here."

He shrugged. "I'm often here these days."

I nodded in understanding. "The investigation, I'm sure. How goes it?"

"Well enough, I suppose. I'm just getting started."

"I hope you find the person or creature responsible. The attacks have everyone on edge."

"I'm sure."

"What do you think it is?"

Sheriff Tavish looked off in the distance, lost in his thoughts. "An animal, I think. Something large and hungry."

I shivered. "Hungry?"

He nodded. "Starving, more like. With the late spring, it's probably famished from going so long with little food. Give it a few more weeks, and I'm sure the attacks will stop."

"I hope so. Mama nearly didn't want me to come here today, except she needed supplies. So here I am, foraging for her." I smiled. "But at least I get to visit my grandmother later, so the work is worth it."

"Oh? Who is your grandmother? And where does she live?"

"My Lola Cerise? Just on the edge of the forest, by Cedarbrook." I frowned. "Haven't I told you that already?"

"Have you? Forgive me, miss. It's been a busy few days."

"I understand. It's been busy for me, too." I chuckled. "I hope you didn't forget my name."

"Of course not. But I was hoping ..."

When he didn't finish, I prompted, "Yes, Sheriff Tavish?"

He smiled at me, suddenly shy. "I would be honored if you would call me by my given name, instead of being so formal."

"Y-you want me to call you ... Hunter?"

"Please. I would be honored, Miss—"

"Oh, you can drop the 'miss'. Just Claret is fine."

"Claret." His soft, velvety voice sent shivers down my spine. He winked at me. "I wouldn't want you to get in trouble with your family. We can drop the titles when we're alone, here in the woods. But I'll make sure to call you Miss Claret in town."

I smiled. "Agreed."

He knelt down beside me. "What are you doing?"

I sat back, frustrated. "Trying to gather some berries for Mama. But this shrub seems to have run out."

"Ah. Well, there are some over there."

My eyes followed his pointing finger. Sure enough, there was a thicket of wild blueberries growing farther into the woods.

I stood up, excited. "Oh, that's perfect!" I scooped up my basket, taking two steps before my mind caught up to my feet. I hesitated.

"What's wrong, Claret?" Hunter asked me.

Although it was nice thinking of Sheriff Tavish as just Hunter, a tingling sensation crawled down my spine that had nothing to do with those happy feelings. I shook my head, as if that could shake off my unease. "It's nothing. Something silly, really. It's just—Mama always warned me about not leaving the road. It's too easy to get lost in the woods, unless you stay on the path."

I looked down at my still-not-full basket, undecided. "But it's already been half a day, and this is all I've found ..."

"That bush isn't far from the road," Hunter pointed out. "And I'll help you."

I smiled gratefully at him. "Thank you. Hunter." For saying his name, I was rewarded with an answering twinkle in those striking green eyes.

We set to work gathering blueberries. With Sheriff Tavish—I mean, Hunter—helping me, the task went faster. We didn't talk much, but just being around him was pleasant.

Every so often, Hunter would point out another shrub or tree or plant, something that was on Mama's list. Delighted, we continued to forage.

My basket grew heavy. I checked it, realizing it was nearly full to the brim. I chuckled. "Hunter, I think I'm good for the day. Any more and I'd have to use my cloak to carry things. If you have any—" I broke off as I straightened and looked around.

Hunter was nowhere to be seen. I was standing in gloomy deep woods, with no sight of the path through the forest. I would have followed the blueberry thicket back to the road, but I had strayed from it, following Hunter's suggestions of other things to gather.

My heart beat faster. Was I lost?

"Hunter?" I called out. "Hunter, where are you?"

No response.

With the increased tree cover, it was hard for me to tell what time of day it was. I also wasn't sure how long I had been foraging since I had left the road. I shivered, cold without my red cloak to cover me.

And it felt awfully quiet around here.

"Hunter?" I called again, but not as loudly as before. When I still didn't get a response, I tried to retrace my steps.

Let's see ... I turned left to get these walnuts. They were close to where Hunter pointed out the mint. But was it ten steps, or twenty, to the thicket?

"Claret."

I jumped at how close Hunter's voice was. I turned, and he was right by my side. I hadn't even heard him join me. "Hunter. I thought I had lost you." I had to stop myself from throwing my arms around him and giving him a big hug, I was so relieved.

"It's all right, Claret. I'm right here."

"I can see that. How did you move so silently? And where were you?"

"Gathering some more for you. Here, give me your basket." When I held it out, he poured an abundance of nuts into it. Chestnuts, hazelnuts, acorns. Even a few pine cones. The basket threatened to spill over with his bounty.

"Wow," I said, eyeing everything as it spilled from his hands. "I didn't realize you had found so much."

He shrugged modestly. "I'm good at woodcraft."

I smiled. "That explains why I didn't hear you, then."

He grinned in confirmation.

"Well, Hunter—or should I call you Mister Woodsman?—if you're so clever, help us find the road again."

"That's easy." He waved his hand in dismissal. "I know exactly how to get us back to the road. Follow me."

With that, he confidently set off, with me on his heels. I wouldn't have been able to get back to the path without his help. There were more turns than I remembered, and it felt like we walked for quite some time. It hadn't felt that far going deeper into the woods, but then again, I hadn't been paying too much attention. I had relied on Hunter to be my eyes.

We reached the road again, and I was relieved to see my red cloak still hanging from the tree, like a bright flag beckoning me back.

I promptly put my basket on the ground and grabbed my cloak, throwing it around my shoulders and fastening it at the neck. "Oh, that's so much better. I was getting cold back there."

Hunter gazed at me, but his eyes seemed unfocused.

I waved a hand in front of his face. "Hunter? Hunter, are you all right?"

He blinked. "Oh, sorry, Claret. I was just thinking about ... something. It's no matter. Are you going back to Woodside?"

I shook my head. "No. It's late in the day, and Cedarbrook is closer. Besides, I want to visit my lola. What about you?"

"I was planning on returning to Woodside, yes. But I can escort you to Cedarbrook, if you like."

I did like, but I also didn't want Hunter caught in the woods at sunset. "No, you should get going. You've got a longer trip than I do. I'll be all right."

"Okay, then." He seemed reluctant to leave. I didn't blame him. I felt the same way.

After an awkward pause, I said, "Well, I'll get going, then."

I pulled the hood of my cloak up over my head, then bent down and picked up my basket. I made sure the cloth was tucked firmly over the top, keeping the contents secure, then turned to Hunter. "Farewell, Hunter. I hope to see you when I return to Woodside."

Inspired, I added, "And you're always welcome at Rowena's Bakeshop. Or at my Lola Cerise's."

"You can count on it," he said. "Goodbye, Claret."

I gave him a little wave, then started walking towards Cedarbrook. A few steps away, I paused and turned around.

Hunter was looking down the road after me, but not at me. Perhaps he was lost in thought again. I waved again, but he didn't react.

Odd. Who would have thought Woodside's new sheriff was such a daydreamer? Smiling to myself, I continued on my way.

CHAPTER 11

MY LOLA'S CHEERY LILT greeted my knock.

"Who's there?"

"It's Claret, lola."

"Oh! Come in, come in!"

I waited, but the door didn't open. So I tried the handle and found it unlocked. Again. Frowning, I pushed open the door and went inside.

"Claret!" Lola Cerise shuffled towards me. "I'm so happy to see you, my dear!"

I embraced her. "I'm happy to see you too, lola." I stepped back, frowning. "But your door was unlocked again. I thought I told you to keep it locked? There's been another attack in the woods. Someone from Cedarbrook this time."

"Oh really?" she said. "I hadn't heard. That's a bit of nasty business, isn't that."

"All the more reason for you to lock your door."

She chuckled as I set my near-overflowing basket on the table. "Sit, sit. I'll make some tea, and we'll talk. Have you seen that handsome sheriff again lately?"

I blushed. "Actually ..."

Lola Cerise bustled around the kitchen, getting our tea ready, while I recounted my recent meetings with Sheriff Tavish. I mean, *Hunter*. I blushed again as his given name nearly slipped from my lips.

My grandmother giggled and "ohh"ed and gasped at the appropriate moments, relishing my stories as if she herself had lived through them. "Such a shame, that you weren't able to spend more time with the sheriff. What happened at the festival anyway, that he was called away so quickly?"

"Oh," I said, realizing I had glossed over the details of Mister Feldan's arrival. I had only told Lola Cerise that someone had been brought to Woodside, injured. "Mister Thoms found a man in the woods who had been attacked by the same mysterious thing that's been haunting the woods lately. A Mister Feldan. Poor man. Even delirious, he was so concerned about possibly losing his red cap."

Lola Cerise stilled. "Feldan's back?" she muttered. "He must have been on his way—"

She stopped. Speaking louder, she said, "He didn't lose his cap, did he?"

"No, he still had it," I said, wondering at my grandmother's strange reaction. "He said someone would have his hide if he lost it."

I chuckled, trying to ease the tension. "Probably much like you'd have mine if I lost my cloak. I took it off in the forest when Sheriff Tavish and I were gathering berries, and I nearly—"

Lola Cerise rounded on me, fiercer than I'd ever seen her.

"Claret! What do you mean, you took off your cloak?"

I hesitated, surprised at the force of her words. "It was hot, lola. It was just easier to move around without all that heavy fabric."

Lola Cerise moved so fast that I barely had time to take a breath. She cupped my face between her hands as she stared deeply into my eyes. "Claret. Claret, my dear. You must never, *never* take off your cloak in Littlewood Forest. Ever."

Unsettled by her intensity, I stammered, "W-what do you mean? Why not?"

"Because there will be powerful creatures that want to hurt you, my dear, by virtue of who you are and what you represent. And until you come into your own, you will lack the power you need to fight them. Which is why I gave you that cloak. To protect you."

"What do you mean?" I whispered.

My grandmother took a deep breath, then shuffled back to the kitchen. She picked up the tea tray, but her hands were shaking so badly I could hear the cups rattle. I jumped up and took the tray from her, bringing it to the table.

Lola Cerise sat down, blowing out a shaky breath.

"Lola? What is it?"

She slowly raised her eyes to meet mine. "My dear Claret. How much do you remember of the old stories?"

I blinked. That wasn't a topic I had expected to discuss. Ever since I was a child, my lola would tell me stories of the Fae, the untamable magical beings that lived in the woods, the water, all around us. They influenced the land and its people, and to run afoul of them was to court disaster. But to befriend them, or impress them—that could reap benefits that lasted a person's entire life.

At least, according to her. I had never run into any of these mythical creatures—not for lack of trying. But eventually I grew up, and grew out of the tales.

Or so I had thought.

Slowly, I said, "Just little bits and pieces. Always be polite, to everyone, because you can't be sure they're not a faery in disguise. Don't forget to leave out little offerings on the high feast days, lest you forgo blessings for a year. Luck compounds luck." I paused. "I know there were many others, but that's all that comes to mind right now."

She patted my hand, pleased. "Even recalling those lessons are good enough. Why do you think I always told you those stories?"

I shrugged. "Because ... they were amusing? They kept me out of trouble? I don't know, lola."

She laughed. "True, those were some of the reasons. But mostly because it was the easiest way for you to learn about your heritage. My dear Claret, I am one of the Fae."

"Excuse me?" Perhaps I hadn't heard her right.

Lola Cerise smiled. "As I said. I am Fae. Your mother is half Fae. You are the result of her union with a fully Fae man. You, my dear, are three quarters Fae."

I? Part Fae? What did she mean?

"But—" I blurted out the first thing my mind could grasp. "My father is dead. He can't be a Fae."

My grandmother sighed, her eyes sad. "Those things are not contradictory, my dear. They can both be true, or not."

I guess I always assumed my father was human. My mind reeled as I tried to make sense of all of this. "I've never seen you perform any magic!"

"Nothing flashy, true. But there are a lot of little magics that you probably never even noticed." She waved a hand around her house. "What do you see?"

I ran a finger along the top of the table. "Well, for one thing, you've let things get dusty again."

"A little dirt never hurt," she chided. "Look a little closer."

I did, slowly surveying her house. Besides her obsession with all things red, I saw—"Wait. Crocus *and* hibiscus, blooming at the same time? I didn't think that was possible."

"It is, if you're a caretaker of the woods," Lola Cerise said. "Anything else?"

My eyes kept straying to one of the knickknacks on the shelf. There was one, a cute little cat peeking out of a pot, that I'd always admired. But now, as I stared at it, something about it seemed off.

The cat moved.

No, wait. The cat hadn't moved. It was something—some*one*—else. A small head peered around the figurine cat's head, blinking at me with wide violet eyes. Pointed ears marked it as non-human—although its diminutive size already helped me figure that out. Behind its tiny humanlike body, I could see shimmery green and purple wings.

When it realized I saw it, it gave a little shriek and flitted away. I tracked its movement, seeing ...

More.

More creatures. Tiny little humanlike flying ones. A stout, hardy-looking being with a long, shaggy beard, no bigger than a toddler. A tall, thin creature that looked like a walking tree, so covered in vines and leaves it blended in with my lola's plants.

I blinked, not daring to believe my eyes. But now that I could see these wondrous beings, I couldn't unsee them.

I turned to my grandmother, still in shock. "Lola," I whispered. "I-I think I'm going crazy. I'm ... seeing things."

Again. Unbidden, a distant memory of my five-year-old self seeing beings much like these came back.

"No, you're not," she said solemnly. Around us, the little creatures relaxed somewhat and started coming out of their hiding places.

"But grandma ... who are all these people?"

Lola Cerise puffed up proudly. "These are the minor Fae that are under my protection. For I am the Scarlet Lady, the official Keeper of Littlewood Forest."

Chapter 12

MY EYES WIDENED AND my jaw dropped. "Keeper? Of the forest? What are you talking about, lola?"

Lola Cerise held out a hand. The little winged humanlike creature I had seen earlier flew over and alighted on her open palm. "As I said. I am the Keeper of Littlewood Forest. As my mother was before me, and her mother before that. As my daughter was supposed to be, although things worked out differently. But there is still hope for Littlewood's future."

She leveled a serious gaze at me. "For her daughter will be the Keeper, after me."

This was too much for my mind to follow. I sat down and put my head in my hands, massaging my temples. "Lola, I think you'd better start at the beginning."

Lola Cerise chuckled and handed me a cup of tea. "Here you go, my dear. You might need this."

She was right. I did need a cup of tea. Several, in fact.

Five cups later, my head was reeling from everything my lola had told me. And she still wasn't done.

Apparently, my great-great grandmother was Fae. And not just any Fae. She had been the official guardian of the nearby forest, appointed by none other than the Fae king himself. As such, my relative's life was bound to the forest's—if the forest died, then so too would my ancestor. And vice versa.

Although the Fae were long-lived—their lives spanned centuries, as opposed to humans' decades—eventually they succumbed to age and time. She had passed down her magical abilities to my great-grandmother, who had then passed it to my Lola Cerise. All three women were fully Fae, and had full and perfect Fae powers.

But then Lola Cerise had done the unthinkable, and fallen in love with a human man.

"I loved my Randwyn dearly." My grandmother lovingly ran her fingers over the plain wooden frame that held a small painting of her and my late grandfather. I only vaguely remembered him, as he had passed away when I was three. "And he was fiercely devoted to me, and your mother. But being with him had an unforeseen consequence—Rowena was born without any magic."

"Really? How did you know?" I wondered.

"She couldn't see the creatures we are tasked with watching over." Lola Cerise waved a hand around the room, at the various beings—*Fae*, I corrected myself—that flew or walked or slinked or sat. "And not for lack of trying. I can only surmise that Randwyn's wholly humanness suppressed any Fae magic Rowena might have inherited. We waited and waited for her magic to appear. So many years, so many tears. But no powers ever awakened."

She leveled an assessing look at me. "Not like you, my dear."

I shook my head. "I don't understand. How can I see them when Mama can't? And what does all of this mean?"

"What do you know about your father?"

The question took me off guard. "Not much. Mama said he died shortly after I was born. There are no portraits of him anywhere in our house. Mama doesn't like talking about him. She says it's too painful."

Lola Cerise's eyes were sad. "It's painful because it's a lie. He didn't die, my dear. He left you and your mother in Woodside while he returned to Faerie."

I gasped in shock. And yet, somehow, some part of me knew, deep down, that my grandmother's words were true.

"What—why—?"

She put her hands up, as if she could ward my questions away.

"I do not know the details, nor did I ever push Rowena for them. It hurt me to see my daughter hurting, so I didn't pry." She sighed. "I just know that your father left this realm, but not before he gave you a gift."

She took a deep breath. "His Faerie blood awakened something in you that Rowena, with her human father, lacked. You've always been curious and believing of my stories, and at one time, when you were very young, you were able to see your future charges. Now that you can see them once more, I know for sure that you will be able to take on the mantle of Keeper of Littlewood Forest when I go. You've proven that with your ability to see, really see, all the Little People."

She chuckled. "That's why it's called Littlewood Forest, after all. For the Fair Folk, the tiny Fae that call these woods their home."

"But ... Mama ..." I protested weakly.

Lola Cerise shook her head sadly. "As I said, she can't see them, or hear them, or sense them. Her frustration over it led her to believe that my stories were nothing more than lies meant to drive her crazy. The more I insisted she try, the more she resisted. Now her heart is so set against it that even if she suddenly inherited my magic, she still would deny the presence of the forest Fae."

Everything became crystal clear to me. My mother's reluctance to have me visit Lola Cerise regularly, and her sometimes near jealousy of our close relationship. But also the guilt and sadness that tinged her demeanor whenever she talked of her mother, or gave me baked goods to take to my lola.

When I was a child, and Mama would accompany me on these weekly visits, Mama had always been tight-lipped and disapproving when Lola Cerise would tell me stories. As I got older and could visit Lola Cerise on my own, my grandmother had still told me the stories, but I had learned not to recount them to Mama when I returned home.

Tears pricked my eyes. I tried to blink them away, but one slipped down my face. "I'm sorry, lola. I had no idea."

Her answering smile was bittersweet. "I know, my dear. I know."

We sat in silence for a few moments. I took a sip of tea, my eyes darting all around the room. A shy creature, with long green vines for hair and a vaguely feminine form made of bark and twigs, waved at me from the small tree in the corner. I tentatively waved back.

A high-pitched giggle caught my attention, and I turned my head sharply to the left to follow the sound. A tiny flying human with oversized gossamer wings flitted around my head, then landed on my shoulder. Cross-eyed, I looked down at the diminutive Fae creature.

"That's a pixie." Lola Cerise indicated the being on my shoulder, then pointed to the one that had waved at me. "And that's a dryad."

She went around the room, introducing me to all the Fae. I tried my best to remember their names and what manner of creatures they were, but I found myself mixing them all up.

Lola Cerise giggled. "Don't worry. You'll learn who, and what, they all are in due time."

"I hope so." I sighed and eyed her sidelong. Teasingly, I waggled my eyebrows at her. "Are you sure I'm not dreaming? Did you add something to my tea, perhaps?"

In response, she reached over and pinched the back of my hand, hard.

"Ow!"

"How real did that feel, hmm?" said my grandmother, unrepentant.

I put my teacup down and rubbed the back of my hand. A small red crescent moon showed where her fingernails had pinched me. "Okay, okay. I promise not to doubt you—or myself—again."

"Good." She sat back, satisfied. "Now that it's clear *who* you're meant to be, we should address the *how*."

"What? What do you mean?"

She waved a hand at the neat rows of books lined up on a nearby shelf. "Take a look."

Curious, I stood up and did as she suggested. My eyes wandered over the familiar spines. Many were as I remembered—handwritten recipe collections, an old primer that my grandmother had used to teach me my letters, a collection of essays from a writer whose work Lola Cerise loved reading in the weekly newspaper.

I blinked as the writing on some of the book spines wavered and changed.

"*The Care and Feeding of Your Faerie Friends. Woodland Fae: An Introduction. Magic and Faerie Folklore?*" I turned to Lola Cerise, confused. "These weren't here before. Were they? Or did I just never notice?"

My lola's face was serene. "A bit of both, my dear. They aren't accessible, unless you have awakened Fae blood. I and all the other Faerie creatures you see in this room can see those titles and read those books. Rowena couldn't, because her Faerie side never awakened. But yours has, so you can."

I ran a wondering finger over the newly formed titles. A few of the books hadn't changed, but the majority of them had. I grinned. "I guess I have a lot of reading in my future."

An answering grin spread across my grandmother's face. "That's my girl."

I plucked a slim volume from the shelf. It was bound in red cloth—what else? I would expect nothing less. Gold lettering spelled out the title: *Faerie Lore and Legends.* "This looks interesting. May I borrow it?"

"Of course, my dear, of course. Help yourself." Her eyes twinkled. "Study hard. There may be a test later."

I chuckled at her jest, then sobered. "But then, who are these unknown enemies I needed a red cape for protection from?"

The twinkle faded from Lola Cerise's eyes. "The Fae live in that Other Realm which is near to our world, yet not. Littlewood Forest is one of the places where the border between our human world and their magical one runs thin, and it is easy for the Fae to cross into our world, or vice versa.

"We Keepers have many roles. We make sure the minor Fae of the forest are safe and their magic stays strong. As the belief in magic and Faerie waxes and wanes, so have the forest Fae. And yet, if any from Woodside or Cedarbrook wander into the Other Realm, it would go badly for them, so we must make sure no humans are lost to Faerie.

"And finally, if any unsanctioned Fae come over to our world with their pure unchecked power, they can wreak great havoc, even in a place that doesn't believe in their existence. For some time, we've been fortunate that hasn't happened. But I always wanted to be prepared, which is why I made you that cloak, with all its magical protections.

"And I'm glad I did, for I fear that our good fortune has ended."

CHAPTER 13

Before I could ask her to explain further, Lola Cerise clapped her hands. "But enough melancholy talk. This is a time for celebration! In fact—" her eyes twinkled as she gazed at me "—I believe it is the right and proper time to pass on the title to you, my dear Claret."

"What?" Startled, I breathed in wrong, then started coughing. I took a sip of tea that had gone cold long ago. I grimaced at the taste, but it did the trick, settling my throat. When I had recovered enough, I said, "Why me? Why now?"

"Because it's time and past for a new Scarlet Lady to be recognized," Lola Cerise said. "I'm certainly not getting any younger. The forest Fae can see you—and more importantly, have accepted you."

An answering giggle came from somewhere nearby. Behind the curtain, I thought.

"Besides." My grandmother turned uncharacteristically serious. "My ability is waning. I've been the Scarlet Lady for some time now, but it wasn't meant to be forever. I would need to pass on the mantle sooner rather than later." She sighed. "These attacks that have been happening in Littlewood Forest ... if I was even just a few years younger, still at my full strength, they would not have happened. Now, I can feel that evil creature testing my protections, piercing through them ... and I am powerless to stop it."

"Oh," I breathed, a sad understanding washing over me. "It's not your fault. Things happen."

"Not on my watch. At least, not before." She patted my hand. "But it won't be that way when you take on the title."

I looked down, overwhelmed at the new responsibility I would be undertaking. And sad at the thought of my dear grandmother getting older, more frail and powerless. Nobody could stop time's inevitable march, not even otherworldly magic.

"Come, my dear. It's not that bad. And I'll be here to guide you, until you are fully ready." Lola Cerise patted my hand.

"Okay, then." Nerves and excitement warred in my body. I blew out a breath, trying to steady myself. "What do I need to do?"

"It's simple, really. We just need a few things." She instructed me to fetch a small, sharp knife from the kitchen, an old towel, and some bandages from the closet at the end of the hall.

I brought everything back, depositing it on the small wooden dining table.

"Perfect, my darling." She stood up, scooping up a lit candle. "If you would be so good as to bring everything with you. Let's go."

"What? Where are we going?"

Lola Cerise gestured towards the cottage door. "Into Littlewood Forest. There's only one place where this can be done. And you should know about it, anyway. Come."

I hastily shoved the bandages in my pocket, before wrapping the knife in the towel and tucking the whole bundle under one arm. Then I grabbed my cloak and put it on. Lola Cerise had already exited the cottage, and I could see the slight glow of her candle moving towards the forest.

At the forest's edge, Lola Cerise turned and motioned to me. "Come, Claret. The night isn't getting any younger."

"But ..." I hesitated. "What about the creature that's haunting the forest, attacking people?"

My grandmother's face was serene. "We'll be all right. But a little bit of caution couldn't hurt. Stay quiet, and follow me."

I choked back further protests and obeyed my grandmother.

In the darkened woods, I had no idea where we were or how long we walked. Every tree seemed to be a phantom shadow ready to strike. But Lola Cerise continued on, calm and confident, her little lone candlelight the only thing keeping the oppressive darkness at bay.

Slowly, I realized the darkness was receding.

I looked up. Had we entered a clearing where the moon could shine down?

But no. We were still somewhere deep within Littlewood Forest. The moon and stars were nowhere in sight.

So why was it getting brighter?

Lola Cerise stopped. "Here we are."

I gasped as I got a good look at what "here" was.

Two large, luminescent cedar trees stood before us. The glowing trees formed the frame of a shimmery silvery-white archway. I couldn't see what was beyond the pale light between the trees. Except I didn't think it was more of Littlewood Forest—the light of this large doorway looked like it disappeared into vast white nothingness.

Before the doorway was a fallen log, just a few paces in front of the gate. One side of the log had been smoothed over to create a flat, level surface, creating a natural, impromptu altar.

No, not impromptu. As I examined it closer, I saw unusual markings carved into the wood, running around the entire length of the altar.

"Lola Cerise, what is this place?"

She chuckled. "This, my dear, is an interstice. A gateway to Faerie. It is a place where the borders between the Other Realm and ours runs thin, and people can cross into Faerie, or vice versa. The magic of Faerie spills into our world from here, and here our humanity streams into Faerie, grounding them. Although many times our worlds are at odds with each other, we also need each other. Without us, the Fae would untether and eventually fade away. And without the Fae, we would lose our sense of beauty and wonder."

She pointed at the altar. "Here, Faerie magic meets human power, tying the two worlds together. It keeps the forest alive and the gateway between the worlds open. Other interstices that serve as bridges between the two worlds have similar conduits, to merge and focus our often opposing magics. It is necessary to ensure both sides are balanced and stable."

I eyed the smooth, unbroken surface of the altar. "What happens if the magic is taken? Or separated?"

Lola Cerise sighed. "Then the gateway will dim, and eventually close. The forest will die. The tether will snap, and the backlash will drain the nearby Fae—on both sides of the portal—of their magic."

"And the people of Cedarbrook and Woodside?"

My grandmother spoke with haunted conviction. "Those who don't die outright in the first few moments after the untethering will become mere shells of themselves. Absent of joy, absent of love. No better than cornered, feral animals."

I fell silent. I had assumed that the sleepy towns of Cedarbrook and Woodside had always been as they were, but it was possible my unnaturally long-lived Fae grandmother had lived through what she was warning me about.

I looked up at the silvery-white gateway, mulling over my grandmother's words.

Lola Cerise held her free hand out to me. "Here, my dear. Help an old woman, please."

I sprang to her side and helped her over to the altar. She leaned against it, panting slightly. "My mind may feel young, but my body certainly doesn't."

"Lola? If you'd like to go back—"

"Not yet, my dear. Let's do what we came here to do, first."

She placed the candle down, then indicated I should do the same with the items I had brought. The candle's meager light was hardly necessary against the bright shimmer spilling from the gateway, but Lola Cerise used it to sterilize the knife, holding its blade against the flame. When she was finished, she put the knife down on one of the towels to let it cool.

"You're right-handed, is that correct?" When I nodded, she smiled. "Just like your lola."

She picked up the knife, and with one swift movement, sliced open the palm of her right hand.

"Lola!" I gasped. I made to pick up a bandage, but she waved me away.

"In a minute. Now you, dear."

Reluctantly, I held out my right hand, hissing when the knife sliced into my flesh. Bright red drops of blood appeared instantly, mirroring the blood dripping from my grandmother's palm.

"And now, place your hand against mine."

I pressed my palm to Lola Cerise's. Our blood smeared and intermingled.

"I, the Scarlet Lady, Keeper of Littlewood Forest, do hereby recognize you, Claret Pangati, as my successor, the next Scarlet Lady of Littlewood Forest. Do you accept this responsibility?"

"Uh ..." My voice came out in a little squeak. I cleared my throat and tried again. "Yes. Yes, I do."

Warmth began to spread from where our palms touched. It wasn't overwhelming or unpleasant, just a little touch of heat, almost like I had put my fingers to the flickering candle.

"Good. As such, my powers are your powers, and my knowledge is your knowledge. The wild magic of Littlewood Forest and its denizens are yours to command and call forth whenever you have need. Should you ever betray your calling, that same wild magic will seek you and destroy you. Do you accept this bane?"

I didn't really want to, but I didn't think I had a choice. So I just said meekly, "Yes."

The warm feeling trailed down my hand, through my arm.

Lola Cerise smiled. "Then go forth as the new Scarlet Lady."

Now the warmth spread throughout my entire body. I felt lighter, brighter.

"Put your hand on the altar. With me, now."

Together, we placed both of our cut hands, palm down, on the altar.

A rushing sound filled my ears, and I heard a sudden chorus of voices surrounding me. "All hail the Scarlet Lady of Littlewood Forest!"

The wood glowed underneath our hands, outlining them in the same silvery-white as the Faerie gateway. The strange symbols I had noted earlier flared to life, first the white of Faerie, then red. Perhaps to symbolize my position as the new Scarlet Lady?

The colors mixed together into a rich rose hue. Then, to my surprise, the glow turned golden, spilling in all directions to cover the entire altar. With one last pulse of color, the golden hue turned darker and faded, becoming the reddish-brown of freshly cut cedar wood.

The chorus crescendoed, then stopped abruptly.

The woods were once again as they were—the doorway to Faerie in front of me, my Lola Cerise beside me, both of our hands lying flat against the altar's smooth wooden top.

"Oh, my." Lola Cerise sounded surprised. "I wasn't expecting that."

"What happened?" I wondered aloud. "What weren't you expecting?"

"What happened is that you are now the new Scarlet Lady, Keeper of Littlewood Forest. The forest has recognized you, and you are now one," Lola Cerise said proudly. Then she paused and studied me. "And, my dear, it seems you are more powerful than even I thought."

"What do you mean?"

"Those of Faerie are made of magic. It flows freely in our world and through our veins, ethereal and potent. Humans possess their own innate magic, but due to culture and tradition, not every mortal can access that magic. Some learn through light or dark ritual, or by sheer accident. Many more never learn.

"But your magic has not only been awakened, your magic is a mix of both worlds. Something unique and rare. I don't even know how I'll be able to teach you how to use it, although I'll certainly try."

I eyed the now faded altar warily. "Is that why that table glowed? And what were those strange symbols?"

"That altar is a totem of the union between Faerie and the mortal world," Lola Cerise explained. She smiled. "Kind of like you. Made of the cedar wood found here in Littlewood Forest, it is imbued with Fae magic—as evidenced by the symbols carved into and around it. Our mingled blood awakened it and allowed it to recognize you as the incoming Scarlet Lady. Over time, as you grow into your powers and duty, you will be able to access the magic here freely. And, I dare say, more deeply than I have ever been able to access it. But for now, to reach it quickly, your blood would be required."

I stared down at my hand. *My blood. Red ... for life.*

Looking around, I realized the area had taken on a sharper quality, as if before I had only had viewed things with a dull impression, but now could see things as they truly were. The forest smelled more crisp, and I could sense where the Fae creatures of Littlewood Forest were, safe in their hidey-holes and homes.

"Everything feels so ... new," I wondered.

My grandmother laughed. "You'll adjust to it, in time. But that awareness will never go away. You'll just be able to call it forth when needed, and dampen it when not. Don't worry, my dear. I'll show you how."

She withdrew her hand. I did too, and was surprised to see that the cut in my palm had closed seamlessly, as if no injury had ever been inflicted.

"Wow," I breathed. I began to gather everything up, pausing as I came to the bandages. "I guess I didn't need to bring these."

"It never hurts to be prepared, my dear."

I looked around, half expecting something to happen. "Now what?"

My grandmother yawned. "Now? We sleep. Let's go back."

CHAPTER 14

DESPITE MY NEWFOUND KNOWLEDGE about my heritage and my parents—not to mention my new awareness of all the extra residents in my grandmother's cottage—I slept well that night.

In the morning, as we lingered over breakfast, I asked, "Lola, I've always been curious. Is there any reason you've stayed here in this cottage, instead of moving in with Mama and me? I know she asked you, repeatedly, for a time, until she finally gave up on you ever leaving."

Lola Cerise sighed and looked around her cozy little cottage. "This is the home that my Randwyn built when we were first wed and I accepted the job to become the Scarlet Lady. I wove all our love and magic into this home, and it's always kept me safe. It's also located in an area that's not quite Cedarbrook and not quite Woodside. Much like Littlewood Forest—of Faerie and humanity, all at once. It's the perfect place for a Keeper like me to watch over her forest."

I looked forward to learning more about my eventual duties and Fae heritage, although my enthusiasm was a bit dampened, knowing I might not be able to share any of it with my mother. At best, she would be uncomprehending but neutral. At worst, talking about it would just drive a further wedge between her and my grandmother.

In fact, as a general rule, Lola Cerise cautioned me to be choosy in who I told about my Fae heritage. With my mother, it was simply a courtesy, a way not to hurt her. With others, they might take me for a madwoman, or a witch. In our sister towns of Cedarbrook and Woodside, magic was not entirely frowned upon, but not entirely embraced, either.

"And," Lola Cerise said, "there might be a rare few who can see the things you see all the time, as you now can. A human can sometimes get a glimpse into the Faerie realm, but those times are so sparse that when it does happen, he or she might dismiss it as dreaming. If you meet someone who has your special sight, take note, for they too might be of Faerie."

Speaking of those of Faerie, Lola Cerise counseled me to visit Mister Feldan. "Please tell him I hope he feels better soon, and tell him to come see me as soon as he is able."

I made ready to leave for Woodside. As I hefted my near overflowing basket, I commented, "Perhaps this would be easier to carry in my cloak. I could make a sling, and—"

Lola Cerise hushed me, her eyes bright and intense. "No, my dear Claret. You must never take off your red cloak in the forest."

"It was only a joke," I said uneasily, wondering how I had upset her.

"Not to me, it isn't." She touched the soft crimson fabric that hung around my shoulders. "I made this for you. I made this—do you understand? It's faery made, with magical properties. Red for concealment, for luck, and with all the most potent charms and blessings I could imbue it with."

I laughed. "Red, to conceal? Red has to be the flashiest color there is, lola."

"Not to some, it isn't. Not to some."

I wanted to know what she meant—indeed, her cryptic words introduced more questions than answers—but she shooed me out the door. "We've wasted enough of the day as it is. Get going back home, safely and swift."

"All right, lola." She walked me to the front door, where I kissed her wrinkled cheek. "Don't forget to lock the door after I leave."

"And you don't ever take off that cloak until you're clear of the forest!" She put my hood up, settling it around my head. She then crossed her arms and gave me a stern look. "Promise me!"

"Okay, okay. I promise."

I chuckled and waved, then turned and headed into the woods.

Not an hour into my walk, I regretted my promise. Despite the trees' shade, the day was unusually hot, more akin to summer rather than the first stirrings of spring. The basket weighed heavily on my arm, and my hand was cramping from carrying it.

Sweat trickled down my face. I was hot and miserable, and only getting more hot and more miserable with each passing moment.

It's too bad Sheriff Tavish—I mean, Hunter—isn't around to help again. His company would definitely make things more pleasant.

A fallen log lay near the side of the road. Taking advantage of the convenient resting spot, I sat down and put the basket on the ground, massaging my poor, aching hand. Miraculously, I hadn't spilled any of the basket's contents, but its heaviness meant I had been walking more slowly and carefully than usual.

It must be getting on midday soon. And goodness, it was such an unseasonably hot day....

I wiped the sweat from my brow. Well. I had promised Lola Cerise I wouldn't take off my cloak. But I hadn't said I wouldn't remove my hood. That was still wearing my cape, wasn't it? I pushed the hood back from my face.

I sat there for a few moments, enjoying the peace of the woods. The occasional birdsong, the buzzing insects.

And then an uneasy feeling crept down my spine.

The forest had grown still and quiet, as it had several days ago when I had been attacked by the unknown creature.

But it's broad daylight, my mind protested. Still, I couldn't deny the absence of life around me. Or the chill of fear that had overtaken me.

I looked around, but saw nothing. No movement, no shadows. I didn't hear anything, either. No twigs snapping underfoot, no creature breathing or growling.

But I felt like I was being watched.

I drew my hood up again, and carefully hefted the basket. As quietly as I could, I stood up and left the fallen log, heading back down the road towards Woodside.

The feeling that I was being watched stayed with me for a while longer, but the further I got from where I had rested, the more the sounds and sensations of life in the forest came back. I nearly cried when an errant blue jay flew across my path. I was safe now, wasn't I? Surely I was safe.

But I kept my hood up until I emerged from the trees and saw the familiar buildings of Woodside.

Mama was glad to see me—and overjoyed at the bounty I had brought home.

"Claret! This is incredible!" she gushed, eyes wide, as I poured out the basket's contents on the bakery counter. She beamed at me, then gave me a big hug. "I'll be able to finish the mayor's order, and have plenty left over for the bakeshop's every day stock. Thank you."

"Of course, Mama."

"What's this?" She picked up the book I had borrowed from Lola Cerise. I had tucked it away in the basket, and it spilled out along with the other items. "It looks familiar."

I held my breath, my heart sinking at the inevitable conversation. But Mama just looked at the title, then smiled. "J.F. Barrow's *Musings on Cedarbrook*. I remember reading this at your grandmother's. A lovely history of the town."

I blinked, surprised. Craning my neck a little, I snuck a peek at the book's cover. Had I picked up the wrong book? But no. The gold letters still boldly proclaimed the book to be *Faerie Lore and Legends*.

Looking at my mother's happy face, I decided against correcting her. There would be time to tell her about my discussion with Lola Cerise later.

I surveyed the pile of nuts, berries, and plants that threatened to spill over the side of the counter. "Do you need any help?"

"You've helped me quite a bit," she said, still smiling. "But if you wouldn't mind sorting these out for me, that would be wonderful."

I nodded and got to work. The bakeshop was closed—I had returned home right as Mama was assisting the last customers of the day—but Mama still had several hours of work ahead of her. She didn't mind it, though. "Baking makes me happy," she had told me once. "If I didn't have to deal with the customers, I would be very happy. But someone's got to eat all of that food!"

Soon enough, I had sorted out the different items into various jars and baskets, ready for Mama to use. Once that was done, she shooed me out the door. "You've done enough. Go enjoy the rest of the day."

I didn't need any more urging. Clutching *Faerie Lore and Legends* firmly in my hands, I escaped out the bakeshop door and into the sunshine.

A NOTICE

T O THE CITIZENS OF Woodside:

In light of the recent attacks growing in frequency, I advise you to curb the majority of your activity in Littlewood Forest. With the recent killing of a mother and her teenage son, please understand that no one is truly safe in the area.

Solo travel especially is ill advised. If you must traverse the woods, go with a companion—or several. Increased numbers might help protect you where weapons seem to fail.

It is also ill advised to hunt in Littlewood Forest at this time. For your safety, it is best to cease any prolonged time in the woods.

If anyone would like to assist our new Sheriff Tavish in his hunt to bring down the attacker or attackers, please inquire at the mayor's office.

Signed,

Joven Marley, Mayor of Woodside

CHAPTER 15

I HEADED DOWN MAIN Street, towards the small Muno River that bordered
Woodside. It was my favorite place to go when I wanted to be by myself, and
a surprisingly quiet spot, save for the occasional fisherman.

Besides, heading into the forest was out of the question. The community of
Woodside was still reeling from the shock of learning that one of our own was
the newest victim. Mistress Arabelle, a seamstress, was dead, killed by the creature
haunting Littlewood Forest. Her fifteen-year-old son Martin had been found
nearby, weapon drawn. He had obviously died trying to defend his mother from
their attacker.

Both Mistress Arabelle and Martin had been found in the same condition as
the Cedarbrook man had been—scored by deep gashes on their faces and arms,
pale from massive blood loss. Yet strangely left intact, like the man Mister Tabend
had found.

And their horrified final expressions ...

The entire town had turned out yesterday to bury the two people. But
although Mistress Arabelle and her son had been laid to rest, the rumors were
alive and active. Some still argued that the deaths had been the cause of a crazed
wild animal, but more and louder voices insisted that something strange was
happening in Littlewood Forest. Something dark, and sinister, and unstoppable.

I had overheard the sheriff and the mayor talking after the funeral. Having been aware of the strangeness of the mysterious creature's attacks, they were now worried about the rumors flying around Woodside. Both Hunter and Mayor Marley had agreed, privately at least, that the creature wasn't searching for food, but something else.

I shook my head, wanting to clear it of such dark thoughts. Dwelling on their deaths wouldn't do me any good.

I approached the riverbank, wondering if I would have to share it with a random fisherman or two. But today I was in luck. No one was around when I arrived, and I had my pick of several choice spots. I settled in the crook of a large oak, enjoying the soothing sound of water streaming by as I opened my book.

Despite its slim size, *Faerie Lore and Legends* had an amazing amount of information within its pages.

The first part described common Fae creatures, or minor Fae, many of whom I recognized from my grandmother's cottage.

Major Fae, such as the Faerie royals and many of the lords and ladies of their court, had considerably more magical ability. They tended to stay in Faerie, but had, on rare occasions, left the Other Realm to attend to affairs outside. But, the book emphasized, it was quite uncommon—and only under the most dire circumstances.

It also detailed a few Fae creatures that, due to certain circumstances, had passed into accursed status. The writer had also been a fairly good artist, and carefully drawn sketches accompanied the majority of the descriptions.

The second half of the book explained Faerie curses and blessings. Such as the notion that most Fae could not abide iron. Depending on the size and magical ability of the Fae, it could burn them, or irritate them, or bind them.

One thing of note was that the Fae could not lie. They could—and often did—say misleading things that were not quite lies. But if asked specifically, in a direct manner, a Fae had to speak the truth.

The book brought up the same point my Lola Cerise had mentioned, that the Fae and human worlds were closely linked. Mortals benefited from the magic of Faerie, be it good or bad, that found its way into our world. The Fae needed the grounding influence of humanity—and more importantly, its belief in the Fae and the Faerie realm.

I thoughtfully studied the page. *But times have changed from when this was written,* I realized. Magic wasn't widely used or accepted in Woodside, having been diminished to mere folk tales or minor herbology. It wasn't that religion had wiped out belief in magic, like it had in other countries. But the "old ways," as my Lola Cerise would have referred to them, weren't as widespread as they used to be.

Perhaps that's why the Fae of Littlewood Forest remained in this area, I thought. *They don't need to have strong magic. They just need to serve as a tie between the Fae and humans.*

One passage caught my eye:

Although the two worlds have a complimentary relationship, it has been demonstrated, time and again, that Faerie's reliance on the mortal world is greater. Humanity's history is rife with periods of disbelief in magic or the Fae, and while it has caused Faerie to suffer, it has not had the same adverse affect on the mortal world. This has led to the creation of interstices between the two places, allowing the Fae to have an anchor in the human realm.

Interstices. A space between the two worlds. Lola Cerise had said that Littlewood Forest was such a place.

And I, the new Scarlet Lady, was the guardian of that special, sacred place.

It was quite a responsibility, one that both delighted and alarmed me. I could only hope, under Lola Cerise's tutelage, that I would eventually prove worthy.

I turned my attention back to the book.

A final thing of note was how the Fae viewed the color red. It was considered a lucky color, especially among the minor Fae. Although green was, understandably, the predominant color among forest Fae, they would often wear red—an armband, a cap, a belt—to signify their allegiance with the Seelie Court. The Fae, as known magic-wielding tricksters, were not necessarily good or bad by human standards, but the Seelie Fae were more sympathetic to mortals (for the most part) than their more malevolent counterparts, the Unseelie Fae.

Lola Cerise had mentioned that she had created my red cape with Faerie charms and blessings. And that it was supposed to protect me as I wandered through the woods. Although protect me from what, I didn't know. I wondered if she had also made the red hat Mister Feldan—the man who had been attacked on the day of the Spring Festival—had been so worried about.

The book continued to detail blessings and curses, namely for the most powerful Fae.

Regarding the accursed Fae: their great power is tempered by nature's limitations. A powerful spell caster might be able to alter the weather, their environment, or even time or death, but to do so, would be drained of power and vulnerable to attack for several days. Or a mighty predator could be a most fearsome hunter, but be unable to distinguish colors or abide the sunlight. Not every accursed Fae has the same limitations, but the manner of Fae creature one is dealing with can give clues as to what their weaknesses might be.

A shadow fell over the page. I looked up.

Chapter 16

S PEAKING OF HUNTERS ...

Sheriff Tavish—Hunter—looked down at me. "I apologize for startling you."

"It's all right, Hunter." The name slipped out before I could think. My eyes grew wide, as did the sheriff's. There was an awkward silence.

"Miss—I mean, Claret." His voice turned uncertain. "If that's all right with you?"

"Of course it is," I said quickly. I mean, we had talked about this already. But somehow, now that we were back in Woodside, it felt different.

A huge smile blossomed across his face. "I looked for you yesterday evening, but I didn't see you around Woodside." There was a slight question in his voice.

"I was visiting my Lola Cerise," I reminded him. "And I want to thank you again, for your help."

"Oh, of course." He still sounded a little confused, but with a bit of self-censure, almost as if he were saying to himself, *Silly me. How could I have forgotten?* "And, of course. I'm always happy to help."

"Are you on your way somewhere? If not, would you like to join me?"

He hesitated, then nodded. "I would love to. Claret."

I felt a small thrill at hearing him say my given name. But still—"You're right, though. It's probably best not to use first names in front of other people."

Hunter paused. "Ah, yes. Of course."

I waved at the surrounding area. "Please, sit."

He did so, choosing a small rock near my tree. I noticed a brace of rabbits, freshly caught, hanging off his belt. "You went hunting?"

Hunter's eyes followed mine, as if he had forgotten what he was carrying. "Oh. Yes. I did."

"Didn't you see the notice?"

Hunter frowned. "Notice?"

"Yes. Warning everyone to stay out of Littlewood Forest, unless absolutely necessary. Mayor Marley posted it just a day or so ago. But he doesn't consider hunting necessary, at least for a little while. With what happened at the Spring Festival ..."

"Oh, yes. That's right." The sheriff didn't seem that concerned. He shrugged. "It's just a good idea to have fresh game around once in a while."

His words struck me as odd, but I didn't press the matter. Hunter coughed and changed the subject. "What are you reading?"

I flipped up the book, showing him the cover.

"*Faerie Lore and Legends*." He read the title out loud, then looked at me curiously. "An interesting choice."

"It sounded interesting," I said. "You can see this?"

"The book? Or the cover?"

"The title." I pointed at it, just to be clear. "You can see what this says?"

"*Faerie Lore and Legends*," he repeated. "The gold lettering is a bit faded, but yes, I can read it."

"But, how—?" I didn't want to ask him if he had Faerie blood, as that would be an untoward question. And a person having Faerie blood didn't ensure that they could see the forest Fae or read my grandmother's magical books. After all, my mother was half Fae and couldn't see the book's true title.

"Most everyone in Woodside or Cedarbrook is connected to the Fae in some way," he said, answering my unspoken question. "It's just a question of how close the connection is, and whether or not their innate magic has been awakened. Some people in both towns go their whole lives living with unawakened ability. That's not the case in my family, though. We have deep roots in Woodside, as I told you when we first met."

"Oh." I ducked my head, sheepish. "I didn't know. I'm ... I'm still learning about all of this."

"I understand. Learning that magic is real, and not just tales from your childhood, is rather intimidating. And exhilarating at the same time. When magic ... first touched my life, it really upended my view of the world."

An undercurrent of sadness laced his tone. I wondered at what had happened when he discovered the reality of magic. Would it be okay to ask him about it?

He shook his head, as if shaking off unhappy memories. "But all that was a long time ago. My point is, you get used to it, and you learn to recognize the little Fae touches all around you in everyday life. Indeed, I don't think Cedarbrook and Woodside would have prospered as long as they have without the Fae. The towns need the forest as much as the forest needs the towns."

"You mean the people?"

"The people, and the land." He waved a hand, indicating the river, the trees, and the town nearby. "The Fae have always been drawn to humanity—humans' short lives have made them bold and hardy in a way that those of Faeriekind, powerful but fragile, are not. Humans, in turn, have always been enticed by their perfection and beauty, something that mortals lack."

"There's plenty of beauty in the world," I argued. "You don't think all you see before you is beautiful?"

He blushed, and belatedly I realized the trap my words had set for him. I looked down, embarrassed.

He coughed awkwardly, drawing my gaze back to him. "There are many things around me that I would consider beautiful." The warm look in his eyes made me blush. "But the Fae possess a beauty that is beyond human comprehension. And when the Fae set their minds to it, they can use their glamours and magic to cause mortals to go insane."

"Oh. I see." Sort of. I hadn't seen any Fae at my grandmother's house that were deadly beautiful, but maybe, because they were minor Fae, that wasn't their domain? Or maybe, because I had Faerie blood, I was immune to their charms? I didn't know. I made a mental note to ask Lola Cerise about that later.

"But enough about that," Hunter said, shaking himself slightly like he was shaking off the previous topic's heaviness. "I want to hear more about you. You and your family. You seem very close to your grandmother."

"I am. After my father—" I hesitated. Should I tell him that I had just learned my father hadn't died, but had left my mother and me and returned to Faerie? I could barely believe it, myself.

"After what?" Hunter asked gently.

I decided against it. Lola Cerise had told me to be careful, and even though Hunter and I had an easy camaraderie, we were still fairly new to each other.

"Was gone," I continued, "my mother threw herself into running the bakeshop. I spent a lot of time with my lola, until I grew old enough to help Mama without getting underfoot and ruining her baked creations. Although—" I smirked "—I'm not sure growing up helped that last bit."

"I'm sorry about the loss of your father," Hunter said. "I'm surprised your grandmother didn't just move in with you and your mother when that happened. It can't be easy, for either you or her having to travel back and forth. And she's all by herself, living on the edge of a dangerous forest."

I didn't know how to explain that away. Now that I knew that Lola Cerise was the Scarlet Lady, Keeper of Littlewood Forest, I understood the reason why she had stayed in her solitary cottage next to the wood. But again, I couldn't tell him that. Could I?

"It's not for lack of trying," I said. "Mama asked her multiple times over the years, but lola always turned her down."

"Any reason why?"

"It was the home she and my grandfather had built. She didn't want to leave." It was mostly the truth.

"Do you think she'll want to move in with you and your mother, now that the forest has become dangerous?"

"Oh," I said, flustered. "I don't know. Maybe. I haven't asked her."

"You should. At least if she's living with you, you know she's safe."

"True," I said noncommittally. I eyed him curiously. "Why does it matter to you so much?"

He shrugged. "I know we haven't known each other long, but I ... am concerned about your wellbeing. And your family's as well, since they matter to you."

I smiled. "I thank you for your concern."

An awkward but happy silence fell between us. I cast about for something to say. "So. Um. How is the investigation going?"

The warmth in Hunter's eyes faded. "Not well, I'm afraid. I've read the reports and talked to those involved, but nobody had anything concrete to tell me."

"You told me the other day that you thought it was a starving animal. Have you identified what kind?"

He blinked, as if my words had caught him off guard. "Oh ... I have a few ideas. Nothing specific, though. But I'm hoping these might help." He held up the rabbits. "It's not much, but it could be used as a lure."

I raised an eyebrow. I wouldn't have wanted to lure whatever was out there right to me, but then again, I wasn't the sheriff. But I refrained from saying that aloud. Instead, I asked, "And how is Mister Feldan? Have you been able to interview him?"

"I've visited him every day since he arrived, but he goes in and out of consciousness. Nothing but ramblings from an agitated, incoherent mind." Hunter sighed. "He would probably recover faster at his home in Cedarbrook, but I did hope to have at least one conversation with him before he leaves."

Remembering Lola Cerise's request, I said, "Before he goes, would it be all right if I saw him?"

Hunter paused, looking a bit confused. "I wasn't aware you knew Mister Feldan."

"I don't," I admitted. "But I believe he is a friend of my Lola Cerise. Perhaps, if I mention her, it might bring him comfort."

"I see. Well, I suppose it couldn't hurt. When would you like to visit with him?"

I stood, tucking my book in my skirt pocket. "How about now?"

CHAPTER 17

"MISTER FELDAN? I'VE BROUGHT you a visitor."

Hunter rapped lightly on the patient's door. But only silence met his words. The figure lying in the bed didn't make a sound, or move.

Doctor Zonta, standing just behind Hunter, frowned. "Sheriff Tavish, I don't know if this is a good idea."

"Mister Feldan?" I called out hesitantly. "My name is Claret Pangati. My mother runs Rowena's Bakeshop here in Woodside. And I think you know my grandmother, Cerise? She lives in Cedarbrook."

The man stirred slightly. A raspy voice said, "Cerise? You're her granddaughter?"

More rustling came from the bed. Realizing Mister Feldan was trying to sit up, I hurried to his side to help him. Hunter and the physician both came to join me, but Mister Feldan waved them away.

"Out, out," he said, with a surprising amount of force behind his voice. "I'll visit with Miss Claret here, and only her."

Doctor Zonta frowned and opened his mouth, but Hunter spoke first. "As you say. We'll give you a few moments to visit."

The sheriff and the physician both left the room, closing the door behind them with a quiet click. I pulled a chair over to the bed and sat down.

Mister Feldan and I regarded each other. His red cap sat firmly on his head, partially hiding his salt and pepper hair. The room wasn't particularly cold, so I surmised he wanted to wear his cap constantly so he knew where it was.

"I'm glad to see you're feeling better, Mister Feldan," I said politely.

The Cedarbrook man nodded his thanks at me. "So you're Cerise's granddaughter. Did she send you?"

"Yes. She sent me with a message for you."

Mister Feldan raised an eyebrow. He glanced at the closed door, then flicked his fingers at it.

Nothing changed. The door stayed closed, Mister Feldan and I stayed where we were. And yet, I knew something had changed. Like catching the whiff of one of my mother's baked creations on the air, I perked up, alert.

"What did you do?" I wondered.

Mister Feldan nodded, satisfied. "So you felt that, did you?"

"Yes." I glanced towards the door, but it stayed firmly shut. If Hunter or Doctor Zonta had felt whatever it was that Mister Feldan had done, they gave no indication.

"I cast a spell so the two outside can't hear our true conversation," Mister Feldan said. "If they do try to listen in, they will only hear innocuous talk about the weather, or the recent Spring Festival. Harmless things."

"Oh. I see." I gave the door a speculative glance.

"Well, then. What did Cerise say?"

"She wishes you well, and wants you to visit her as soon as you are able," I recited.

Mister Feldan nodded somberly. "I'd like nothing more than that. But healing has been slow going. Today is the first day I feel like myself somewhat."

His eyes flashed, unsettling me. "What are you?" I whispered.

In answer, Mister Feldan pulled off his red cap.

I gasped.

His face elongated before me, his cheekbones growing higher and sharper. His eyes turned a dark gold, the pupils turning into vertical slits like a cat's. On top of his head, the twigs or leaves I had seen before were now more prominent. But they weren't twigs. They were—

"Horns?" I queried.

"Ears," Mister Feldan said. He pushed back his hair, and I realized his ears—his human ears—had disappeared. The pointed ears on top of his head twitched, as if to underscore his point.

"I am a cait sidhe," he explained at my questioning look. "Fae born, I can transform into a cat at will. I serve as a messenger and a liaison between the Seelie Court and those who have left Faerie to live in the mortal realms but still swear fealty to the Seelie rulers, King Finvarra and Queen Oona, may they reign forever.

"I reside in Cedarbrook, with my pet cat." Mister Feldan chuckled. "My fellow Fae in the area know that I have no such pet, while my human friends wonder why my 'pet' is so shy and is always hiding when they visit."

I giggled. "Understandable."

Mister Feldan's mirth faded. "When the attacks started happening, your grandmother sent me back to the Seelie Court to apprise them of the situation. But when I arrived, the Seelie Court was in disarray, our rulers in hiding. They, too, had been attacked by some creature that caught them unawares. I spent some time back in Faerie, trying to piece together what had happened."

He paused, gathering his thoughts. But his story had me riveted. I breathed, "What happened? Do you know?"

He shook his head slowly. "Not entirely. How much do you know of the Fae? Of minor and major Fae?"

"Not much, I'm afraid. I just learned about my grandmother's heritage yesterday. And I've only just started studying this." I pulled the *Faerie Lore and Legends* book from my pocket and showed it to him.

Mister Feldan nodded, pleased. "That's a good start. So you've read about minor and major Fae, then?"

"Yes, but I didn't quite understand it."

He smirked. "Unless you've spent some time in Faerie, it can be a bit complex. But I'll do my best to explain." He tapped his chin in thought. "Minor Fae have very specific, limited power. And their power is often focused on just one area.

For example, the minor Fae your grandmother watches over are all related to the nearby forest. One Fae takes care of the trees, whereas another keeps the water pure. Their magics work in harmony, with each other and with humans. In addition, the minor Fae are the Fae most likely to be tied to mortals in some way.

"The major Fae, like our Seelie king and queen, have more magical ability, and are able to use their power in a multitude of situations. Of course, each Fae's ability varies, as not everyone has the same amount of power. But the major Fae are more powerful, and that power does not always play nice with humankind. Woe to the mortal who befalls a Fae's wrath."

I nodded, excited. "Yes, the book mentioned that the major Fae rarely leave Faerie. But I didn't realize that was due to their magic."

Mister Feldan chuckled. "It's not that the magic of the major Fae is anathema to humans. But there's little reason for them to leave the Beautiful Country for the mortal realm. Be glad for that, Miss Claret. The Fae, especially the major Fae, are known for being capricious. They'll just as easily curse you as bless you."

"Oh, I see." And I wondered how the major Fae would treat me, as the future forest's caretaker, once they met me. I put the thought aside. No sense in borrowing trouble. I would deal with it when it happened. If it happened.

"Then there are the accursed Fae."

"Do they have even more power than the major Fae?"

"Yes, and no." At my confused look, Mister Feldan smiled. "I'd say they have as much magic as any other of the major Fae. But the accursed Fae serve as warnings to us. Often they are the result of Fae power gone horribly wrong."

He pointed at *Faerie Lore and Legends*. "What that book doesn't tell you is *where* the so-called accursed Fae come from. They are those who overstepped in trying to gain power, and paid a price when the royals exacted their justice. They often go into exile or hide themselves away."

I frowned. "Does every punishment from the Crown result in a curse?"

"Not necessarily. Most punishments are fairly routine—imprisonment, a stripping of power. At times, the royals will place a curse on someone, but again, those are often mild. Maybe changing the offender into an animal, or making them do something foolish for a while.

"But there are times when the king or queen punishes someone, and the punishment goes awry. What was meant to be a simple removal of ability backfires and distorts into something else. Thus is an accursed Fae born. Those wretched souls have great power, but their lives burn fast and hot, like a candle. They are rare, but a new accursed was created recently."

"Who?" I wondered, even though I had no knowledge of the Faerie court.

Mister Feldan shook his head. "I'm not sure. It was hard to get information, for most of the court is in shambles. The accursed are usually expelled from Faerie, but on the day of expulsion, the accursed got free. Several Fae courtiers were injured or killed trying to stop it. It made an attempt on Queen Oona, prompting King Finvarra to spirit her away. I have yet to discover where they have hid themselves. I left Faerie, intending to tell Mistress Cerise what had befallen the Faerie court. On my way to see her, I too was attacked."

Mister Feldan's horrifying news rendered me speechless for a few moments. Even though I hadn't ever given the existence of Faerie a thought until just a day ago, I was still distressed to learn about what had happened.

I found my voice and my footing at the same time. Without even realizing it, I had sprung to my feet, ready to run out the door. "My lola has to know about this, right away!"

Mister Feldan reached out to me, his hand shaking. "Wait. Cerise does need to know, but you need to know some things too, before you run off. My red cap didn't work."

Before today, I wouldn't have understood what his statement meant. But now that I knew that Lola Cerise was the appointed Fae guardian of the neighboring forest—and that apparently red was a lucky, protective color for the Fae—I grasped the gravity of what he was saying. "Are you sure? Lola said—"

"I was attacked just after sunrise." Mister Feldan twisted his precious red cap in his hands. "It has always kept me safe, even at night, during the height of Unseelie powers.

"I figured if I traveled during the day, I would be fine. The creature that attacked me was unusually fast, more than the usual wildlife that roams these woods. And it drained me of nearly all my magic, which would have killed me. I don't know why it didn't complete the task, only that I am fortunate that it stopped when it did.

"The enchantments your grandmother wove into my cap should have rendered me near invisible, especially in the daylight. Whatever is out there is able to pierce the spells of safety that Cerise, a powerful Fae enchantress, created. No mere mortal predator can do that. I fear that the creature haunting our woods is the escaped accursed Fae."

CHAPTER 18

A FTER HEARING MISTER FELDAN'S disturbing news, I was eager to visit Lola Cerise and tell her everything he had told me. But although I begged and pleaded, Mama wouldn't let me leave again.

"I need your help getting ready for Mayor Marley's event," she said. "You can visit your lola after the town's anniversary celebration is over."

I chafed at her words, but I understood. The mayor's event was in just a few days, and Mama would be spending every spare moment preparing for it. I could help her by overseeing the day-to-day tasks of the bakeshop and keeping the place clean and organized.

Mister Feldan's news is already a few days old, I reasoned. *One or two more days can't hurt.*

The rest of the week passed in a flurry of activity. The days were long—I would wake up early, before sunrise, to get things ready. And then crawl into bed late at night, exhausted. Hunter stopped by the bakeshop every day, a faithful customer, but except for a few brief moments of conversation—usually about the day's baked goods—we didn't visit much.

Perhaps I could ask him to accompany me to Cedarbrook to see Lola Cerise when the mayor's event is over. I smiled to myself. *Mama would* love *that.* I blushed. *And so would I.*

The day before the mayor's event, a messenger from his office came by the bakeshop. "Mayor Marley would like to know when Madam Pangati will come by to pick up the cart and horse for tomorrow's celebration."

Mama was in the back, baking and fretting, which she had been doing all week. Fortunately, she was able to multitask, otherwise her worrying would have ensured that nothing got made. As it was, I didn't want to bother her. "I'm her daughter, Claret. I'll be the one picking up the cart and horse. When is the earliest I can get them?"

"The stable master is usually in at least an hour before sunrise."

"Perfect. I'll come by then."

The day of the mayor's event dawned. Well, not quite. I was up early again, although the sun wasn't. I sat up in bed and yawned, giving my pillow one last loving glance before I sighed and got out of bed.

I got dressed and made my way quietly down the stairs and out of the house. If Mama heard me leave, she would insist on going with me, and I wanted to let her rest.

The balmy spring air greeted me as I opened the back door. A pleasant surprise, considering it was still dark out. I left my cloak hanging on the hook by the door. I didn't need it to keep warm, and I wasn't going into the woods. Closing the door gently behind me, I made my way to the front of the shop.

"Oh! Hunter. Hello."

The sheriff stood by the bakeshop door, half of his handsome face highlighted by the street's yellow lamplight. "Claret. It's good to see you again."

I giggled. "Silly. I've seen you all week. Just not for more than a few minutes."

He nodded in acknowledgment. "I hope you don't mind me being here. I wanted to see you again, and I thought perhaps if I waited until the shop opened ..."

"Oh, the bakeshop isn't open today. A rare occurrence, I know. It's the day of Mayor Marley's celebration in the town's civic center." I raised a surprised eyebrow. "I can't believe you forgot."

Hunter shrugged. "There's been so much happening, it just slipped my mind for a bit."

"I understand." I smiled sympathetically, then waved a hand at the quiet street. "I'm headed to the mayor's office now, if you'd like to join me?"

"I'd love to."

Hunter fell into step beside me, an easy silence falling between us. After a moment, I said, "How goes the investigation into the attacks?"

"Same as always." He sighed. "If I only had a lead to look into, or some new information ..."

"Oh!" I said. "I didn't have a chance to tell you, since I didn't want to recount our conversation in front of Doctor Zonta. And then things at the bakeshop have been so busy. But Mister Feldan had plenty of interesting things to say. In fact—"

"Mister Feldan yet lives?"

I blinked, confused. "Well, yes. Unless things have changed since I visited with him? But he seemed to be in fairly good health when I saw him a few days ago. You've seen him daily, I thought. How is he doing?"

Hunter coughed. "Oh, I haven't been by since ... well, since our last visit. The, uh, investigation has kept me occupied."

"Of course." But privately I wondered at Hunter's words. He didn't strike me as a flighty person, but I also had to admit that, for all that I was drawn to him, I still didn't know him that well.

Silence descended on us again, but this one felt heavy and awkward. Wanting to bring us back to our usual easy camaraderie, I said, "I'm glad you came by this morning. I always enjoy spending time with you ... Hunter."

He smiled at me, a wide, toothy grin. "I feel the same way, Claret."

A warm tingle ran down my spine.

"I'm glad I didn't have to wait until the shop was open, either," Hunter continued. "Not that I don't want to purchase your mother's lovely pastries. But it's nice to see you outside of store hours."

"Don't feel that you can only come by when the bakeshop is open," I assured him hastily. "You're welcome at our shop anytime. And I'm sure my Lola Cerise would love to meet you. You are welcome there too."

Hunter paused. "Cerise, you say?"

I cocked an eyebrow at him. "Did you forget my grandmother's name already?"

"No, no. It's not that. I just ... can't believe I didn't make the connection before. Cerise is also the name of a color, yes? A bright reddish-pink."

I chuckled. "It is. And wait until you see her house. It's decorated in reds of all shades. It's a good thing she was named for a shade of red, for it's her favorite color."

"And the bakeshop ..."

"Is named after my mother, Rowena."

"Another shade of red, a bit darker."

"Yes. And it's my lola who came up with my name—"

"Claret. Also a type of red."

I nodded. "Red runs in the family, apparently."

"Apparently," he echoed. "Am I truly welcome in both your shop and your grandmother's house?"

"Of course. I've told you once before, and I meant it. In fact, when the mayor's event is done, I'm going to go visit her in Cedarbrook. Would you like to join me?"

There was another pause, and then Hunter gave me another big smile. "I can think of nothing I'd like more."

My cheeks warmed. I hoped Hunter wouldn't be able to see it in the lamplight. Fortunately, I was spared from coming up with a reply, as we had arrived at the stable near the mayor's office. I went inside the stable while Hunter waited outside.

"Good morning," I said to the stable master. "I'm here on behalf of Rowena Pangati, of Rowena's Bakeshop. The mayor said we could borrow a horse and cart for today's event?"

The stout man grunted. "Sure, sure. I have a horse right here. Cart's around the corner. D'you need help hitching her up?"

"I have a ... friend with me. If we can't do it, then I'll come find you."

The stable master grunted again as he led my borrowed horse out of her stall. The placid speckled mare looked about as excited as I was to be up so early. Soon the stable master had her harnessed and ready. Handing me the reins, he said, "This here's Willow. She's sturdy and obedient, she shouldn't give you any problems."

"Thank you." I led Willow out of the stable. Hunter wasn't waiting right outside the doors, but then I caught sight of him pacing back and forth. I waved at him, nodding towards the horse. "Can you help me secure her to the cart? The stable master said it's around the corner."

Hunter pointed at something I couldn't see. "Yes, it's right here." He disappeared behind the stable.

Still leading Willow, I headed in Hunter's direction. Turning the corner, I saw the promised wooden cart. Hunter stood beside it. "Perfect," I said, walking forward.

But Willow wouldn't follow me. I tugged on the reins again, but met only resistance. Confused, I turned to see what the issue was.

Willow—the supposedly sturdy and obedient beast—snorted and pawed at the ground nervously, her head jerking from side to side.

"Willow?" I said uncertainly. "Come on, girl." I tried to get her to move.

The horse snorted again, her wide eyes rolling back in her head so the whites showed.

I turned back to Hunter. "I don't understand what's going on. She was fine just a moment ago. Can you help me with her?"

Hunter started towards us.

Willow screamed, an unexpected, high-pitched sound. She began to buck, straining on the reins.

"Woah, woah!" I cried out. I reached a hand out, intending to soothe her, but she was flailing about so wildly, it took all I had to hold on to her.

Hunter stilled where he was.

"What's going on out here?" The stable master hurried towards Willow and me. Grabbing the reins from me, he led the horse a few steps away. "Willow, girl, it's all right. It's all right."

The horse calmed down somewhat at the familiar voice of the stable master. With flared nostrils and big eyes, she kept throwing nervous glances towards the cart.

"What happened?" the stable master asked me.

"I don't know," I said. "I brought her outside, and she didn't want to go anywhere near the cart."

"Huh." The stable master scratched his chin. "That's never happened before. Willow's the best horse I've got. Good with kids and new riders alike. Hard to scare, too. A snake got in the stable once and it spooked every other beast, but ol' Willow here barely gave it a glance. For something to frighten her ..."

"Miss Claret." Hunter was at my side. I hadn't even realized he had moved. A few feet away, Willow snorted and flared her nostrils. "I'm afraid I have to take my leave of you. I have some things to attend to before I can go to the mayor's event. Now that the stable master is here, will you be able to handle Willow and the cart on your own?"

I nodded. "Yes, Sheriff Tavish. Thank you for your help this morning." I smiled at him. "I hope to see you later today, at the celebration."

"You can count on it." He nodded at me, then at the stable master. With that, he strode away.

"She seems to be doing better," the stable master said, patting Willow. "Let's get her hitched up."

After the stable master secured a now calm Willow to the wooden cart, he helped me up onto the box seat.

"You don't think she'll spook again, do you?" I asked. She was fine now, but if she got scared again, I didn't know if I would be able to handle her by myself.

"Nah, it looks like she's back to her sweet self again," he said. "Really, nothing short of the otherworldly could spook this old gal." With that, he gave her one last pat and sent us off.

I pondered his words as we headed to the bakeshop.

CHAPTER 19

B Y THE TIME WILLOW and I reached the bakeshop, sunrise had come and the streets were stirring with people. Mayor Marley's celebration was to go from just after sunup to sundown, and the citizens of Woodside were headed to the civic center to attend.

As we approached, Mama yanked open the door. "There you are! I was getting worried."

I halted the cart and jumped down, tying Willow's reins to a nearby post. "My apologies, Mama. I had some trouble hitching up Willow here to the cart this morning. She was a bit skittish."

Mama eyed the horse suspiciously. "She won't run off or go too fast, will she?"

I shook my head. "She shouldn't. The stable master assured me that she's a good, calm horse. She must have been spooked by a bee or something earlier."

Mama shrugged and sighed. "Well, come on, then." She hurried back inside, with me at her heels.

In short order, we had the cart loaded and ready to go. My story about Willow's spooking had Mama fretting, and she kept turning around nervously to make sure the trays of baked goods were still upright and intact. Luckily, the trip back to the civic center was uneventful. Willow didn't startle, the cart continued at a steady pace, and the food arrived unharmed.

Four of the mayor's clerks greeted us on arrival. Two helped Mama and me step down, while the other two began unloading the cart.

Mama and I hovered nearby, but one of the clerks said to my mother, "Don't worry, Madam Pangati. We'll take care of setting all of this up. We'll also make sure the empty trays and baskets are delivered back to your bakeshop, so you don't have to worry about collecting them. You and your daughter can go and enjoy the festivities. The mayor will send payment this week. Not tomorrow, since it's Daypito and the office will be closed, but after that."

"Thank you," Mama said.

The clerk nodded, then waved at someone behind us. "Hello, Sheriff Tavish."

I turned to see the sheriff approaching. He nodded at all of us. "Good morning. What a perfect day for the mayor's event, don't you think?"

The clerk chuckled. "Indeed it is. If you'll excuse me." He hefted a tray of food and left.

"Well met, sheriff," Mama greeted him. "A pleasure to see you, one of my best customers."

"It's easy, when there are so many delightful things at your shop." He smiled at me warmly. Instantly I felt my face heat. "Speaking of delightful, I'd love to take you around the celebration if you're free, Miss Claret."

"Oh! I don't have to work a booth this time, but Mama—"

"Actually Claret, I'm feeling a bit tired," Mama said. Huh. Funny, she didn't sound tired. And I doubted she had worked off her nervous energy from earlier.

I glanced at Mama sidelong. She winked at me, then let out a huge, loud yawn. I resisted sighing. *Not obvious at all, Mama.*

"I'm going to head home to take a nap. I'll come back to the celebration later," she continued.

"I can accompany you," I began, but she waved my words away.

"No, no. You stay here and have fun. Take your time." She waved at me, then the sheriff. "I'll see you both later." With that, she hurried away.

Hunter and I stood there in an awkward silence. I cleared my throat and cast about for something to say. "Oh. It looks like they're done unloading the cart."

"Oh, I know this horse," Hunter commented. "The mayor was kind enough to loan her and the cart to me when I had to haul away a bunch of debris from the office. She and I are old friends."

He reached out and stroked Willow's nose. The mare nickered softly, enjoying Hunter's attention.

The clerk who had spoken to us earlier returned, having delivered his basket of food. "Ah, she likes you. That's a good girl. But say goodbye now, Willow. I've got to take you back to the stables."

With one last pat, Hunter stepped back from Willow. The clerk took her reins and led her away.

Hunter crooked his arm. "Shall we?"

I placed my fingers on his arm and smiled up at him. "Yes, let's."

We looked over the civic center, decked out beautifully for Mayor Marley's event. Even though the festivities had only just begun, the area was already packed with people.

As we walked into the crowds, Hunter commented, "Woodside really likes its celebrations, doesn't it?"

I giggled. "It really does seem like that, doesn't it? The Spring Festival is an annual event that brings Woodside and Cedarbrook together. But this one is a bit different."

I pointed at a colorful banner that hung between two lampposts. Its brightly painted words greeted people entering the area: "Happy 200, Woodside!"

"Today marks the two hundred year anniversary of Woodside's founding," I said. "I mean, Woodside has been around longer than that, a few decades at least, just as a smaller, unnamed village. But this is the town's official 'birthday.' I think, since it's a milestone year, Mayor Marley wanted to recognize it as such."

"Two hundred years, huh? My, time flies." At my quizzical look, Hunter pointed. "Look at that juggler! I'm impressed."

We wandered over to join a small group that had formed to watch the juggling man up close. As we marveled at his skill—he kept adding more and bigger objects to his rotation—Hunter asked me in a low voice, "Will you be working at the bakeshop tomorrow, Miss Claret?"

"Normally I would be," I said. "But since the anniversary celebration was such a big order, Mama decided to take a rare day off. Tomorrow is Daypito. I usually visit my lola on Daypito."

Hunter nodded gravely. "I'm worried about the recent increase in activity from the woods. I'd be happy to accompany you to Cedarbrook, if you'll let me."

I smiled. "That would be lovely. As I've said before, I'd love for you to join me."

To my surprise, he frowned. "You—you told me that? When?"

I nudged him playfully. "This morning, silly. Or don't you remember?"

Hunter's frown deepened. "No ... No, I'm afraid I don't recall you saying that."

I laughed. In a teasing tone, I chided, "You'll have to work on your memory, Sheriff Tavish."

He joined in my laughter. "I suppose I need to. Otherwise I'd be a pretty poor sheriff. No wonder my investigation isn't going anywhere."

Instantly, I felt bad for my teasing. "Oh dear. I'm sorry. I didn't mean—"

He reached out for my hand and squeezed it. "It's all right. I know you didn't mean anything by it."

"Thank you." I expected Hunter to drop my hand, but instead, he laced his fingers through mine.

We spent the next few hours walking around the mayor's celebration, pleasantly reminiscent of our time at the Spring Festival. We had just finished a light lunch when I realized that Mama hadn't returned.

"She's probably here somewhere," Hunter said. "It's just so crowded."

"True, but it's not that big of an event. After all, we've already gone around twice," I pointed out. "I know she's tired, but she wouldn't want to miss this."

I looked down the less crowded Main Street. "Perhaps I should go see if she's okay."

"I'll go with you."

"You sure?"

"Of course." Hunter stood up, brushing crumbs off his lap. "Let's go."

We headed back to the bakeshop. A few people were out and about, all headed towards the civic center.

"Late risers," I giggled. "I guess they're all just now going to the anniversary celebration."

Hunter chuckled along with me. "Better late than never, I suppose."

By the time we reached Rowena's Bakeshop, the already sparse crowd was nonexistent. I stepped in front of Hunter, fishing in my pocket for the key. "I hope Mama won't be upset if I wake her up."

I was about to go around the back, to our private entrance, when I spotted the front door.

It was open.

CHAPTER 20

"Claret? What's wrong?"

I could barely hear Hunter over the rushing noise in my ears. I shook my head to clear it as I slowly approached the door. "I don't know," I said. "But the shop is closed today."

Perhaps we had forgotten to shut it when we made the morning's bakery delivery. Maybe? Frantically, I thought back to a few hours earlier. But no. I distinctly remembered Mama locking the door behind her once we had finished loading up the cart.

Perhaps Mama accidentally left it open when she returned? But since we always used the back door to come and go, I highly doubted she would have come this way. She had no bakeshop business after our delivery, since the shop was closed. So there would be no reason for her to use the front door.

I reached out to open the door wider, but a hand on my arm stopped me. "Let me go first," Hunter said.

He stepped in front of me, drawing a dagger with one hand as he slowly opened the door with another. Sunlight glinted off its silvered edge.

My brow furrowed as I heard a crunch underfoot. Hunter stepped to the side, allowing me to enter.

A strangled cry escaped me as I got a good look at the shop's interior.

The wooden shelves had been smashed and splintered, spilling the little glass jars and other items we had on display. The jars had shattered, and sticky jellies and jams dripped down the broken shelves and spread all over the floor. The countertop had also been destroyed, with a crater the size of a large, meaty fist in the center.

While I stood there, frozen, Hunter moved farther into the shop. He walked behind the counter, his keen eyes assessing the place as he went.

I dashed to the door that separated the bakeshop from our private residence. It was, surprisingly, still locked.

"Mama?" I called out. "Mama, are you there?"

I tried the door a few more times before my sluggish brain caught up to me. *Oh, yes. Of course. My key.*

I reached into my pocket for the key. Hands shaking, I drew it out—and then promptly dropped it. I reached down to get it, but my quivering, clammy fingers didn't help me. I dropped it two more times before I finally picked it up.

Just as I was about to unlock the door, a low shout came from the kitchen.

"Claret! Claret, quick!"

I hurried towards Hunter, stopping short in the doorway. My eyes widened.

"Mama!"

I knelt next to her, uncaring of the broken crockery on the floor. Mama lay on her side. Her dark hair had fallen out of its usual bun and obscured her face.

"Here, help me," I said to Hunter.

He grabbed a linen towel from the counter and wrapped it around his hand, carefully sweeping aside debris to clear a space on the floor. I brushed Mama's hair aside, leaning close to her face to listen. "Oh, thank goodness. She's breathing. She's still alive."

Together, we carefully moved Mama onto her back. I blinked back the sudden tears that sprang to my eyes. Shallow cuts scored my Mama's face, and I could see a bruise blooming on one cheek. *Most likely from falling—or being hit by something. Or someone.* I swallowed hard. She possibly had more injuries than I could see at first glance.

"Mama?" I said tentatively. No response. I repeated myself, louder. "Mama?"

Still no response. She didn't even stir at the sound of my voice. If I hadn't heard her steady breathing for myself, didn't see the slow rise and fall of her chest, then I would have thought she was dead.

"Mama, wake up. Mama, can you hear me? Mama?"

Hunter reached across and put a steadying hand on my shoulder. "I don't think she can, Claret."

The tears that had threatened earlier now spilled down my cheeks, unchecked. "What do we do? Why won't she wake up?"

I turned back to my mother, lying unconscious in front of me. "Mama, wake up!" I wailed like a five-year-old child—and felt just as helpless. "She's not waking up!"

Two strong arms wrapped around me, holding me still and safe. I melted into the warmth of Hunter's chest, his comforting scent of cedar and vanilla overpowering the sickly sweet smell that permeated the bakeshop. *Cedar*, I thought inanely. *Like the trees in the forest.*

"Shh, shh," Hunter soothed me. "It'll be all right. I'll go get the physician—"

"No!" I yelled. "What if whoever did this comes back?"

Hunter stilled. "I don't think they will. But I understand your concern. How about you go get Doctor Zonta, and I'll bring your mother to her room?"

"Okay," I sniffled. "But then you'll be by yourself if the intruder returns."

Almost to himself, Hunter growled, "I'd like to see them try. I'd have quite the welcome waiting for them." He composed himself, then said more calmly, "I'll be fine. Don't worry about me."

I nodded. "Okay, then. Let me unlock the house for you. You can go on in. Mama's room is at the top of the stairs, first door on the right."

Hunter helped me to my feet. I held open the door for him while he carefully carried Mama through the destroyed bakeshop and into the house. I followed after. The sheriff seemed distracted as he held my mother. He froze in the doorway, his expression distant.

"Hunter?" I waved a hand in front of his face. "Hunter, hello!"

He blinked, startled out of whatever thoughts had stolen his focus. "Ah, forgive me. Which way am I going, again?"

I pointed out Mama's bedroom once more, then left, running towards the physician's office as fast as my feet could carry me.

Fortunately, Doctor Zonta was in his office. He grabbed his bag and was out the door before I had even finished telling him what had happened. Together we hurried back to Rowena's Bakeshop. Upon seeing the shop's state, he whistled.

"Oh my, Miss Claret. I'm so sorry to see so much destruction."

I nodded numbly as I led the doctor through the bakehouse, into our private residence, and up the stairs. "Thank you, sir. My mother is in here."

I ushered the physician into my mother's bedroom. Hunter, who had been sitting by her bedside, stood up and offered Doctor Zonta his chair. As the doctor got to work, Hunter and I moved out into the hallway.

"Any change?" I asked him anxiously.

He shook his head. "I'm sorry."

I dabbed at the tears dotting my cheeks. When had I started crying again? "Thank you for helping her. For helping us."

He enfolded me in a hug. "Of course."

A discreet cough from the bedroom doorway caused us to jump apart. "Pardon me," Doctor Zonta said. "I've had a chance to look Madam Pangati over."

I turned hopeful, expectant eyes on him.

But the physician shook his head sadly. "I'm afraid it's not good, miss. Your mother has sustained several injuries. I counted two broken ribs, and there is swelling around her left ankle that suggests she may have twisted it. But those things will eventually heal, with time and rest.

"Of bigger concern to me is that she won't respond to anything. I take it you both have tried to wake her?" At our nods, he frowned. "As I thought."

"Perhaps, when she fell—" Hunter began.

"No. If her affliction was of a normal nature, she would at least respond, however subtly, to some sort of stimuli. But she seems to be as one dead, although she is still alive. No, I fear a different sort of malady has befallen her."

CHAPTER 21

B
EYOND THAT, THE DOCTOR could not explain, even though both Hunter and I peppered him with questions. Without an exact knowledge of what my mother had gone through, he couldn't begin to guess at what was wrong, let alone how to help her.

"She should continue to rest. Make sure she still eats and drinks to keep up her strength. Keep talking to her, try to reach her with your voice. That's all I can tell you, for now."

Hunter and I followed the physician downstairs. Rather than make him go through the destroyed bakeshop again, I opened the back door for him. "Just go around the corner, and you'll be back on Main Street."

The doctor gave me a small smile of comfort. "Chin up, Miss Claret. Please keep me informed if anything changes in your mother's condition."

"I will. Thank you again, doctor."

With a nod of his head, the physician slipped out the door into the afternoon sunshine.

I sighed and closed the door. Turning, I saw Hunter staring at me.

No, not at me. At my red cape, which hung next to the back door.

"That's a lovely cape," Hunter commented. He reached a hand out towards it, almost as if he were in a trance. Then he caught himself, and paused, dropping his hand.

"I'm sure if you ask my grandmother nicely, she'd make you one," I said lightly.

"Your grandmother made that?" He studied the cape, but didn't try to touch it again.

"Yes. And she also made Mister Feldan's red cap." I ran a loving hand down the vibrant, soft fabric. "I always wear it when I visit her. It pleases her to see me wear it."

"I do recall seeing you in it a time or two. I guess—I never really noticed it, until now."

I giggled. "It's a bright red piece of fabric. How could you *not* notice it?"

"A fair point." He looked towards the bakehouse, whatever spell my red cape had over him broken. "I'm sure you're wanting to clean up in there."

I sighed. "Not particularly, but it has to be done. Eventually."

"Before you do, I'd like to look at everything a bit more closely."

I gave him a sharp look. "What do you think you'll find?"

He shrugged. "I'm not sure. But I would remiss at my job if I didn't examine the shop and the damage."

"I understand." I paused, then said, "Do you need my help?"

"Not at this point," Hunter assured me. "Go be with your mother. If I need anything, I'll let you know."

I nodded and trudged upstairs. Mama lay still in the same spot I had left her, barely breathing. I touched her cheek, my heart breaking as my fingers ran over the cuts and bruises there. Her face was shockingly cold despite the afternoon sun pouring through the window.

In the back of Mama's closet, I found two extra blankets. I pulled them out and placed them over Mama, hoping the additional warmth would help. But her hands and face were still so cold, and I feared nothing would be able to help.

I heard footsteps coming up the stairs. Soon, from the doorway, Hunter's voice floated over to me. "How is she?"

I sighed. "No change. And she's so incredibly cold. I don't know why."

"Maybe we should have kept her downstairs, by your fireplace. If you need more blankets, let me know."

"Thank you." I stared at my mother's still face for a few more moments before looking up at Hunter. "Are you done downstairs?"

"Sort of."

That caught my attention. "Sort of? What do you mean?"

He took a deep breath. "I'd like you to look at something with me."

Curious, I stood and followed him downstairs.

Back in the bakeshop, Hunter led me around the area, pointing out his observations. "Whoever did this was quite strong, as evidenced by the destruction and the force behind it."

He indicated some broken jars on the far side of the room. "There was either a lot of passion or a lot of strength behind this. But I'm inclined to believe the intruder was physically strong, because of this."

He pointed at the broken countertop. "Even the town's blacksmith, using his hammer, wouldn't be able to create a dent this deep or this big. It doesn't look like a tool did this, anyway."

"It reminds me of when Mama beats the dough with her fists," I said tentatively.

"I'm inclined to agree. But who or what could leave a handprint like this, I'm not sure."

I looked around the destroyed bakeshop. "Did you find anything else of import?"

He shook his head. "Not really. Nobody in Woodside strikes me as being able to do this kind of damage, but I'll keep an eye out." He sighed. "I'll also question your neighbors, to see if they may have seen anything. But with how quiet the streets were on the way here, I don't have much hope. Pretty much the entire town is at the anniversary celebration today."

I knew he was probably right, but I still held on to the slim hope. "I'm sure one of them stayed back, and saw something."

"Indeed." He gave me a sympathetic smile. "Before I go, would you like me to help you clean up?"

"No. Thank you, though." I smiled grimly. "Your time is better spent finding out who did this than helping me clean up their mess."

"All right. I'll come by at first light tomorrow, then, to escort you to your grandmother's."

"Great. Thank you." I paused. "Hunter, do you ..."

When I didn't continue, he prodded, "Do I what?"

"Do you think Mama will be okay?" *And me*, I silently added.

"I don't presume to know more than the town physician," Hunter said slowly. "But if your mother is afflicted by something else, maybe something magical? Then perhaps we should look to the Fae for answers."

"How do I find them?" I asked, even as I was thinking, *Lola Cerise. The creatures of the forest that she watches over. Maybe they know.*

Something in his eyes flickered. "I'm not sure. Although the Fae sometimes have dealings with humans, they're just as wary of us as we are of them."

"I see." Privately, I resolved to ask Lola Cerise tomorrow. Hunter might be the town's sheriff, but he hadn't been in Woodside long. My grandmother, having lived her whole life in Cedarbook near the forest, would have more insight.

I hoped.

Hunter took his leave shortly thereafter. I surveyed the damage one last time, shaking my head at how extensive it was. It would take time and money to restore the bakeshop, two things Mama and I didn't have much of.

Sighing, I grabbed a broom from the kitchen and got to work. I actually welcomed the physical work. If I was concentrating on *sweep, pile, dispose, repeat*, then I didn't have to think about Mama's condition.

Sunset approached as I finally finished cleaning the bakeshop. Certain things, such as fixing the shelves or the countertop, would have to wait until I had the materials or could hire some help. But at least the floor and shelves were free of the glass, spilled food, and other debris that had been littering the place.

I pulled the curtains shut against the coming night. Although, with the long slashes down the fabric, they wouldn't do much good. I made a mental note to repair them soon.

Finally, I walked over to the bakeshop door so I could lock it. It hadn't been practical earlier, as I had been going in and out of the shop for the past few hours to toss the trash. Now that I was done cleaning, I could close up the shop. *For who knows how long*, I thought sadly.

I started to lock the door when I realized something. I opened the door and examined the side and the handle in the golden sunset light. Frowning, I ran my fingers down the door, over the handle, and then over the door frame. Everything was smooth and intact, and when I closed the door, it fit perfectly in the frame. The lock still worked. And though I searched thoroughly, I couldn't find any signs that the intruder had forced their way in.

Had Mama willingly let the intruder in? How else would they have gotten into the bakeshop?

And why hadn't Hunter noticed this?

CHAPTER 22

T HE NEXT MORNING, AT first light, Hunter knocked on the back door to
 our private residence.

I grinned at him as I opened the door. "Right on time."

He grinned back. "I try."

I grabbed my red cape from its hook by the door, slung it around my shoulders,
then slipped out of the house. "I feel so odd, going to my lola's empty-handed."
It was one of the rare occasions when I wouldn't be bringing her a basket full of
Mama's baked creations.

"I'm sure she'll understand. I'm looking forward to meeting her."

"And I know she can't wait to meet you."

We kept up a light, easy chatter as we walked through the town. I wondered if
Hunter had talked to my neighbors, but I didn't want to ask him about it while
we were still in Woodside, even if said neighbors were probably still sleeping in
their beds.

We left Woodside and reached the forest's edge. Even though the sun was up,
the morning chill hadn't burned off yet, and the tree canopy obscured some of
the light and heat.

"It's colder than I expected," I said, pulling up my hood.

I had gone a few feet when I realized Hunter wasn't next to me.

Confused, I turned around. The sheriff was still walking, a few paces behind me. But he was moving slowly, as if he was disoriented. As I watched, he put a hand out tentatively, sweeping his hand out in front of him and to the side.

"Hunter?" I said.

At my voice, the sheriff turned his head sharply towards me. He stared in my direction, uncomprehending for a few moments, before his face lit in a relieved smile. "Claret! There you are. I was worried I had lost you."

My hood fell back as I walked over to him. "Silly. I wouldn't have run ahead without you."

He massaged his temples. "My head hurts," he muttered. "I must be tired, to not notice you standing right there."

"It's all right." We started walking again. Even though I was still cold, I left my hood down so I could look at him easier.

After a few moments, Hunter said, "I talked to your neighbors."

"Wow, already?"

He nodded. "After I left your shop, I went to my office so I could write down some notes. Since my office is in the civic center, I knew when the event ended, and returned to your area at that time."

"And? Anything?"

He shook his head. "Nothing, I'm afraid. They were all at the anniversary celebration, for pretty much the entire day."

"And no one saw anything?"

"Unless they're lying, no. One woman who lives across the street from you—Mistress Kirkston, I think her name was—saw your mother return home, but then Mistress Kirkston left for the event and didn't return until sundown. She didn't see anyone in the area, either lurking around or heading that way while she went to the civic center." He paused. "Do you have any reason to believe that Mistress Kirkston is lying?"

I sighed. "No. Mistress Kirkston is a sweet lady, and has always been a good neighbor. I'd say that about any of the people who live near us. They've never given us any trouble, and we haven't given them any trouble."

He nodded. "I'll take that into consideration. Although I won't completely discount that perhaps one of them did it—it's not unusual for neighbors to have grudges that take years to come to light."

He was right, but the thought made me sad. I hated the idea that one of our neighbors could be that duplicitous.

"Are you particularly close to any of your neighbors? Do you perhaps show favoritism to one over another? Are any of them aware of your routines, or where you keep your valuables?"

Thinking back to the destroyed shop, and the subsequent cleanup, I said slowly, "Nothing was stolen. Just broken. And the door that leads from the bakeshop to our home was still locked. If someone wanted to steal money or jewelry, the first place they should have gone was into the private area. We don't keep money in the shop when it's closed."

"Speaking of closed, we found your mother in the shop, and not in your home. I thought she wanted to rest. Why was she in the shop, do you think?"

I smirked. "Mama *said* she wanted to rest, but she doesn't know the meaning of the word. She actually finds working—baking—restful. Even though the shop was closed for the day, she probably wanted to get ahead of the next day's baking."

"Ah." I could hear the laughter in Hunter's voice. "You don't share that love, I take it?"

I chuckled. "The last time I helped Mama in the kitchen, the biscuits came out hard and burnt, and there was too much sugar in the jelly-filled pastries. Mama doesn't really like me helping out anymore."

His laughter poured forth in earnest, a lovely, rich sound.

One thing he had mentioned earlier sparked a memory. "That reminds me. You asked if any of our neighbors knew where we kept the valuables. Besides not knowing that, none of our neighbors have a key to our house or the shop. And we don't hide keys on the grounds, either."

He eyed me sidelong. "What are you saying?"

"The door wasn't forced open. Or hadn't you noticed that while you were looking around?"

Hunter frowned. "I had noticed, but I thought perhaps one of your neighbors had a key. Or that your mother had left it unlocked."

"She might have, but I doubt it. Since the shop was closed for the day, she wouldn't have wanted anyone to come in. And when she's deep in her work, she hates interruptions."

"Hmm."

We didn't say anything more after that, both of us lost in our thoughts.

In the silence, I slowly became aware of voices that had been whispering to me since we had passed the halfway point of our walk.

"Claret ... Claret ... beware."

"He's on the prowl. Must hide ..."

"Red everywhere, and still not enough to protect her."

"Hide away, all. Hide away, now!"

Who is he? I wanted to call out. If Hunter hadn't been with me, I would have. Instead, I looked around, trying to determine where the voices were coming from.

"Claret? Is everything all right?"

With a gasp, I wrenched my attention away from the voices and back to Hunter. "Yes. Yes, I'm fine. I think the excitement of the past day is finally catching up to me."

He gave me a sympathetic smile. "Much has happened recently. I'm sure after today's visit with your grandmother, things will settle down a bit."

"Yes. I won't have to work in the shop, just keep a vigil by my mother's side until she wakes up." I sighed. "I can't run the bakeshop without her, nor do I want to. But it also can't stay closed indefinitely."

"Worry about that if the situation arises," Hunter advised. "No sense in borrowing trouble."

I nodded. "Of course."

We had reached the edge of the forest, and I could see my grandmother's modest cottage just a few feet away. I pointed. "There it is. My Lola Cerise's house."

"It's absolutely charming."

"Isn't it?" I chattered happily as we approached. "Wait until you see the interior. Lola Cerise loves—"

I stopped short. My skin instantly prickled as I stared, dismayed and disbelieving.

My grandmother's front door hung open.

CHAPTER 23

"Lola? Lola Cerise, are you there?"

I pushed the open door wider, continuing to call out as I stepped into the house. "Lola Cerise, are you—"

The rest of the question died on my lips as I looked around my grandmother's house.

The wooden dining table and chairs had been upended and smashed. Red wallpaper hung off the wall in slashed ribbons. All of my grandmother's knickknacks were strewn across the floor, broken or trampled.

Lola Cerise was nowhere to be seen.

"Lola? Lola!" I ran down the hallway, even as Hunter, behind me, called out my name.

A quick peek into the kitchen revealed more destruction, but no Lola Cerise. Nor was she in her bedroom, which was just as destroyed.

But deserted.

I ran back into the front room, where Hunter still stood just inside the doorway. "I can't find her! She's not here!" I burst into tears.

Hunter put his hands on my shoulders. "It will be okay. We'll find her, Claret."

I sniffled and wiped at my tears. "How?"

"First things first. I'll get Constable Piera. He needs to know what's happening in his area, and I don't want to step on any toes. I can ask around in the town while I'm there, see if anyone has seen your grandmother."

"Okay. Thank you." I paused, looking around. "I'll stay here, clean up a little—"

"Not yet. Both the constable and I will want to look at everything more closely. Why don't you come with me?"

I shook my head slowly. "I'll stay here." For some reason, I just felt like I needed to be here. Even though I would just have to sit and wait for Hunter to return. Even though whoever had broken into my lola's house could come back at any time. I was probably safer with Hunter than here, alone in the house, but … "I'll look around and see if anything's missing. But I won't touch anything."

"Good idea."

He left. For a few moments I stood in the center of the room, still too numb to do anything.

Claret.

I blinked, confused.

The voice that was calling me wasn't one I recognized, but I heard it clearly in my mind as if it had been spoken aloud.

Claret.

My eyes swept the room carefully. From the potted tree in the corner, a pair of bright eyes stared at me from the trunk. Several pixies peeked out from behind one of my grandmother's little ceramic knickknacks. I felt something brush against my knees, but saw nothing.

"It's all right." My voice sounded painfully loud as I spoke into the waiting silence. "I'm here to help. Please come out."

A gnome, no higher than my knee, shimmered as he appeared in front of me, twisting a pointed yellow cap in his hands. He stared up at me, eyes wide and fearful. The pixies slowly fluttered away from their hiding spot. The eyes I had seen in the tree moved forward, solidifying first into a face and then the slender body of a dryad.

The otherworldly creatures continued to stare at me.

I cleared my throat. "Please. I want to help you. And I need your help. I don't know what happened to my grandmother."

And suddenly the little cottage filled with noise.

"Bad-bad-scary-bad!"

"... Just walked in ... couldn't stop 'em ..."

"Had to hide. Otherwise we would have been taken, too."

"So much blood ..."

"Wait, please! I can't understand what you're all trying to say," I said over the din. "Please, one at a time."

One of the pixies flew around my head, clearly agitated. I held my hand out, and the little Fae creature alighted on my open palm. I slowly brought the pixie up so it was level with my eye. "Can you tell me what happened?"

Instead of answering, the pixie shuddered and sat down, curling in on itself.

I felt a tug on my dress somewhere around my knees. Looking down, I saw the gnome staring up at me.

"Can you tell me what happened?" I asked him.

"As much as I know," he said.

"Then, please. Anything you know will be welcome." I cocked my head at him. "What's your name?"

"Veronn." He cleared his throat. "It's a bad business, miss. A bad business, indeed."

The day had been deceptively normal. Veronn, along with some of the other minor forest Fae, had spent the day visiting Mistress Cerise, as was often his custom. As evening approached, the Fae left the little cottage to make it back to their homes before nightfall.

Although Mistress Cerise had offered them places to stay in her home, her Fae visitors rarely did so. They preferred their forest homes, for comfort and to keep them connected to their magic. As Veronn explained, all Fae were tethered, in a way, to their element. Water Fae to the rivers and lakes, earth Fae to the forests. They could leave, for a time, but if they stayed away too long it drained them of their magic. Being in their true home was the only way to ensure their magic was replenished. And Mistress Cerise's house, while located near their forest, was not their true home.

Veronn had settled into his home for the night, a lovely, cozy place nestled high in the branches of a stately oak tree. But even though he was snug and warm in his bed, he couldn't sleep. Every time he was about to drift off, something would jerk him awake.

He found himself staring out the window, although he didn't recall getting out of bed and walking over to do so. All was quiet in the forest, and nothing seemed amiss as he surveyed the tree tops lit by moonlight.

But he still felt restless, and he didn't know why.

He found himself outside his tree home, again without quite knowing how he got there. Even stranger, he wasn't the only one standing in the dark forest, blinking in confusion. There was Nellah, the dryad. And Kaer and Oonie, the pixie twins. All frequent visitors to Mistress Cerise's woodside cottage.

And all of them were staring down the road, towards Cedarbrook.

But the scream galvanized them into action.

It wasn't an audible shout. Any traveler through the woods, or the citizens of Cedarbrook, wouldn't have heard it. But each of the Fae present, tied as they were to their forest and their forest's caretaker, heard the agonized scream in their minds.

Mistress Cerise was in trouble.

The Fae hurried towards Cedarbrook. Each new scream caused them to stumble or recoil in fear, but they forced themselves to push through the pain.

They broke through the trees, but halted at the sight of the cottage.

For a large figure, cloaked in shadows, was making its way out the front door. And draped over its shoulder was the limp and lifeless form of Mistress Cerise.

CHAPTER 24

F OR A MOMENT, VERONN and the other Fae just stood there, paralyzed by
fear and indecision.

The mysterious figure had nearly crossed the threshold. And Veronn knew
that, should that happen, Mistress Cerise would be lost to them.

With loud shouts, the forest Fae charged towards the imposing form filling the
cottage doorway.

The dark creature snarled, revealing long, sharp teeth. It pinned them with a
piercing red gaze. The Fae halted as the paralyzing fear returned....

... And when they came to consciousness again, the creature was gone.

And so was Mistress Cerise.

"Wait," I said into the silence that followed Veronn's tale. "I don't understand. You
saw the ... *thing* ... that took my grandmother, but you weren't able to stop it?"

I tried—and failed—to keep the accusation from my voice.

Veronn hung his head. "I'm so sorry, miss. But none of us could stand against
something that powerful."

"And you don't know where it went? Or what it was?"

"Since it overcame us with its magic, we missed seeing which direction it ran."

The two pixies landed on my shoulders, one on each side.

"Hello, miss. I'm Kaer," the one on my left said in my ear. "As for what it was, it was not a creature from the mortal world, we're sure of that."

"And I'm Oonie," the one on my right said. "We may be minor Fae, but we have our own tricks and magic."

"And we are stronger than we look, for we draw on the magic of our forest nearby."

"But whatever took your grandmother had more power than any of us."

In unison, the pixies solemnly said, "Only a Fae of the royal court, or an accursed, could have overpowered us like that."

I stilled, remembering Mister Feldan's story. An accursed Fae, escaped from Faerie and loose in the mortal realm. A multitude of emotions washed over me. Pain over my lola's abduction. Regret that I hadn't come sooner, with the knowledge Mister Feldan had given me.

And anger.

Anger at the cold, distant Fae royals who had allowed such a powerful, dangerous creature to be created. Anger at them for thinking the best solution was to throw it into the human world, full of fragile mortals who couldn't fight against such a beast. Anger at said creature for daring to come to Cedarbrook and steal my loved one.

And anger at myself. If only I had visited right away, once I had Mister Feldan's news. If only I had put two and two together and protected my mother better.

Because, if what the forest Fae told me was true, then it was possible that the bakeshop intruder was the same accursed Fae that had taken my grandmother. I didn't know why it would have targeted my mother—perhaps it thought Lola Cerise lived with us in Woodside, instead of by herself in Cedarbrook?—but I did know there was quite a bit of power behind the violent damage the shop had sustained.

And Doctor Zonta had said that whatever afflicted my mother was beyond his ability to diagnose. Doctor Zonta had been Woodside's physician for many years, and had seen many ailments. If he didn't know what it was ...

The more I thought about it, the more I thought Hunter was right. My mother's malady had to be of a magical nature.

"When did this happen?" I asked the group.

Veronn said, "The night before last."

So, two days ago. Lola Cerise had been taken the night before my mother was injured in our bakeshop, during the Woodside anniversary celebration.

And that also meant the bakeshop disturbance was not because the intruder was trying to find Lola Cerise in Woodside. They would have already known that my grandmother didn't live with my mother and me. So, what was the purpose behind that incident?

Up to this point, all the attacks had occurred in the forest, and mostly at night. With my grandmother's cottage so near the forest's edge, it made sense that the creature might go after her eventually. But our bakeshop had been broken into during the day. And my mother and I lived near the town's center, so it was surprising that no one had seen anyone in the area. Perhaps the two attacks were unrelated, then?

When Hunter returned, I would ask him. He might be able to see a connection where I couldn't.

"Have you all been here the whole time?"

The dryad Nellah nodded shyly from her corner. "We've waited here for Mistress Cerise to return," she said in a high, light voice. "We'll need to go back to our homes soon, to replenish our magic. But we won't stay away for long. We'll come back every day and night, until she returns."

The gnome nodded in agreement, as did Kaer and Oonie. The pixies' wings brushed against my cheeks, a light feathery touch.

"I thank you all for your concern," I said, deeply touched by their fierce loyalty. "And I thank you for the information. When Sheriff Tavish comes back—"

There was a brisk knock on the door.

Hunter's voice called out, "Miss Claret? I've brought the Cedarbrook constable."

My Faerie friends instantly reacted, diving into or ducking behind various hiding spots around the room.

"Come in," I replied, even though the front door was still slightly open. I probably should have closed it after Hunter left, but I was still reeling from shock—first from seeing the cottage's condition, and then from the story my new Fae friends had told me. Since the mysterious figure had apparently already gotten what it wanted—my Lola Cerise—it seemed unlikely it would return to her cottage.

I hoped.

Hunter stepped inside, followed by another person. The short, rotund man's eyes darted all around, quickly assessing the interior.

"Hello, miss. The name's Piera. I'm the new constable around these parts. Got hired about a week ago." He took off his cap and nodded in my direction. "Sheriff Tavish here apprised me of the situation."

"I don't suppose you've seen my grandmother," I said, but he was already shaking his head before I finished talking.

"I'm sorry, miss." But his demeanor shifted, and his eyes slid away from me.

I felt suddenly wary. "What? What is it?"

"Truth be told, miss, I don't ..." He mumbled something I couldn't catch.

"You don't what?"

Constable Piera coughed a little, uncomfortable. "I don't normally come out this way, on my rounds."

"Why not? This is part of Cedarbrook, isn't it?"

"Ye-es," the man said slowly, as if the word was being dragged out of him. "But your grandmother is the only one who lives this far from town. And ..."

"And?" I prompted, when he didn't continue.

Constable Piera took a deep breath. In a rush, he said, "And there's talk that Mistress Cerise is a witch."

CHAPTER 25

I BLINKED, UNSURE OF how to take the constable's confession. It wasn't that we frowned upon magic. Cedarbrook and Woodside, having grown up in the shadow of the mystical forest that lay between the two towns, acknowledged that magic existed. But it wasn't something that had every day bearing on our lives.

The great magicians had faded into legend, giving way to simple herbalists and physicians who relied on passed-down wisdom, not great shows of power. Both towns' magical histories, if they had ever had any, were now in the past. Magic had been reduced to superstitious stories, mostly about minding the Fae in the forest and being careful not to upset them or get tricked by them. And not everyone believed the Fae existed. After all, how many had actually seen them or encountered them?

So, in our current time, the lack of every day magic meant that the townsfolk didn't believe magic existed.

Or if it did, they distrusted it.

The thing was, the constable wasn't wrong. My grandmother *did* possess a bit of magic, due to her Fae background and her position as the forest's caretaker. I knew, from having grown up living near Lola Cerise—and the fact that, until recently, I hadn't even suspected her Fae connections—that she had never shown that power to the people of either Cedarbrook or Woodside. But apparently, humans could still sense it.

Constable Piera mistook my silence as judgment, for he hurriedly continued, "Mind you, miss, she is a lovely woman, from all the townsfolk tell me. Kind as can be, at the rare times she's seen in town. But a bit reclusive, living here on the edge of the forest. And though she's getting on in years, never needing anyone's help, despite the offers."

His voice lowered to a whisper. "But there are the rumors, miss. Dancing lights in the cottage at odd hours. Strange creatures sometimes seen coming or going. Those rumors would be enough to keep anyone away."

A giggle floated on the air. "Silly man," I heard Oonie say, even though the pixie was well hidden. "People should mind their own business and not spy on their neighbors."

"They only get what they're asking for," Kaer agreed.

"Hush," Veronn said.

Constable Piera stiffened. "What was that?"

"What was what?" I asked innocently.

He frowned. "I thought I heard ... never mind."

I wondered what, exactly, he had heard. The Faes' actual conversation? Or just unusual, unnatural sounds?

Constable Piera was still staring at me, waiting for my response. Or absolution. Clearing my throat, I said, "Quite understandable. It's easy to mistake such things as signs of something odd."

"Rightly so, miss." And that was the end of that topic.

A quarter of an hour had barely passed when the constable announced, "Well, I've seen all there is to see here. I'll head back into Cedarbrook now."

Surprised, Sheriff Tavish said, "That's it? But what have you concluded?"

"I'm afraid not much, sir," the constable said. "It's as you told me, sheriff. Things disturbed, Mistress Cerise missing. I'll ask around in Cedarbrook if anyone's seen anything. That's the best I can do."

Hunter frowned, but merely said, "As you say, constable. Thank you for coming out here."

The two men stepped outside. Hunter closed the door slightly behind him, but I could still hear them talking in low tones just beyond the front door.

"Stupid human," Oonie commented. "Only seeing what he wants to see."

"What do you mean?" I asked, keeping my voice down so the men wouldn't hear me.

"Humans can see Fae things, if they really want to." That came from Kaer. "Some just choose not to believe. Silly, superstitious people."

Veronn sighed. I could hear centuries of weariness in that one little sound. "Hush, you two. Stop it. Do you want the entire town of Cedarbrook out in our forest hunting us down? If they're spooked enough, they'll come looking, and none of us will be safe anymore."

"Best to keep them on their toes," Oonie grumbled, but quietly.

The conversation outside stopped. Hunter pushed open the cottage door and reentered as I caught a glimpse of Constable Piera walking away.

"Well, he was helpful." I didn't bother to keep the sarcasm from my voice.

Hunter nodded in agreement, a frustrated sigh escaping his lips. "Hardly worth the time it to took to go fetch him. In fact, I think it took longer to get him and bring him back than it took for him to look around."

"I wouldn't want him to get tainted by my Lola Cerise's *magic*." I spat the word out, annoyed. "'All there is to see.' The cottage is destroyed, an elderly woman has been taken, and the Cedarbrook constable is letting his baseless prejudices get in the way of doing his job properly. He barely looked at anything, much less did a thorough investigation."

"Taken?" Hunter echoed, giving me a sharp look. "How do you know your grandmother has been taken? And by whom?"

Oh, dear. While I did trust Hunter, I wasn't sure how much of my Faerie heritage I should disclose. It was still too new to me, and there was much I had to learn. There was Lola Cerise's warning, as well. In my annoyance with Constable Piera, I had let my caution slip. I could tell him now, but I found I was reluctant to expose my new Fae friends to curious eyes. Even if they were eyes I could get lost in.

I'll tell him later, I decided. *After I ask the minor Faes' permission to mention them.*

I shrugged, waving a hand around to indicate the cottage's interior. "It's obvious, isn't it? Anyone can see that a struggle occurred, and she was most likely overpowered. But she's not here. So she was mostly likely taken by whoever broke in."

"That does make sense," Hunter agreed. I breathed a bit easier.

He continued, "But we shouldn't rule out other possibilities, gruesome though they may be. Have you looked around outside?"

I shook my head.

"I'll go investigate, then." The sheriff ducked through the front door, closing it behind him.

The moment the door shut, my Fae friends emerged from their hiding spots.

"He won't find anything," Kaer scoffed.

"He might," Oonie said.

"I doubt it."

"But, maybe—"

"It can't hurt to look," Veronn said, firmly putting an end to the pixies' bickering. "Anything he finds—or doesn't find—will just give credence to Miss Claret's words."

"Ah, yes. About that," I said. "Would it be all right with all of you if I told Hunter—I mean, the sheriff—the truth of how I know what happened to Lola Cerise? He wouldn't tell anyone else about you, I'm sure of it. Not if I asked him not to."

The minor Fae all paused, considering. Then, Nellah spoke up in her soft voice.

"If you please, miss, it's not a good idea. Not unless we could be certain he is a good man, and a friend to the Fae. The consequences otherwise would be too dire." She shuddered.

Veronn explained, "It's hard for us minor Fae, even with our magic, to deal with humans. It's usually more trouble than it's worth. It's the major Fae who willingly consort with humans. And even then, as time has gone on, not as much."

I eyed him curiously. "But you talk to me, and I'm only part faery."

"Ah, but you're of the line of forest keepers, and thus a friend to us. Then, too, you've hardly needed any convincing we're real. Your grandmother's word, and one look at us, was all it took for you."

"Well, of course. I can see you all, plain as day. Can't anyone else, even if they're fully human?"

"Some can, if their hearts are in the right place. Others mistake us for ghosts, goblins, or similar. Humans are more likely to believe in the dark creatures, and hunt us minor Fae as such."

I understood now what Veronn was getting at. "So belief in you is tied to your magical ability?"

He nodded sadly. "And as that belief has waned, so too has our magic."

"And our willingness to mix with humans," Kaer piped up.

"Which is why Mistress Cerise's disappearance is most disturbing," Veronn said. "We need the tie to humanity. Without our forest guardian, our magic will ebb and fade. And without our magic, we will die."

CHAPTER 26

S HERIFF TAVISH RETURNED, HIS face grim.

"Did you see anything?" I asked.

"No, nothing," he said. "The windows on the sides and back are intact, but since it seems obvious that the intruder entered through the front door, that's to be expected. But ..."

When he didn't elaborate, I prompted, "What? What is it?"

He shook his head, as if to clear away whatever thoughts were troubling him. "It's nothing. I think I'm just tired. Are you ready to go back?"

I took a deep breath, my eyes sweeping around the wrecked cottage. In various places, I could see the bright, watchful eyes of my Fae friends. I turned to Hunter. "Yes, let's go."

I followed the sheriff outside. As I turned to close the door, my foot brushed up against something. I looked down, my eyes widening as I spied a glint of gold in the sunlight.

Curious, I knelt down. My brow furrowed as my fingers closed over thin, cool metal. I recognized it as my Lola Cerise's favorite necklace, a gift from my grandfather.

And next to the broken chain I had just found were footprints. From the look of them, they came from a large creature. What kind of creature, I didn't know. My eyes followed the prints, noting that they went straight into the forest.

"Miss ... uh, I mean, Claret?" Hunter called out.

I looked up. Hunter stood at the forest's edge, watching me curiously.

"Coming." I stood, shoving the slight gold chain into my pocket. As I hurried over to Hunter, I kept my eyes down, following the footprints. They led to the tree line, but looked like they disappeared beyond that.

"Claret? What is it?"

"You don't see them?"

"What are you talking about?"

I pointed at the tracks. "There! Right there! They're headed in a straight line from my lola's house into the forest."

Hunter's gaze followed my finger, but when he looked back up at me, his face was filled with confusion. "I don't see anything."

I stared at him, incredulous. But he was completely sincere.

He really doesn't see them, I thought in wonder. *Maybe he's right and I'm wrong? Maybe I'm just overtired and seeing things?*

I looked again at the ground. The footprints were there, plain as the daylight streaming down and illuminating them. Gingerly, I touched one of them. My fingertips brushed against dirt, grass—and a slight indent where the ground had sunk underneath the weight of the print.

I'm not going mad. But I don't know how to convince him otherwise.

I straightened, brushing my hand against my skirt. "I must just be imagining things," I said, trying to sound nonchalant. "Let's get going."

Hunter gave me a funny look, but turned and headed into the forest. With one last glance at the mysterious footprints, I followed after him.

The unnatural quiet of the house unsettled me.

I had finished cleaning up the bakehouse, but with my mother indisposed, it would have to stay closed for a while. Also, the counters and shelves needed to be repaired before we could open it to patrons again.

There wasn't much I could do in the house besides daily chores and making sure Mama was warm and fed. Both of which took hardly any time at all.

And yet somehow, despite that feeling of time passing imperceptibly slow, soon I saw the shadows lengthening outside of our still, somber home. I'd have to feed Mama her dinner, eat some myself, and then get ready for bed. I didn't know what I would do on the morrow. I wanted to find my Lola Cerise, but I also had to make sure Mama was taken care of. Perhaps I could ask Doctor Zonta to look in on her? He would need an update anyway.

Although I had no idea where to even begin looking for my grandmother. The footprints had led into the forest, I was sure of that. But even though I had surreptitiously kept a lookout while on the return walk with Sheriff Tavish, I hadn't seen any more tracks, not on the road nor leading deeper into the forest. As crazy as it seemed, the large creature that had abducted my grandmother had just vanished.

Round and round my thoughts spun, never settling on any concrete course of action. My churning thoughts kept me company as I made dinner for my mother and myself, fed her, then cleaned up the dishes and went through the rest of my nightly routine.

By the time I settled into bed, I was exhausted from repeatedly pondering the same inconclusive thoughts. I was nowhere nearer to a solution for any of the problems that had sprung up in the last few days, and I fought the growing fear that I never would be. I put my musings aside and fell into a troubled sleep.

My eyes flew open even as my body tensed. I concentrated, trying to see if I could catch the noise that had woken me up.

I lay in bed for a few moments, my eyes adjusting to the surrounding dark. Perhaps I had imagined it.

But I hadn't. There it was again. A heavy shuffling somewhere below me. A wooden floorboard had creaked, giving away the intruder.

Who was downstairs, in the bakehouse.

Carefully, I slid out of bed and made my way to my bedroom door. I eased it open quietly and slipped out of my room.

I was halfway down the stairs when I realized that I hadn't bothered to grab a robe before I left my bedroom. Not that I wanted to take the time to change before confronting whoever was in the bakehouse. But I was wearing a long white nightgown that would surely draw the intruder's eyes like a beacon.

I paused, unsure of what to do. If I went back upstairs, would I miss the chance to learn more about the intruder? But I didn't want to enter the bakehouse so conspicuously.

My eyes landed on my red cape, hanging by the back door in its usual spot. Ah, perfect!

I grabbed my cloak as I passed by, throwing it over my shoulders as a makeshift dressing gown.

As I approached the door that separated the private residence from the bakeshop, the sounds of someone moving about grew louder. As did the sounds of various objects being moved around. Apparently, whoever had broken into the bakeshop a few days ago had returned to complete the job. Except I didn't know what they wanted or what they were looking for.

Slowly, so as to minimize the sound, I unlocked the door and turned the handle. I grabbed a heavy brass candlestick from a nearby side table, then pushed open the door.

CHAPTER 27

I BRACED MYSELF, BRANDISHING the candlestick in front of me.

But nobody came at me.

Relaxing somewhat, my eyes swept the room.

The first thing I noticed was the door to the bakeshop was open. Just a bit, enough that I could see a sliver of moonlight through the crack. But even odder—the doorway seemed intact. The door hadn't been bashed in, it wasn't hanging off its hinges. Whoever was in here had gotten in through the door, but without having to force their way inside.

I frowned, frantically thinking. I *knew* I had made sure the door was locked when I was done cleaning, and I hadn't touched the bakeshop door since then. Mama and I didn't leave keys outside, so there would be no hidden keys in flowerpots for an enterprising thief to find. And I had all the building's keys—for the bakeshop door, for our back door, and for the door that separated the shop from the residence—with me, in my pocket.

The second thing that caught my eye was the moonlight streaming through the windows at the front of the shop. I thought I had drawn the curtains, signifying to outsiders that Rowena's Bakeshop was closed. And again, since cleaning and closing up the shop, I hadn't been in here. But whoever had entered had pulled the curtains back, probably to aid them in their search.

The last thing I realized—and fortunately, for me—was that the sounds of searching were coming from the bakeshop's kitchen, around the corner and out of sight from the entryway where I stood. I was alone in the room. For now.

I quietly closed the door behind me, slipping the key into my pocket. If something bad should befall me here, at least Mama would be safe upstairs, behind a locked door.

I hoped.

Putting that thought aside, I crept towards the kitchen.

Low snarling and snuffling made my skin stand on end. What manner of trespasser was this? Bad enough, to have to confront another human, one desperate and depraved enough to break into our shop. But these unnatural noises sounded ... otherworldly.

I got a good look at the intruder in the kitchen and instantly froze.

Kneeling on the ground was a large man-like creature. Broad shouldered and covered in dark reddish-black fur from top to bottom, I caught a glimpse of wickedly sharp claws digging through dirt and broken stone. Like the now broken countertop in the bakeshop, the normally pristine stone floor had been smashed in the middle by a heavy blow. No doubt from the creature's meaty fist.

I gave an involuntary, startled gasp.

The creature stopped and looked up. Its glowing red eyes locked on mine. Its lips peeled back in a menacing snarl, revealing fangs as sharp as its claws.

I froze. The creature was frightening, yes. But something about it seemed familiar, particularly about the eyes....

And then the beast sprang at me.

Startled, I stumbled back, my hip catching on the countertop just outside the doorway to the kitchen. I yelped as my knees buckled from the sudden pain and I dropped my candlestick weapon. I fell to my knees, having just enough presence of mind to crawl between the two counters that served as our service area.

But my unexpected injury ended up being my salvation. The crimson-eyed creature grabbed at empty air, then looked around wildly, trying to determine where I had gone.

Sucking in air through my teeth, I kept crawling, only wanting to put as much distance between me and the creature as I could. As I did, I thought through my options. I could try to get back into the house, but that would require taking time to unlock the door, as it locked automatically and required the key to open it from either side. It had been made that way on purpose—after all, we didn't want any patrons wandering into our private home—but now I silently cursed its design.

There was a second reason to reject that door, as well. I didn't want to lead the creature right back to my mother so it could harm her again.

There was no door through the kitchen, although there was one window. But that was above the oven, and escaping through that would be slow and awkward. It would be too easy for the creature to catch up to me and pull me away.

That only left the bakeshop's front entrance. Or one of the front windows, although the door made more sense. If a clear path presented itself, I decided, I would make a run for the door and hopefully escape to find help before the creature caught up to me.

The creature's footsteps sounded uncomfortably close, but they weren't behind or in front of me. Rather, they were right beside me, give or take a few feet. It was parallel to me, with just the bakeshop counter between us. If I kept crawling this way, I would run right into it.

I was halfway between the kitchen and the door to the residence. I paused and sat back, my heart beating wildly. Besides its heavy tread, there was another sound that I was just beginning to be aware of—an odd *clack-clack* sound that kept time with its walk. With dawning horror, I realized that the creature must have claws on its feet *and* its hands, and it was the sound of those foot-claws against the hardwood floor that I was hearing.

With shaking hands, I drew my hood up over my head. It wouldn't do much to conceal my already dark hair, but it comforted me to be completely covered with my grandmother's gift.

I turned to look back the way I had come. And blinked in surprise. Although my eyes had adjusted to the darkness quite some time ago, and the moonlight bathing the bakeshop had helped me see as well, it was still hard to see things in some parts of the bakeshop. Such as the dark well between the two counters I was now sitting in.

But now I could see everything so clearly, it was as if daylight had come. Experimentally, I pulled my hood down. The world faded back into indistinct grays and blacks, and it was only my familiarity with the shop that let me know what it was I was viewing. I put my hood back up. The darkness faded away from my sight again.

Interesting. I had never known that was a feature of wearing my cloak, nor had Lola Cerise ever mentioned it. And as I rarely went in the woods at night, I wouldn't have had occasion to discover this. Or perhaps it was tied into my newfound knowledge of my Faerie heritage? If—*when*, I told myself sternly—I saw my grandmother again, I would have to ask her about it.

As quietly as I could, I crawled back the way I had come. The *clack-clack* of the creature's clawed feet continued down the length of the counter, away from the kitchen. Away from me.

I reached up and grabbed the counter's edge, slowly rising to my feet. I barely breathed, afraid of giving myself away by any little noise. If I was lucky, the creature would keep its back to me just a little bit longer ...

But I had forgotten about the open curtains.

Light flooded my eyes, and I squinted against the brightness. After a moment, my eyes readjusted, and I realized that the moonlight, combined with my newfound night-sight, was responsible for the unnatural brightness in an otherwise dark room. I froze, staring at the creature, knowing that by standing in the moonlight I was an easily seen target.

The creature turned.

I held my breath and braced myself.

CHAPTER 28

B UT INSTEAD OF THE attack I expected, the creature stayed where it was.

Its eerie red eyes swept over the area where I stood, not quite landing on me. Confused, I stayed where I was, staring. How could it not see me? The front window's curtains were wide open, and I had unwittingly stood up right in a patch of moonlight.

The beast lifted its nose to the air and sniffed. Nostrils flaring, it hissed. It sniffed again, more deeply, but seemed a bit confused. As if it could catch some unfamiliar scent, but just barely.

Its head turned this way and that, scanning my side of the room. But still, though it was looking in my general direction, it hadn't actually spotted me.

My eyes widened with dawning realization. It knew, generally, where I was. But, for some reason, it didn't know where I was specifically.

My cloak.

That had to be it. Lola Cerise had said she had woven magical protections into it.

Like helping me see in the dark.

And keeping me hidden from a predator's prying eyes.

I sent out a silent sentiment of gratitude. *Thank you, Lola Cerise. Wherever you are.*

But I knew staying in place, even if it seemed like the creature couldn't see me, wasn't wise. Carefully, I began to make my way towards the bakeshop door.

Across the room, the beast growled, low and menacing.

I kept up my slow creep towards the front of the shop, while trying to keep my eyes upon the creature. Some long-buried instinct told me turning my back on this beast might be a bad idea.

The creature stalked towards the area I had just been standing in. Hearing the scraping *click-clack* of its clawed feet sent chills down my spine.

Breathe, Claret. Breathe. Keep moving.

Without warning, the beast swiped at the empty air. Had I still been in that spot, or nearby, my face and chest would have been sliced open by those horrifyingly sharp claws.

Realizing that its intended prey was no longer there, the creature threw back its head and howled, angry and frustrated.

Forget trying to be slow and quiet. My panic spiked; I needed to get out of here, *now*. This thing was out for blood—mine—and I had no intention of staying here one moment longer, giving it more time to find me.

I bolted for the door.

Hearing my hurried passage, the beast's head turned sharply in my direction. Its nostrils flared as it caught my scent, more sure this time.

I felt a brush of wind as the beast swiped at me, just missing me. My shoulders slammed into the bakeshop's door as I leapt, throwing all my weight into the jump.

The door, already ajar, swung wide open. I landed heavily on the street outside, my left side tingling from taking the brunt of my fall.

But my injuries would have to wait. The creature, hard on my heels, stood in the shop's entryway, sniffing and surveying the area.

For me.

What to do now? Pain clouded my thoughts, but there was nowhere I could really hide. The street outside the bakeshop was lined with other shops and residences, but no convenient hiding spots. I also worried that if I moved, I would attract the creature's attention again.

So instead, I burrowed deeper into my cloak, pulling the hood further down my brow, as I curled into a ball. I bit my lip, willing my heartbeat to slow, afraid that my breathing would give me away. If I was to meet my end, I at least didn't want to look it right in the glowing red eyes.

The beast sniffed again, slow and deliberate. Its claws *click-clicked* against the hard ground and it took a few steps. First towards me, then away as it continued sniffing around.

Please don't find me. Please, don't find me.

I closed my eyes and thought invisible thoughts.

The footsteps paused. Then they started again.

Moving in my direction.

Maybe I should have made a run for it. Even if that would have led to my ending quicker.

The footsteps stopped, mere inches from where I lay. If the creature continued on, it would walk right into me. Above me, I could hear the creature's heavy breathing, and shrank into myself further, recalling its sharp fangs.

I've failed you both, Lola Cerise, Mama.

And then I heard the sound of gravel crunching underfoot, and the sound of breathing stopped. The air suddenly felt lighter as the feeling of dread that had hung over me disappeared.

What ...?

I counted to twenty, then slowly uncurled myself and turned onto my back, hoping the cloak's magic was still protecting me. I fully expected to be staring up into the slavering face of the mysterious creature—followed by its fangs and claws tearing me apart.

But to my surprise, I was alone.

I sat up, pushing my hood back as I looked around in wonder. My left arm screamed in pain, and I was fairly sure my left hip would show bruises in the morning.

And speaking of the morning, the night sky was noticeably lighter. Sunrise would be here soon.

I startled at the sound of footsteps running towards me. Stupid of me, to think I was safe. I reached for my hood, knowing it was futile—the beast would have already seen me—

"Claret!"

Hunter dropped to his knees beside me. "What's happened? Are you all right?"

I shook my head. "Someone—some *thing*—broke into the bakeshop during the night. When I went to investigate, it ... it tried to attack me."

"Oh, my. Are you hurt?"

"My arm," I groaned.

"Can you stand?"

I started to, but my legs refused to cooperate.

"I'll fetch Doctor Zonta."

"No!" I surprised both of us by grabbing the sleeve of Hunter's coat. "Please don't leave." What if that thing came back? I didn't want to be here, by myself, if it did. But I was still too shaken to stand, much less walk over to Doctor Zonta's office.

The sheriff looked down the street, torn. "But if you can't stand ..."

He stood. As I started to protest, he held up a finger. *Wait.*

"Do you have the shop key?"

I obediently fished it out of my pocket and handed it over.

Hunter jogged over to close and lock the bakeshop's door. He returned, giving me back the key. I had just finished tucking it away when I felt two strong arms scoop me up gently.

"Hold on. I'll go as carefully as I can," he said. "We'll be there in no time."

I breathed deep, finding comfort in the sheriff's vanilla-and-cedar scent. The first rays of sunrise spilled over the horizon, one beam lighting his handsome face in a lovely, golden light. He grinned down at me, his smile as bright as the growing sunlight.

I rested my cheek against Hunter's chest, finally letting myself relax after the tension of the night's events.

CHAPTER 29

WHEN SHERIFF TAVISH APPROACHED the physician's office, carrying me wrapped in my scarlet cape, it caused quite a stir.

I could see a few of the doctor's neighbors peeking through their curtains, watching the event unfold with interest. Doctor Zonta had just opened up for the day, and his eyes widened when he saw me.

"Miss Claret!" He regarded the sheriff gravely. "Sir, what has happened?"

"I'm afraid I don't really know," Hunter admitted. "Those answers will have to come from Miss Claret herself."

"Well, then, the answers can wait. Bring her this way, if you please."

Hunter followed the man into a familiar room. I had been here just a week or so ago, to meet Mister Feldan. The room's single bed was neatly made—the cait sidhe was no longer present. I hadn't thought to look him up during my recent visit to Cedarbrook, assuming he was still in Woodside. While I was glad he was well enough to leave, I also wished he was present. I could use some advice right now.

Hunter gently laid me on the bed, helping me get settled, then he left the room to allow Doctor Zonta to look me over.

A meow from one side made the man frown. A large black cat with a white spot on its chest sat in the open window.

"Shoo, you," the doctor said, swatting at the animal. The cat hissed but jumped away just as Doctor Zonta closed the window.

"Pesky thing," he said. "Appeared a few days ago. I can't have an animal here—I have to keep my instruments clean. But it won't leave me alone."

I nodded, only half paying attention to the doctor's chatter. I was more worried about the state of my arm, which the doctor had uncovered while talking.

My left arm looked a mess—all bloodied, and still throbbing from landing on it. But once the doctor cleaned me up, I was relieved to find it wasn't as bad as it looked.

Part of my arm sported a long scrape, and the bright red bruised spots on both my arm and hip were beginning to turn purple. But I would be fine, as long as I babied my left side a bit. And didn't run away from any more mysterious night visitors.

Doctor Zonta smeared a strong, bitter-smelling salve over my bruised skin, then stepped back.

"We'll that soak in for a bit, then I'll come back in for one last check," he said. "After that, you'll be able to leave."

"Thank you, doctor," I said.

The physician left, closing the door behind him. Hunter didn't come back in—perhaps to allow me a chance to rest? I wouldn't have minded his company. The doctor hadn't said how long I'd be waiting, and there was nothing to do in the austere room besides sit on the bed and stare at the wall. Or, as a marginally better option, out the window.

A soft meowing through the glass caught my attention. The black cat had returned, perhaps sensing that Doctor Zonta had left. It reached a paw out, patting at the glass.

Curious, I opened the window. The cat immediately jumped inside. As it landed on the floor, it transformed into the slight figure of Mister Feldan. His trusty red cap sat atop his silvery hair. He pulled it off and held it between his hands as he bowed slightly to me.

"Mister Feldan!" I said. "It's good to see you again."

"Likewise, Miss Claret," he said. "As much as I hate to see you injured like this, I'm glad that you're here."

I eyed him curiously. "Have you been looking for me?"

"I have," he said. "I left here several days ago, and returned to Faerie, then came back. I went to the bakeshop to find you. But the place was closed, and I couldn't figure out a way to get in."

"Oh," I said, realization dawning. "We may have just missed each other. My mother is ... currently indisposed. That's why the shop is closed. I went to visit my grandmother, to give her your news, but ... she was not there."

A long silence fell between us. Then, from Mister Feldan: "I think you'd better tell me everything."

As succinctly as I could, I outlined the events of the last few days for Mister Feldan. His face grew darker during my recitation. When I finished, he said, "What would you have me do, Miss Claret?"

Confused, I asked, "What do you mean?"

"With Mistress Cerise gone, you're the rightful Keeper of the Forest. The new Scarlet Lady. Miss Rowena was never eligible, and even if she was, she is unable to fulfill that duty right now." Mister Feldan stared at me, his yellow cat-like eyes unsettling in a human face. I hadn't noticed them before—or he had masked them well with a Fae glamour—but now that I was aware of what he truly was, it was hard to see him as an unassuming human again.

His words weighed on my heart. Yes, he spoke truth. But that didn't mean I welcomed it.

I fought the panic rising within me. I wasn't my Lola Cerise. I didn't know what to do as the Scarlet Lady. My grandmother was supposed to have guided me into this new role. I was supposed to have more time to learn, to understand, to grow. But instead I had no time at all.

Lola Cerise was gone and the Fae of Littlewood Forest were looking to me to help them.

Mister Feldan's earlier words pierced through my despondent fog.

"Wait. You said that you went back to Faerie? And returned to find me? Why?"

"After the good doctor released me from his care, I decided to go back to Faerie, instead of to Cedarbrook." He hung his head in shame. "Hearing your tale, I now wonder if I made the right decision. Perhaps if I had returned to Cedarbrook and met with Mistress Cerise with my news, she would still be here."

"Don't blame yourself," I said. "Neither of us could have known what would occur."

"But she would have known what to do. I mean no offense, miss, but you are right. You are truly powerless and untried against the creature that you now face."

"Do you know what it is, then?" Any information was better than none. Perhaps the knowledge would help ease my worries.

"Yes." His face was grim. "The reports from Faerie all say the same thing. It is a lycan."

CHAPTER 30

*I*T'S A LYCAN? I thought. Then, recalling my reading, *Oh, dear.*

Lycans had been mentioned in the *Faerie Lore and Legends* book I had borrowed from my grandmother. A type of werewolf, they were considered a rarer and stronger form of their cursed canine cousins. In general, werewolves were subject to the lunar cycles. Their power grew as the moon grew towards fullness, with the full moon giving them the height of their power. However, with that power came a body change that they couldn't fight.

Lycans, however, could change their forms at will.

New werewolves were made when bit by a werewolf, but lycans were unusual cases. Created when cursed by great magic, they leaned into their werewolf side, embracing the darkness that had created them instead of merely trying to manage it or live around it. This gave them stronger abilities and increased power, with the downside being that their time was limited. Without a near constant supply of magic, they would eventually wither and die. It was hard to maintain such a supply, which was why lycans were thrown into the mortal world, where the chances of them finding an endless source of magic were slim.

As well, over time a lycan would go mad, their mind broken from the weight of so much power. It was possible for them to live on, nearly immortal, as an unusually strong and deranged wolf.

Neither option sounded that great to me.

Knowing what we were facing didn't make me feel any better. If anything, I felt even more panicked.

"So what should I do?" I asked Mister Feldan.

The cait sidhe frowned. "I don't rightly know, miss. Go carefully. Arm yourself with silver, if you can. And ..."

When he didn't continue, I prompted, "And?"

He tapped his chin thoughtfully. "Every accursed has a weakness. A trade-off for their immense magical power or physical strength. For a lycan, such a fierce predator ..."

Mister Feldan twisted his red cap in his hand. "Some of the most dangerous predators have poor eyesight. Can't see things clearly, or can't distinguish colors. That's why Mistress Cerise made me this, why she loves red so much. It's a lucky Faerie color. And for certain creatures, they can't see it well, or see it at all."

A creak in the hallway made us both jump. The low murmur of men's voices floated towards us, muffled by the wooden door to my room.

I gasped. "Doctor Zonta and Sheriff Tavish! They're coming!"

"Be watchful and wary, Miss Claret," Mister Feldan said, his form beginning to shimmer. "And be careful of who you invite into your home. It may be a legendary Fae, but even the royals of Faerie cannot enter someone's abode without an invitation."

With that, his human body winked out. A moment later, a black cat with a tuft of white fur on its chest and two white paws appeared in his place.

I settled back into the bed just as there was a knock on the chamber door.

"Miss Claret?" came the physician's voice.

Mister Feldan, now in his feline form, jumped onto the windowsill. I held out a hand in thanks. He rubbed his head against my palm, then ran off.

"Come in," I called out.

Doctor Zonta entered, followed by Hunter, who hovered just outside the doorway. Seeing the open window, the doctor frowned. "Fresh air is always a good prescription for my patients. But I hope that pesky cat didn't come back to bother you."

"I wasn't bothered at all," I said with perfect truth.

He examined my skin, satisfied that the salve was doing its work. Giving me a little pot full of the same thick ointment, he said, "Apply this once a day for a week, and that should ease the hurt in your muscles."

"Thank you." I tucked the salve away, then said, "Can I leave now?"

The doctor chuckled. "Of course, miss. And how's your mother doing?"

I sighed. "No change, I'm afraid."

"I'll stop by tomorrow, to check up on both of you."

"Thank you," I said again.

The physician helped me stand, then addressed Hunter, still standing in the hallway. "Make sure she gets home safe, young man."

The sheriff chuckled. "Yes, sir."

After Doctor Zonta saw us out, I stood on the office doorstep, looking around uncertainly.

"Miss ... uh, Claret? Are you all right?"

I gave Hunter a reassuring smile, although I wasn't actually sure. "I-I will be. I think."

"Let me take you home."

After a few steps, the sheriff realized I wasn't following him and turned around. "Claret?"

I tried to move in his direction, but I couldn't move. "I don't want to go home," I whispered, realizing. I knew I'd have to, eventually. But for now, I didn't want to be back in there, silent and unsafe, the ruined bakeshop a reminder of this morning's attack and my mama's condition.

The sheriff was quick to return to my side. "It will be all right," he said, gently taking my arm to steady me. I hadn't even realized I was shaking until that moment.

"Are ... are you sure?"

He frowned, but his eyes were gentle. "It will be, eventually," he repeated. "I will do all I can in my power to ensure it."

I sniffled. "Thank you."

"How about we go to my office?" Hunter suggested. "You can see the changes I've made since you were there last."

His voice turned endearingly shy. "And if you like, I could show you the progress I've made on the investigation so far."

And I could be somewhere a little more neutral than back at home. Although looking over Hunter's notes might trigger a negative reaction. Still, it would be interesting.

And it really was adorable, how much he wanted to share his work with me.

So I nodded. "That sounds interesting. Yes, let's do that."

We headed towards the city center. After a few moments, I added belatedly, "Thank you."

Hunter gave me a quizzical look. "For what?"

I shrugged, feeling suddenly shy. "For ... everything. Looking out for my mother and me. Trying to help me with my grandmother. Helping me now. Just ... everything."

He ducked his head modestly. "It's my job. I'm the sheriff of Woodside, I'm supposed to look out for its townsfolk. Although sometimes," he muttered in a lower voice, "I'm not sure I'm doing that good of a job at it."

I started to protest—*of course you're doing a good job*—but he continued, "But I do have to admit that I might be interested in the welfare of certain citizens more than others."

I blushed at his intense sidelong look. "Well. Um. Thank you. Again."

Hunter chuckled, but didn't say anything else.

As we walked towards the sheriff's office, I noticed more people out and about. Well, it *was* a work day, and most of Woodside was probably heading to jobs or to do business in the civic center. I got a few funny looks from passersby—after all, I would normally be in Rowena's Bakeshop, working, instead of in the middle of town—but nobody stopped us to ask why I wasn't back home. For which I was quite thankful.

Hunter unlocked his office door, saying, "It's mostly finished, although I'm not entirely settled in yet."

He swung open the door. I gasped, then clapped my hands in delight.

"Wow, this place looks amazing! You've done wonders with it!" I said.

Hunter's mostly finished office was a far cry from the decrepit mess I had helped him clean. The cracks and holes in the walls and ceiling had been repaired, and the walls had been washed and repainted with a fresh coat of paint. The floor also gleamed, with new pieces of wood flooring to replace boards that had rotted.

Sitting in pride of place was a stately cedarwood desk with a matching chair. Two more chairs sat opposite the desk, presumably for visitors. A wall-to-wall bookcase made of the same red-brown cedarwood as the desk stood behind Hunter's desk. I noticed how empty the bookcase was—only one shelf held a few books and knickknacks.

"Thank you. I couldn't have done this without you." Hunter grinned, leaning back against the desk. I sank down in one of the visitors' chairs.

I grinned back, waving a hand at the lone, somewhat full shelf. "I see you're still unpacking."

Hunter smiled. "Actually, that's all I brought with me." His smile faded. "I ... didn't see a point in bringing more when I left."

His cryptic statement reminded me that I still barely knew the new sheriff, despite the time we had spent together since his arrival. I tilted my head, curious. "Why not?"

Hunter regarded me. The silence drew out between us. Usually I felt comfortable in his presence, happy to not fill the quiet with inane talk. But now, I could feel something brewing underneath, something he wanted to tell me but wasn't sure how.

Finally, he spoke. "Miss ... uh, I mean, Claret. There's something I need to tell you. I—"

An urgent knock startled us both. As we turned to look, a woman burst through the office door. "I'm looking for the new sheriff," she said.

Hunter straightened up. "That would be me."

"I'm here to make a report. Something tried to attack me last night."

CHAPTER 31

I JUMPED OUT OF my chair as I recognized the speaker.

"Mistress Tabend? Are you all right?"

The plump matron blinked, surprised to see a familiar face in the sheriff's office. Her brown hair, streaked with grey, was pulled up in a messy bun. Her usually crisp cream-colored apron was wrinkled, hastily tied over an equally wrinkled grey dress. I was surprised to see Mistress Tabend in such a state. One of our best customers, who visited the bakeshop on a near daily basis, she was always impeccably turned out whenever I saw her.

Mistress Tabend fell into my arms. "Oh, Claret! I'm happy to see you, safe and well!"

"What do you mean?"

She choked back a sob. "I was coming back home from Claralynn's sewing circle. It got out later than usual ... she's been having so much trouble with her rascal of a brother, and she needed to talk about it."

Sheriff Tavish held out the second chair for Mistress Tabend. She slowly sank into it, still telling her tale.

"I was the last to leave, and it was already dark by then. But I didn't think anything of it. Woodside is safe enough, and I wasn't going far. I certainly wasn't going into the forest. I've seen the signs around town.

"As I started walking home, I realized something was following me. I would catch it out of the corner of my eye, keeping pace with me in the shadows. I froze, not sure if I should run or hide."

"Something? Not someone? What made you think that?" Hunter was all business now, but his voice was gentle as he questioned Mistress Tabend.

The poor woman shuddered. "It can't have been human. Not with the sounds it was making, the snarling and the heavy breathing, from a chest larger than a man's. And its eyes ... red, glowing. Unnatural."

My blood ran cold. Mistress Tabend's description sounded a lot like the creature that had broken into the bakeshop recently.

"So then what happened?" Sheriff Tavish asked.

"I screamed and started running. Which, looking back, may not have been the smartest move. But what could I do? I dropped my sewing basket, picked up my skirts, and ran for all I was worth. I didn't stop until I got to my house, but that ... *thing* ... was right on my heels. I barely got the door unlocked and shut behind me. Even then, it prowled around my house for a while longer, trying to find a way to get in."

"It didn't, did it?" I asked breathlessly.

Mistress Tabend shook her head. "No, although I had a frying pan at the ready to bash it over the head if it did."

I stifled a giggle at the thought of the matron lurking just behind her door, wielding a cast iron pan as an instrument of doom.

She continued, "It eventually tired of trying, and moved on. But I didn't sleep a wink, waiting for it to return."

"What about your husband?" I asked. "You didn't wake him up to help or investigate?"

She shook her head. "He's on a two week trip in the south right now. He should be back in a few days."

Mistress Tabend's husband was a traveling merchant, often leaving for several weeks at a time. Their two grown children had moved away from Woodside years ago, usually coming back to visit during the end-of-year holidays.

She stood, brushing back a few strands of hair that had fallen across her face. "I should get back home. I hope that thing doesn't return tonight. I just didn't know what to do ..."

"You did the right thing, coming to see me," Hunter said. "I'll accompany you back, and if you don't mind, I'd like you to retrace your steps from last night."

"Of course. And thank you." Mistress Tabend stepped outside.

Hunter paused before following, turning to me with a questioning look.

I hesitated, unsure of what to do. "You don't need my help, do you? I don't want to get in the way."

Sheriff Tavish shook his head. "No, it's all right. Do you want to go back home? If so, I'll need to lock up."

"Uh ..." I didn't really want to return home just yet, but I couldn't say that in front of Mistress Tabend without introducing a bunch of explanations.

"Or you can stay here," Hunter offered. His sympathetic eyes warmed me. He knew—and understood—my reasons. "I can give you the key."

"If you don't mind ..."

"Not at all." He fished a brass key out of his pocket and handed it to me. "Don't feel like you need to wait for me. I might be a while. Just remember to lock the door if you leave."

"But won't you need to get back in?"

He grinned and held up another key identical to the one in my hand. "I have a second key. I'll get yours back when I see you next."

My face lit up in an answering smile. "Perfect."

Hunter left. For a few blissful moments, I just sat in the quiet of his empty office, enjoying the stillness and the slight sound of my breathing.

But soon boredom overtook me. I hadn't expected, when Hunter extended the invitation, that I would go to his office and just sit around, waiting for him.

I could leave. Hunter trusted me enough to give me a key. And it was full daylight out.

But I still didn't want to go back home. Not yet.

I stood and wandered around the office. Even though it was clean and orderly, there wasn't much to look at—as Hunter had said, he hadn't brought much with him. I surveyed the one shelf that held anything of interest.

I skipped over the first few books, which were treatises on the science of investigation. Although the one on famous unsolved cases looked interesting.

The next book caught my eye. It was titled *Faerie Lore and Legends, Vol. 2.* Volume Two? I hadn't realized there were more.

With nothing else to do, I plucked the book from the shelf and settled into a chair to read. As I opened the book, a strange scratching sound reached my ears. I startled, thinking the monster from last night was at the door, trying to get in.

But all I saw was sunlight streaming in from the office windows. There were no menacing footsteps, no big lurking shadows. I was truly alone.

I flipped through the book. Curiously, only part of the book contained text and pictures—the front third. The last third of the book was blank.

Why bother printing a book with a bunch of blank pages?

The scratching sound was louder now. I glanced nervously at the door, but I still didn't see or sense anything amiss outside. I looked down at *Faerie Lore and Legends, Vol. 2*, as the pages fell open to the center.

To my horror and amazement, words were appearing across the blank page, scrawled in a fine, spidery writing. I finally recognized what I was hearing: the sound of a fountain pen as it moved across paper.

Before my eyes, the book was writing itself.

CHAPTER 32

M Y JAW DROPPED AS the book fell from my hands. The book flipped closed on the floor.

I rubbed at my eyes, disbelieving. I must be tired. Yes, that was it. It had been a stressful few days, and now that I finally had a moment's peace, my eyes were playing tricks on my mind. That had to be it.

Cautiously, I picked up the book and opened it to the middle. Fine lettering was still forming slowly across the cream-colored paper. The soft scraping of the invisible pen nib sighed from the page. I stared at it, my vision swimming slightly as I tried to make sense of what I was reading.

Frustrated, I set the book on the table.

The pages rustled. Startled, I glanced over at the book. The pages rustled again, sounding almost ... impatient.

"I'm ... sorry?" I said sheepishly, my voice sounding too loud in the quiet of Hunter's office. "I ... don't know what you want?"

Oh, great. I'm talking to a book. Maybe I should go home.

With a final swish, the book fanned its pages until it was open to its beginning. I eyed the book, but didn't pick it up. Its spine lifted up slightly and thumped against the desk, as if to say, *Well? What are you waiting for?*

"Oh, my. I'm sorry," I said again. "Uh ... thank you?"

The book's pages fanned slightly, sounding smug.

I picked up *Faerie Lore and Legends, Vol. 2* and began reading.

A few pages in, my head was spinning.

Whereas the book I had borrowed from my grandmother was a static history book, the new volume I had found on Hunter's shelf was *alive*. I didn't know any other way to describe it. Aside from its ongoing writing, it contained a more recent—and intriguing—history of the Fae.

Of note was a section on Faerie politics. A list of Fae courtiers, along with the names of their children, spanned the length of three pages. I wondered why anyone would think the list important.

Realization dawned as I stared at the list. Although I'd never been to court—the fancy doings of our royals were not for the likes of my family, and Woodside was well away from the kingdom's center—I was sure some poor scribe was tasked with keeping the lists of our kingdom's courtiers up to date. And that list could change often, as people moved away, fell into disgrace, or died. It would be a nuisance, but do-able.

With the Fae's longevity and near-immortal status, a listing of that realm's lords and ladies would seldom change, if ever. They rarely bred, so any children were highly prized and often coveted by others. My book had mentioned changelings, those monstrosities left as replacements by the Fae when they stole unfortunate human babies from their cradles.

So, I surmised, in Faerie it would be a mark of honor for a courtier to have their families listed along with them. And judging from these few pages, there weren't many Fae families. Many singular lords or ladies, and an equal amount of couples. But just a small amount of families.

One surname stood out to me.

Tavish.

My finger traced the short genealogy.

Lord Percival and Lady Katerina Tavish. Two sons, Hunter and Hudson. Their ages were unlisted, and Hudson's name had been crossed out with a single thin black line. I scanned the other pages. There were very few cross-outs, and there was no clear logic behind the scratched out names.

What could it mean? I'd have to ask Mister Feldan when he returned. Without knowing the depth of Faerie politics, I could only guess. Those who had died, somehow? Those who had fallen into disgrace?

Hunter hadn't mentioned having a brother. Then again, we hadn't really discussed his family at all. Perhaps he hadn't mentioned a brother because his sibling had died, and it was too painful to talk about it.

But seeing Hunter's name on this list gave me pause. If this was true, then Hunter was of Faerie. *And* he was nobility. I didn't know if he was fully Fae or just part Fae, like me. But with his high Other World connections, he must know more than he had been letting on.

Why didn't he tell me?

I frowned as more implications set in. Did he know who and what my Lola Cerise was? Mister Feldan? Had Hunter been able to see the minor woodland Fae in my grandmother's cottage? Had he seen the footprints that led into the forest? And if so, why had he acted like he couldn't?

And why would he come here, to sleepy little Woodside, to be the sheriff of a human town? He had told me he was here to investigate the attacks, but to what end? Why would a Fae noble have that much interest in human affairs, even if it did include a Fae? He could have just left my grandmother, the forest Fae, and the human constable in Cedarbrook to deal with things.

Under the Tavish listing was a description of an area. I looked it over.

The Tavish holdings are bordered by the Muno River on the east, and includes the entirety of Littlewood Forest.... I realized the listing outlined an area that included all of Woodside, Cedarbrook, and Littlewood Forest.

The Tavish holdings? What did the book mean? This area was under the rule of King Josten IV, who resided in the capital city over a week's ride away. Due to our location, Cedarbrook and Woodside were fairly autonomous, only sending in taxes once a year. For the most part, the king left us alone, and no nobles had overseen us for several decades. I frowned, trying to recall my history lessons. I didn't recall any nobles named Tavish in our area's history.

Hmm. How curious. Eagerly, I flipped through more pages.

Another page was titled, *Keepers*. I skimmed the alphabetical list, my eyes catching on "Cerise, Scarlet Lady of Littlewood Forest." Interesting that her full name was not recorded. As I studied the rest of the list, I saw that other guardians were named similarly, with just their first name marked down next to to their title and location.

A bit of superstitious lore came back to me. Something that, back in the days when we minded the Fae, Lola Cerise said to be careful to do.

Never tell anyone your real, full name, unless you know they are completely trustworthy.

Something about names having power, and your true name having the most power of all.

I shook my head, unsure if I was even remembering Lola Cerise's words correctly. If only I could ask her.

I turned back to the book. Two names had been crossed out, with new names scrawled next to them. Neither of them were my grandmother's.

Please, please ... *let that be a good sign.*

I looked again at the Scarlet Lady listing and my jaw dropped. As I watched, a new entry appeared next to it. Now, the record read, "Cerise, Scarlet Lady of Littlewood Forest. Recognized successor: Claret."

But at least Lola Cerise's name hadn't been crossed out. I turned the page. This page was labeled In-. I wasn't sure "In" what, or how long the handwritten list was, for the majority of the page had been torn out.

I studied the pages that came before and after the ripped one. They didn't give me any hint of what the missing one could be about. The left-hand page was blank, while the right side page looked to be about a new, different subject.

"Maybe the scribe messed up while writing," I mused aloud. "Smeared a line, spilled ink on the page ..."

In my hands, the book's paper rustled indignantly.

"Oh!" I said, startled. "Uh ... I'm sorry?"

The pages fluttered a bit softer, sounding mollified.

"I take it you wrote this? This entire book?" I ran a finger down the spine.

The pages fluttered again, smugly. Amazing how an inanimate object could sound pleased with itself.

"What happened to this page? Why is it torn out?"

There was a soft sigh from the book, which lifted the edges of the top four pages. I held my breath expectantly. But the book didn't talk to me, nor did any words appear on the paper.

The pages flipped forward to the middle, where the invisible pen had been busy scratching out words earlier. I frowned, unsure of what the obviously sentient book was trying to convey. The words hadn't changed from earlier. They still looked to be some sort of historical record that held no meaning for me.

I sighed, a louder imitation of the book's. Whatever spirit was trapped within the tome, it appeared it could only do a limited amount of things. Communicating clearly with me was not one of them.

A scratching sound at the door caused me to jump up hastily.

CHAPTER 33

It DIDN'T SOUND LIKE Sheriff Tavish at the door, but nevertheless, I startled guiltily. He hadn't explicitly told me not to touch anything, but he also may not have liked me going through his belongings.

The scratching noise started again, followed by a funny, low *thud-thud*. Now that I paid closer heed, I realized the noises were coming from ground level, not higher up where I would have expected a person to be knocking.

I left the book on the table, still open and merrily writing away, and slowly opened the door, curious to see the source of the sound.

A black and white cat rushed into the sheriff's office. It sprinted around the room, then sprang onto one of the wooden chairs. From there, it leapt onto Hunter's desk, just narrowly missing the faery-made book.

The book emitted an indignant *scratch-squeak*. Hastily, I scooped it up and closed it, then placed it back on the shelf.

Meanwhile, the cat didn't notice or care about the near-destruction it had left in its wake. Instead, it jumped from the desk onto Hunter's cot, where it began licking one paw unconcernedly.

I laughed. "Mister Feldan!"

The cait sidhe purred, pleased I had recognized him. As he continued to groom, the air around him shimmered, and soon the form of the man was sitting on the cot.

"What are you doing here?"

"Well, mistress, we didn't have a chance to finish our conversation back in Doctor Zonta's office."

I frowned. "Didn't we?"

He shook his head. "No, mistress. You are the new Scarlet Lady. The Keeper of Littlewood Forest. I am one of yours, and yours to command. What would you have me do?"

Ah, yes. That's right. He had asked for direction back in the physician's office, but I had been so distracted by my own woes I hadn't answered his question. The most important one, really.

"My first priority is to find Lola Cerise. But I don't know where she might be. Or how to find her, especially if there is a lycan on the loose."

I paused as an idea came to me. "You're a messenger, are you not?"

At Mister Feldan's nod, I continued, emboldened. "Then let me send you back to the Faerie court with a message. Tell them what has happened to my family, and request they send help. If we truly are facing an accursed Fae, then we will need more power than the forest Fae or I can provide."

I took a deep breath and stood tall. "Tell them that Claret, the Scarlet Lady of Littlewood Forest in Cerise's absence, sent you."

Mister Feldan grinned and bowed. "A fine idea, Mistress Claret. I will go immediately."

"How long will you be gone?"

The cait sidhe frowned. "I'm not sure. I'll return as soon as I may, but with the royal family in hiding ..."

"I understand." I sighed. "I'll be so worried until I hear back from you, but there's not much I can do."

"I'll come to Woodside and find you. And the forest Fae are very aware of everything that happens under the Littlewood trees. They'll know the moment I return, and can get a message to you."

"One more thing, before you go."

"Yes, mistress?"

"What do you know about the Tavish family?"

Mister Feldan paused. "An old, esteemed family. Their lands lie in close proximity to the human world, although, like most noble Fae, they would rather focus on Faerie affairs than mortal ones. The current Lord Tavish has served as an advisor and confidant to King Finvarra and Queen Oona in the past, but recently retired from active court duty. Why do you ask?"

I blushed, embarrassed at having to admit to snooping. "I ... found a book recently that had a genealogy of Faerie nobles. I saw a listing for the Tavishes, including our new sheriff and a name that was crossed out. A Hudson Tavish."

"Ah. That would be one of the Tavish sons, I believe."

"But why was his name crossed out?"

Mister Feldan frowned thoughtfully. "I haven't paid attention to Fae politics as of late. But my guess is, if he is crossed out of the listing, he must have died. I can look into it when I go back to Faerie, if you like."

"Please do so. And, as you say, go carefully."

Mister Feldan nodded, his form shrinking in on itself before my eyes. Soon the man was replaced by a black and white cat, who jumped down from the cot and came towards me, purring and rubbing his head against my leg. I smiled and reached down to scratch the cat's head. Mister Feldan's purring grew momentarily louder, then he slipped out the still open door, just narrowly missing a newly returned Sheriff Tavish.

"Woah!" In trying to avoid tripping over the fleeing cat, Hunter nearly lost his balance. His arms flailed. I reached out to help him steady himself. "Thank you."

For a moment we just stared at each other. Bright emerald eyes, framed by dark lashes, gazed down at me. I could really get lost in those eyes....

Belatedly, I realized I was still holding onto his arm. I coughed, embarrassed—and to give me an excuse to let go. I stepped back. "How did it go with Mistress Tabend?"

His face darkened. "Well enough, I suppose. The most useful thing I can report is that we found her missing sewing basket."

I frowned. "No news on the creature?"

He shook his head. "Everything looked as she said. Large tracks along the path, following her home. Those same tracks lurking about her house. Gouges in the wood where it tried to get through her front door."

His gaze turned thoughtful. "I didn't realize how close Mistress Tabend lives to you and your mother."

"She's one of our best customers, probably because she's just a few doors down."

"Hmm." Hunter ran a frustrated hand through his dark hair, leaving it sticking up at various angles. "Whatever is haunting the forest is bold enough to come into town. One time might have been a coincidence, but this is twice now. Perhaps I should keep a watch overnight."

"Tonight?"

He sighed. "Every night. Until it returns."

Looking at his drawn face, my heart hurt in sympathy. "Will you be roaming about Main Street all night, then?"

"Not if I can help it." He paused. "The creature seems to be drawn to your area of town. It stands to reason it might look for a new target, or return to Mistress Tabend's."

Or return to Rowena's Bakeshop. But we both knew better than to say those words aloud.

I nodded solemnly. "You're welcome to keep vigil in our shop, then. And I would be happy to keep you company during your watch."

He hesitated. "I wouldn't want to put you in any danger."

"I want this creature to be stopped as much as you do." I shrugged, a bit embarrassed. In a smaller voice, I added, "Besides, I don't know that I'd be able to sleep in my house after what's happened."

A long silence fell between us.

I looked down at my hands. My breath hitched as Hunter took my hands in his.

"Come, I'll walk you home." He took a deep breath. "And then, if you're up to it, I'll come by this evening. I thank you for your generous offer of using your shop as a base while I keep watch."

A slow smile bloomed across my face. "Well. I suppose it's a good idea for me to get more rest, then."

He grinned back. "Yes. A good idea, indeed."

CHAPTER 34

B Y THE TIME LONG lines of golden light streaked across the floor, signaling sunset, I was awake and ready to go. I flung open the back door after hearing the second knock.

Hunter blinked in surprise. "Well. Good evening." He chuckled. "I thought you'd still be sleeping."

"Oh, no. I've been busy." I stepped back to allow the sheriff to enter.

He lowered his voice as he walked in. "With what?"

"Just making sure we have food for the night." I waved a hand towards the staircase. "And you don't need to whisper. Mama is still ... indisposed."

He gave me a sympathetic smile, catching the sadness in my voice. "She'll be all right. We will make sure of it."

That *we* wasn't lost on me. My cheeks warmed as I ducked my head, pleased.

Hunter followed me into the shuttered bakehouse. I went to pull back the curtains, intending to let the fading light in, but the sheriff stopped me.

"Don't open them fully," he said. "If that creature is out there at this moment, it might notice any activity in this building."

I dropped my hand. "But how will you see in here?"

He smirked as he tweaked the curtains just open enough to his satisfaction. "That's kind of the point."

"Understood." I looked around. "Would you like a chair or something, then?"

We moved two straight-backed wooden chairs into the bakehouse, positioning them by the window, but didn't sit.

"Should I get a light?" I wondered. Already it was dim out, and although the lamplighter would come around soon, it wouldn't provide that much light in the shop. The nearest street light was a few doors down from our bakery.

But Hunter shook his head. "It would only draw attention. No, I'm afraid we're in for a long night of sitting in the dark."

"Oh, dear." Realization hit me, and heat rushed to my cheeks. Suddenly, I was glad the shop was dark, so Hunter couldn't see my face.

"What is it?"

"I didn't think about it, when I offered to help you keep watch ... but I probably shouldn't be alone with you, in the dark, like this."

"I ... didn't think about it, either. I can leave, if that's—" There was a slight rustling as Hunter turned to go.

I reached out and touched his elbow. He stopped moving. "No, that's okay. I guess ... I mean, it's for a good cause. Maybe we should just ... keep it to ourselves?"

Hunter stepped closer, closing the small distance between us. His head dipped towards me. His lips were impossibly near. "If you're sure."

My breath hitched at his nearness. I whispered, "I'm sure."

His lips met mine, soft and questioning. Hesitant at first, I melted into the kiss, losing myself in Hunter's heady cedar-and-vanilla scent.

When the kiss ended, we both just stared at each other.

Hunter cleared his throat. "Perhaps I shouldn't have done that."

"No ... no, it's all right."

"If your mother found out ..."

I joked weakly, "Well, we're already on first name terms. What's one more secret?"

He chuckled, "When you put it that way ... honestly, I was surprised you insisted we drop honorifics."

I blinked, confused. Mistaking my hesitation, Hunter continued, "I mean, I don't mind. I like that we're less formal, even if it is only in private. I just—"

"But ... you said ..." I stopped. "I thought that's what you wanted."

"What I wanted? I was just following your lead."

"But that day in the forest, when we were gathering ingredients—"

"What day? What are you talking about?"

I felt a bit hurt. How could he have forgotten that day in Littlewood Forest? It had been a special memory in my mind. And dare I say, even romantic. But apparently it hadn't meant as much to him as it had to me.

Perhaps he was playing with me? But the question in his eyes was sincere.

"Just a few days after the Spring Festival ... I was out in the woods getting berries and nuts for Mama, and you were out there as well. We spent a while looking for everything ..." My voice trailed off. "Don't you remember?"

Hunter gripped my shoulders, surprising me with the sudden force. "Let's say I don't. Remind me, please. Tell me everything."

Unbidden, tears sprang to my eyes. I swallowed hard. "All right. Like I said, it was after the Spring Festival, and Mama was running low on ingredients for Mayor Marley's order. So she sent me into Littlewood Forest to get them. I was picking berries when you said hello."

I pulled up my sleeve, showing him the long scratch that ran the length of it. It was mostly healed, but there was still a faint line to mark it. "I was so startled I accidentally brushed my arm against the bush's thorns."

Hunter shook his head as if he couldn't believe anything I was saying. "I don't remember any of this, Cl—Miss—uh, Miss Claret."

We were back to titles again. Had I done something wrong?

I guess that day in the forest really didn't matter to him. What was that kiss, then? Did that matter to him?

As if sensing my distress, Hunter said, "It's not what you think. I—"

Movement outside caught our attention.

A large shadow loomed, imposing, outside the bakehouse window.

I gripped Hunter's arm. "What should we do?" I hissed.

He patted my hand, but all of his attention was on the hulking figure outside. "Stay where you are," he breathed into my ear, barely audible. "Don't move unless you have to."

"But—"

He put a finger to my lips and shook his head at me, a silent warning. Although I was shaking uncontrollably—I would have climbed out of my skin if I could—I understood what he meant. The bakehouse was completely dark, except for a small pocket of moonlight right by the window. And from where we were standing, the creature would not be able to see us, nor us it. We were only aware of it because its movement outside had attracted our attention.

But if we moved a few steps to our right, we might be able to catch a glimpse of it through the crack in the curtains.

The creature's heavy footsteps stalked slowly towards the bakehouse door. I held my breath, feeling incredibly vulnerable. I had no weapons, and I had stupidly left my trusty red cape hanging on its hook by the back door.

The steps stopped.

We turned to face the door.

CHAPTER 35

H UNTER REACHED AN ARM back, indicating I should get behind him. His other hand rested on his belt, where a dagger was sheathed. While I was sure it was sharp and dangerous, it would be no match against the beast I had encountered the other night.

There was a curious clicking sound. My eyes widened in horror as I realized that, somehow, the creature outside was unlocking the door.

Frantically, I patted my pockets. My keys were still on my person. Mama's keys, as best as I could recall, were upstairs, lying on her nightstand. I remembered seeing them there when I had checked on her earlier today. I had also secured all the windows for the night before coming downstairs to help Hunter with his nighttime watch, so I doubted Mama's keys had been stolen. And we never kept spare keys outside the bakehouse or in the back near our private door.

Slowly, the door started to creak open.

I cowered behind Hunter. An errant thought flitted through my mind. *Could I use one of the chairs as a weapon? Or would it be better to run?*

But if it came to that, I couldn't leave Hunter behind.

A small sliver of light spilled into the bakehouse from the slit in the ever widening door.

I tensed, ready to do ... something. Anything.

But then—the creaking ceased. The door paused in its slow opening. On the other side, I could hear the creature's heavy breathing, a strange, staccato sound.

The door fell back into the doorframe as the pressure opening it on the other side stopped.

I held my breath. Any moment now, the creature would burst through the door ...

But it didn't. Instead, the beast's footsteps moved away.

Hunter and I looked at each other sharply, confusion mirrored on our faces.

"I'm going after it," he whispered, drawing his knife. The blade glinted in the faint moonlight.

"With just that?" I pointed at the weapon.

He ignored my question. "Lock the door behind me, and don't let anyone in. Not even me, unless you can verify beyond doubt that it's me. I'll be back soon."

"Wait, Hunter—"

But he was gone before I could finish speaking.

For a few heartbeats, I just stood there, frozen in fear. Hunter would be out there, in the dark, with that *thing* ... and there was nothing I could do about it. I hated feeling so helpless and alone, just waiting to see what would happen.

Stop it, Claret! I chided myself. *Go help him!*

Hands shaking, I did as Hunter had instructed, shutting and locking the door. For good measure, I wedged one chair under the door handle.

I hurried into the kitchen, rummaging through the drawers in the dark. I didn't want to take the time to find a light, nor did I want to attract the creature's attention with it. Going by feel, I found what I was looking for—a small knife, easy to carry and conceal.

Thank goodness I didn't cut myself on this while trying to find it.

I moved from the bakehouse into the private residence, taking care to lock that door as well. I dragged the hallway end table across the floor until it partially covered the pathway. It wouldn't stop a strong, determined supernatural creature, but I hoped it would slow it down, at least.

I grabbed my red cape, tying it around my neck hastily as I slipped out the back door. Should I lock it behind me? But if I needed to get back in a hurry ... the creature didn't seem to know there was a back entrance to the building. I hated leaving things to luck like this, but I also didn't want to cut off my only means of quick retreat.

Please, let Mama be safe.

I headed out into the night.

Out on Main Street, I looked in both directions. I didn't see either the creature—thankfully—or Hunter. But that didn't mean they weren't nearby. Shivering, I drew up my hood. Standing in the mix of moonlight and lamplight, my presence was probably quite obvious to anyone watching the road. Pulling my hood over my head would do nothing to conceal me, but it gave me a small measure of comfort.

Glancing down at the ground again, I gasped.

My cloak's magic must have lent some sort of magical boost to my eyesight, or perhaps it revealed things previously hidden. Glowing bright before me were unusually big footprints, bigger than any human's I had ever seen. They tracked to and away from the bakehouse, all from the same direction—Littlewood Forest.

Mixed in with the creature's prints were smaller ones, also illuminated. Indentations from human-sized boots.

Hunter's.

I set off towards the edge of town.

As I walked, I was acutely aware of the sound of my footsteps against the road's gravel. The area around me was quiet. Too quiet. Not that I expected birds to be singing in the dead of night. But I couldn't stop the prickling sensation that crawled down my spine. Was I being watched? Or was it just my overactive imagination?

Main Street was also curiously dim. Only a few lamplights shone, weak against the sinister night. What had happened to the town lamplighter? He was always so conscientious about his job. Had he fallen asleep before finishing the job?

Or had something worse happened to him?

I stayed close to the shadows, hoping they would help keep me hidden. Although I also feared that, at any moment, something would reach out and grab me from the dark. Which way was safer?

Probably neither.

I was at the edge of Woodside. A few more steps would take me out of the relative safety of the town and into the darkness of Littlewood Forest.

The glowing footprints pointed directly into the forest, but disappeared beyond the tree line. I hesitated, unsure if I should follow. If the beast had gone away from the path—which was highly likely—then I might easily wander around the dark forest for hours.

A high-pitched shriek came from within the forest.

My eyes widened. Had that sound been from Hunter?

Or from one of my little Fae charges?

A breeze emerged from the woods, even though the night hadn't been windy. It blew towards me, kicking up leaves as it went. As it reached me, I could have sworn I heard it sighing.

"Claret ... Mistress ... help us."

This time I recognized the voices. Veronn, the gnome. Oonie and Kaer, the pixie twins. And Nellah, the shy dryad.

Lola Cerise was missing. My mother—who couldn't see the minor Fae anyway—was unconscious. Sheriff Tavish was gone, presumably in Littlewood Forest hunting the creature that had been terrorizing our town.

And my new Fae friends.

I grasped the handle of my knife. Swallowing down my fear, I entered the dark woods.

CHAPTER 36

THE MOMENT I STEPPED foot into Littlewood Forest, I couldn't help but think, *This was a bad idea.*

The woods were so dark, I could barely see a few paces in front of me. Small pools of moonlight dotted the road or parts of the forest where the trees didn't grow as thick, but it wasn't enough to see by. Perhaps I should have brought a lantern, even if that would have made me an obvious target.

I surveyed the ground. Before my disbelieving eyes, the glowing footprints from outside the forest appeared on the road.

But the only prints I could see were the creature's. I couldn't tell for sure if Hunter was still tracking the beast.

I'm sure he is. He has to be.

Another faint shriek echoed through the trees.

Hold on, my friends. I'm coming.

Although what I would do when I got there, I had no idea.

I tamped down my nerves and negative thoughts. Taking a deep breath, I followed the tracks deeper into the woods.

An uncanny greenish-yellow light emanated from the ground from the creature's illuminated footprints. For a time, the tracks formed a straight line down the forest path. Then they veered off to the right, disappearing into the woods. The greenish-yellow glow ended just a few feet from the road.

I paused. Should I continue to follow the footprints? But what if I couldn't pick up the trail? I didn't want to take my chances by leaving the road and trying to locate the tracks in the forest. My skills in woodcraft were limited to finding nuts and berries for my mother, or avoiding poisonous leaves. Mama and Lola Cerise had always warned me to stay on the road, lest I get hopelessly lost in Littlewood Forest.

Perhaps I should go back. The footprints that had led me here would be able to lead me back, at least. I didn't like leaving Hunter or my little Fae friends alone and possibly in trouble, but I couldn't help them if I were in trouble myself.

I turned around, intending to return to Woodside. My hand flew to my mouth, stifling the cry that threatened to spill out of me.

The glowing footprints were gone.

They might have still been there, but if they were, they were no longer lit. I'd have to make my way back to Woodside in this complete, imposing darkness.

I turned back, towards Cedarbrook. And saw a faint light just up ahead.

I made my slow, careful way to where I thought I had seen something. Yes, there it was! More footprints, glowing that sickly greenish-yellow.

I let out a silent, relieved breath. Thank goodness I had a trail to follow once more.

I hurried along, the illuminated tracks my only companion in this dark forest. All would be well. I would find Sheriff Tavish. I would find my Fae friends. And, eventually, I would find my lola....

The tracks disappeared again, this time going to the road's left.

I paused. Perhaps more glowing tracks would appear again, just like before.

I waited for a few heartbeats, willing the footprints to appear.

But they didn't.

I turned to look behind me. As I had expected, those tracks were now gone too.

Great.

I was alone, in the middle of a dark forest, with a lycan on the loose. And it was nearing midnight. The lycan, already strong, would be at its full power for several hours.

And I was all alone.

All right. Okay. Breathe, Claret. Breathe.

Just put one foot in front of the other. You'll know if you stray off the path. Just walk straight ahead. It will be fine.

I hope.

I slowly shuffled along, my senses straining to catch any awareness of Hunter, my Fae friends, or the lycan. With the stifling dark stealing away my sight, my nerves were on edge.

Leaves rustled to my left. I turned my head sharply, even though I couldn't make out anything. *What was that?*

Something moved to my right. My breathing came in shallow gasps. Was I surrounded? By what?

Oh, my. What if there is more than one lycan out there?

I had to rein in my runaway thoughts, or I'd go mad. Panicking wouldn't help me right now.

Should I keep moving? Or stay absolutely still?

I took two tentative steps forward. Nothing stirred nearby, so I kept walking. Slowly, carefully, trying ever so hard not to be heard or attract attention.

A twig cracked to my left.

My heart raced so fast, I could practically hear the blood pumping. And if I could hear it, I'm sure the creature could as well.

Forget it. Forget caution. Gripping the knife as best I could in my sweat-soaked palm, I picked up my cloak and skirt with my other hand and started running.

My unseen tracker gave chase in the trees, paralleling my blind flight down the forest road.

I kept running, fear giving me speed. I didn't even know if I was going in the right direction. Perhaps I was headed towards Cedarbrook, or maybe I had gotten turned around and was heading back to Woodside. I didn't care. Every part of my being screamed, *Get out of here! Now!*

Tears streamed unbidden down my cheeks. It was probably good it was so dark; my sight would have been compromised anyway by my crying.

And then something jumped out of the trees and slammed into my side. I heard a grunt from my unseen assailant as they ricocheted off me.

My breath whooshed out of me as I fell, hitting the dirt road hard. Pain lanced through my arm and my hip. For a brief moment I saw stars. I had fallen on my left side, and my still-healing bruises let me know they didn't appreciate the new bumps and jolts. Fortunately, I hadn't fallen on my knife, but the impact was enough to make me to drop it.

Oh, no.

Frantically, I felt around for the weapon, sending up two silent prayers. *Please, help me find it, fast. And not by the blade.*

The wind swirled above me as the thing that had hit me regrouped and approached me.

My hand closed on something hard—and thankfully not sharp. I grabbed the knife's handle, gripping it so tight my hand throbbed.

Hearing its passage, I tensed. I sensed it coming closer … closer …

"Aarrgh!"

With a scream, I sprang up and slashed at the presence. With my one arm bruised—and maybe even injured more seriously—I didn't have as much power behind my jump as I'd have liked. Still, I felt the knife make contact with something.

The thing I had slashed yelped in pain.

"Don't come any closer!" I shouted. Like that paltry command would stop a supernatural being.

"Miss … uh, Cl-Claret?"

I nearly dropped the knife in surprise.

"Hunter?"

CHAPTER 37

"I MEAN, SHERIFF TAVISH. I mean—" I stopped, reined myself in. I was in shock and I was babbling, which wasn't helping anyone.

I had to focus. Hunter was hurt.

And it was all my fault.

I took a deep, somewhat steadying breath. First things first. "Are you all right?"

Okay, that was a stupid question. But it had to be asked.

Hunter's low groan lanced the darkness. "I'm not sure. Give me a moment."

I heard the rasp of metal as the sheriff unsheathed a weapon. Unexpected light flared out, and I turned my head too late, temporarily blinded.

When I turned back, my jaw dropped open, disbelieving.

Pale silver light spilled from Hunter's hand, illuminating his agonized face and shaking hand. The light was coming from—

"Is that your dagger?"

"Ye-es," Hunter said, his voice as shaky as his hand. "Here, can you hold it?"

Hastily, I reached out and took the glowing weapon from Hunter, switching my paltry kitchen knife to my other hand. I turned it over and back, marveling. "How is this possible?"

"I'll explain later," Hunter replied through gritted teeth. "In the meantime, if you don't mind?"

"Oh! Oh, yes, of course."

I held the dagger up, the flat of the blade facing me. A cold greyish-white glow bathed Hunter's arm.

"Oh, my goodness. Sheriff, I am so sorry."

A rip in his shirt revealed a nasty-looking gash in Hunter's upper right arm, just below his shoulder. Blood oozed from the open wound, and from Hunter's gasp at my tentative touch, I knew it was painful.

"It's a good thing I'm left-handed," Hunter joked weakly.

"Let me make a bandage—"

"You can just use the rest of my shirt." Hunter nodded at his torn sleeve. "It's probably not worth repairing, anyway."

I bit back yet another apology. Instead, I waved the glowing knife slightly. "Is it all right if I use this?"

"Sure."

I slipped my knife into my pocket and turned my attention to Hunter's shirt. "Okay, hold still."

Carefully, I used the glowing knife to cut away the rest of the fabric without hurting Hunter further. Despite my movements, the knife gave me a nice, steady light to work by. Hunter heeded my words and stayed perfectly still, only flinching slightly at one point when my fingers accidentally brushed against the still bleeding gash.

"Oh, dear! I'm so sorry."

"It's—" Hunter hissed through his teeth. "It's fine."

We both knew he was lying, but it was nice of him to try to reassure me. I finished cutting the fabric, then handed Hunter's knife back to him while I bandaged his arm. The light wavered slightly when I tightened the binding. "We're nearly done. Just a little bit more ... there!"

I stepped back as Hunter moved his arm experimentally. "Thank you."

I started to apologize again, but Hunter shook his head. "Don't worry about it. You didn't know it was me. Anyone else would have done the same."

"What are you doing out here?" I asked him.

"I could ask you the same thing. I distinctly remember telling you to stay back in the bakeshop."

"You told me, but I didn't tell you I would."

He smirked. "A fair point. I see I'll have to pay more careful attention to your words in the future." He paused, then added cryptically, "That's a good skill, by the way. Don't lose it."

"I ... won't," I said, unsure of what he meant. "Did you find ... it?"

"Sort of. I was on its trail, but I lost it soon after I entered Littlewood Forest. The woods are ... disorienting ... at night. My apologies. I thought you were the creature."

"And I thought *you* were the creature, so I suppose we're even."

"So, why are you out here? You would be safer back in your home. And my arm would have been too," he said ruefully.

I hesitated. Should I tell him the truth, that I was looking for the tiny Fae that were my new friends and now responsibility? "I thought I heard something."

Sheriff Tavish gave me a funny look. "You heard a noise in the forest, all the way from inside Rowena's Bakeshop?"

I sighed. "All right. I was worried about your safety."

The grin that blossomed across Hunter's face was worth the admission of worry. He looked positively gleeful. I was fairly sure that if his arm hadn't been injured—and it hadn't been undignified—he would have clapped his hands in delight. "You were worried about me?"

"Yes. Not that you can't handle yourself, but ..."

My voice trailed off weakly as Hunter closed the slight distance between us.

"You were worried about me." His voice was quiet, and although he repeated the question, he already knew the answer.

"Yes," I breathed.

Hunter's lips brushed mine, soft and warm and sweet. "I should be mad that you followed me out here, but I'm ... touched."

I didn't know what to say, so I just smiled.

"But it's dangerous out here. You need to get back to Woodside." His gentleness faded into frustration. "I suppose I'll have to escort you back. I've lost the creature's trail, anyway—"

At that moment, another high-pitched scream echoed through the trees.

Hunter stiffened.

"Did you hear that?" I whispered.

He nodded grimly. "I need to investigate that. But I can't let you go back alone."

"I'll go with you. It would be safer if we stick together." I hoped. "Besides, if anyone should go back, it's you. You're injured."

Hunter hesitated. I could tell he wanted me to return to Woodside, but he couldn't take the time to see me safely back to the town. Nor could he afford the time it would take to argue with me about it. "All right, let's go. But stay close."

We hurried down the road, in the general direction of where the sound had come from. As we went, I adjusted my cloak, which had gone askew when I fell, and pulled the hood back over my head. Enough of the night air's chill had seeped into my bones already to make my movements stiff. I didn't want to get any colder, if I didn't have to.

We hadn't gone far when Hunter stepped off the path. I froze, unsure if I should follow.

Realizing I wasn't with him anymore, Hunter turned around. "Claret?"

"I ... don't want to get lost," I said, remembering the last time I had left the forest road. Granted, it had been daytime. And I hadn't been in pursuit of a crazed lycan. But still ... I had nearly gotten lost then.

Hunter walked back to me and held out his hand. "You won't get lost," he promised. "I'll be with you."

As I looked into his emerald eyes, which had a metallic tinge thanks to the dagger's light, I recalled that other time in Littlewood Forest. And how Hunter had gotten me back to safety.

Placing my hand in his, I let him lead me off the path and deeper into the forest.

Hunter's hand felt warm and reassuring around mine. Although Littlewood Forest was full of deep, menacing shadows, I relaxed a little. As long as I was with Sheriff Tavish, all would be well.

As we walked, I could hear small, labored noises from Hunter as he tried—and failed—to mask his pain. He was holding the glowing dagger with the hand attached to his injured arm, and the strain was definitely showing.

Finally, I said in a low voice, "Here, let me hold the light."

"Thanks." Relief laced Hunter's voice as he passed the knife to me.

"This is an unusual weapon," I remarked.

"We're tracking an unusual creature," he retorted.

"True." Since he was playing coy, I decided to get straight to the point. "You obviously know more about this creature than you've been letting on. Knives don't usually glow in the dark, at least not the ones I've seen around Woodside. Hunter, what's going on?"

The sheriff sighed heavily but didn't respond. The silence stretched on, punctuated by the occasional soft crunch of leaves underfoot.

Just when I had given up on an answer, Hunter said quietly, "Do you know what we're hunting?"

I paused. "Yes. A ... a lycan."

He looked at me sharply. "How did you know?"

How could I tell him, without giving away my grandmother's heritage, or Mister Feldan? "I was reading about them in my *Faerie Lore and Legends* book. The description made sense, with what's been happening in the area."

Hunter nodded, although I wasn't sure how convincing my explanation had been. "I see. Well, you're right. It is a lycan."

He paused. "My brother."

CHAPTER 38

I GASPED, NOT QUITE believing what I had just heard. "Y-your brother?"

"Yes."

I bowed my head under the weight of Hunter's grief. In that one little word, I could feel his boundless sadness. My heart broke for him.

"May I ask ...?"

"How? Why? When?" He laughed bitterly. "There are many questions, but few answers. But I can try nonetheless."

"It's all right. You don't have to tell me."

Hunter took a deep breath. "No, I want to. It will be good to talk about it. I haven't been able to discuss it with anyone, for a long time."

I squeezed his hand in silent support as he told me his story. His quiet voice cut through the darkness as we picked our careful, slow way through the forest.

It should have been a triumphant homecoming.

After returning home from his pilgrimage, Hunter was looking forward to reuniting with his family, particularly his beloved older brother, Hudson.

It was the first time the two had ever been separated. Growing up as the twin sons to Lord Percival and Lady Katerina Tavish, they shared a special, unbreakable bond.

But as was custom in their country, when the boys reached their age of majority, they settled into their respective roles. Hudson stayed home, learning the skills that he would eventually need as Lord Tavish's heir. Meanwhile, Hunter embarked on the two year traditional grand tour that younger siblings often took, with the expectation that Hunter's travels would help him as an advisor to Hudson one day.

And now, finally, he was returning home.

He was greeted at the door by a familiar face.

Anton had been the family's butler for as long as Hunter could remember, and in some ways served as a de facto parent for the twins when Lord Percival and Lady Katerina were away. For their duties as courtiers to King Finvarra and Queen Oona of Faerie's Seelie Court kept them busy, often taking them away from their children for days or weeks at a time.

A rare smile bloomed across Anton's normally stolid countenance. "Master Hunter! Welcome home, sir."

Hunter laughed as he pulled Anton into a hug. "It's great to see you again, Anton. Where's the rest of the household?"

The smile slipped from Anton's face. "You'll find His Lordship and Her Ladyship in the solar." The butler reached for Hunter's valise. "Let me help you with that."

"There's more in the carriage outside." Hunter waved a hand at the conveyance behind him. "My apologies to Jeannie and George in advance. I collected more on my travels than I thought."

Anton paused. "Jeannie and George are no longer with us."

"Really?" Hunter frowned. True, many things could change during the course of two years. But, like Anton, Jeannie and George had served the Tavish house for a long time. "Have they been hired away?"

"No." Anton hesitated again, obviously struggling with how much to say. "They were let go. Along with most of the staff. Due to lack of funds."

"What? Why? What's happened?" This was a surprise. Although Hunter had gotten the occasional update from his family during his travels, the apparently sorry state of the family fortune had never come up. *I would have remembered that.*

But why hadn't his parents or his brother said anything?

"I am afraid I am not at liberty to say, sir," Anton said, hiding behind formality. "But if you go see His Lordship, I'm sure he'll explain."

"He'd better." Leaving poor Anton to deal with the carriage full of luggage, Hunter hurried towards the solar.

As he drew closer, he could hear muffled weeping coming through the slightly open door, punctuated by his father's deep voice.

"Katerina, my love. All is not lost. We'll find a way to come back from this, I promise."

"How can you make a promise like that?" came Lady Katerina's shrill response. "We are ruined, Percival. Completely ruined." Hunter's mother began crying again.

"I know it may seem that way, but—"

Standing just outside the solar, Hunter coughed loudly, then knocked for good measure.

"Come in," Lord Percival said, curt and barely civil.

Hunter pushed open the door, getting a glimpse of his parents for the first time in two years.

The long-lived Fae aged very slowly, although some preferred to use glamours to mask their true faces. Lord and Lady Tavish, a handsome couple, had no need for such magic, even though they were both several hundred years old. If they had been human, one would have easily assumed they were in their late thirties or early forties.

But in two years, both Lord Percival and Lady Katerina had lost their youthful appearances. Streaks of grey liberally laced Lady Katerina's mahogany-colored hair, and worry lines crossed her once-smooth forehead. Lord Percival had fared no better, if the dark circles under his eyes and his thinning hair were any indication.

The solar looked just as rundown as his parents. The dingy, peeling wallpaper and the dirty windows surprised him. Usually this room was impeccable. Come to think of it, the foyer and the hallways had also been in bad shape. Hunter wondered if the rest of the Tavish home was just as neglected.

Upon seeing her youngest son, Lady Katerina hastily put aside the handkerchief she had been dabbing her eyes with and stood, holding her arms wide. "Hunter! Oh, my dear, you're back!"

Hunter walked into her welcoming embrace. "It's good to see you, Mother." He looked over his mother's shoulder at Lord Percival. "And you as well, Father."

Lord Percival clapped his son on the back. "Well met, son. I'm glad you made it home safely."

"What a lovely surprise," Lady Katerina said, still holding her son tightly. She pulled back to study his face, cupping his cheeks in her hands. "We didn't expect you back for a few more weeks."

"I sent a letter ahead to let you know I was finishing my tour early," Hunter said. "Didn't you get it?"

Lady Katerina didn't respond. Instead, she released Hunter and sank back down into her chair, biting her lip.

Lord Percival said, "We've had to let go of most of the household staff. Anton is doing the duties of at least five servants. Things like correspondence collection have gone to the wayside recently."

"But wouldn't someone come by occasionally to deliver letters or packages?" Hunter said, confused. "Giving them a few coins for their service isn't a big burden."

Both his parents refused to meet his eyes.

"Mother. Father. What's going on?" Hunter asked gently. "When I arrived, Anton seemed upset about something, but refused to elaborate. But it's obvious something has happened ..."

A heavy silence fell. Hunter didn't dare breathe, waiting for his parents' response.

Finally, Lord Percival said, "We're in a bad way. Our family fortune is dwindling, and we have no allies in court anymore. Few want to associate with your mother or me, lest the shadow of the scandal that has tainted our name falls on them."

No wonder Anton had been on edge, and his parents were so distraught. If the Tavish family had fallen into disgrace at the Faerie court ...

"That's bad news, for sure, but it's not insurmountable," Hunter rallied. "Now that I'm home, I can help Hudson. We'll just focus on building up our lands, living quietly out of the court's notice, and in time, everyone will forget whatever happened and we can regain our good reputation."

At that, Lady Katerina burst out sobbing. Lord Percival said slowly, "While that would normally be a fine plan, I don't think it will work in this case."

"Why not?"

"Because." Lord Percival swallowed hard. Hunter's blood ran cold. For his normally steady and stoic father to show even the slightest break ... whatever had happened must have indeed been dire.

And when his father spoke again, Hunter felt like his heart stopped, turned brittle, and broke in two.

"Hudson was caught, with several others, in a conspiracy against the king and queen. He was imprisoned in the palace while the royals investigated the extent of his involvement. We spent all we had—and then some—to try to buy his freedom.

"But the evidence against Hudson was too incriminating. The punishment was severe and swift, and he was stripped of his status and powers, cursed forever for attempting to harm the Faerie royals.

"However, the curse backfired, and warped him into an accursed Fae, twisted with dark power. When such things happen, there is only one conclusion, as prescribed by Faerie law. An accursed is not allowed to stay in the realm of Faerie, and must be cast out.

"On the day of Hudson's banishment, he overpowered the royal guards and attacked the Fae royals and members of the court. Two guards were killed, with a few courtiers and Queen Oona injured. Hudson was finally subdued and cast out of Faerie, but not before swearing to return for his revenge."

A weighted silence fell between us. While all of Hunter's tale disturbed me, one point in particular stood out.

I asked, "When they banished Hudson, where did they send him?"

Even before Hunter spoke, I knew the answer.

"The only place any disgraced Fae can go. Into the human world. Specifically, into Littlewood Forest."

CHAPTER 39

"WHY?" I GASPED. "WHY here? I understand that an accursed Fae needs to be somewhere with little or no magic, for everyone's safety. But why pick this area?"

Hunter raised an eyebrow. "That was not the question I expected you to ask."

Belatedly, I realized I had betrayed the depth of my Faerie knowledge. I looked down and shrugged. "I ... I've done a lot of reading lately."

He smiled. "I'm glad. It saves me a lengthy explanation. You've read all of *Faerie Lore and Legends*, I take it?"

I nodded, not adding that I had also read its magical companion, the second volume that was on his office bookshelf.

"Then you know much already. But one thing that few know is that accursed Fae are bound, not only by limitations on their ability, but by their location. They are tethered to a place that holds significance for them, usually a family homestead or a place they've spent most of their life in."

My eyes narrowed. I had my suspicions, but I wanted to hear him say it outright. "What aren't you telling me?"

"You're a sharp one, Claret. You're right, I haven't been completely open with you." Hunter sighed. "Parts of Faerie overlap with the human world. Usually around the interstices, where the two worlds meet. One such place is here. In the human world, you know it as the towns of Woodside and Cedarbrook, with Littlewood Forest in between. In the land of Faerie, these are my family lands."

"The Tavish holdings." We said it at the same time.

Hunter raised an eyebrow at me. "How did you know that? Or was that a very lucky guess?"

I smiled sheepishly. "Not quite. I ... I read your book. The second volume of *Faerie Lore and Legends*? While you were assisting Mistress Tabend."

Hunter frowned, and for a moment I thought he would reprimand me. Which would have been warranted. After all, I had been poking around his things. But then he smiled. "I'm impressed. If you were able to read it—and understand it—that means you won it over. If it didn't like you, it would have made sure all its scribblings were gibberish."

"It's a very lovely book," I said politely.

Hunter smirked. "I'll make sure to tell it you said so. It'll love you even more. But then again, that's pretty easy to do."

I blushed. Hunter's smile grew wider, then slowly faded as a new thought came to him. "I'm worried about Hudson. With each passing day, he loses his mind more to the beast he's become. Soon it will be too late to slow the curse and try to save him. And if he could easily overpower the Faerie royal guards, then the humans in Woodside and Cedarbrook stand little chance against him."

"Can a Faerie curse be removed?" I wondered.

"It's difficult, and often requires very specific items or circumstances. It is possible, though. But first, I have to find him."

"Why has he been attacking all the animals and people in the area?"

Hunter fell silent for a moment. "An accursed needs magic to stay sane, and magic is innate. Which means, to access a living being's magic, blood must be spilled. I'm guessing that my brother is trying to find Faerie magic in whatever he can get his hands on. But so far, all of his kills have been mundane beings, with little to no inherent magic. He's probably starving right now, in a manner of speaking."

"I see. What are you going to do when you do find him?"

Hunter sighed. "I don't know. I don't think I can know until I see what state he's in. If he's not too far gone, then maybe returning back to the Tavish lands will help remind him of who he is. But if he is ..."

His voice broke on a choked sob. Poor Hunter. I squeezed his hand again, not sure what to say to make him feel better.

He squeezed my hand back. "Thank you."

We continued on in silence. Surrounded by darkness punctuated only by the knife's silver glow, it felt like we had been wandering in the woods forever. I didn't even know what we were looking for, exactly, or how to find it.

And yet, I found that I was the one leading us. With sure steps and an ever-growing confidence, I gently guided Hunter towards ... something.

Just ahead of us, a shadow peeled itself from a tree and started walking our way.

I brandished the knife, trying to appear threatening. Hunter let go of my hand, reaching for a second weapon at his hip.

"Please don't hurt me," came a quiet, feminine voice. "I'm not here to cause you any harm."

"Nellah!" Recognizing the shy dryad, I quickly lowered my hand.

"You can see her?" Hunter asked me, incredulous.

"I-I'll explain in a moment."

I turned back to the dryad. "Nellah, what's happened?"

"Veronn is hurt. He needs help. We could sense you in the forest, so I came to find you."

"You knew I was here?"

Nellah nodded. "We are tied to you now, as you are tied to us. Don't worry. You'll come to understand, in time."

Realization washed over me. That earlier feeling of certainty. Somehow I knew, without knowing how, that the earlier shouts were a cry for help. Calling out to me.

It must be some special ability I've acquired, now that I'm the de facto Keeper of Littlewood Forest, I thought. *If Lola Cerise were still here, she could explain it all to me.*

Then again, if Lola Cerise were still here, I wouldn't be the forest's keeper.

I could mull over all this later. Right now, Veronn needed my help.

"Take us to him," I said.

"Come."

Hunter and I followed the dryad deeper into the woods. Nellah's steps were silent, and without the dagger's silver light I would have been unable to track her passage.

"Who is Veronn?" Hunter whispered.

"A friend. He knows my grandmother." The sheriff would see for himself, soon enough.

"A friend," Hunter repeated. "Like this dryad is a friend? You're human, or so I thought. How are you able to see such friends?"

"I couldn't before, not until recently." I paused. Hunter had been open with me about who he was, and his heritage. Lola Cerise had cautioned me to be careful ... but Lola Cerise wasn't here right now. I took a deep breath. "As you are of Faerie, so am I."

Hunter's sharp intake of breath was the only indication of his surprise.

I snuck a sidelong glance at him. His face displayed open curiosity and ... something else. But he didn't say anything, just waited for me to continue.

"My grandmother Cerise, also of Faerie, was tasked with guarding Littlewood Forest. Which she has done, for most of her life. The mantle of keeper was supposed to go to my mother Rowena, but it skipped her and has come to me. My mother cannot see the minor Fae that call Littlewood Forest home. But Lola Cerise can. And so can I."

Still Hunter didn't speak. When I glanced at him again, his brows were drawn down in consternation.

"Sheriff? What is it?"

"Oh, Miss ... I mean, Claret," Hunter breathed. "If that's true, then you are in terrible danger."

"What do you mean?"

"I didn't know," he muttered. "If I had known ... but I don't know if it would have changed anything."

"What are you going on about?" I couldn't keep the frustration from my voice.

There was silence while Hunter gathered his thoughts. Then: "How much did your grandmother tell you of her duties? Of Littlewood Forest?"

"Just a few things, before she was ... taken."

"I see. Like what?"

I frowned, trying to recall that conversation. "She said there are several places where the boundary between Faerie and the human realm is thin. Littlewood Forest is one of those. And that the keeper must make sure no humans are lost to Faerie, or it will go badly for those poor souls. Finally, that the Fae rely on humans' belief in them to stay strong in their magic."

"Then you actually know quite a bit." Hunter sounded impressed. "But what your grandmother didn't tell you is the significance of your position."

"I'm part Fae, and can see the little Faerie creatures that live in the woods." I shrugged. "What else is there to know about it?"

"It's more than that. You might not be able to wield great magic, like the accursed Fae or the—"

"I know I can't. At least, I don't think I can." I thought of the minor magics my lola could work, such as the charms on my cloak or Mister Feldan's cap. Even the red basket cloth, the one Mama considered lucky. The bakeshop had certainly prospered over the years, with few setbacks. Thinking of all those red items, I wondered what simple spells were woven into Lola Cerise's red cottage walls. Would I be able to someday do those things, too?

"But, by virtue of who you are, you have immense, inherent power. As keeper, you are the bridge between the Fae and human realms. You can touch the magic on both sides—the raw, wild magic of Faerie, and the magic of belief in humans."

"I can?" My head spun. "Does that mean—"

"That it's the same for your grandmother? Yes, possibly. It depends on the balance within her, human to Fae. Which explains why she was targeted by the lycan." He paused. "By ... my brother."

"But why?"

He didn't say anything for a long moment. Then: "Hudson needs pure Faerie magic, but it is hard to find it, and in the quantity he needs it, on this side of the border. Littlewood Forest has some Fae magic, but it is diluted by its ties to humanity. That tie is represented in the Scarlet Lady. She who is of two worlds, who binds the two worlds together."

"Why should that matter?"

Hunter's explanation came reluctantly. "I planned on bringing my brother back to Faerie, but if he returned that way, he would be under my authority, and he would need my help to return. If he can undo the binding and get rid of the humanness mixed in with the forest's magic, then he will have access to a large amount of pure Faerie magic. Enough to push back the madness, perhaps even enough to break through the gateway and return to Faerie unchecked. No one—on either side of the gate—would be safe from him then."

His next words chilled me. "The only way he can undo the binding is by killing the Scarlet Lady."

CHAPTER 40

NELLAH POINTED AT A clearing just beyond the trees. "Veronn is over there."

I hurried into the clearing. The gnome lay sprawled on the ground, a few feet from one of the trees that lined the area.

"Veronn!" Kneeling next to him, I tried to assess the extent of his injuries. But I was no physician. He didn't look like he had any open wounds, but he didn't wake.

"Let me take a look at him." Hunter knelt beside me.

"You have training in the healing arts?" I asked in surprise.

"Not exactly," he said. "I just wanted to ... ah!"

I glanced at the sheriff. Satisfaction warred with sadness on his face.

"What is it?" I wondered.

"I suspected, but I needed to be sure. Obviously, your friend has been attacked by the lycan. But there's an added layer to it, and I can tell—the magic afflicting him has my brother's magical signature all over it."

A memory rose in my mind. Hunter, helping me after the lycan had broken into Rowena's Bakehouse and attacked my mother. Hunter, distracted and unfocused as he carried Mama up to her bedroom. Hunter, completely unsurprised as Doctor Zonta announced that Mama had been afflicted by something mysterious and untreatable by normal means.

"You knew, didn't you?" I said. "That day, when my mother was struck down by the lycan. You could sense your brother's magic, couldn't you?"

He nodded. "I sensed he was in the area, but that confirmed it."

"Why didn't you tell me?"

Hunter just looked at me. I squirmed under his gaze.

"Okay," I grudgingly acknowledged. "I understand. I wasn't that forthcoming with information, either."

He smiled gently. "You had good reason not to be. As did I. But we need to work together on this. So, no more secrets?"

I smiled back. "Agreed."

Nellah sniffed the air. "We are past the midnight hour. Dawn will be here in a few hours."

I glanced up at the night sky. With the clouds covering the moon, I couldn't see where it hung in the sky. But I trusted Nellah's assessment. And with the bone-weary exhaustion I was now feeling, I knew she was right.

We took a few more moments to try to wake Veronn, but no matter what we did, he didn't respond.

I sighed. "I think the only thing we can do is bring him back to my house. There, I can look after both him and Mama."

Hunter nodded in agreement. I turned to the dryad. "Nellah, where are we? Can you help get us back to the road?"

"Yes. And I will escort you back to Woodside and help you keep watch. The trees will tell me if the lycan approaches."

"All right, then. Let's go." Hunter scooped up the gnome, hissing in pain when his shoulder injury made itself known again.

"I can carry Veronn," I offered, but Hunter shook his head.

"He's not that heavy. I just need to be mindful of my shoulder." He shifted Veronn in his arms so the gnome's weight was more on his good arm. "*Now* let's go."

Nellah led the way, a sure-footed and decisive guide. By unspoken agreement, none of us spoke. Only the occasional leaf or twig crunching underfoot broke the silence.

As we walked, my mind wandered. Once I got Veronn settled in, I would happily crawl into bed and sleep well past sunrise. That glorious moment couldn't come soon enough.

Eventually, we found ourselves back on the forest path. I was bleary-eyed, my energy flagging. I had nearly dropped the glowing silver dagger twice, only catching myself at the last moment.

"I'm so glad to see the road again," Hunter commented. "It will be easier walking from here on."

"Woodside is this way," Nellah said. "Come."

We started in the direction the dryad had indicated.

We hadn't gone far when I tripped on an unseen rock. I bumped into Hunter, accidentally brushing up against his injured arm. He yelped and stumbled as well, momentarily losing hold of Veronn.

Hastily, I reached out to steady both the sheriff and the falling gnome. Nellah, hearing the commotion, turned to help. Between the two of us, we stopped Hunter from dropping Veronn, although it was a close thing.

"I'm so sorry," I said. "Is everyone all right?"

"I think so," Hunter said. "It's a good thing you didn't nick any of us with that knife."

"I know. Please." I hated how whiny I sounded. "I know we really shouldn't stop, but I'm so tired. I need to take a rest. Just a little one?"

Hunter frowned. "I don't think that's a good idea."

"I understand. But ..."

Hunter took a deep breath. "But you and I are both tired. Maybe overly so. We're not far from Woodside, maybe a little over an hour's walk away."

I nearly burst into tears—an indication of how exhausted I was—but steeled myself to continue.

"We'll stop and rest," Hunter said. "Just for a few moments. And then we press on, with no more stops."

"Agreed," I said, relieved.

Nellah helped us find a fallen log just off the road. Unceremoniously, I plopped down on it, grateful to have a bit of time to sit. Hunter sank down next to me, carefully settling Veronn on his lap, before rolling his shoulders and massaging his neck.

"I can carry Veronn from here," I offered.

"What about the light?" Hunter said.

"If you don't mind holding it. I should give it back to you, anyway."

Hunter shook his head. "Keep it. You might need it."

"Don't you?"

He patted the second knife sheathed at his hip. "I have another, similar weapon. If I need it back from you, I'll let you know."

"Shh!"

That came from Nellah, who had remained standing. While we had rested, she had placed her hand on a nearby cedar tree, closing her eyes and communing with it.

Now her eyes flew open, wide and apprehensive. "It approaches!"

CHAPTER 41

HUNTER AND I LOOKED at each other. The knife's silver light reflected in his emerald eyes, causing them to appear an unsettling shade of otherworldly grey. In that moment, I could truly believe he was Faerie nobility.

The sheriff started to lift Veronn from his lap. "Here, take him. Get out of Littlewood Forest as fast as you can and get to safety. I'll meet up with you in town later."

I cradled Veronn in my arms as I stood. "But what are you going to do?"

Hunter drew his dagger from its sheath. "I'm going to find my brother."

"But, Hunter! Wait—"

But he had already disappeared.

Dismayed, I looked at Nellah. "I guess we should go?"

The dryad shook her head. "There is no time. We must hide. Hurry!"

Hide? I looked around frantically. *Where?* I didn't relish the thought of running back into the dark, deep woods, but if that was the only way ...

I turned to look back at Nellah and gasped.

Her hand was on the trunk of the cedar tree again. But instead of communing, a part of the tree's trunk swung open, revealing a darkened hollow just big enough to fit Nellah, Veronn, and me.

I must be dreaming. That's it. I'm beyond tired, and now I'm imagining things.

Nellah stepped into the cedar's recess. "Come, mistress. We will be safe in here."

At my hesitation, she motioned frantically at me. "Hurry, Claret. Hurry!"

Still wondering, I followed the dryad into the tree. The tree bark shut soundlessly behind me. Nellah put her hand on the seam of the magical door. Was she talking to the cedar again?

Then I saw the fine sheen of sweat beading on her forehead, and noted how stiff and alert she held herself. She was communing with the tree again, using her magic to hold the door shut.

And not a moment too soon. We had barely just hidden ourselves when we heard a low snuffling sound. Snapping twigs and the crunch of dry leaves marked the passage of the lycan, who was sniffing around outside the cedar.

The snuffling grew distant as the creature moved away, focusing on a different area to explore. I breathed a bit easier. Just a few moments more, and we'd be safe ...

The beast returned to our tree.

It snarled. Then a curious scratching reverberated through the cedar, shaking me with its loud echoes.

Nellah hissed in my ear, "The knife! Turn off its light!"

Belatedly, I realized I was still holding Hunter's knife in my hand, even while cradling Veronn in my arms. "I don't know how to make it stop!" I whispered back.

"Put it out!"

I should have asked Hunter for instructions on how to use this thing.

There was nowhere I could place Veronn's still form in the cramped hollow. Nellah needed to concentrate on keeping the tree shut against the lycan. And I could barely maneuver in this space.

So I did the only thing I could think of. I dropped the knife on the ground, nearly slicing my leg. The knife's silver light burst upwards, until I stepped on the blade.

My foot didn't quite completely cover the weapon. A thin sliver of silver glow outlined my boot, but at least most of the light was dampened.

I held my breath, scared to make any sound. Nellah closed her eyes and pressed both hands to the tree bark door, her mouth moving silently.

The scratching stopped, then devolved into a few confused sniffs that circled our tree.

A low snarl stopped my heart.

But when I heard the creature's steps move away, its snuffling slowly sounding farther away, my heart started beating again.

Nellah's eyes met mine. She kept her hands firmly on the tree trunk, but shook her head at me. *Wait. Not yet.*

To pass the time—and steady myself—I started counting in my head. *One ... two ...*

I had reached *one hundred seventy-four* when Nellah cautiously pushed open the door, just enough that she could put her eye to the open seam and assess the area. After a few more seconds—*one hundred ninety-one*—Nellah opened the door wider.

"It's gone," she said quietly. "Let us proceed."

I stepped out of the hollow, taking in a deep breath of the cool, fresh night air. My shoulders and arms were beginning to ache from holding Veronn for so long. I turned back to the cedar in time to see the tree bark door swing shut.

"Thank you for protecting us," I said to the tree.

Its fernlike leaves rustled at me, as if to say, *You're welcome.*

Nellah was already back on the road. "It's not much farther. Come."

I hurried after her, saying, "But what about Hunter? We can't just leave him alone in the woods with that ... thing."

"We must," she said simply. "We have no choice. He made the choice for us. Do not fret, mistress. He will return."

I hope.

But I kept my worried thoughts to myself. Instead, I focused my remaining strength on walking back to Woodside and getting Veronn—and myself—to safety.

We walked as fast as we dared, although every shadow seemed to jump out at me and Veronn's body weighed on me like I was carrying a boulder, not a little gnome. Every so often, Nellah would veer slightly off the road to touch a tree, then continue on. Every time, my worried eyes would follow her, but she would silently glide back to the path and continue on.

It's better than hearing bad news. My feet felt made of lead. If the lycan came back, I lacked the energy to hide again, let alone fight it.

The path lightened ahead, and with it, the constant feeling of dread I had been carrying all night.

Nearly home. I squared my shoulders and tightened my arms around Veronn. *Nearly there.*

At the edge of Lakewood Forest, Nellah stopped. "I dare not go any further into a settlement of mortals. I fear being seen, or worse."

"I understand," I said. "Thank you for your help, Nellah."

"I will send Oonie or Kaer in a few days to attend to you and Veronn. If you require my assistance, you can send word through one of them."

I frowned. "Aren't *they* worried about being seen in Woodside?"

She chuckled, the sound a curious mix of sighing wind and twigs rubbing against each other. "They are bolder than I am, to be sure. And they are easily mistaken for butterflies or dragonflies. I am much harder to disguise."

I giggled, a high-pitched release of pressure after the tension of the long night. "I see. Well, thank you again."

"Be well, Scarlet Lady." Nellah touched her fingers to her forehead in a gesture of respect, then melted into the forest. I started towards home, eyeing the slowly brightening sky with relief.

Balancing Veronn's weight carefully against one arm, I opened the back door and pushed it the rest of the way open with my hip. I could practically hear Hunter chiding me, *Why didn't you lock it?* But I was too relieved that my hasty leaving earlier meant that I had one less obstacle now.

Closing the door with my foot, I made my weary way up the stairs. Just a few steps more, and I would be able to sleep. Although I wondered if sleep would come. My nerves were still on edge, and I worried about Hunter's safety in Littlewood Forest. I wouldn't truly be able to rest until I knew for sure that he had made it back unharmed.

Back in Mama's room, I plucked an extra pillow from her bed and placed it on two wooden chairs, settling Veronn into the makeshift bed. I grabbed a shawl from her wardrobe, tucking it around the gnome's still form as a blanket.

I hope that's comfortable. Perhaps I could borrow a cot from Doctor Zonta, although I had no idea what excuse I would give him to obtain it.

Now that I had seen to Veronn, the remnants of my adrenaline fled. I wanted nothing more than to go to bed, preferably for days. I wanted to wait up for Hunter, but he would understand if I didn't answer the door right away. I would seek him out after I woke up.

As I headed downstairs, I heard a scratching sound at the back door. I paused on the staircase, head cocked as I strained to listen. The scratching noise occurred once more, then stopped.

Curious. We didn't have any pets, so it couldn't have been a dog or cat wanting to return home. The few stray animals in Woodside gave the townspeople a wide berth, preferring to forage in the forest.

I tweaked the window curtain aside and peered out. No one was there.

CHAPTER 42

PERHAPS I HAD IMAGINED things. With everything that had happened over the last few hours, my mind was certainly overacting.

I had just locked the door when I heard a muffled knocking. Frowning, I realized it was coming from the front. And whoever was doing it must have been banging on the bakehouse door, since I could hear it all the way back here.

There's a big handwritten "Closed" sign in the window. Can't people see it? I thought crossly as I headed into the bakehouse. And since we'd been closed for several days, I had thought everyone knew we were still closed.

Apparently, I had thought wrong.

Still annoyed, I glanced out the window to see who was outside. Weren't they going to get an earful?

But my ire dissipated when I saw Hunter, hand poised to knock again.

I flung open the door. "Sheriff Tavish!"

The man startled, squinting in my direction. But he seemed to be looking past me, not at me.

"Sheriff?" I reached up to brush a lock of hair from my face, forgetting that the cloak of my hood was still up. In my eagerness to get Veronn settled, I hadn't even taken the time to hang up my red cape or remove my shoes, two things I usually did immediately upon returning home.

My hood fell back. Hunter's gaze focused on me and he gave me an easy smile. "Since when are we back to formalities, Claret?"

I blushed. "Since ... well, I don't know."

"May I?" He nodded at the bakeshop's interior.

"Oh! Of course." I stepped aside to give him room.

Hunter stepped inside, his sharp eyes taking everything in. "Are you all right?"

"I should ask *you* that. I didn't want to leave you, but ... did you find the lycan?"

A shadow passed over Hunter's eyes. "Not quite. A few times I thought I had him, but he kept eluding me."

"Oh." Part of me was sorry, but another, bigger part of me was glad. "You'll find your brother, I'm sure of it."

"You can trust in that," he said. "I won't stop looking until I have him in hand."

I raised an eyebrow at Hunter's choice of words. I hadn't thought he wanted to exact any sort of judgment on Hudson. But perhaps there was a deeper undercurrent to their relationship than Hunter had originally let on.

"I hope when you do, he'll tell me where my lola is. And how to lift the magic from Mama and Veronn."

A smirk played about Hunter's lips. "Don't you worry, Claret. I'll make sure he does."

What had happened after Nellah and I had left him in Littlewood Forest? The normally gentle Hunter Tavish seemed downright angry about something.

I started to ask him why, but a jaw-cracking yawn interrupted me.

"Oh, my," I said. "Sorry about that. I'm so tired ..."

"I understand. It's been a long night. I won't keep you, I just wanted you to know I got back to Woodside safely."

"I'm glad." I paused. "Will I see you soon, then?"

He hesitated. "I'm not sure. I need to get some rest, then figure out the best course of action. I was so close ..."

"I need to tend to Veronn, anyway," I put in hastily. "If anything changes, I'll let you know."

"Please do. And I'll let *you* know if I get my hands on my brother."

Again, I wondered at his hostility. But neither of us were in any state to get into a deep emotional conversation right now. I'd have to gently pry into this matter later.

"Good night, then. Or should I say good morning?" I chuckled. "I hope I hear from you soon. Oh, that reminds me. Was that you poking around the back door earlier?"

"Oh, yes. I couldn't get in, so I thought I would just come around to the front."

"Huh." Something was bothering me, but my brain was too fuzzy to figure out what. "That's all right, I suppose. It's just that, with the shop still being closed, I'd prefer to keep the front completely shut up."

"Understandable." He ran a hand through his already messy dark hair. My eyes fell on his upraised arm.

"When did you remove the bandage?" I asked. It was way too early for any of the Main Street offices to have opened, although for an emergency, Doctor Zonta would have gotten up. But Hunter didn't seem to be in any pain.

He glanced at his upper arm as if seeing it for the first time. "Oh. I stopped by my office before coming here."

"Oh. Okay." I glanced at his sleeve again, which was intact. He must have changed shirts as well.

"I need to go," Hunter said. "I'll see you soon."

I smiled. "I can't wait."

Hunter leaned down, touching his lips to mine. I blissfully met his kiss. *A girl could get used to this.*

Or could she?

Hunter pulled me close. His kiss, which had started sweet and gentle, suddenly turned deeper. Demanding. Insistent.

Hungry.

Some buried primal instinct rose up within me. At first, I eagerly let myself get lost in his kiss.

But then his arms tightened around me, holding me so firmly I had trouble catching my breath. His ardor changed from enticing to ... frightening.

I tried to pull away, but he wouldn't let me go.

My thoughts exploded. What was wrong with Hunter? Usually so reserved and respectful, it felt like he wanted to devour me.

Once more, I tried to wrench myself free. But Hunter couldn't—or wouldn't—respond to my subtle signals. So, as he pulled me towards him again, instead of fighting it, I leaned into the motion.

My shoulder smacked into Hunter's chin. It startled him enough that he loosened his hold on me, and I took advantage of his momentary distraction to step back and out of his embrace. For good measure, I scrambled backwards several more steps.

We faced each other across the bakeshop.

"Oh! I don't know what came over me," Hunter said, sounding a bit more like the man I had come to know. "I guess I got carried away." He smirked. Before, I had found it charming. But now, it seemed ... sinister? "You have that effect on me."

I fought to get my racing heart and frantic breathing under control. "Part of me didn't mind. But another part ..."

He looked out the still-open bakeshop door. "I need to get going."

I didn't move.

"Please don't be angry with me. I couldn't bear it." His smirk melted into a smile, and I could feel an answering thaw in my heart.

"I'm not," I reassured him.

"Good. Am I forgiven, then?"

I nodded, but my feelings were still in turmoil.

Hunter stepped towards me, palms up in a gesture of peace. When I didn't move away, he tilted my chin up, his emerald eyes looking into my eyes. Or my soul. "I'll return soon," he promised, then sealed that promise with a short but rough final kiss that left my mouth feeling bruised.

"Goodbye." Hunter exited the shop. I followed after, framed in the doorway as I watched him leave.

When his form had disappeared from sight, I turned and headed back inside. As I closed and locked the bakeshop door, something Hunter had said earlier resurfaced in my thoughts.

He had said he couldn't get in the back way, through the door that led directly into the house. Why not? Because it was locked?

No, that can't be right, I realized. I had left the door unlocked all night while I was with him in Littlewood Forest. And in my haste to help Veronn, I hadn't locked it when I returned home. In fact, the only time it had been locked was when Hunter had shown up this morning. And I had only locked it after I had heard something or someone at the private back entrance.

Perhaps his arm had been hurting so much, he couldn't work the handle? But that didn't feel right either. It wasn't like both his arms were injured. And when I had seen him just now, he didn't even seem to be in that much pain anymore.

My head throbbed, a sure sign that I was exhausted. There was sure to be some obvious reason I was missing. I'd ask Hunter about it later. If I remembered.

Trudging upstairs and into my room, I only had enough energy left to tug off my boots and sling my red cloak over a chair before I fell into bed and a deep, dreamless sleep.

CHAPTER 43

WHEN I WOKE UP, sunrise was just breaking through my window.

I sat up in bed, feeling a bit groggy. I could happily go back to sleep for a few more hours.

Then it hit me. Sunrise? Wait. I had gone to bed at sunrise. Had I not gotten any sleep at all?

But I felt fine. Actually, quite well rested.

Shaking my head to clear my mind fog, I grabbed my boots and cloak from where I had carelessly tossed them earlier. Hands full, I ducked my head into my mother's room.

Mama and Veronn lay still in their respective beds.

"Mama? Veronn?" No response.

I sighed as I quietly closed the bedroom door. Eventually, I'd have to make sure my two patients were fed. But I wasn't sure what food was in the house, nor was I feeling particularly hungry.

After I headed downstairs, I started to hang my cloak back up in its proper spot by the back door, but stopped. Instead, I ran a questioning hand down the fabric. It had held up remarkably well despite the madness of the last few days. No tears or snags that I could see.

But when I took a whiff of the fabric, I sneezed and scrunched my nose. I would definitely have to wash this before I ventured out in it again.

Come to think of it, it was probably time to do the washing anyway. I sighed again and glanced out the window. Doing all the washing would take a good part of the morning, and I'd have to hurry if I wanted to make sure I got to the market before it closed in the afternoon.

Fortunately, there wasn't much to clean, just a small pile of clothing that was primarily mine. I washed everything—my goodness, my red cloak hid a lot of dirt and dust—and then hung the lot outside, in the back. Hopefully the fresh spring air would dry everything quickly.

With that taken care of, I left the house, the bakehouse basket hanging off my arm. A glance overhead told me that it was now noontime, and the streets were accordingly busy.

Mister Maerton, the fruit and vegetable seller, greeted me as I approached. "It's lovely to see you, Miss Claret."

"Likewise, Mister Maerton," I said.

"And how is Mistress Rowena doing?"

I gave the merchant a sharp look, but there was no gleam of gossip in his eye, just polite concern. Inwardly, I sighed. I couldn't have expected news of Mama's condition to stay quiet, especially since the bakeshop had been closed for several days. But it was still too raw and uncertain for me to want to discuss any details.

"She's as well as can be, I suppose," I said. "Just keeping an eye on her and making sure she's comfortable. That's why I'm here at the market. I've let food run low a bit. I'm just glad it's Daydalawa and the market is open."

Mister Maerton gave me a funny look. "Today is Dayapat. You were smart to come today, since the market will be closed tomorrow."

Dayapat? The fourth day of the week, already? I frowned, counting back mentally. Sheriff Tavish and I had gone to see my Lola Cerise on Daypito, the seventh day, considered the day of rest. That night, the lycan had broken into the bakeshop, and the next morning, on Dayisa, the first day of the week, Hunter had investigated the attack on Mistress Tabend, and then we held an all-night watch in case the lycan returned. Which meant ...

I had slept for two days. *Two days.* I must have been more tired than I realized.

"Miss Claret. Miss Claret?"

I realized Mister Maerton had been calling my name for some time. "I'm sorry, Mister Maerton. What were you saying?"

The kindly merchant gave me a sympathetic smile. "You're going through a lot, my dear, what with Rowena unable to work and the bakeshop closed. Tell you what. Hold out your basket."

I obeyed. Mister Maerton pushed back the red cloth covering and began heaping produce into my basket.

For a few moments, I just watched, uncomprehending. Four apples, two bright red and two green Granny Smiths. A head of lettuce. Some potatoes. Onions. Leeks. A bunch of carrots....

"Wait," I said. "I only came for a few things. I can't afford all of this."

He waved away my protests. "I don't want any coin. You just take this home to your Mama and make sure she gets better. And if you need anything else, you stop by my stall anytime."

Sudden tears pricked my eyes. "Oh, Mister Maerton. Thank you. Thank you so much."

He finished filling my basket and resettled the cloth over it, tucking the ends in to secure the contents. "We in Woodside need to watch out for each other."

I nodded, my throat too thick to continue speaking.

I stepped away from Mister Maerton's stall and looked around. My basket was full enough now that I didn't need to continue shopping. And although I needed to get back to take care of Mama and Veronn, I wasn't in any rush to get back. Just the two still forms of loved ones and a big, dark, partially destroyed bakehouse were waiting for me when I returned.

But I didn't feel like looking around the market any longer, either. I didn't want to make small talk with the merchants and have to field their questions. I didn't want to have to avoid their overly curious gazes or pitying eyes.

The market, which was held every day except for the fifth day of the week, Daylima, was held in the open civic center square, where Woodside had hosted the earlier Spring Festival and town anniversary events. The mayor's office was in the area. As was the sheriff's.

Thinking of Hunter, I decided to stop by to see him. He hadn't come by the bakehouse in the last two days—or if he had, I hadn't woken to admit him. It would be good to see how he was faring. If he'd had any luck finding Hudson.

And, if I was being honest with myself, I also wanted to make sure things were all right between us. Our last encounter had ended a bit ... awkwardly. At least, to me.

Perhaps now that some time had gone by, and we were both in a better frame of mind, things would be better?

I hefted the basket and headed towards Sheriff Tavish's office.

A few feet from the door, I paused, tugging on my skirt to straighten it. I ran quick fingers through my hair, hoping that tamed it somewhat.

Taking a deep breath, I stepped up and rapped on the door. "Hello? Sheriff Tavish?"

No one responded.

I frowned and knocked again, once more calling out.

Still no response.

Normally I wouldn't have considered that odd, except I knew Hunter's office still doubled as his home. So the likelihood of him not being in were slim.

Experimentally, I tried the handle.

Not only did it open easily, but it broke off in my hand.

My eyes widened. Now I knew for certain something was wrong. Hunter wouldn't have left his office unlocked. And he had recently repaired this door. I recalled how proud he had been to show me around the clean, furnished, and newly restored office. He hadn't done shoddy work.

The sound of rushing blood filled my ears. Heart pounding, I pushed the door open fully.

CHAPTER 44

"SHERIFF TAVISH?" I CALLED out as I stepped inside. "Hunt—"

My words died on my lips as I got a good look at the interior.

Much like Rowena's Bakeshop had been, Hunter's office was completely ravaged.

Splintered wood was scattered in the area where the chairs near Hunter's desk had been. The cot, which had served as a temporary bed, was now a mess of long white ribbons, complete with a smashed wooden frame. Piles of white cloth and feathers from a former pillow littered the floor.

The few books on the shelf had been dashed to the floor, lying askew with bent pages and broken spines. Angry half circular indentations marred the once stately wooden shelves, ensuring they were beyond repair.

The big wooden hand-me-down desk had also suffered the unknown intruder's wrath. The top of the desk, like the shelves, had been smashed by a large fist. The left hand drawer had been pulled out, its few contents strewn on the floor. I spotted a cracked bottle of ink and a quill that had been snapped in half.

I knelt down and picked up the bottle. A thin seam of liquid black beaded on the outside. I'd have to decant the ink into another bottle soon, or it would leak all over.

As I started to gather the tossed books, a faint scritching reached my ears. *Faerie Lore and Legends, Vol. 2.* The poor thing was still writing, its constant jotting currently sounding slow and distressed.

I picked it up, shaking the book out a little and then dusting off the cover. The pages fluttered at me in thanks.

I ran a loving hand down the spine. "Of course, little book."

The quill-scratching noise picked up a little, jaunty and happy. I smiled as I set the book aside on the desk.

The right hand drawer caught my attention.

Unlike the rest of the desk, it was still intact, and closed. Curious, I reached out, fully expecting it to be locked.

It opened easily at my touch. It hadn't been locked, which may have explained why there were no claw marks or fist indentations. But when I pulled it open, there was nothing to see. The drawer was empty.

Well, that wasn't surprising. Compared to Mayor Marley's office—or any other Woodside business—the sheriff's office was fairly sparse. And Hunter had said he hadn't moved to the town with much.

I pushed the empty drawer back in. Or tried to, anyway. Now that it was free of the damaged desk, it didn't quite fit back in. Upon closer inspection, I saw that the drawer's frame was a bit warped.

But I didn't care. I was determined to get that drawer back in the desk. If I was being honest with myself, I needed to put all my pent up stress and fear *somewhere*. Might as well be that poor little desk drawer.

I jammed it in with all my strength. "Aaarghh!"

With a sickening crack, the drawer split in two. Apparently I was stronger than I knew. Half of the drawer was now folded over, with the paneling and handle swinging to the side.

Revealing a formerly hidden false bottom.

My eyes widened. I peered in between the wooden slats. A thin piece of paper lay nestled in the hiding spot.

Curious, I reached two fingers in and carefully extracted the single sheet. Once I had secured it, I smoothed out the cream-colored paper and read.

H—

With the misfortune that has befallen our family, swift and decisive action must be taken before the situation devolves further. Should you decide to venture into the human realm, seek out the Scarlet Lady, the Keeper of Littlewood Forest. With her strong ties to both the Fae and human worlds, she may have the answers you seek.

If you cannot find her right away, I understand she has family in the area. They may be able to locate her. Or one of them may have taken up the mantle of Keeper of Littlewood Forest. After all, it has been awhile, and time flows differently between the land of Faerie and the mortal world.

You will know the true Scarlet Lady by her name and her power. If she is alive and well, then her protections over Littlewood Forest will be strong. If they are fading, then know that her power is fading as well. She will need to name her successor, and soon, before all the power of the forest fades along with her.

Finally, remember that a bit of blood may keep your brother's madness at bay. That knowledge may prove useful, should you find him.

Yours—

The signature was illegible. But the firm pen strokes made me think that perhaps the letter, terse and to the point, had been written by Hunter's father, Lord Percival.

I pondered over what I had just read. *You will know the true Scarlet Lady by her name.* What did that mean?

I recalled how Lola Cerise's cottage was an explosion of reds. Dark or bright, if it fell in the red color family, it could be found in my grandmother's house. When I was a child, I had once asked her about it, and she had giggled and said, "What can I say? I like my namesake."

Mama had said, "Perhaps a little too much." Since her name, Rowena, was derived from the red-berried rowan tree. And, when I was born, Lola Cerise had insisted I be named Claret.

Which was another shade of red....

The sound of the office door opening made me look up. And then hastily get to my feet. "Oh! Hunter, I'm so glad to see you!"

For it was indeed the sheriff, walking through the door. He stopped, narrowing his eyes when he spotted me.

"Sheriff? Is all well?"

His expression smoothed out, so quickly I wondered if I had imagined his earlier ... anger? Irritation?

At me? Or at something else?

"Claret. I'm glad to see you as well." He frowned as he looked around. "Were you here when this happened?"

"No. I arrived just a bit before you did. I was coming to look for you."

Hunter waved a hand around the office. "I'm embarrassed you have to see this place in such a state."

Such a state? His office had been destroyed. Why was he acting like it was just a bit of everyday clutter? "Hunter, this is horrible. Who would do such a thing?"

He looked around. "Someone with nothing to lose, I suppose."

"I suppose," I echoed. "Anyway, I'm glad you're all right."

"I'm fine, Claret. But thank you for worrying about me."

As he walked towards me, I noticed how fluid his movements were. He wasn't favoring his injured arm, which I would have expected. "How is your arm doing?"

He rolled his left shoulder. "Much better, as you can see."

Something about the motion bothered me, but I couldn't pinpoint what. "Oh, I'm glad."

He glanced at the letter in my hand. "What's that?"

I blushed, embarrassed at being caught snooping. "It's your letter. I found it in the desk, here." I indicated the now-broken drawer's secret compartment. "It caught my eye. I hope you don't mind ..."

"I ... didn't realize that was there. May I see it?"

I handed him the letter. He read it carefully, a frown tugging at his lips. At one point, his eyebrows flew up, and he looked at me. Then back at the paper. Then at me again. Assessing.

I squirmed, feeling uncomfortable under that shrewd gaze, and not knowing why. This was just Hunter, after all. My dear friend—and maybe something more. I had nothing to fear from him.

So why did I feel so uneasy?

"Who is it from?" I asked, to break the silence. And the tension that had come over me.

"My father," he said dismissively. I nodded. My guess had been correct.

"Are you and your father close?"

"We used to be. Before—" He stopped himself. "Well, the past is past. It doesn't matter now."

I recoiled from the bitter heat in his tone.

"Claret." Before, when he would say my name, it felt like a caress. A sweet promise. But this felt different. It was slow and deliberate, like he was testing it.

Tasting it.

"Y-yes, Hunter?"

"I'm really glad I found you." He echoed his earlier statement, but this time it also felt different. Predatory. Dangerous. I was the trapped mouse to his stalking cat, unable to hide and only waiting for the inevitable pounce of death.

"You are?"

"Yes. I have news of your grandmother."

My sense of apprehension grew, warring with feelings of relief. "You do? How is she? Where is she?"

He smiled. I had always found it endearing, but this time I wondered why I had never noticed how big and toothy his smile really was. Or how his green eyes flashed with something mesmerizing and wild. I could get lost in those eyes ...

"She is in Littlewood Forest. Unharmed."

"What?" I had to stop myself from running past the sheriff and straight into the forest. "What do you mean? Is she back home? We should go get her, right now—"

He held up a hand. I choked back whatever else I was going to say. "She is not back in her cottage, no. And to retrieve her, it will be ... complex."

"I don't understand."

"You will, in time. It will be easier to show you than explain it all now. I will need your help, anyway." He looked out the window. "I suggest you go home and rest. I will come by in a few hours and take you to her."

"But ..." A number of things ran through my mind, preparations that might be needed. "If she's injured, how will we transport her? I can see about borrowing the cart and horse again from Mayor Marley's office—"

"No need. Where we are going, no creature from the mortal realm would be willing to follow."

"Wait. Do you mean ...?"

"Yes. Your grandmother is caught between the human and the Faerie worlds."

CHAPTER 45

Despite my two day rest, my legs felt sluggish and my eyes heavy as I trudged back to Rowena's Bakeshop and my home. Perhaps Hunter was right, and I did need more rest.

Or maybe I had fallen under a spell of some sort? Something in his mesmerizing green eyes ...

I had to laugh at myself. Hunter was no more a mage than I was the queen of Faerie.

When I got home, I checked the clothes hanging on the line. Some had dried already, mostly thinner and lighter clothing. I grabbed the wicker basket I had left by the clothesline and pulled down the dry clothing to fold later. However, my red cloak and two skirts still felt damp. I'd leave them on the line for a bit longer, and bring them in before I left with Hunter.

I unlocked the back door and entered the house. And then paused, listening.

A strange skittering noise echoed from upstairs. What could that be? Crazily, I thought, *What if it's the lycan?* Did I have Hunter's dagger? No, I had left it in my bedroom ...

The skittering sounded again. And it sounded like it was coming from my mother's room.

I quietly dropped the basket by the stairs and slowly crept upstairs. My eyes scanned the area. Was there anything I could use as a weapon? It was still light out. It should be weak during the daytime, right? Hopefully, if I could take it by surprise ...

I peeked around the slightly open bedroom door.

"Veronn! Veronn, you're awake!"

The gnome turned with a surprised scowl that quickly changed into joy at seeing me. "Miss Claret! You don't know how happy I am to see you. I woke up, in this strange house that smelled of humans and dead wood. The lady on the bed wouldn't wake and tell me where I was—"

"Ah, yes. I can see how being in a strange place would have caused you distress. You're in my home, Veronn. And the woman over there is my mother. She's been unconscious for several days. Hunt—I mean, Sheriff Tavish and I—think it's a result of being attacked by the lycan."

Veronn shuddered. "That makes sense. That beast ... a nasty piece of work, that."

I sank down on the edge of Mama's bed. "What happened to you? Nellah led the sheriff and me to you the other night. We found you in Littlewood Forest, lying in a clearing."

The gnome rubbed the side of his head, as if reliving the attack. "I'm not entirely sure. All I can remember ... it was nighttime. I couldn't sleep. So I left my tree, took a little stroll under the stars." He paused. "You know of the gateway to Faerie, yes?"

I nodded. "It's where my lola bestowed the title of Scarlet Lady on me. And the forest recognized me as such."

"Yes. A place of great Fae magic, as any of the gateways are. While I rarely cross into Faerie anymore, I sometimes go there when I'm feeling unsettled or homesick. That night was one of those times. The gate beckoned to me, and I sought its comfort.

"But it didn't feel right. Usually it's soothing and melodic, but this time ... it was jarring. Like the wrong notes were being played, and the melody couldn't figure out how to resolve itself properly. I went towards the trees, and I saw ..."

"What?" I asked, after a long, uneasy pause.

"The altar ... there was a figure lying on top of it, and a large shadow looming above it. The air tasted foul, and I could feel the forest crying out in pain and confusion all around me. I started towards the altar—and then the shadow turned. Bright red eyes pinned me in the dark. Something sprang at me. I yelled a warding spell ... and then I don't remember anything after that."

Oh, my. I wondered ... "Who was atop the altar?"

Veronn shook his head, then winced. "I did not get a good look before the creature tried to attack me. I just know that I saw something I shouldn't have."

Silence fell between us. I glanced at my mother, her thin chest rising and falling ever so slightly under her blanket. The lycan had attacked both her and Veronn, but she was still not waking. Why?

Veronn had mentioned a warding spell. Perhaps that had taken the brunt of the lycan's attack. Mama had no such protections, nor did we have any such safeguards in the bakeshop.

And, I thought guiltily, *she is not the Scarlet Lady. Lola Cerise is—or was. As I am now. Which means we might be able to tap into magic to protect us, but Mama cannot.*

Veronn moved towards the bedroom door. "I need to get back to the woods. To my tree."

"Veronn, wait a moment."

The little gnome stopped and looked expectantly at me.

I studied him from head to toe. Although I could tell he was still shaken, overall he looked fairly well and ... unharmed.

I ran a finger down my cheek. "You weren't ...?"

Veronn answered my unfinished question. "No," he said, that simple word conveying the same surprise I felt. "Not that I can tell, anyway. I think ... I think the creature wanted to harm me, but it couldn't touch me, for some reason. And then—"

He stopped, frowning. "I don't remember anything after that. But when I woke up, here in your home, I felt perfectly fine. Other than a slight headache, probably from the magic used on me."

How odd. I wondered how the lycan was unable to touch Veronn, while it had no problem injuring or killing other humans or animals. I thought back to the attack on Mister Feldan. Like Veronn, he had fallen unconscious from a magical attack—but the lycan had not cut his body like it had Mistress Arabelle, Martin, and the Cedarbrook man.

What prevented the lycan from finishing his attack on the Fae of Littlewood Forest?

"If that will be all, Mistress Claret, I'll get going."

Veronn's voice brought me out of my musings. I followed him into the hallway. "Are you sure you're well enough? You're welcome to stay as long as you need."

His voice echoed back to me as he stumped down the stairs. "I'll heal faster if I'm back in my tree, connected to the forest's magic. And once I am hale again, I can help you search for Mistress Cerise."

"Oh! Good news—Sheriff Tavish knows where my grandmother is. He will take me to her later."

Veronn turned around, peering up at me from the bottom of the staircase. "He does? How? And where is she?"

I shook my head. "I don't know, exactly. He said she was caught between two worlds, Faerie and human." I paused as a thought occurred to me. "He must mean the gateway, where the forest recognized me. Well. I'll know for sure when he shows me tonight."

The gnome frowned, making his already gruff face look positively thunderous. "Go carefully, then, Mistress Claret. Have you a weapon?"

I nodded, remembering the silver knife Hunter had loaned me. The one that I had left behind in my bedroom.

"Carry it with you. And keep a watchful eye out."

"A-all right," I said, surprised by the vehemence in Veronn's voice.

He hesitated. "If I may speak freely, mistress?"

"Of course, Veronn. Always."

"There has been too much strangeness happening in Littlewood Forest lately. I would feel safer if I and the others met you and your companion in the woods tonight. With your permission, I will gather the other Fae, and we will find you. Just in case you need us."

"That is an excellent idea, Veronn." I watched the little gnome swell with pride, and smiled. "I would feel better knowing all of you were looking out for me."

"It will be done," Veronn said.

"Oh, Veronn, that reminds me—do you know if Mister Feldan has returned?"

Veronn frowned. "The cait sidhe messenger? No, I haven't seen him in a while. Were you expecting a message from him?"

"Perhaps. I asked him to go the Faerie royals for help against the lycan." At my words, Veronn flinched, and I realized he and the other forest Fae might not have known the manner of creature we were facing.

"Would you like me to watch for him?"

"Yes. Or one of the other forest Fae, if the watch goes too long. And the moment he returns, come and tell me."

"It will be done."

I held open the back door for him, standing in the doorway to watch him leave.

He took a few steps into the backyard, pausing when he saw my red cloak billowing in the breeze. "Is this the cape Mistress Cerise made for you, all those many years ago?"

"It is," I said. "I'm sure you've seen me in it often."

"I have. And I can feel the magic emanating from it. Mistress Cerise wove all the magic of Littlewood Forest into it, as much as she could. We all contributed to it."

I eyed the cape with a new eye. "I didn't know that."

"Oh, yes, mistress. We are a part of you as much as you are a part of us. The Scarlet Lady and the Fae of Littlewood Forest are ever and forever connected."

"Wow. Thank you for telling me that." I touched the cape lovingly. It was one of the few ties I had left to my Lola Cerise right now.

"Take care of it, mistress. It's quite valuable."

"I will. Once it's dry, I'll bring it inside."

Veronn paused, then shrugged. "All right, mistress. I'll be going, then."

I waved goodbye to the gnome, then went back inside. I started running through all the things that needed to be done before I left. First, make sure Mama was fed. Perhaps change into something warmer, since the woods would be cold at night, even with my cape on. Oh, and make sure I had Hunter's knife on me—and maybe another weapon. If Lola Cerise was hurt, should I bring bandages? Extra clothes for her? Or ...

My mind swirled with all the preparations. By the time I was done completing my list, I felt even more exhausted than before. I fell into a chair in our back parlor, intending to sit down for just a few moments—

—And startled awake to a knocking on the back door.

"Claret?" Hunter's muffled voice came through. "Claret, are you there?"

I sat up, rubbing my temples. I, unfortunately, had quite the headache. Usually a sign of sleeping too little—or too much. But there was no time to wait and hope it would subside. I would just have to work through it.

The knocking came again. "I'm coming!" I called out. Groaning, I heaved myself out of the chair and towards the door.

Hunter stood at the back door, his tall frame filling the doorway. He smiled cheekily. "I see you fell asleep."

"You're the one who suggested I rest," I said, a bit cranky.

"So I did. Are you ready to go?"

"Yes. Let me just get my things." I turned and grabbed my basket, packed with bandages and biscuits for Lola Cerise. The red cloth was tucked firmly around it. I slipped a hand in my pocket, reassuring myself that Hunter's knife was there. It was.

Hunter was still standing where I had left him. I wondered briefly why he didn't come inside—after all, he'd been in my family's private residence several times by now—but perhaps he was trying to hurry me along by staying outside.

With the basket over my arm, I headed back to the door. Hunter moved aside to give me room to exit. "Let me just grab my—"

I stopped short as I stared at the clothesline. In the fading light, I could see two skirts hanging there.

But no cape. The spot where it should have been was empty.

My red cloak was gone.

CHAPTER 46

"**W**HAT'S WRONG?" HUNTER ASKED me.

"M-my cloak," I stammered, still not quite believing my eyes. "It's gone!"

The sheriff's eyes narrowed as he stared at the clothesline. "It's not one of those?"

What an odd question. I supposed, from a certain angle, a skirt could look like my cape. Maybe. The length, the drape of the fabric could fool someone at first glance.

But the skirt colors were all wrong. One skirt was a deep green, reminiscent of the cedars of Littlewood Forest. The second skirt was a deep golden yellow, like a black-eyed Susan.

Neither were the bright, eye-catching red of my Lola Cerise's beloved cloak.

"Those are my skirts," I said slowly, glancing sidelong at Hunter. "Aren't they pretty? They're my favorite color."

"Oh, yes, I can tell," he agreed. "You've a light brown one there—" he pointed at the green skirt "—and a darker brown one too." He motioned at the yellow skirt. "Very practical. A nice, neutral color you can wear with anything."

"Yes," I echoed, even while my mind screamed in warning. I pasted on a smile. "I'm nothing if not practical."

"Well, I'm sure it will turn up," Hunter said. "But if you get cold, I'm happy to lend you my cloak."

"Thank you."

We left, heading straight for Littlewood Forest. Hunter didn't try to engage me in small talk, for which I was grateful. My thoughts were in turmoil, and I needed a few quiet moments to sort them out.

He couldn't tell the difference between my green and yellow skirts. When I tested him, he thought they were the same brown color.

And earlier, in his office, when he said his arm felt better, he looked at his left arm. But I know it was his right arm that was injured.

And how could he not care about the fact that his office had been destroyed? Why didn't he know about the hidden letter? If it was truly his office, he would have known about the drawer's false bottom. And the letter from Lord Percival Tavish.

My mind kept churning as I recalled more and more discrepancies.

When we met in the woods … he couldn't see me clearly once I had my cape on. But once I had taken it off …

I invited him to visit both Rowena's Bakeshop and Lola Cerise's cottage. And then both places were ransacked, my loved ones injured or taken.

Humans did not need express permission to enter a place. But those of Faerie did.

I thought back to my first meeting with Sheriff Hunter Tavish. He had easily walked into the bakeshop and delivered Mayor Marley's message to my mother. No invitation needed.

But wait, I thought. *Hunter is of Faerie … so how was he able to enter the bakeshop?*

Well. Hunter had been hired by Mayor Marley to investigate the attacks, to stay in Woodside. Lola Cerise had told me the Fae could only enter if invited by someone who had a deep connection to a certain place. As the town's leader, Mayor Marley had a connection to all of Woodside, and had probably extended a blanket invitation to Hunter upon his employment.

And I had invited Hunter into my grandmother's house when she went missing.

The man walking beside me hadn't entered the private back residence, even though the door had been wide open. Hunter could, and had, because I had allowed him. I had even held the door open for him.

But this man hadn't come in.

Because I had never actually extended an invitation for him to come inside. I had done so for the front bakeshop and my grandmother's home. But not for the private residence.

As to how this man had gained entry to the sheriff's office, I could only guess. Somehow, he had extracted an invitation, probably from the mayor. Or had forced one from Hunter.

My mind reeled.

It explained why Hunter had been confused when I called him by his given name, instead of Sheriff Tavish, as was proper and polite.

Or that day with the mayor's horse, Willow.

Or ... or ...

I tried to keep my breathing even and steady, even though my heart was now pounding so hard it was sure to beat right out of my chest. Had this man stolen my cloak? It was possible. I hadn't heard anyone outside until he knocked, I had been so sound asleep. He could easily have taken it and hidden it.

Or even destroyed it. The thought brought tears to my eyes.

But if he had, how would I find out? And how could I get it back? Should I confront him? Or just play along for now?

I eyed the sky nervously. Sunset approached, and soon I would be back in the darkened forest. Trying to find my grandmother. With a man who I now suspected was not Hunter. But Hudson Tavish. His twin brother.

The lycan.

Hudson could be lying to me about my Lola Cerise. But if it was truly him—and I was sure it was—he would also be my best chance of finding her. Somehow.

I touched my pocket surreptitiously, just wanting reassurance. Yes, I did have Hunter's silver knife. And I recalled Master Feldan's advice to carry silver. While I was no match for Hudson physically, no matter what form he was in, perhaps the dagger would be enough to keep him at bay long enough that I could run away.

Thinking of Hunter, a sudden chill ran down my spine. If this was Hudson ...

... then where was Hunter?

Every fiber of my being screamed at me to *run, hide! Get away from this beast as fast as you can!* But I knew I couldn't, not until the time was right. If I tipped my hand too early, then the lycan Hudson could easily harm both my Lola Cerise and Hunter. I didn't know where either person was, or what condition they were in.

I needed information. So I would wait, and watch, and get away when I learned what I could.

As we walked, a cold fog began to creep through Main Street. Fog wasn't necessarily unusual in Woodside, especially during the spring or fall. But today had been hot and dry, with no rain. And something about this fog seemed strange. It sparkled in the fading light, like a bunch of fireflies were floating around in it.

I yawned, even though just moments ago I had felt rested and alert from my nap. "Funny weather we're having."

Hudson eyed me sidelong. "Yes, I suppose so. I rather enjoy it, though. It makes a sleepy town feel even ... sleepier."

Had I imagined the slight emphasis he gave sleepier? Or the malicious glint in his eyes when he spoke?

Even though night was coming on, one could usually find at least a few people on Main Street, walking home or to friends' or neighbors' houses. But all of Woodside seemed shut up, quiet, and ... sleepy.

I yawned again, then caught myself, horrified. What was going on?

The sun had already disappeared behind the trees as we reached the edge of Littlewood Forest. Hazy purple twilight surrounded us. The fog danced along the road leading into the woods, the little twinkling lights entrancing. Beckoning me in. I shivered.

"Would you like my cloak, Claret?" Hudson offered politely. His hand touched the clasp, ready to remove his cape if I just gave the word.

I shook my head. I didn't want any part of this strange, dangerous man. "I'll be all right once we start moving."

"As you say." He smirked. "Claret. What a lovely name. All the women in your family are named for a shade of red, aren't they? Your grandmother, Cerise. Your mother, Rowena. And you. Claret."

"I was named after the light, rose-colored wine that was popular when I was born," I said. I was babbling, but I couldn't help myself. My head—my whole body, really—felt sluggish. There was a strange, sickly sweet smell on the air, and my earlier headache was now back in full force.

"I see. Yes, that is a good wine. Delicious. Light and delicate, like you." He opened his mouth wide in a grin, and for a horrified moment I thought he was going to devour me. "Did you know, in some circles, claret means blood?" He licked his lips. "Claret. Yes, it really is a beautiful name."

"Th-thank you."

His hand—the one attached to his uninjured right arm—dropped. Was he taunting me? Did he know I suspected him? It felt like he wasn't even trying to pretend to be Hunter anymore.

Once we started down the road into Littlewood Forest, there was no turning back. I didn't know what game Hudson was playing, but I knew with a sick certainty he wouldn't easily let me go.

But what else could I do?

"Shall we, Claret?" Hudson's mesmerizing green eyes pulled me. Coupled with the already heady feeling from the unusual fog, I felt disoriented, drowning in that gaze.

Go carefully. Veronn's warning echoed in my mind.

I closed my eyes briefly against that entrancing stare. Thought of Lola Cerise, waiting and helpless. Of Hunter, somewhere in the forest. Of the very charming predator standing beside me.

To find my loved ones, I would willingly become the prey. But not for long. For it was time I changed from being the hunted into being the hunter.

"Yes. Let's go."

CHAPTER 47

WE STARTED DOWN THE forest path, the fog snaking around our ankles. I fought the shivers that threatened again. I couldn't show weakness in front of Hudson.

Although I had a feeling I was utterly failing.

The unexpected weight of his hand on my shoulder caused me to startle.

"A bit jumpy, are we, Claret?" He chuckled, a throaty low grumble that was equally seductive and scary.

"It's just harder to see with the sun gone," I said. "I didn't think to bring a light."

All right, that last bit was a lie. I did have a light—Hunter's dagger—but I wanted to keep that a secret. For now.

"Don't worry, I have excellent sight. I can see better in the dark than most." Hudson's shadowed green eyes glittered in the growing twilight. He waved a hand. "But also, nature provides."

He was right. The sparkling fog from Woodside, which was definitively thicker in Littlewood Forest, had somehow solidified into a tapestry of tiny twinkling stars surrounding us. We didn't need a lantern, not really. Once my eyes adjusted, I realized the little lights provided just enough illumination for a few steps ahead.

"Come." Hudson's hand slid down my shoulder, clamping down firmly on my upper arm. I'm sure he meant for it to feel like a protective, guiding gesture.

It didn't. Instead, the heat and pressure gripping my arm reminded me that, now that he had me so close, Hudson wouldn't let me go.

I swallowed hard. *Stay calm, Claret. Don't show fear.*

Hudson guided me, sure and steady, deeper into the woods. I was overly conscious of his hand clamped around my arm. To calm myself, I tried to concentrate on something—anything—else. The earthy scent of Littlewood Forest, now mixed with an unusual sweetness I didn't normally associate with this area.

The deepening shadows felt sharper, somehow. Perhaps it was a reflection of the odd sparkle in the air?

Underneath it all, I had a new growing awareness. I could feel the presence of dozens of tiny beings, most of them deep in slumber. Even the leaves of the surrounding cedars seemed to be speaking, although I couldn't quite decipher their murmurings.

With a jolt, I realized I didn't need Hudson's guidance. Wherever we were headed, whatever was calling to him—it was calling to me too.

I tried to resist it. At first. If it was something Hudson wanted, then I wanted no part of it.

My skin crawled with a heightened sense of danger. Was it from Hudson's too close presence? Or was it from the growing realization that was slowly stealing over me?

We were no longer in Littlewood Forest. At least, not the Littlewood Forest I knew.

We turned right, down the path. As if to underscore my thoughts, my eyes were met by an overpowering silver-white glow.

And when we entered the clearing and I saw the two silent cedar sentinels, it felt like coming home.

I knew this place. This was where my grandmother had passed on the mantle of Scarlet Lady to me. Where Littlewood Forest itself had acknowledged me as its new Keeper.

The gateway to Faerie.

"Lovely, isn't it?" Hudson sounded smug, as if my calmness confirmed something he had suspected.

As we drew closer, I saw the wood altar with the strange carved symbols where I had undergone the transference ritual with Lola Cerise. Strange that I had never noticed it was long and large enough to hold a person.

For a supine figure lay across its top.

And that figure was—

"Lola Cerise!"

I gasped and moved forward, momentarily forgetting that someone was holding onto my arm. There was a momentary jerk of surprise as my companion tightened his grip, then reluctantly let me go.

If I had any doubts of which Tavish brother was accompanying me, they fled in that moment.

Hunter wouldn't have held me back. If anything, he would have pushed me forward, rushing with me to see if Lola Cerise was all right. His concern would have matched mine.

Hudson, though, hadn't wanted to let me go. But he needed to keep the charade going. Not that I was going to be leaving the area any time soon. Not when I had finally found Lola Cerise again.

And not now. Now, when I noticed the other figure leaning against the fallen tree altar.

Hands bound, head lolling to the side. Bruises marred his still, handsome face, and one eye showed signs of swelling. I noted the empty sheaths at his side, and wondered where his weapons had gone.

"Hunter?" I breathed.

He didn't respond.

I reached out to try to shake him awake—

And a heavy hand clamped around my wrist.

"I wouldn't do that, if I were you," Hudson snarled.

I yelped and tried to wrench myself away from him, but it only made him tighten his grip. The pressure of his fingers made spots dance before my eyes.

Still holding me none too gently, Hudson hauled me onto my feet and pulled me close. His eyes drew me in, so similar to his brother's, but lacking Hunter's warmth and gentleness. As I stared, crimson began to creep into the edges of Hudson's emerald eyes.

"Do you like what you see, Scarlet Lady?"

I gasped.

"Oh, I know who you are. And I can tell, my dear Scarlet Lady, that you know who I am."

"Yes." I aimed for bold and defiant, but the squeak at the end betrayed my fear. "But what do you want of me, Hudson Tavish?"

His lips pulled back in a twisted parody of a smile, revealing teeth that were too pointed and long to be a human's. I turned my head, not wanting to look at those horrid, huge teeth.

I shuddered at the sudden feeling of rough fingers and sharp nails against my chin. Hudson held my chin between his thumb and forefinger, turning it ever so slowly until I was forced to face him again.

"Look at me, Scarlet Lady. Don't shy away. *Look at me.*"

Reluctantly, I met his gaze, noting that even more red had overtaken his eyes. I let my eyes roam over the rest of his face, the hand holding my chin captive, his arm. His skin looked darker, rougher, as his lycan form began to show. A random thought floated into my mind. I had thought he was able to control his other self at will. Why was he having trouble keeping it at bay now?

Unless he *wanted* me to see it.

"This is what I am," Hudson snarled, shaking my chin for emphasis. "This is what those royals have made me become."

"It's no less than you deserve," I spat back. His red eyes kindled. "Oh, yes, I know what you did. What you tried to do. But I'd rather you were back in Faerie, and leave us humans be. Woodside and Cedarbrook have nothing for you."

"Believe me, my dear. I want what you want." Surprisingly, Hudson released me and stepped back. I eyed him warily, wondering what he was about. Could I distract him and run? But I couldn't leave behind Lola Cerise and Hunter. Could I overpower him? But how?

He started to slowly circle me. "I don't want to be here, in the human world, any more than you want me here. But King Finvarra, may his name forever be cursed—" he spat on the ground, as if trying to rid his mouth of the taste of the Faerie king's name "—put me here. To die a slow, agonizing death, starved of the magic of Faerie. Just enough crumbs to barely sustain me, but not enough to allow me back into the Other World."

He stopped just behind me. His breath, heavy and hot, brushed against the top of my head. "See that portal?"

My head turned to look, unresisting. Almost as if I couldn't help myself.

The gateway to Faerie glowed, its blank white depths beckoning to me. Despite the sharp sense of danger emanating from it, I wanted to run headlong into it. I just knew there was something beautiful and mesmerizing beyond that sea of silver-white....

"Do you know how maddening it is, to be so close to Faerie and yet unable to return?" Hudson's voice had dropped to a menacing whisper. "No matter how much blood I obtain, I'm not strong enough to break through it. The animals of the forest weren't enough. The human townspeople weren't enough. I tried to take your mother's, but she was protected somehow. Same with that gnome. I thought his Fae blood would help me. I thought, after I had gotten that cait sidhe, that perhaps I could break through their magical protections. But I couldn't. I couldn't break through the magic."

He eyed the still form on the altar. "Even your grandmother. Once I had the Scarlet Lady in hand, I should have been able to break her connection to the forest. I should have been able to use her blood to awaken the altar and the Faerie magic. But when I tried ..."

He snarled, his body jerking slightly towards Lola Cerise. For a moment my heart stopped, and I was afraid he would harm her. But he settled back down, growling, "I couldn't kill her. I tried. But she resisted me, somehow. Even unconscious, with her guard down. She resisted me."

My eyes widened in realization. It wasn't Veronn, my mother Rowena, or my grandmother Cerise who had been able to protect themselves, physically or magically, from the lycan. Hudson was right—with Lola Cerise in this state, she should have been vulnerable.

So who was protecting them?

Me.

It was me.

My Lola Cerise, through the virtue of her calling as the Scarlet Lady of Littlewood Forest, had been the protector of the woods—and our family. But her power had been fading. As was her ability to protect the forest. Until she transferred the mantle—and her magic—to me.

I don't know how to use that magic, a part of me whispered in fear.

But he *doesn't know that*, another part whispered back.

I'd have to learn how to use that magic pretty fast, or I, and all those I held dear, would soon be at Hudson's mercy.

For I knew, from the feral look in his bright crimson eyes, he would have no mercy.

CHAPTER 48

MY GAZE SHIFTED FROM the glowing gateway to Faerie to my grandmother's still form on top of the wooden altar. Perhaps it was a trick of the eerie silvery-white light, but she looked so incredibly pale....

"Interested in my guest, are we?" Hudson breathed behind me. "Or should I say, *guests*?"

"Please—" I didn't even know what I was begging for.

"Go ahead." Hudson waved a hand at Lola Cerise.

I stepped over to the altar. My breath caught in my throat as I got a good look at my grandmother.

Lola Cerise's normally tanned skin had an unnaturally pale, waxy cast to it, contrasting with the dark bruises that dotted her body. Dried blood outlined cuts on her arms and face, similar to the ones Hudson had given his earlier victims. But unlike those poor souls, the cuts on my grandmother were shallow and small, as if Hudson had tried to tap into her blood's potential magic and failed.

She wasn't bound, unlike Hunter, who was sitting propped up against the altar. I reached out a tentative hand, intending to touch her shoulder.

But my hand wouldn't make contact.

Disconcerted, I put my hand out again. And again, I couldn't touch Lola Cerise.

I slammed my palm against the open air. Although I couldn't see an actual barrier, my hand met solid resistance. I pulled my hand back, trying to shake out the stinging sensation.

I rounded on Hudson, who was still behind me. Standing way too close.

"What have you done to her? And to your brother? Release them both, this instant!" My voice shook, undercutting my bold words.

"You didn't say please," Hudson taunted. "Funny. Neither did Hunter. Not that I would have listened, anyway. It's better this way without him underfoot, getting in my way. Constantly being an annoyance." He shook his head mockingly. "I suppose that's just a trait of younger siblings."

"How did you—"

"Capture him?" Hudson grinned, showing way too many sharp teeth. "He made it easy. Coming after me in the night, when I'm at my strongest. Really, I should thank him."

I stared at Lola Cerise, just out of my reach behind that unseen magical barrier. Were my eyes fooling me, or was she still breathing? "She's alive," I whispered. "She's alive."

"She is, although she shouldn't be," Hudson said, sounding like he was discussing the weather. "But I think I have an idea why I couldn't kill her."

I held my breath. Had Hudson figured it out?

"I need the altar to awaken. And for that, I need the blood of the Scarlet Lady. Only then can I access the pure Fae magic that I know runs deep in this place. And just to make sure the worlds are no longer bound together, any who can claim the title of Scarlet Lady must die."

Hudson was still too uncomfortably close. I wanted to take a step back—take a million steps back—but I needed to put on a brave front. *Never turn your back on a predator. Never show fear.*

Hudson stretched out a hand towards my face. I flinched, but all he did was grab a lock of my dark hair and run it through his fingers.

I willed myself to stay perfectly still.

"Pretty," he said dismissively. "I can see the appeal."

"What's that supposed to mean?" I snapped. Then I promptly bit my tongue when Hudson's crimson eyes swung to meet mine.

"Humans have always held an allure for the Fae. Just like the Fae have always fascinated mortals. Although there have been multiple attempts to sunder the Faerie realm from the mortal one, they have never been successful."

He eyed the portal, almost as if in a trance. "Our worlds depend on each other. In fact, although it pains the Fae to admit it, we need you more than you need us. You can exist in a world without magic. But we cannot exist in a world without belief."

I narrowed my eyes. "What are you trying to say?"

He continued on in a dreamy tone. "They'll realize how wrong they were to cast me out. When I tap into the magic of this place, I'll return just in time to see their horrified faces as they slowly die. It will be so satisfying, even if I die with them."

My eyes widened. He meant to close the interstice that was Littlewood Forest! "But what will that do to the woods? To the Fae that live here?"

He snorted. "Who cares? The world—*your* world—will be better off without any of them. You won't even notice that they're gone."

In a way, he was right. Most people *wouldn't* notice the minor Faes' absence. But I would notice. My grandmother would notice. And over time, when the wonder and vibrancy had faded from Littlewood Forest, the rest of the townsfolk would feel it. They might not know quite what had happened, but they would eventually feel the loss just as keenly as my grandmother or I would.

"Although," he continued on in a singsong tone, "it is war. This is only the first battle. And there are always casualties in war."

"What do you mean?"

He shrugged. "When I destroy this gateway, there will be repercussions. Any living thing within a day or two's ride of here will feel the effects. All that magic has to go *somewhere* ... and it won't be Faerie."

Within a few days' ride? That was a wide area—and certainly included both Woodside and Cedarbrook. Not to mention Littlewood Forest. All three areas would be decimated by the magical backlash.

I needed to keep Hudson from closing the gateway. But how? For now, all I could do was keep him talking.

"I don't see how closing this interstice will affect Faerie," I said defiantly. "So you cut off Littlewood Forest? Big deal. I'm sure it will take more than one closed gateway to hurt the Faerie royals."

"Perhaps. But this is the gateway closest to court. And it *will* hurt them."

He pulled a folded piece of paper from his pocket and shook it out. Despite its worn appearance, the jagged edge on the creamy white paper and the delicate, wispy handwriting matched that of the Fae-written book I had seen in Hunter's office.

My eyes fell on the top of the page. *-terstices* was scrawled at the top, along with a three-column list of some sort.

In the leftmost column, *Littlewood Forest* caught my eye. Next to it, in the middle column, were the words *Scarlet Lady*. And then a check mark in the third column.

There weren't a lot of locations listed on the page. From my quick glance, I estimated ten, at most.

The *Faerie Lore and Legends, Vol. 2* book I had perused in Hunter's office had had a torn page. At the top of that had been the letters *I-n*. I had assumed the page meant "in something". But it had actually been part of a word.

Interstices.

I sucked in a breath. Hudson had a list of all known gateways between the Faerie and human worlds.

The lycan grinned, showing way too many long, sharp teeth. "You know what this is, then." It wasn't a question.

"Are you mad?" I breathed. "Do you mean to destroy all of these places?"

"I won't have the time, and with my tether to this place, I can't." Hudson pointed out. "But before I die, I plan on passing this on to my allies in the fight against the Faerie court. They can carry on and close all the gateways, and eventually destroy all of Faerie."

"You *are* mad," I said. "You're willing to destroy two worlds just for your silly revenge."

His hand came down on my shoulder, hard. I stiffened, suddenly acutely aware of his large hands—and the claws that were currently hidden.

"And I would destroy two hundred more," he breathed into my ear. "Two thousand. Whatever it takes."

"What about your family?" I threw out desperately. "They're back in Faerie—"

"And they can stay there and rot with the rest of them," Hudson snarled. "When I was captured and then cursed, where were they?"

"They tried—"

"Not hard enough." His fingers curled around my upper arm. I couldn't stop the small yelp of alarm that escaped my lips. "They were more worried about their ruined reputation than saving me from King Finvarra's machinations."

I glanced at Hunter, who still hadn't stirred. The story he recounted differed from Hudson's retelling, and I wondered which story was true. Perhaps both of them—the actual truth probably lay somewhere in between both accounts. Or maybe Hudson's version was tainted by his bitterness and anger.

Hudson's red gaze followed mine. "Or did you mean my dear brother?" He snorted. "Some help he was. Gallivanting all around Faerie, and then some. While I was trapped in the Tavish lands."

"But—" My thoughts spun. Hudson's hand clamped down on my shoulder wasn't helping calm my mind any. "I thought that it was customary for your family—"

"To leave? To abandon each other?" Hudson's breaths came in rapid pants, and a repressed heat laced his usually deep, languid voice. His hand tightened around my arm. I didn't like the unhinged, dangerous look that had crept into his already wild eyes. "That's not family. That's not how family treats each other."

He really is insane. It wouldn't matter what I said. No amount of cold, sane logic would convince him that there might be another side to his reality.

In an effort to distract him—could I get him to release me?—I blurted out, "What do the check marks mean?"

He paused for a moment, confused—but didn't let go of me. Then he remembered the wrinkled piece of paper in his free hand. He studied it briefly, then looked back at me. "It's a marker of whether or not a known magical item is located at that interstice."

"Why should that ... matter?" My heart was beating so wildly, I was having trouble breathing.

"I would assume it wouldn't," Hudson answered, almost absent-mindedly. He appeared to be working something out, and it was drawing his focus. "But it's a useful bit of information to have, anyway. For the Keepers would have tied the magic of their interstice into whatever item they created. So it would be worth having the item ... and destroying it. Otherwise, it could prove to be problematic later. The only thing is, the exact nature of said item isn't included in the list.

"But I do know what the Scarlet Lady created." His crimson eyes sharpened on my face as he growled, low and menacing.

"Where is your cape?"

CHAPTER 49

M Y EYES WIDENED AND my breath caught in my throat. I felt light-headed, then a feeling of dread spread over me. Hudson didn't have my cape? When I had noticed it was missing from the clothesline, I had assumed he had been the thief.

And I certainly didn't have it, or I would have donned it well before now and stayed safe and hidden.

So if Hudson didn't have my cape, who did?

"You were with me when I realized it was missing," I said slowly. "So why would you think I have it now?"

He snorted. "A pretty lie to throw me off track. But I know you hid it before I got to your home. Besides, you stupid girl, I cannot touch it."

Was he lying? A memory surfaced, of running through the woods as the sun set. Of a creature reaching out towards me—and pulling back after touching my cloak as if stung.

Hudson couldn't have taken my cloak, not if he couldn't hold it. His next question echoed the one in my head.

"So ... *where is it?*"

I don't have it, I nearly started to say. My mind raced. Should I insist that I didn't know where my cape was? Would Hudson even believe me? He seemed convinced that I was lying to him.

But what would he do if he knew, with certainty, that I didn't have my cape? It might send him over the edge that he was already so perilously perched on.

Best keep that knowledge to yourself, I decided. *It might be the only advantage you have over him. Slight as it is.*

I stiffened my spine and stood up a bit straighter. In what I hoped was a defiant tone, I said, "I don't believe I shall tell you."

His fingers squeezed my poor arm even more, forcing an involuntary gasp from me.

"Ow," I said. "Let go of me. You're hurting me."

"Where is your cape?"

"I-I've hidden it."

"Give it to me."

"No."

"Then I will help you remember," he snarled, and swiped at my face. Instinctively, I winced and turned away.

But his hand didn't make contact. Surprised, I turned to look at Hudson. He swatted at the air near my head, but didn't touch me.

Couldn't touch me.

"How are you doing that?" he snarled, frustrated.

I didn't answer. Mostly because I didn't know, myself.

Hudson's anger ceased, becoming an eerie, deliberate calm. "It's no matter. I think it will be so much more satisfying when you're too weak to stand, begging me for mercy."

He pushed me towards the altar and my Lola Cerise. I fully expected to ricochet off the invisible barrier that was keeping me from my grandmother, but instead my body hurtled through the air, only stopping when my legs slammed into the low rise of the wooden altar.

Surprised, I turned around to launch myself—well, if not at Hudson, at least away from the altar. But I didn't go more than a few steps when I hit that unseen wall.

How had he done that?

I reached my hands out in front of me, dismayed when they met an invisible resistance. I spread my arms wide, even running a few steps this way and that, but the barrier followed everywhere I went. Balling my hands, I raised my fists and beat them against the air. But I couldn't break out of my magical, indiscernible prison.

"Let me out!" I screamed.

"I will," Hudson said. "Eventually. When all your power has been leached away, and I can use it as I please. Then I'll let you out.

"Although by then, you probably won't be awake enough to even realize you're free. If you're even alive."

He walked away, the sound of his fading laughter sending despair spiking through me.

With Hudson gone, I could breathe easier—but only a little. For the dark magic Hudson had placed around the altar, no doubt a twisting of the forest's Faerie magic, had turned it into a prison for Lola Cerise and me that also served as a conduit to siphon away my strength.

With each passing moment, I felt myself growing weaker.

My poor grandmother had already been here for several days. How much magic did she have left? It couldn't have been much, considering her power had already been waning when she transferred the Scarlet Lady title to me.

And as I considered her still form, her pale face, and her barely audible breaths, I worried—how much life did she have left?

I sank down to the ground, leaning my back against the unforgiving wood of the altar. Lola Cerise's limp hand flopped over the side. I reached up and grasped it, surprised at how cold and stiff it was. I held her hand to my cheek, heedless of the tears spilling from my eyes. Maybe my warm tears and flushed cheeks would help warm her up.

"I'm so sorry, lola," I whispered. "I don't know how to get us out of here. Hudson will be back any moment. I've failed us, lola, and now the entire forest will suffer for it."

Still crying, I closed my eyes and leaned into my grandmother's unmoving hand. I felt so tired. It would be so easy to just let myself sleep ... for however long.

CHAPTER 50

A TAPPING SOUND SLOWLY pierced my thoughts.

I groaned, not wanting to move, not even wanting to open my eyes long enough to see what was causing the sound. But the tapping kept happening, more insistent.

Blearily, I opened my eyes and looked up. All I could see were the darkened trees, looming above me.

The tapping was no more than some cedar tree branches? Not worth the effort it took to look at them. I sighed, even that small sound taking too much energy from me. I closed my eyes. My mind was so sluggish, my body so weary....

A loud *smack!* made my eyes fly open.

A diminutive figure—decidedly *not* a cedar tree—stood before me. Well, not right before me. Just mere feet away, on the other side of the invisible barrier.

"Veronn!" I cried out. Or tried to. His name slurred on my lips, and my head lolled to the side. Whatever Hudson had done to alter the magic of Littlewood Forest, it was strong, and it worked fast.

"Mistress Claret!" The gnome's voice sounded fuzzy, like I was hearing him from underwater.

That's odd. I'm not drowning. Am I?

I could hear more tapping, but distantly. I tried to reach out to Veronn, to say his name again, but my mouth refused to work properly.

"Hold on," I thought I heard him say. I couldn't be sure. My mind, already feeling fuzzy, gave in to the inevitable bliss of unconsciousness.

I came to when rough hands gripped my wrist.

"I've waited long enough," Hudson snarled.

I tried to protest, but all that came out was a weak whimper. My grandmother's hand, my only comfort, was ripped from mine as Hudson hauled me unceremoniously to my feet.

"Tonight, the Scarlet Lady line ends. And with it, the connection between mortal and Faerie magic. The woods will be unprotected, and I will have my fill of Faerie magic, at last."

Before I could stop him—not that I could have, dizzy and weak as I was—Hudson protracted his sharp claws and slashed a line down the center of Lola Cerise's right arm.

I screamed.

Bright red waves of blood poured down her arm and onto the altar. The wood greedily lapped it up, and some of the strange symbols began to glow.

I fought to get free, but Hudson easily held me at bay while he scored another set of lines down my grandmother's left arm. More blood soaked into the altar, igniting another set of silver-white symbols.

"Lola ..." I breathed, horrified at how fast her blood flowed.

"I thought so." Hudson seemed oblivious to anything but the altar, now coming to life. "I couldn't get at her before. The Scarlet Lady's protective magic was still alive and well. I thought it was in *her*—but it was in *you*."

"Please, please, let her go," I pleaded, but my words fell on deaf ears.

"What does it matter to you?" Hudson's feral smile was fearsome to behold. "You'll be dead, my dear."

He raised his free hand high, ready to slash down on my neck. The silver-white glow of the Faerie portal glinted off his sharp claw.

I squeezed my eyes shut, bracing for the blow and my inevitable fate.

And then Hudson gave a startled shout. His grip on me fell away.

Surprised, I whipped my head back to see what the commotion was.

The lycan was no longer menacing me. Instead, his arms were flailing about his head as he growled at the air, grumbling incoherently as he fought an unseen foe.

No. Not unseen. My eyes caught the lightning quick fluttering of gossamer wings. High pitched giggles floated on the air, unexpected music to my ears.

"Oonie! Kaer! Watch out!" I called to the pixie twins.

Gleeful laughter was the only response.

Hudson growled again and swiped a meaty hand at Oonie. His fingers made contact, beginning to curl around the pixie. I gasped and took a step towards them.

A shimmer of light darted in the air, right at Hudson's face. Sparkling dust blew into his eyes. He abandoned Oonie, instead stepping back to swipe at his face. Snarling furiously, he tried to wipe the dust away, but to no avail.

A frantic tug at my skirt made me look down. "Veronn!"

In a low voice, the gnome said, "Hurry, Mistress Claret. While he's distracted." He jerked his head towards the woods.

I scrambled after Veronn, only glancing back once to see how the pixie twins were faring. Hudson was flailing about, trying to find one, if not both, of them to take his mounting anger out on. From his unsteady, slow movements, I could tell he was still blinded. Whatever magic the pixies' dust contained, it was potent. I only hoped it would last a little bit longer.

Veronn led me to where the trees grew closer together. Now that we were safely hidden, for a time at least, all the questions that were building up inside me burst forth.

"What about Lola Cerise and Sheriff Tavish? What do we do about Hudson? How—"

Veronn held up a hand to curb my questions. I immediately fell silent.

"Mistress, please. We'll go back for them. But first—"

"Wait, Veronn. I just have one more question. And it's very important."

"But, Mistress. I need to tell you—"

I shook my head. "Please, Veronn. Listen to me. My cape is missing. Do you know where it could be?"

The gnome didn't answer me right away, and for a heart stopping moment, I feared he would say that my cape was lost, destroyed, or—impossibly—in Hudson's clutches.

And then I realized Veronn was pointing at me.

No, not at me. At something behind me.

I turned, and then I saw it.

Draped over a low branch hung my red cape.

CHAPTER 51

I GAPED, DISBELIEVING MY eyes. I squeezed them shut, sure I was imagining things. But when I opened my eyes again, my red cape was still there.

Waiting for me.

The Scarlet Lady of Littlewood Forest.

I grabbed it, marveling. "Veronn, how did—"

"Forgive me, Mistress Claret," the gnome said. "I took it for safekeeping. With the lycan on the loose, I thought ..." He looked down, shuffling his feet in shame. "I'm sorry."

"I'm glad you did," I said, running my hands lovingly over the velvety fabric. "If you had left it there, Hudson might have destroyed it."

"I meant to return it to you sooner. But when I went back to your home, you were already gone."

I knelt down and hugged him. "Thank you, Veronn."

I stood and shook the cape out, putting it on and drawing the hood over my head. The fabric settled around my shoulders, its familiar weight comforting.

Veronn bowed. "I'm that glad to serve by your side, Scarlet Lady. But—what now?"

What now, indeed? I had no better idea now of what to do than I had just a few moments before.

But I did know I felt better having my cape back and securely tied around me. As my grandmother's gift and legacy to me, it felt like she was holding me in her embrace. I sensed all the love and care and magic she had so carefully stitched into every inch of the fabric.

Tied to her by blood and to Littlewood Forest by my new vows, I could feel the ancient, wild magic of the woods coursing through me. Already I felt somewhat stronger, renewed by my calling as the Scarlet Lady. But it would be some time before I was fully myself again. Hudson's dark magic had drained much out of me, and as I was still untrained as a Keeper, I didn't know the full extent of what I could do. So I also didn't know what abilities I might be missing.

Veronn was still watching me, waiting for my command.

I opened my mouth to speak—

—When a high-pitched scream pierced the air from beyond us, back where the wooden altar lay.

Instantly, we both ran towards the sound.

But when we broke through the trees and back into the clearing, Hudson was gone.

I looked around wildly, but didn't see the lycan. Meanwhile, Veronn was examining the ground around the altar.

"Mistress Claret! Come quickly!"

Alert to his alarmed tone, I hurried over to him. Next to the altar, in a pool of shadow just outside the glow of the lit symbols, lay Oonie.

"Oonie!" I knelt down next to the fallen pixie. "Is she—"

"I'm not sure, mistress." Veronn wrung his hands in worry. "I tried to rouse her, but she didn't respond to my voice or my touch."

Oh, dear. I looked over Oonie's still form. Her body sprawled at an unnatural angle, suggesting broken limbs. Or worse. If she wasn't waking up, could it mean ...?

Gingerly, I scooped up the little creature, cradling her between my hands.

For a moment, Oonie didn't stir, and I feared she truly was dead. But then, her wings shivered, tickling my palms. Her eyelids fluttered—once, twice—before she opened them fully, looking around in a daze.

"Oonie, are you all right?" I whispered.

Her eyes met mine, wide with ... shock? Fear?

"Mistress Claret, how did you do that?" Oonie's voice trembled.

"Do what? What do you mean?"

"I was unconscious," the pixie said. "The lycan went after Kaer ... I tried to stop him, but he swatted me out of the air. I hit the altar, and screamed from the pain in my back. Then everything went black."

"Veronn tried to wake you, just now. Maybe you—"

But Oonie shook her head, then winced at the movement. "I wasn't aware of anything until you held me in your hands. I could hear someone calling to me, telling me to awaken. And with the way I had hit the wood, flying through the air ... I'm sure my back was broken, yet I feel fine." She sat up and moved her body experimentally. She looked at me, surprised. "It barely hurts."

"Can you fly?" I asked.

She fluttered her wings. "I don't think so. Not yet, anyway. I need a little more time to recover."

Veronn held out his cupped hands. "I'll take Oonie, mistress."

I gently transferred the pixie to Veronn's outstretched hands, then stared at my own hands in wonder. If I could heal Oonie, could I heal Hunter? Lola Cerise? Or would it be better to go after Hudson?

I could practically hear Lola Cerise's voice in my head. *There's strength in numbers, my dear.*

"Veronn." The gnome snapped to attention. "Leave Oonie here. I need you to track the lycan. Don't engage him, unless absolutely necessary. But just find out where he is, and return to warn me when he's on his way back."

Veronn nodded, placing a protesting Oonie on top of the altar. "It would be better if I go. I can fly faster than you can run, Veronn. And you shouldn't go after the lycan alone."

"You just said you can't fly yet," Veronn pointed out, already moving away. "Besides, I won't be alone."

At the edge of the clearing, he knocked on the trunk of one of the cedar trees. A familiar lithe figure stepped out from under the branches. The dryad Nellah nodded gravely at me, then disappeared into the forest behind Veronn. Oonie pouted, crossing her arms as she glared after them.

"Oonie, could you keep a lookout, please?" I suspected that much of Oonie's hurt over being left behind stemmed from her concern for her twin, Kaer.

"Of course I can." The pixie's angry pose softened into one of alertness. She flew into the trees, her movements sluggish and weak.

With that settled, I knelt down next to the still unconscious Hunter. I could barely hear him breathing, but the shallow rise and fall of his chest gave me hope. I took one of his hands in mine. It was unnaturally cold, reminding me of my poor grandmother lying atop the altar.

Although I held Hunter's hand for a few moments, he didn't stir. Perhaps it had been too optimistic of me ... but holding Oonie in my hands had worked. Was it because she hadn't been unconscious as long as Hunter? Because she was smaller?

I couldn't exactly hold Hunter in my hands, nor did I know how long it would take to wake him.

I touched his face. My fingers met his chilled cheek, and I was appalled at the waxy cast to his skin.

And his brother would return, any moment now....

I placed a hand on Hunter's chest, over his heart. His heart beat, sluggish and nearly imperceptible. Instinctively, I knew. I was too late, and he had been here too long. Within a few more moments, he would be gone.

Tears pricked my eyes.

"I'm sorry," I whispered. My mind swirled with memories. Our moonlight kiss when we were keeping watch in Rowena's Bakeshop. And then later, also in the shop, but in the daytime.

But that last kiss hadn't been with Hunter. It had been with Hudson, posing as his brother. I didn't want that kiss with the false sheriff to be my last memory of the true Hunter Tavish.

I leaned forward, meeting Hunter's cold lips with my own. Warm tears coursed down my cheeks and onto my mouth, mingling with the kiss.

Nothing happened, but then again, it had been wishful thinking on my part. I pulled away slowly, reluctant to say goodbye.

I startled at an unexpected touch on my hand—the one against Hunter's chest. Something was covering it. I glanced down, opening my eyes.

A human hand, larger than my own, and blessedly familiar. Warm fingers curled around mine, holding my hand tightly. I looked back up to see Hunter smiling at me, the silvery-white light of the Faerie portal kindling a loving glow in his eyes.

"Hunter," I breathed. "I thought you were nearly—"

"Dead?" His eyes locked on to mine. "You're right, I nearly was. But something called me back."

"The magic of Littlewood Forest," I guessed. "It's a part of me now, although I don't know how to use it properly."

"Maybe? But I don't think so."

"What, then?"

He smiled, and I felt an answering grin spread across my face. He reached out to caress my cheek.

"You. It was you."

CHAPTER 52

Now that Hunter was awake, I turned my attention to Lola Cerise. But no matter what I tried, I couldn't rouse her.

"She's lost too much blood," I cried. "I should have tried to stop the bleeding instead of running ... I should have—"

"Anything you would have tried with my brother nearby ... would have failed." Hunter panted slightly, which turned into weak coughs. When his coughs subsided, he added, "I think the tainted magic in this place affects your grandmother more deeply than it did me."

"What do you mean?" I looked frantically between his weak figure, still slumped against the side of the altar, to my lola's still one atop it.

"The gateway between the worlds is not meant to be open for very long," he explained. "It's only supposed to stay open long enough for someone to pass through to one side or the other. But Hudson's kept it open for days now, weaving the magic of Faerie deep into Littlewood Forest."

"But Littlewood Forest is part of Faerie. Isn't it?"

"It is, and it isn't." Hunter struggled to stand. I made to help him, but he waved me away. "Littlewood Forest has just enough Fae magic to keep its little citizens alive and well. But its ties to the mortal world make its magic anathema to the pure Fae. The humanness draws those of Faerie, but also dampens the power of Faerie magic."

"How do I wake her up?" I shrieked.

"You don't."

I stiffened at the sound of the unfortunately all-too-familiar voice. Hunter, leaning against the altar for support, did his best to stand straight. I gripped the altar, too, my knuckles turning white with the effort. Both of us did not want to show weakness to the predator who knew quite well we were at his mercy.

Hudson stalked into the clearing, one side of his form bathed in silvery-white, the other half in shadow. His claws, fully on display, glinted dangerously at his sides.

I gasped. Dangling from one claw was a pointy yellow cap.

"Where did you get that?" I demanded.

Hudson turned towards me, his head cocked in confusion. Had something happened to him while he was in pursuit of Kaer? He squinted in my direction, disoriented.

A weak cough from Hunter caused Hudson to look over at him. His gaze sharpened as his lips pulled back in a sneer.

"Brother," he greeted Hunter. "I didn't expect to see you on your feet again."

"You didn't expect a lot from me, did you?" Hunter was desperately trying to mask his labored breathing. "That's partly why we're in this mess now."

"A mess? You underestimate me."

"Where did you get that hat?" I asked Hudson again.

He glanced over at me, but that hazy look clouded his eyes again. His eyes roamed over the area where I was standing, never quite landing on my face. When he spoke, he sounded distracted. "I took it from a pesky gnome who was following me in the forest. There was also some annoying pixie keeping watch on the periphery. I put it to sleep."

"What have you done with the gnome? Where is he?"

The lycan looked back at Hunter, as if his brother had spoken and not me. He waved his claw lazily, and the hat flew off the tip, landing in a little crumpled heap near the trees. "I took care of him. He won't be bothering me again." He laughed evilly. "Hearing his bones break was so satisfying. Perhaps the Scarlet Lady is closer to death than I thought."

I choked back a sob. A rushing sound filled my ears as an uncontrollable rage came over me. I tensed, ready to launch myself at Hudson, with no care for caution—but Hunter's hand over mine stayed me.

"Speaking of pests, where is the girl?" Hudson asked his brother.

Hunter and I exchanged an astonished look. How could Hudson not see me, standing mere feet away from him?

The sheriff shook his head at me, ever so slightly. *Don't speak. Don't give anything away.*

I nodded back, letting him know I understood.

"Don't you know?" Hunter challenged Hudson.

Hudson sighed in exasperation. "If I knew, I wouldn't be asking, now would I?" He looked around the clearing with a frown. "I could hear her speaking earlier, but I don't know where she's gone."

"Ah, I see the lycan's curse has befallen you," Hunter said. "Keen hearing, but poor eyesight. Unless at night?"

"This dratted gateway isn't helping things any," Hudson grumbled. "It's practically as bright as day here."

"Do you still have trouble distinguishing your greens from your reds?" Hunter's tone was casual.

"It's only gotten worse since the curse took me," Hudson confided. "What's the point of becoming a powerful being if you have such limitations?"

"It's just nature at work. There must always be a balance. Limitations."

"Balance. Limitations. Such ugly words."

Nature at work. Limitations.... Hunter's words caught my attention. Where had I heard that before?

Not heard. Seen.

Faerie Lore and Legends—the first volume, the non-magical static book I had borrowed from grandmother—had highlighted the balance Hunter had just mentioned. What had it said?

Regarding the accursed Fae: their great power is tempered by nature's limitations ... a mighty predator could be a most fearsome hunter, but be unable to distinguish colors or abide the sunlight....

My eyes widened. How could I have not realized sooner? I thought back to those moments when I had encountered Hudson, particularly in Littlewood Forest. Of course, I had thought he was his brother Hunter, and had attributed his confusion to daydreaming. But could it have been something else?

As quietly as I could, I began to back away from the altar. Hunter's hand had been covering mine on the top of the altar, and he startled at my movement.

"What?" Hudson's eyes narrowed suspiciously.

"My hand slipped. On all the blood covering this altar," Hunter replied pointedly. "Speaking of which, Hudson, what was your great plan? You awaken the altar, you steal the forest's magic, and then destroy the gateway? Some plan."

"I was going for expedience, not elegance."

Still moving carefully, I circled around to Hudson's other side so he was now standing between Hunter and me.

The sheriff shook his head sadly. "Oh, Hudson. It's not too late. Come home, and we can see about removing your curse. Mother and Father—"

"Mother and Father turned their backs on me! They would sell me to the highest bidder if they thought it would buy their way out of their disgrace. The disgrace that they made sure I knew I brought on them," Hudson said bitterly.

"They love you, brother. As do I. Please, turn from this madness, and we'll—"

"No!" Hudson lashed out towards Hunter. Hunter didn't flinch or step back. He just stood there, leaning against the altar, meeting his crazed brother's gaze. Hudson's claw stopped just short of slashing Hunter, but it wasn't for lack of reach. The lycan could have easily hurt his brother if he had wanted to.

Perhaps his restraint meant he still cared for his brother after all.

I slipped my hand into my pocket, feeling around for the knife. Fortunately, when Hudson had imprisoned me earlier, he hadn't thought to search my pockets. Maybe he had assumed that I was powerless without my cloak.

He wasn't that far off from the truth. My cloak really does lend me strength, somehow. But even without it, I'm not entirely without resources.

My fingers found the hilt of the silver knife. Slowly, carefully, I drew it out.

The symbols that ringed the altar were still lit, except for one final section.

Hudson turned to Lola Cerise. "It's not enough. Shouldn't there be more magic?" He looked around wildly. "If I can't find the girl, I'll use what I have."

He raised his claw to strike.

CHAPTER 53

HUNTER GAVE A SHOUT and launched himself at his brother. Hudson's slash went wide, down the center of my grandmother's chest instead of right at her heart, where the lycan had originally intended.

I screamed. I was supposed to be in hiding, but I couldn't help myself.

More blood—how was it possible that there was any left in my lola's body?—gushed forth, spilling down her arms and onto the altar. Frantically, I moved to the other side of the altar to get closer to the wound. I put the silver knife to one side and pressed my hands to her chest, hoping against hope that I might be able to stanch the bleeding.

Hudson growled and threw Hunter aside. Hunter landed on the ground, groaning at the impact.

"Get in my way, and you'll regret it, brother," Hudson snarled. "Don't think for a moment that I'll hesitate to kill you, too."

The lycan looked around. "Where is she? I heard her, just now. *Where is she?*"

"Perhaps your hearing is going, just like your eyes," Hunter taunted.

Hudson took a few menacing steps towards his brother, still on the ground. "Don't toy with me. Even cursed, I have more power than you'll ever dream of."

"Oh?" Hunter straightened and looked beyond Hudson, towards the altar. "If you're so powerful, then why did the altar fail to fully light?"

Hudson's head whipped around. For a heart-stopping moment, I froze, certain he could see me standing behind the altar.

But his eyes swept the area, skipping over me. Instead, his gaze focused on the small grouping of unlit symbols that Hunter had so helpfully pointed out.

"The old lady's blood should have worked," he grumbled, moving forward to examine the altar. "Why didn't it work?"

"So much for your grand plan," Hunter chuckled weakly. "Just give up already, Hudson."

Hudson's eyes kindled, the crimson gaze of his lycan self piercing through his normally emerald eyes. His breath started coming in short, heated gasps. Maybe from his position behind his brother, Hunter couldn't tell that Hudson was getting agitated. But I could see it.

And I also foresaw that it was a very bad idea to enrage a lycan.

Hunter, now standing, moved slowly towards the altar. "Come on, Hudson. There's nothing for you here. We'll find a place in Faerie for you to hide ... I'll help keep you alive until we can remove the curse. Let's go home and—"

"No!" Hudson screamed. "I won't!"

His voice fluctuated strangely, dropping from his light baritone into something deeper, more sinister. Horrified, I watched as Hudson's form began to change before me.

Wiry red fur, so dark it looked nearly black, sprouted along Hudson's arms, his neck, his hands. Over his face. His body contorted, growing broader and bigger than his original human form. His nose elongated into a canine snout, his now overly large nostrils sniffing the air.

Was it possible that his claws had become sharper and longer? Or maybe it only seemed that way because they now fit in properly with the rest of his werewolf body.

Hudson snarled, revealing long, dagger-like teeth. His red eyes gleamed as he scanned the area slowly, still sniffing around.

"She's here. I know she's here."

I held my breath, wondering how long it would take Hudson to figure out I was standing right in front of him.

Hunter started talking faster, trying to distract his brother. "Hudson, what are you talking about? There's no one here except us. Change back, and we'll go through the gateway. Back to Faerie. Back home."

"Not until I get what I came here for," Hudson growled, looking down at my grandmother's still form. "I need to kill the Scarlet Lady. I need to untether the worlds. And I need magic. Whatever I can get."

Hudson's claw flashed. Instinctively, I flung myself over my grandmother, tears streaming down my face.

But Hudson wasn't out for more blood. Instead, he scored a line into the altar, gouging the rugged wood with his outstretched claw. A silver-white shimmer, similar to the glow coming from the gateway to Faerie, seeped out of the newly formed split. He bent over, greedily lapping it up with his tongue.

I slowly straightened, eyeing the white light spilling out of the altar. A memory teased the back of my mind, dancing just out of reach.

I looked at Lola Cerise's still form, remembering. Her joy whenever she saw me, arms always open wide for a hug. Her teaching me woodcraft, so I could assist my mother better. Her pride when she presented me with the red cloak I now wore, the symbol of her ongoing love and protection.

My red cloak ...

What was it the Fae were so fond of saying? Red for safety. Red for life.

Red for life....

Red was a lucky color for the Fae. Red, the color of blood and love and passion, symbolized life. And humanity, with its bright but brief flickers of life in the vast sea of time, was the epitome of life and living to the fullest.

Lola Cerise and I had stood before this very altar, cutting our palms to invoke the ancient combined magic of Littlewood Forest and Faerie. That magic had recognized me as her heir.

Now that I was remembering, my mind started racing. Hudson wanted Faerie magic, unmixed with human power. He thought that the partially awakened altar meant he wasn't getting the full amount of Fae magic.

But all the symbols had come to life when the altar had recognized me. With a jolt, I realized the last set of symbols represented the human side of the binding.

What would happen if Hudson got what he wanted—the complete magic of the fully awakened altar?

Bent over as he was, his full concentration on the silvery magic spilling from the partially awakened altar, Hudson didn't notice his brother sneaking up behind him. He suddenly shot up, back bowing as he screamed in agony. A thin line of silvery-white trickled down his lips and chin, the stolen magic a sparkling contrast to his dark red fur.

Hunter danced back, narrowly avoiding getting swiped by those fearsome claws. He held a dagger in each hand, one a dark, dull grey, the other lighter and brighter than its companion. The lighter one, which resembled the silver knife that Hunter had loaned me, was now wet with Hudson's blood.

"I didn't want it to come to this," Hunter said. "I don't want to hurt you. Cease this madness, and come home with me."

Hudson growled and stalked towards his brother, staying just out of reach of Hunter's silver blade.

The two brothers circled each other warily. Then Hunter slashed at Hudson, nicking the lycan's arm and earning a yelp. I could see the wound in Hudson's side, from where Hunter had stabbed him earlier. Surprisingly, the bleeding had stopped and the cut already looked better. Perhaps it hadn't been that deep? Although from Hudson's reaction, I had thought it quite painful.

Even the new cut on Hudson's arm didn't look that bad. In fact, it was already healed, its edges lined in shimmery silver-white....

Could it be that the altar's magic was healing Hudson instantaneously?

If that was true, then this fight was futile. No matter what Hunter did, he wouldn't be able to overpower his brother. It would just be a matter of time before Hudson had the advantage. All Hudson had to do was wait, and Hunter, already weakened from his earlier ordeal, would eventually succumb.

Hunter gave a strangled cry and dropped to the ground. He groaned and struggled to rise, but a swipe of Hudson's paw made Hunter fall silent.

Hunter, get up! my mind screamed. But he didn't, and my blood ran cold. *Please don't be dead.*

Hudson straightened up. "I didn't want it to come to this, brother," he said, parroting Hunter's earlier words.

Stepping over his brother's prone body, he turned to face the altar.

And looked directly at me.

Just breathe, I willed myself. *He can't see you, remember?*

Indeed, with my red cape and his color blindness, I was practically invisible to him. As had been demonstrated time and again. Perhaps if we were in the shadows, it would be different. But the glade was so brightly lit, it may as well have been daytime.

So I had nothing to fear. As long as I stayed quiet, he wouldn't know I was there.

So why was he just standing there, staring at the spot where I stood?

And why did his gaze make me feel so uneasy?

Slowly, he began moving towards the altar.

"It's funny," he said, seemingly speaking to the air. "When I was forced into this blighted human realm, I could feel my power weakening almost immediately. Me, a descendant of one of the Great Ones of Faerie! And a firstborn, at that. Back in the Other World, my magic was as strong as any of the fops who call themselves courtiers.

"But here, my weaknesses quickly overtook me. What paltry magic I could find was barely enough to turn the forest's magic to my will. I despise being so weak."

He was closer now. A few more steps, and he would be standing before me again. He licked his lips as he approached.

My breath caught. Was he looking at the altar?

Or at me?

"But having some Faerie magic back—pure, wild, raw—makes me feel like a new person. Stronger. Faster. And able to see things like I never have before."

My blood ran cold. He was definitely looking right at me. I felt like a rabbit caught in a snare, watching the satisfied hunter as he approached to deliver my fate.

Hudson, I could tell, delighted in my terror. He stopped on the other side of the altar, facing me across my grandmother's body. He flashed a sinister smile.

"Hello, Claret."

CHAPTER 54

*B*REATHE, I TRIED TO tell myself, but my body was no longer listening to my mind. Even if Hudson had been unable to see me, he would have definitely heard my panic.

"What's wrong, Claret?" He feigned sympathy, but I could hear the malicious undercurrent in his voice. He had me, and he knew it. "Don't be frightened."

"Don't be patronizing," I snapped. "We both know you intend to kill me. At least treat me with some dignity."

"My, my. Aren't we the feisty one. I can see why my brother has taken a liking to you." He spared a glance for Hunter, still lying on the ground. "Too bad he won't have a chance to say goodbye. Don't worry, I'll tell him all the details of your death."

In that moment when Hudson looked away, I moved. I didn't have much of a plan besides *Get away from here, now!*

A dull thunk sounded behind me. I tried to keep going, but I couldn't go any further. I was stuck.

Or more accurately, caught.

My cloak was pinned to the altar. A knife that I recognized as Hunter's stabbed through the fabric and into the altar's wooden top.

I tugged at my cloak, but it refused to budge. The fabric was too thick to tear easily. Not that I would have wanted to rip my grandmother's precious gift, if I didn't have to. I pulled at the knife, but it was stuck fast, well embedded in the wood. My hands, slick with blood and sweat, refused to grip the weapon's handle.

Hudson chuckled, clearly enjoying my distress.

"I'd have used that one—" he pointed at the silver dagger I had left atop the altar— "but I can't abide touching it. Much like your cloak."

He came around to my side of the altar, giving my cape a wide berth. Standing in front of me, he smirked. "Really, I'm disappointed. First my brother, now you. Hardly any challenge at all. I'll remember to be grateful to you both when I'm strolling back into Faerie."

He eyed my cape with distaste. "Now, I don't suppose you'd be willing to take that off? I'm afraid I've run out of non-silver knives."

In response, I gathered the free part of my cloak around me. Since he couldn't tolerate its touch, I was going to make this as hard as possible on him in my final moments.

Thank you, Lola Cerise. It's not much, but it's something.

Hudson glared at me. "No?"

I snorted. "So you can kill me sooner? Not likely."

He sighed. "I didn't think so." He flexed a claw. "So, a bit of a challenge, after all. This will hurt me something fierce, but in the end, it will be worth the pain."

He raised his hand to strike.

"Wait!" I called out.

Hudson paused. "What is it? I've never been fond of someone's 'final words', but if you feel you must, I'll allow it."

"You can't kill me. Not yet. You need me."

The lycan's red eyes narrowed. "Continue."

I gestured at the partially lit altar. "That. It's not fully awakened."

"I know. But there's some magic there for me to access."

"Just some? Is that good enough?"

Hudson lowered his arm. "What are you saying?"

"I can kindle the last set of symbols. I can give you full access to the altar."

He smirked. "I know that, too. I just need your blood."

"No," I said quickly. "I mean, yes, you need my blood. But you need me alive as well. Only I can call forth the magic that will awaken the altar completely."

Hudson hesitated, looking between me, the altar, and my grandmother atop it.

"I tried it with the old one, and it didn't work," he muttered. "What if the young one is right?"

I held my breath. Had I persuaded him?

"All right," Hudson said. "Do as you say. Light the symbols and unlock the altar fully. But if you're lying—"

"I'm not."

"I'm going to kill you anyway."

"I know." I steeled myself to meet his crimson gaze. "You've already hurt the ones I love. What do I care now if you leave annihilation in your wake when you leave? You might be doing the area a small mercy."

For a long moment, we just stared at each other. Finally, he nodded at the altar. "Begin."

"Could you give me the knife, please?" I looked at the dagger that held me prisoner.

Hudson snorted a laugh. "Not likely," he said, sarcastically echoing my earlier words. He showed his claws again. "If you need help cutting yourself open ..."

I shuddered. "No. I need a controlled flow of blood."

He indicated the other weapon, the silver knife. "You have a free blade, there."

Inwardly, I gave a frustrated sigh. It had been a slim hope that he would free me. "All right, then."

"And don't get any grand ideas. Drop the knife on the ground once you're done with it. If you try to slice me with it, it will be the last thing you do."

I picked up the silver dagger. Carefully, I sliced open my palm, hissing slightly at the pain. Hudson growled a warning at me, and I obediently dropped the knife on the ground.

He kicked it away, wincing as he did so.

I held up my palm, now welling with blood. "Are you ready? The magic will be yours for the taking, soon enough."

"Cease your prattle and do it, already."

I nodded and took a deep breath. I placed my hand, palm down, on the wooden altar, over the open seam that was spilling out the white Faerie magic.

The final set of symbols flared to life, turning as red as the blood that had awakened it. Red light mixed with white, encasing the altar in the rich rose glow I remembered from before.

The shimmery stream of magic changed colors, from bright white to a soft blush pink.

"The magic. It's changed," Hudson said. "Why has it changed?"

"Because I, as the Scarlet Lady, have called forth the rest of the Faerie magic from within Littlewood Forest," I said. "Before, you only had the magic from the gateway. Now you have all the Faerie magic in the area."

"Why is it not white, like the gateway?"

"Littlewood Forest is located here, in the human realm. Not the Other World. That's changed it, somewhat. But it's still Faerie magic."

Hudson lowered his head to the altar and gave an experimental sniff. "It smells the same. Tantalizing." His tongue flicked out. "And the taste! Exquisite."

Greedily, he started to lap at the flowing magic.

I backed away, but I couldn't get far, pinned as I still was. I surreptitiously wiped my hands against my cape and tried again to loosen the knife, but it wouldn't budge. Should I cast off my cloak and run? Since Hudson was distracted, maybe I might be able to escape.

A light breeze blew by me, causing me to shiver. Then I trembled more as the wind picked up.

Hudson kept drinking, heedless of my presence and the growing gale in the glade. He wouldn't be stopping any time soon—now that the altar was fully awakened, the magic flowed strong and sure.

Where was this wind coming from? I looked up. The moon and stars winked down at me from a cloudless sky. Not a storm, then.

My eyes were drawn to the gateway. Was I seeing things? I thought I spied some shadowy figures approaching, though they were distant still.

At the altar, Hudson straightened up, having drunk his fill. He didn't bother to wipe his mouth, and the pink lines of magic looked like shimmery streaks of thinned out blood dribbling down his lips and chin and cheeks.

"What is this?" he said, finally noticing the leaves and dirt being kicked up by the strong wind blowing about the clearing. He looked at the gateway, then back at me. "Is this your doing?"

I shook my head. "No. I don't know what's happening, either."

A brawny hand shot out, fur-lined fingers closing around my throat. "You summoned them here, didn't you?"

Summoned? Who? But the words wouldn't come. All I could do was make a strangled sound of protest.

"You foolish, foolish girl. You thought you could best me, but you were wrong. You'll be dead before they ever get here."

Hudson's fingers tightened and began to squeeze.

CHAPTER 55

D ARKNESS CREPT IN AT the edges of my sight.

I had no idea who it was Hudson had thought I had summoned, and it looked like, soon, I would never know.

I'm so sorry, Lola Cerise. Mama. Hunter. And Littlewood Forest. I really thought ...

The wind was now so strong that Hudson had trouble keeping his footing. A large branch whipped by, knocking his arm. Hudson stumbled, losing his grip on my throat.

As much as I didn't want to lose my cloak—again—self-preservation kicked in. My fingers fumbled at the clasp around my neck, opening the cape and setting me free. I fell to my knees, struggling to catch my breath. Spots swam in front of me, but I forced myself to crawl forward.

Where was that silver knife? If I could only find it, I might have a chance....

I spared a quick glance to see where Hudson was.

He had been forced back by the wind, slamming into a tree at the edge of the clearing. He was trying to make his way back to me, but the wind kept pushing him back.

I kept crawling. Although still breezy, the wind was less forceful closer to the ground.

A glint caught my attention.

There! I could see it, a few feet away. Hunter's silver dagger.

The shadowy forms framed in the gateway were slightly bigger now. Getting closer. The intense glow of the portal made it impossible for me to make out any distinct features, but I thought I saw five, maybe six, figures.

Frantically, I crawled towards the dagger. But I was so weak, both from Hudson's attempt to kill me, and from my earlier imprisonment. Now that I was without my cloak, my strength had quickly left me.

So close. I was so, so close. Just a little bit farther. If I stretched my hand out, I could just reach it....

A growl to my right was the only warning I had.

Hudson slammed into my side. He must have also figured out that staying low to the ground was the only way to avoid the wind.

I tumbled, rolling over a few times before coming to a stop, lying on my back. My breath came in heavy pants, and those darn spots were back, dancing in my vision. And had I heard something crack? My chest hurt, and I feared I had bruised or broken a rib.

I turned my head to see Hudson coming after me again. My eyes widened. Crawling, the lycan couldn't launch himself at me, but he could still move fast. I scrambled up onto my hands and knees and moved as fast as I could out of the way.

Towards the silver knife.

Hudson swiped at me, scraping his claw against my leg. I screamed as pain flared through my body. I kicked backwards as hard as I could, feeling a sense of satisfaction when my foot made contact and I heard a yelp.

The figures in the gateway still hadn't come through. Whoever they were, I could have used their help. Assuming, of course, that they were friends and not foes.

"Hurry up!" I yelled at the portal. But the wind carried away my weak, ragged voice.

I kept moving, even though my energy had long since been spent. Wheezing and coughing, I kept my head down and my eyes on the knife.

Hudson's hand grabbed my boot just as my hand closed around the dagger's hilt.

I screamed as I felt my body being dragged. Hudson's hand moved to my ankle, then up my leg, as he pulled me towards him.

"That's it," he growled. "You die now, Scarlet Lady."

"Not if you die first," I shouted. I turned over, slashing out with the knife as I did so.

The silver knife cut across Hudson's face. A bright red gash appeared, his lycan's blood mixing with the dried pink shimmer of the altar's magic still on his face.

Hudson recoiled, putting a paw to his face. I scrambled away, using my free hand to propel me backwards while brandishing the knife in front me.

"Come closer, and I'll let you taste more of this," I promised.

The shadowy figures were now at the portal's entrance. They had solidified into five stately figures, and one smaller one. One by one, they began to walk through.

Hudson spared a brief moment to see who was entering the clearing from Faerie. His red eyes flashed as recognition dawned. Whoever they were, their appearance seemed to have given him renewed vigor.

"Enough!" he spat out. He started to lunge at me—

—And then halted, eyes bulging. Chest heaving, he suddenly had trouble breathing. He collapsed, then lifted himself off the ground on shaky arms.

"What's ... wrong ... with me?" he choked out.

A satisfied smile played about my lips. "You drank from the awakened altar's magic."

"Y-yes, but ..." he panted. "It was ... supposed to ... give me strength."

"It did," I said. "Strength from the combined magic of both the Fae and human worlds."

Hudson stared up at me with wide, horrified eyes as realization sank in. "What ... have you ... done?"

"Given you what you wanted." Looking down at him, my smugness faded. I hadn't wanted his death—after all, he was Hunter's twin brother. But I didn't want him terrorizing my town. Or my forest.

"Clever," he whispered. "I can see why ..." He stopped to catch his breath.

"Miss ... Claret. The Scarlet Lady. Please. Take care of my brother." Then Hudson shuddered and breathed his last.

Chapter 56

I COLLAPSED ONTO MY back, breathing heavily, my strength well and truly spent. The silver dagger, now unneeded, fell from my grasp and onto the ground.

The wind had died down, and now a gentle breeze stirred my hair, bringing cool relief to my sweat-soaked skin.

Leaves crunched nearby. I suddenly found myself looking up into an impossibly perfect face, pale and stern, framed by long, black hair. A silver crown was perched atop the person's head. He held out a slender hand to me, a white sleeve edged in silver trim flowing down his arm and around his wrist.

Hesitantly, I placed my dirty, bloodied hand in his. He didn't flinch or wrinkle his nose at the gross state I was in. Instead, he gently helped me sit up, motioning to one of his companions to come steady me.

"Are you well, miss?" the stranger asked. Even his voice was perfect, melodious and strong.

I nodded. Bad idea. I winced as a headache flared up. Slowly, I looked around.

Next to the beautiful man stood an equally beautiful woman, her raven tresses falling in gentle waves around her face. She also wore a pure white gown edged in silver, with a silver circlet on her head. They were accompanied by a small retinue of guards, who stood watchful. One of the guards knelt next to me, his hand on my back as he propped me up. He offered me a waterskin, which I accepted with a grateful smile.

After taking a long, much needed drink, I glanced at the white-robed pair. "Are you ... are you the king and queen of Faerie?"

A sparkling smile blossomed on the dark-haired man's face. "We are. I am King Finvarra of the Seelie Court, and this is my bride, Queen Oona."

I did my best to bow, although the movement caused my rib to protest. "It's an honor to meet you, Your Majesties. I am Claret Pagnati, the newly recognized Scarlet Lady of Littlewood Forest."

King Finvarra nodded. "Yes. We came here expressly to find you."

"Me?" I squeaked.

"Feldan gave us your message. We came as soon as we could. Although—" the king eyed Hudson's still body "—perhaps it was not soon enough."

"I'm glad Mister Feldan was able to find you," I said.

"He is quite persistent. A good trait in a messenger." King Finvarra's eyes twinkled. He turned and nodded at someone behind him.

My face broke out in a smile as a familiar figure stepped forward.

"Mister Feldan!" I held out my arms to greet him. The cait sidhe, in his human form and with his red cap sitting jauntily on his head, embraced me. "It's so good to see you!"

"Likewise, Mistress Claret. I worried about your safety every moment I was away."

"It was uncertain for some time," I admitted. "I was quite lucky."

"I don't know if it was just luck," Queen Oona said, her voice reminding me of tinkling bells. "It looks to me like you were capable of holding your own. A worthy successor to Scarlet Lady Cerise."

Lola Cerise. I startled, remembering. And then promptly hissed in pain, holding my side.

"My grandmother," I said. "She's lying on the altar. Hudson—the lycan—bled her to awaken the altar's magic. Is she ...?"

Mister Feldan sprang from my side, hurrying over to check on Lola Cerise. From where I was sitting, I couldn't quite see what he was doing. But when he turned back to look at us, his face was grim.

"Mistress Claret. I ... I'm sorry."

I hung my head. I had known, deep down, that there was little chance her frail, elderly body could have withstood such an assault. But still. I had hoped that maybe magic, or a miracle, could help her.

I swallowed hard. There would be time to mourn her properly later. For now, there were other things to attend to. "What about Hunter? I mean, Sheriff ... uh, Lord Tavish?"

At a wave from King Finvarra, one of the guards went to check on Hunter.

"He's stunned, but he's still breathing," the guard called to us. "He's injured, but it's hard to determine the extent."

King Finvarra nodded, as if he had expected to hear that. "We'll take him back to Faerie. He'll get the finest healing there."

A pang hit me. I understood, of course. And Hunter's parents would be happy to see him again. But if he went back to Faerie, would I ever see him again? Now that his true mission was done—finding his brother—he had no reason to return to Woodside.

"What about the lycan?" I asked. "I know he's exiled from Faerie, but if he's no longer a threat ...?"

"We will take him back as well and deliver him to the Tavishes. They can decide what to do with his body from there."

Two guards went to pick up Hudson's body. As they passed by, holding the fallen lycan, my jaw dropped. Hudson's werewolf form had disappeared in death, leaving the broken, human shell of the former Fae noble.

Mister Feldan returned, waiting for instructions.

"Veronn and some of the others are somewhere in the woods," I told him. "They lured the lycan away, but didn't return."

"I'll find them," the cait sidhe promised, and hurried away.

The guards holding Hudson had disappeared through the gateway. The one who had been helping me stood, going over to assist with Hunter.

The king and queen of Faerie regarded me, regal and serene.

"We owe you a great debt," King Finvarra said. "You have rid both of our realms of a dangerous accursed Fae. For that, we thank you."

"But, if you please, Your Majesty," I said. "I don't understand how I did it."

"You are a daughter of both worlds, are you not?"

I paused, confused, until I remembered what Lola Cerise had told me, here in this very spot. *My dear, it seems you are more powerful than even I thought ... Your magic has not only been awakened, your magic is a mix of both worlds. Something unique and rare.* "I ... I suppose I am."

"The lycan needed pure Faerie magic to return," the king explained. "But he didn't know that the altar, drawing on the magic from both worlds, would not have what he needed. Indeed, any Fae who's spent a fair amount of time in the human world, as your grandmother and all the Fae of Littlewood Forest have, would not have what he needed.

"When you gave him your magic, it was something he did not expect to encounter, and was not able to handle. A mix of human and Faerie magic, amplified by the altar, wielded by the Scarlet Lady who was protecting her forest. It overwhelmed him." He smiled. "Even I do not think I would have wanted to experience that."

"Oh. I see." Sort of. If only my Lola Cerise could explain it to me. It was one of her legacies to me, but I would have to figure it out on my own.

"We will take our leave of you now," King Finvarra said. "But before we do, know that you are welcome in Faerie anytime, should you choose to visit. We give you our solemn promise that no harm will befall you or any companions you bring with you. In addition, we pledge to keep you exempt from the possible time change between the realms. If you come to Faerie, time will flow the same in the human world, instead of stopping or moving forward at an unnatural pace."

"Thank you." I hesitated, then said, "I know it's too late for my grandmother. But my mother, Rowena, has been unconscious for several days, by some magical malady the lycan inflicted upon her. The town physician is unable to help her. Would it be possible to send someone from Faerie, who understands magical afflictions?"

"It will be done," the king assured me. "And we will make sure former Scarlet Lady Cerise has a proper burial. Expect our envoys to arrive within the week."

I nodded. "Thank you," I said again.

"It is we who should be thanking you," King Finvarra said sincerely. "Both of our realms were in grave danger. Without your courage and quick thinking, the human and Fae worlds would have suffered widespread and possibly irreparable damage."

With that, the king and queen of Faerie moved towards the gateway. They gave me a final wave before entering the portal. I waved back, then stilled when I saw the guards carrying Hunter through the door.

I touched my fingers to my lips, sending a gentle kiss upon the breeze to the fallen sheriff.

Be well, Hunter. I'll miss you.

CHAPTER 57

THE DAYS FOLLOWING THE events in the clearing blurred by.

King Finvarra kept his word. The Fae envoys showed up in Woodside two days after the Tavish twins returned to Faerie.

Among them was a Fae healer, who knew immediately upon seeing my mother how to help her. She stayed by Mama's side for a few more days, muttering spells, mixing potions and poultices, and shooing me away from Mama's bedroom. "I can't help her if you're constantly underfoot," the healer chided me.

"Is there anything I can do to help?" I asked, desperate to keep busy. I needed to keep my mind and my hands occupied, for I didn't want to think about my beloved grandmother, now back in her woodside cottage, waiting for burial. I didn't want to think about what would happen if Mama didn't wake up.

And I didn't want to think about Hunter, his recovery, and the idea that I would never see him again.

The healer waved irritated hands at me. "I have all I need, and so does your mother. You can go about your other business."

But I had no other business, except to worry.

Fortunately, a familiar black and white cat showed up.

"Mister Feldan!" I practically jumped on the poor Fae after he transformed into his human self. "What news do you have?"

The cait sidhe wore a somber expression. "If you're not busy, Mistress Claret, I would ask that you accompany me back to Littlewood Forest."

"Gladly," I grabbed my cape, now mended from where the knife had torn it slightly, and donned it before leaving the house. With the lycan gone, I most likely didn't need to wear it anymore. But it was one of the few things I had left of my beloved grandmother, and I hated being without it.

But once Mister Feldan and I reached our destination within the forest, my relief over escaping the house turned to sadness.

We were back in the glade, the Faerie gateway looming over us. The altar, now back to ordinary, non-glowing wood, looked mostly unchanged, save for the single deep gouge that marred one long side of it. The blood had been washed or scrubbed away, for which I was grateful. The less reminders I had of that horrible night, the better. Nellah and Oonie were there, along with other forest Fae I had yet to meet.

Three holes of various sizes had been prepared in the ground. One to fit a human close to my measurements. One to fit a being about half my size. And one to fit someone no bigger than my hand.

Three graves. For my grandmother Cerise, the gnome Veronn, and the pixie Kaer.

Tears pricked my eyes as the Faerie envoys carried the bodies of my loved ones into the glade. Although I had been able to protect them somewhat unwittingly, it hadn't been enough. For the rest of my life, I would carry the scars of my failure on my heart.

Gently, the three were laid to rest. Wrapped around my Lola Cerise's fingers was the broken gold chain, the necklace my grandfather had gifted her. I watched, tears streaming down my cheeks. No one gave any grand speeches, or said any prayers or platitudes. Just silence, and the occasional sniffle from someone crying. I found I preferred the quiet, getting lost in my memories of my grandmother and friends instead of having to listen to someone else's impressions of them.

When it was done, one of the envoys waved a hand. Instead of gravestones, the three graves were each marked by a small bed of flowers. Kaer's and Veronn's were covered by bluebells, also known as fairy flowers to those of us in Woodside. The vivid purple-blue flowers brought a sad smile to my lips.

I turned to look at Lola Cerise's grave.

Red foxgloves adorned her final resting place. The bell-shaped flowers reminded me of the red cap that Lola Cerise had made for Mister Feldan, and I pulled my cloak tighter around me. I imagined I could feel her embracing me one last time.

"A fitting tribute to the Scarlet Lady," Nellah said softly.

"Yes," I said, taking in the flowers, the gateway, the altar. I wished, in vain, that I had had more time with my grandmother. More time to learn more about being the Scarlet Lady from her. More time to sit and laugh with her. More time ... knowing that even if I had more time, it would never have been enough.

Upon returning home, I had one consolation. Mama was awake and alert, although weak from her ordeal.

"Claret? What's happened?" Mama asked when I walked into her room.

"How much do you remember?" I said.

She frowned, touching her head, and winced. "Something attacked me ... I fell ... and I don't know, beyond that."

I sat down on the bed, taking her hand up in mine. "You've been out for several days. Rest and recover, and when you're feeling better, I'll tell you the whole story."

"All right." Mama paused. "What about the shop? Have you been running it while I've been indisposed?"

I shook my head. "No, it would have been too much work without you. Besides, the shop was also ... indisposed ... while you were."

She eyed me narrowly. "Why do I have the feeling I won't like the story you have to tell me?"

I sighed. "Because you won't. It doesn't really have a happy ending."

"I see. Well, with all that time on your hands, what have you been doing?"

I paused, not wanting to get into everything that had happened while she was still feeling poorly.

"Oh, I know," Mama said, brightening. "I'm sure you were able to visit your lola quite a bit. How is she doing?"

At that, I burst into tears.

More days, and then weeks, went by.

I'm not sure how word reached the mayor—Faerie magic, or a trick from the envoys, maybe?—but Mayor Marley announced that Sheriff Hunter Tavish had been called away on indefinite business to the capital. But we needn't worry, as the sheriff had assured the mayor that the attacks in the forest had been stopped. In the meantime, Constable Piera would be overseeing both Cedarbrook and Woodside until a replacement could be found. If a new sheriff was even needed.

Mama recovered rapidly, much to my surprise and relief. Soon the Faerie healer declared her "healthy and whole once more" and allowed Mama to get out of bed and even bake again. The baking helped my mother recover faster than the rest did.

The Faerie envoys left, and life in Woodside returned to normal. Well, mostly normal. I made repairs to the bakeshop as best I could, wishing all the while that Hunter was there to help me and then berating myself for thinking about him. Mama and I reopened Rowena's Bakeshop, and business quickly became as brisk as it always had been.

I finally told Mama the news about the lycan, my new calling as the Scarlet Lady, and Lola Cerise's death. She listened, still and stoic, as I recounted everything. When I finished, she asked, "What will we do about your grandmother's cottage?"

The question caught me off guard. I had expected weeping, or anger. Not something so practical. "I-I'm not sure. I don't want to sell it, but ..."

"It might be time for you to have a place of your own," Mama said. "After all, the cottage goes with the calling."

"But what about you? What about the bakeshop?"

Mama smiled, but it was tinged with sadness. "We both know your heart was never in this bakery. It's about time I scaled back, anyway. I'm not as young as I used to be, and I don't know if I'll ever fully recover from the lycan's attack."

"I don't have to—"

"Yes, Claret. You do. Even if you decide not to keep the cottage, at the very least you'd be living in the forest or something. Not here in Woodside. The Scarlet Lady belongs to her forest, as Littlewood Forest belongs to her."

I paused. Mama was right. "All right, then. We'll figure something out in the meantime, until I know for sure where I want to reside. The forest is safe again. I can come back anytime to help you."

Mama smiled, a genuine one this time. "I'd like that."

EPILOGUE

*O*NE YEAR LATER

It was another hectic day at Rowena's Bakeshop. I brushed a tired hand across my sweaty forehead as I walked over to the window, turning the "Open" sign to "Closed".

As she had hinted, Mama had reduced the shop's open days to just three times a week. Which made the place busier than ever, since people knew they couldn't get their baked treats as often as before. To cut down on the hassle, Mama was accepting special orders to be made on her off days. I didn't see how that reduced her workload, but she swore it made her life easier.

I had been staying at Mama's for a few days, but planned on going back to Cedarbrook tonight. In fact, I was glad the bakeshop had closed early, since it meant I could get on the road sooner.

Cleaning and sorting out Lola Cerise's things had been a slow process, but I was nearly done with it. That was actually one of the reasons I had returned to Woodside recently. I had wanted to give Mama some of my grandmother's personal items that I thought she might cherish.

Also, I just wanted to see Mama again. Since moving into Lola Cerise's cottage, I hadn't been been able to visit as often as I would have liked.

I still didn't know if I wanted to keep her cottage. It held too many memories of my beloved grandmother. Lovely memories, to be sure. But each memory was tinged with sadness. I wasn't sure if that ache would ever completely go away.

But I didn't know where I would live. Woodside no longer felt like home. And, aside from my grandmother's cottage, I had no ties to the town of Cedarbrook. As the Scarlet Lady of Littlewood Forest, I had to stay close by, but I didn't know where that would be, exactly.

So I continued to reside in Lola Cerise's former home, missing her fiercely. I was fortunate to be able to visit Nellah and Oonie and the other Fae of the woods, but even then, I needed something to fill my days.

I grabbed a rag and started cleaning the back countertop.

The bell over the bakeshop door dinged. Silly me. I had forgotten to lock the door when I had flipped the sign.

"We're closed," I called out, not bothering to glance over my shoulder.

The door clicked closed. Good. I'd finish wiping this down, then go over and lock the door so no one else bothered us.

I stiffened when I heard approaching footsteps. Hadn't the person left?

"We're closed," I repeated irritably, turning. I was ready to give this intruder a good tongue lashing. "We've sold our last—"

My voice faded as I got a good look at the trespasser.

Dark hair, slightly longer than I remembered. A lopsided smile. And bright, piercing emerald eyes.

Eyes that I couldn't forget.

"Hello, Claret."

I suddenly found myself in Hunter's arms. I don't even know how I got there so fast. One moment I was behind the bakehouse counter. The next thing I knew, I was in his arms, laughing and crying all at the same time.

"How did you ... Where have you ...?" The words wouldn't come to me. I seemed incapable of forming coherent thoughts.

Hunter laughed. "It's good to see you, too."

"I-I thought I would never see you again."

He sobered. "I know."

"What happened? You were injured, and they took you back to Faerie ... and that was that."

"Honestly? That really is about it. I was in a bad way. The healers thought I might not make it. In addition to the physical injuries I had, Hudson's magic packed a pretty mean punch." He sighed. "It took about three months for me to mend, five for me to be completely myself again. Not to mention, we had to bury my brother and take care of other things."

"Other things?"

"Well. With Hudson gone, I'm now the Tavish heir."

"Oh." Somehow that thought had never occurred to me. But it made sense. And then something else came to mind. "*Oh*. Does that mean you have to go back? To Faerie?"

"Yes." Hunter's voice was quiet. "When Hudson was brought home, it devastated my parents. I swear they aged overnight. My father ... my father lost his mind. He is no longer fit to oversee our lands."

"Oh, dear. I'm sorry to hear that." And I was. I was sorry that so much heartache had visited Hunter's family. I was sorry his twin brother was dead.

And, selfishly, I was sorry for myself, that Hunter would have to go back to Faerie permanently.

I pulled back a little. "So, then, why did you come back to Woodside? To say goodbye?"

"In a way. Even though I was here only for a short time, Woodside was good to me." His glance felt like a caress. "Among other things."

I pulled back farther until he was forced to release me. "I see. We'll miss you, then. Thank you for all of your help here. It's nice to be able to wander the woods again without fear."

Hunter looked startled, then chuckled. "Oh, Claret. I'm doing a poor job of explaining myself. You misunderstand me, I'm afraid."

"Oh? Then enlighten me, please."

He took a deep breath. "Yes, I have to go back to Faerie. But I want you to come with me."

I frowned. "I have my duties here as the Scarlet Lady ..."

"Which you can carry out in Faerie, as well."

"How? That's not possible. I know our two worlds are linked, but—"

"You know that the Tavish lands overlap Littlewood Forest and the surrounding area, yes?"

I nodded.

"Littlewood Forest, along with the other interstices, has the distinction of being in both realms. What affects the woods on the human side affects it on the Faerie side as well. It's just that some Fae choose to reside in the human world, while some prefer the Other World. But they can move freely between both sides in an instant. As can the Scarlet Lady. If she so desires."

My mind whirled.

"And as Littlewood Forest is your domain, you would be aware of what is happening in the forest on both sides of the gateway at all times. The only difference between the two realms is my family's domain on the Faerie side, and Woodside and Cedarbrook in this world. Time runs differently in Faerie than here, so you might return to a big change in the human world—"

"But I have King Finvarra's blessing. He promised that I would be exempt from any time change trickery."

Hunter smiled. "Then that settles it. You could easily come to Faerie, and all would be well."

I hesitated, feeling uncertain. "But what would I do in Faerie?"

Hunter cleared his throat, suddenly nervous. "Um. Well. I was hoping you would return with me ... to be my wife."

Silence fell between us. Then Hunter started babbling. "You wouldn't be bored. There's a lot to do, overseeing our holdings back in Faerie. I was supposed to help my brother, but now that's he gone.... Of course, you have your duties as Littlewood Forest's Scarlet Lady. I wouldn't want to take your focus from that. And. And, I love you, and I don't ever want to be away from you again—"

I giggled.

He stopped speaking, eyes wide and wary. "Um. You're laughing. Is that a good thing or a bad thing?"

I giggled harder. "It's a good thing. It's a very good thing."

"Oh. Claret, I love you—"

"You know, you really should have started your proposal with that," I teased, then turned serious. "Oh, Hunter, I love you too. Yes, I'll marry you."

Hunter's eyes kindled. "You will?"

I nodded, laughing as he scooped me off the ground and swung me around. "I can tell your arm is doing just fine. Tell the healers they did a good job with you."

He set me down on my feet. "You can tell them yourself. After all, you'll be heading to Faerie soon."

"Ah, a fair point." I tilted my head, thinking. "You're now Lord Tavish. Does that make me Lady Tavish? Or would I be called by my Keeper title?"

Hunter smirked. "Lady Scarlet Lady? I'm not sure about that."

"It might need some work. Then again, it does make me sound doubly noble. Perhaps I could just drop the second 'lady' and just be called Lady Scarlet. It has a nice ring to it, don't you think? Or maybe—"

Laughing, Hunter pulled me into his arms and pressed his lips to mine. I eagerly lost myself in his kiss, happy to cease any talk of titles or family lands or Faerie.

For this was the moment I had dreamed of and wished for and hoped for. To finally be reunited with my love, a bright future ahead for both of us.

AUTHOR'S NOTE

I'LL BE HONEST—I HADN'T planned on writing a retelling of Little Red Riding Hood. I had other stories I wanted to tell first, and I thought that perhaps Little Red had been overdone.

But then I began to wonder, why did no one ever comment on the fact that Little Red wore a red cloak? I mean, isn't that the most obvious color to wear? There's a reason red is often used in media as the color of love, seduction, or attention. It's bold, eye-catching, and confident. Surely not the color a little girl should be wearing if she wanted to stay under the radar while walking through the forest. And while red camouflage might work in the right settings, most versions of Little Red Riding Hood that I've seen depict her in a typically deciduous forest, with no mention of or real emphasis on the season (for example, fall when the changing colors might hide her better).

And then I thought ...

What if the wolf was color blind?

So I started researching it. And the more I learned, the more I got excited about the concept.

In real life, wolves are color blind and can see yellow and blue, but not red or green. They do have excellent night vision, and see shades of grey better than humans. But they do have red-green color blindness.

Extreme color blindness can manifest in only seeing shades of black, grey, and white. Affected individuals may also have poor eyesight and light sensitivity.

Color blindness, while rare, affects males more than females. About 8 percent of males can have color blindness, with red-green color blindness being the most common. And often fairly mild. For most people, it doesn't really affect their day-to-day lives, or they find ways to get around it, such as memorizing where red and green lights are placed on a traffic light instead of relying on the changing colors to signal them to go or stop.

Finally, I leaned on the idea that nature believes in balance. A predator may be physically strong, but moves slowly. Perhaps it has incredible hearing, but poor eyesight. If a predator (or really any creature) was completely perfect physically, then it could easily overrun other species in the area.

With those ideas in mind, Seeing Red was born.

If you're interested in learning more about wolves or color blindness, here's some extra reading and viewing for you:

What Makes Sense to a Wolf, article from the Pikes Peak Courier — https://gazette.com/pikespeakcourier/what-makes-sense-to-a-wolf-wildlife-in-t he-news/article_b3210fa8-23e3-11ed-a097-e72adb947d3c.html

Different Types of Color Blindness and Distinguishing Them, article from Midtown Optometry — https://midtownvision.com/blog-posts/types-color-blindness

Do colourblind people see traffic lights differently?, video from Antonio the Optometrist — https://youtu.be/3qWzl7-ZE88?si=3yPhjbGbBPQXlwXo

And a fun fact on the name Claret:

Why are Bordeaux wines called "claret"? from Wine Spectator — https://www.winespectator.com/articles/why-are-bordeaux-wines-called-claret-46560#:~:text=Before%20%E2%80%9Cclaret%E2%80%9D%20was%20the%20 nickname,word%20for%20%E2%80%9Cclear%E2%80%9D).

DEAR READER:
THANK YOU

THANK YOU SO MUCH for reading Seeing Red. I hope you enjoyed your adventure with Claret and Hunter as much as I enjoyed writing about it! If this is your first time in the ReTold world, welcome! And if you're a returning reader, I'm so honored you've chosen to pick up this book.

I've always loved fairy tales and fairy tale retellings, and I'm excited to bring you more in this series. And if there's a fairy tale I have yet to touch but you'd love to see retold, please let me know! I love reader recommendations and reading new and obscure fairy tales, or rediscovering old favorites.

Thank you for reading, and please leave a review on Goodreads or wherever you like to buy books and learn about new titles.

Want to be the first to know about new adventures? Let's be friends!

Sign up for the Newsletter: http://www.rachanee.net/newsletter

Instagram: http://www.instagram.com/rachaneelumayno

TikTok: https://www.tiktok.com/@rachaneelumayno

YouTube: https://www.youtube.com/@rachaneelumayno

Twitter: http://www.twitter.com/rachaneelumayno

Join the community on Discord: Kingdom Legacy

READ ON FOR A PREVIEW OF MIDNIGHT ROSE, THE NEXT BOOK IN THE ReTold FAIRY TALE RETELLING SERIES

MUSINGS

CONTRARY TO THE RUMORS, I never killed dozens of people.

Only two.

And, in my defense, one was dying anyway. As for the other ...

Well, everyone likes to *think* they know the truth. But unless you were there, how can you really know?

I was there. And I think about it often. Practically all the time.

And believe me, I have had a lot of time to think about it.

CHAPTER 1

"WELL, IF IT ISN'T my favorite customer! Rose, my dear, how are you today?"

I laughed as I looked around the merchant's stall. I pushed up my eyeglasses and gave the woman a mock stern look. "Ilana, right now I'm your only customer."

"That doesn't mean you're not my favorite." The vegetable seller gave me a big wink. "So, what will you have today?"

I made my selections, then counted out some coins and handed them to Ilana. She placed them in a pouch at her hip, not bothering to count them. She wasn't lying about me being a favorite patron of hers. If she didn't like me, didn't trust me, she would have made a show of counting out the coins before putting them away. All the merchants in this sleepy village of Sonden were like that.

Not that I blamed them. Most of the people living in smaller towns and villages were distrustful of outsiders. It took a lot of time and effort to earn the longtime citizens' trust, but once you did, they were the most loyal of friends and neighbors. Living in a city might have been easier, but a higher concentration of people brought its own set of problems.

Even after all this time, I still hadn't figured out the safest place for me to live. To hide. To be myself.

Or to just ... be.

I said goodbye to Ilana and moved on, only giving the other stalls a cursory glance. I didn't really need anything else, and besides, I didn't like to stay in town long.

"Hello, Rose!"

"It's Rose! Hi, Rose!"

Seven-year-old Karra and her five-year-old brother Arn waved at me, giggling, as they ran past. Their mother, Jeanna, struggled to keep up, but the baby on her hip and the overly full bag on her shoulder weighed her down.

"Karra! Arn! Get back here!" Jeanna huffed. She gave me a tired smile. "Rose. It's good to see you."

"Do you need help with that?" I indicated her market bag.

"If you don't mind." Unceremoniously, she handed the baby to me.

"Oh, I meant—" But Jeanna was already gone, having dumped her bag next to my feet to hurry after her other two children.

In my arms, the baby cooed, staring deep into my eyes. I swallowed hard and willed my breath to stay steady. The infant reached out a chubby hand towards my face, grabbing for a strand of hair that had fallen over my cheek. After happily gumming on the strand's end for a moment, the baby decided to target my glasses, pulling them from my face.

Hastily, I reached up and firmly resettled them on my nose. I swatted my hand, intending to create a barrier between my eyeglasses and the child's little fingers. The baby grabbed one of my fingers and held on to it, their grip surprisingly strong.

I stilled, acutely aware of their weight, their vibrancy.

Their innocence.

Karra and Arn came up to me, running around me in circles while they tried to tag each other. Jeanna followed after, brushing back some dark hair matted with sweat.

"Children," she said, but I wasn't sure if she was addressing hers or making a general statement. She lifted the baby from my arms and settled the infant back on her hip. "You're a natural with babies, Rose."

"Oh, I—uh, thank you."

"If you ever want some extra coin, I'd pay you well to mind my little ones," she said. "It's hard to find people you can trust with your family."

"Th-that's a very generous offer," I stammered. "I'll ... I'll think about it."

"Please do. I'd be more than happy to pay, and pay you handsomely. I can't imagine you earn a lot, minding that old castle."

I shrugged. "It's a free place to stay, at least."

Jeanna raised an eyebrow. "I'm sure it's lonely, too, with no one but the plants to talk to. How is that any kind of life? Anytime you need some people, some talk, you stop by."

"I will. Thank you, Jeanna."

At that moment, Karra reached out and successfully tagged her brother. She jostled me in the process, knocking into my basket.

But her touch was a bit too forceful, and Arn fell to the ground, skinning his knees. The little boy began to wail.

Jeanna sighed. "I think it's time we all went home. Do think over what I said, Rose."

I nodded and said goodbye, then turned and headed down the main road that would lead out of Sonden and into the countryside.

I managed to escape the town with just a few more hellos and goodbyes, but thankfully no more extended conversations. Once Sonden was out of sight, I breathed easier.

It was always like this for me when I went to market. Or just went into Sonden, in general. If there was only some way to conduct my business without having to talk to people, it would be much easier for me.

It wasn't that the people were unfriendly. Far from it. Once they had accepted me, they had been quite generous and welcoming.

I would rather they were shuttered and distrustful towards me. Then I could enter the town, do what I needed to do, and leave quickly and easily. Without feeling the excessive shame, fear, and self-loathing I always did when I was there.

Rose, you've been doing so well. I tried to bolster my spirits as I walked home. *You haven't had any incidents since ... well, since. One day at a time.*

If only one day at a time hadn't stretched into several long decades. If only I could get rid of this never-ending hunger and be normal again.

But ever since ... *since* ... nothing in my life was normal.

And I despaired of it ever returning that way.

Chapter 2

Before

"My children, I'm afraid I have some bad news."

My sisters and I exchanged worried glances, then crowded closer.

"What's going on, Father?" Isa, the eldest, asked. At twenty-two, she was considered quite the beauty, and had many suitors in the city vying for her hand.

My father took a deep breath. "It's been several months, and no word from my ships. They were to return before the winter frost set in, and now ... now, I'm afraid they are lost at sea. And with it, all our fortune."

Isa gasped. Althea, my middle sister, swooned. Just one year younger than Isa, she had a delicate constitution and was prone to fits like these. I barely caught her before she could hit the ground, and between Isa and I, we brought her to the settee and settled her there.

Isa, ever the responsible one, disappeared into the kitchen, returning with a dampened linen towel. She waved at me to move aside, taking my place next to Althea. While I stood nearby, awkward and uncertain, Isa pressed the towel to Althea's forehead.

Father absent-mindedly frowned at my sisters, then turned to look out the sitting room's oversized window. The heavy dark blue velvet curtains were pulled back, allowing a view of sunset over the still-bustling street outside. The winter holidays would be here in a week, and people's preparations were visibly underway. A light snow started to fall, blanketing the world in a peaceful white.

Beyond the cobblestone street, brick homes, and candle-lit shops, we could see a slight view of the harbor, the tall ships' masts standing proudly against the darkening sky.

The harbor. Father's domain. Or rather, Father's former domain, now.

I joined my father at the window. "Is everything truly lost?" I asked softly.

He continued to stare outside, as if the world beyond held all the elusive answers he was looking for. "Yes, Rosie," he said, falling back on the family's nickname for me. He sighed heavily. "I invested everything I had—that *we* had—in those ships, and that cargo. And now, all of it, gone. Forever." He took a deep breath, but it sounded labored.

I looked at him, furrowing my brow when I saw his hand had crept up to brace his chest. "Are you well, Father?"

He took another shuddering breath, then dropped his hand. He turned to look at me, giving me a reassuring smile. "I'm fine. Don't you worry about me."

But I would—and I did. Father's job trading and buying and selling brought with it a lot of stress, but he had always thrived on it. Now, however, the stress of his shocking news made him look haggard and defeated.

I didn't want to worry him more, but I had to ask one last question. "What will we do now?"

His smile dropped, and he turned to look out the window again. "I don't know, child," he murmured, more to himself than to me. "I don't know."

The answer to my question became apparent all too soon.

Father's creditors came knocking on our door, wanting their share of their investments, even though the cargo was lost and nothing had been sold. The families of the lost sailors had to be compensated, as was outlined in the workers' contracts. And the outstanding debts at the various shops that Father did business with regularly had to be settled.

Any savings Father had set aside were instantly drained. Our household staff, including one housekeeper, three maids, one butler, and Father's personal valet, were let go, with small bonuses as thanks for their many years of service.

But the depth of our new financial status hit me when I noticed that several household items were missing.

A tea set. The pianoforte, where our late mother had taught my sisters and me the basics of music. (Isa and Althea were brilliant at it. I, not so much.) Several paintings and the small lacquered side table from the front hall.

I balked when I saw the pale blue settee being carried out from the sitting room.

"Father, no!" I rushed to his side, tugging at his sleeve in a way I hadn't done since I was a small child.

His face was impassive. "We need the money, Rose."

"But ... but ... that's *mother's*." I remembered sitting there with her for hours while she did her embroidery or read me a story. Playing at grown-up tea with her, practicing for the day when I, too, would entertain visitors with such effortless ease as she did. It was one of the last links we had to her, and after losing so much else, I was loathe to let it go.

He turned away. "And she's gone. Like so much else...."

My hands flew to my mouth as I gave a choked sob. I turned and fled to my room, hoping to reach it before the tears came.

I was not successful.

The day we left the city dawned cold and grey. The sky was steel.

Much like my heart had become. Had to become.

We were moving to the countryside with nothing but a single cartful of belongings, mostly personal necessities like clothing that we couldn't find buyers for. Nearly everything else had been sold to satisfy Father's business debts. Even the horses we were riding on and the cart would be sold at our end destination, the money sent back to the city to be used to pay off the final creditors.

The move had been an unexpected bit of luck. An elderly aunt had heard of our family's misfortune, and as a courtesy to her favorite niece, my late mother, had bestowed her equally aging country estate on us. The property didn't seem very promising—just a few acres of wild land that might or might not have been suitable for farming, and a moderate-sized house that had been overrun with rats and spiders and rot. But it was a place to live, especially since our grand city home, with all its lovely furnishings, large rooms, and prominent location, had been sold along with everything else.

Father locked up the house one last time and turned the keys over to the waiting banker. Althea sobbed loudly while Isa pulled her close, patting her shoulder in comfort. I stood nearby, still as a stone statue. And almost as unfeeling.

Father turned to us as the banker walked away. "Well, girls. It's time. Let's get going."

Silently, we mounted our horses. Father jumped up on the cart's bench seat, taking up the horse's reins. A quick flick of his wrist and click of his tongue spurred the horse forward. Reluctantly, sadly, my sisters and I followed after.

SPECIAL THANKS

THE RETOLD SERIES WAS something that had been in the back of my mind for several years as something I wanted to write, but I wasn't ready to write it until recently. And I wouldn't have been able to get to this point (or write *Seeing Red* at all!) without the help and encouragement of the following people:

Tom — I would not have been able to start or continue this writing journey without you. From your thoughtful notes, to your encouragement, and your willingness to answer all my silly questions. I am so fortunate to have you on my team, and more importantly, in my life. Thank you, thank you, thank you!!

My mother — My sweet little senior (along with Lana!). I love that you're always finding ways to get the word out about my work. Thanks for being my biggest fan.

Riley and Lana — I don't think I could even consider myself an author without my two favorite kitties! One to sit in my lap for hours (so I have to write!) and one to meow at me to get the work done. The best directing duo team.

And an extra special many thanks to the following people who were kind enough to back this book on Kickstarter. Thank you for believing in me.

Nicolette Andrews

Alexis Hope

Rebecca O'Neill

Apocalypse Cowboy

Anonymous

Elizabeth Marie

Paul C.A. Graham

Erik

Yesenia Aguilar

Mireya M.

Rob Embrey

Karra leanne

Paul Redfern

Mr. Onoufrios Oikonomidis

Samantha Newberry

Melanie Stark

"Musically inclined" Brian

Anonymous

Servo

Charlotte Irving

ValerieAnne

Makenzie A.

Carol MacLennan-Gonzales

Brian Grimes

Alexandra Corrsin

Rachel Z.

Anonymous

Michallie (Mica) Brown

Karina Krogh

Cristina Marti

Mack Murdoc

Volume

Michael Lynch

Logan

Anonymous

Rafael Alejandro

ABOUT THE
AUTHOR

A WARD-WINNING AUTHOR RACHANEE LUMAYNO is also an actress, voiceover artist, screenwriter, avid gamer, and amateur dodgeball player. She grew up in Michigan, where she spent way too much of her free time reading fantasy novels. She still spends too much of her free time reading fantasy, although now she writes them as novels, narrates them as audiobooks, and creates them as improv for various roleplaying campaigns as well. *Seeing Red,* the first in her new dark gothic fairy tale retelling series ReTold, is her eighth novel. She is the author of the Kingdom Legacy fantasy series, the first of which, *Heir of Amber and Fire,* was honored with the 2024 Spring PenCraft Seasonal Book Award for Best Young Adult - Fantasy/ Sci-Fi. She is also a former staff writer for two comics and a horror video game. You can find her online at her website, www.rachanee.net, or on Instagram, TikTok, or YouTube (@rachaneelumayno).

www.ingramcontent.com/pod-product-compliance
Lightning Source LLC
Chambersburg PA
CBHW021033030726
47496CB00006B/1508